UNHOLY ROLLERS

The demons just stood there, murmuring to themselves in deep-throated syllables that seemed to make the air vibrate. Sun glinted off their smooth hides, shimmering with the tremor of their rumbling. A suspicion grew in the captain's mind. What kind of demons were made of iron? In truth, they looked a lot like machinery— weird, outlandish, gigantic machinery, to be sure, but with identifiable wheels and levers and such.

His speculation ended when one of the things opened up and strange-looking people poured out, as if the demon were regurgitating its last meal of damned souls.

He unsheathed his sword and called his men to ready.

By Leslie Gadallah
Published by Ballantine Books:

CAT'S PAWN

THE LOREMASTERS

THE
LOREMASTERS

Leslie Gadallah

A Del Rey Book
BALLANTINE BOOKS • NEW YORK

A Del Rey Book
Published by Ballantine Books

Library of Congress Catalog Card Number: 88-91121

ISBN 0-345-35576-8

Printed in Canada

First Edition: October 1988

Cover Art by Barclay Shaw

One

It began in a place far from Monn, with an argument Sarah never heard.

Cleo was stomping along a curving walkway ten meters above the ground, her back stiff, her feet punishing the pavement. Reese was following, talking, explaining, his hands moving gracefully as if unseen gestures would soften the rigid spine in front of him.

Night was falling in the Mid-American Enclave. Above and below the combatants, tall buildings began to show glowing windows. Beneath them, the busy street was dissolving into patches of lamplight. The walkway glowed at foot level, casting shadows upward.

They left the walkway along a narrower branch and turned into a rank of impossibly tall Doric columns with bases at ground level and capitals another three stories above their heads. The pillars were a sham, of course. Unsupported stone so high would collapse of its own weight. The soaring, tapered length of them declared the architect's belief that the human spirit should never be bound by such petty limitations.

The door, discreetly labeled "Residence G" on the panel above the frame, swished open as they approached, and slid shut behind them. Halfway down a wide hallway of muted lighting, another door slid open with the touch of Cleo's hand on the identiplate beside it.

A serious trouble with automated sliding doors was that they could not be slammed. A good, soul-satisfying slam of the apartment door would have suited Cleo's temper just fine.

1

Aurelius the cat took one look when they came in, then dived under Reese's desk and dashed for the bed at the first opportunity, to hide among the blankets. When the people were fighting, it was best for the cat to stay out of sight.

"Reese, dammit, it's crazy," Cleo yelled.

Reese smiled at her with that infuriating, patiently tolerant smile of his. "Somebody's got to do it."

"They're barbarians, for crying out loud. Primitive, hostile barbarians. With fleas and God knows what."

"A few fleas aren't going to kill me, Cleo," Reese said.

"Don't be so damned sure," Cleo shot back. "You think you're invincible, a bloody superman? Fleas are plague carriers, you know."

"Thank you. Now I feel better."

Then Cleo felt miserably guilty for bringing it up, a little biological fact she had picked up somewhere. But it was only one of a multitude of dangers she foresaw.

"You go out in the field from time to time," Reese said. "So how come it's so much more dangerous for me than it is for you?"

"It's not the same thing."

"Oh?"

"I go out for a few hours now and then to check out a find. I'm not trying to live in those scummy, Phobish places."

"How long does a fleabite take?"

Cleo didn't trust herself to answer. She turned away from him and stared out the apartment's window at the street below. Every second streetlight was out, an energy-saving measure, for the Mid-American Enclave was desperately short of energy. So was every other enclave. That's why Reese was doing what he was doing, why people in enclaves all over the world were frantically searching for energy resources.

They had lightheartedly dubbed their quest "the Treasure Hunt," and the treasure they sought was abandoned stores of reactor fuel, waste products from inefficient old-style fission reactors, weapons, any fissionable material the Old People might have left behind. At the time of the Separation, no one had anticipated that locating this stuff would become so important. The old books held only hints and vague references to place names that no longer existed, and some maps of doubtful accuracy that might actually be deliberately misleading, given the Old People's passion for secrecy about such things. But they were sure that the forgotten caches existed, scattered around the countryside, buried deep in the earth. The Treasure Hunters were charged with the job of trying to find them.

Not knowing where to look made the Treasure Hunt a wild gamble. What made it hazardous was the Phobes.

Reese came up behind Cleo and put his hands on her shoulders. His strong fingers massaged the tense corded muscles at the base of her neck. "It's not demons and dragons out there, Cleo. Just people. They eat, shit, and make love the same way you and I do."

"Sure," Cleo said. She shrugged him off, turned to take a printout off the desk, and thrust it at him. "Read this."

It was a thin file. Anthropological reports were spotty. What data were available showed a wide range of Phobish societies, from the subtribal to something similar to European Middle Ages feudal, with one and only one thing in common—a hostile terror of everything and anything associated with the enclaves.

Poking around in those communities was insanely dangerous.

"I did read it," he said. "I wrote some of it."

"They hate our guts," Cleo pointed out.

He turned her around to face him, his gray eyes filled with sweet reason, which only served to fuel her anger. He didn't even have the grace to get mad, she thought.

"Let me show you something." He reached into his pocket and came up with a coin-sized electronic bug in a plain aluminum alloy case which he held between his thumb and forefinger for her inspection. "This is my tracer," he said. "As long as I'm carrying this thing, the office can tell where I am. And there's an alarm in case I get into any kind of trouble. Come on, I'll show you."

He led her to the long arc of the communications and entertainment console which separated the living area from the entry. At the moment it was playing a recording of Wheeler's *Rite of Spring* concerto. It had been programmed before they left, when they were feeling more romantic toward one another, to greet them in this manner. But the music had been forgotten in their quarrel.

Reese gave her the tracer. "Push the little red spot on the rim," he said.

Almost immediately the communications terminal responded with an imperative blat, not its usual soft ping requesting attention.

Reese activated the screen, and Irene's extremely irritated face appeared there.

"Just what do you think you're playing at?" she demanded.

"Sorry," Reese said. "It was an accident. It won't happen again."

"See that it doesn't. One more accident, and you're out of the Hunt. Period. It's not some kind of a game we've got going here."

The screen blanked. Reese turned to Cleo, one questioning eyebrow upraised.

"It doesn't look like much security," she said.

Reese attached it to a fine steel chain and hung it around his neck. "Well, to tell you the truth, my love, a full suit of knight-in-shining-armor type armor would be just too heavy to carry around."

Cleo allowed herself a small smile at the thought of him clanking around the Phobish city encased in iron. It would be a little out of keeping with the notion that the Hunters should remain as inconspicuous as possible to avoid trouble with the natives.

"You're going to go whether I like it or not, aren't you?" she said.

"This is the kind of work I'm trained to do, Cleo. It's not so different from any other field trip."

"You realize I'm going to be furiously worried the whole time."

"Please don't."

"Sure," she said again. After a moment, she asked, "When are you going to leave?"

"In a couple of hours. I want to get there before first light."

He looked so wistful that Cleo relented. "So throw the damned cat off the bed. That doesn't give us any more than enough time."

* * *

Cleo was able to put her anger on hold until Reese was ready to go. But as he was gathering up his equipment, it started to flare up again, and it was blazing by the time she was at the window watching the headlight on his transport pod play connect-the-dots with the streetlight until it cleared the perimeter wall and picked up speed.

From there the podway drove arrow-straight to the west.

She stayed at the window until she couldn't see the pod's headlight any longer. "Selfish, stubborn son of a bitch," she said to the window.

She turned and glared at Aurelius. "I don't know if I can deal with this, cat."

TWO

Near the low stone wall surrounding Market Square, a small fire burned. The storyteller sat cross-legged on a short, sheepskin-covered bench with his back against the wall, the firelight adding a touch of youthful gold to his graying beard. Around him, almost invisible in the enveloping night, a crowd had gathered, a motley group representing a cross section of the population of the city of Monn. The people sat on the ground, or squatted near the fire. They were still and quiet, enchanted by the rich cadence of his voice, enwrapped in the illusion he was creating.

The story was about the Old People, the way of things before the Bush Wars. It was a popular tale. The storyteller expected this audience to be generous.

He had reached the place where magic fires cooked the Old People's food without flames. Weaving his words carefully, he drew his audience with him outside the hard realities of daily life and the dark and windy night, to a sweeter, kinder world of another time and another place.

A commotion in the square interrupted him.

He stopped abruptly in midsentence, the fantasy ruined, the illusion in shreds blowing away on the night wind.

Torch-carrying, black-robed men had joined the storyteller's audience, and the listeners stirred uneasily. They looked up at the torchbearers and then at the storyteller.

The storyteller was more than a little annoyed. His status in the community was high enough that interruptions were rare, and he could usually afford to express his irritation when they occurred. But this time he took a deep breath and swallowed his indignation. He raised his expressive hands, palms up, to shoulder level, indicating his surrender. He would go hungry that night, but there was nothing he could do about it.

His audience dispersed, most of them drifting after the torch-bearers heading toward the center of the square.

"Repent," Brother Parker cried, arms spread wide.

Sarah pushed her way through the crowd, wiggling aggressively into small spaces, working her way toward the front, trying to see what was going on.

She called herself Sarah because she liked the sound of the name. She lived as best she could with a combination of small jobs, charity, wiliness, and theft. She slept in the basement of an old, collapsing prewar building and had done so for most of her fourteen years. None of that distinguished her greatly from dozens of other children in the city who lived the same way. On the other hand, she had discovered that smiling got her more from people than sullen anger or wistful pathos ever had, and that did distinguish her. She smiled up at the brawny men who owned the chin-high elbows, and they smiled back at the grubby, elfin child and shuffled around and made a space for her.

In the center of Market Square a rough platform had been built of planks laid across sawhorses. All around the narrow, improvised stage, Brother Parker's followers in their cowled robes—black for the men, stark white for the women—stood looking out at the crowd with beatific smiles on their hooded faces and alert wariness in their eyes. Each of them held a torch, so that the stage was lit almost as bright as day.

In a pen behind the platform a mob of sheep awaited their fate in the morning market with mute misery, torchlight glinting dully in their eyes.

Just ahead of the platform and to one side, the torchlight gleamed on the brass and leather of a mounted troop of Guardsmen. The crowd kept its distance from the nervous horses and only gradually realized that the governor was in their midst. People stared, separately and in groups. The governor kept his attention fixed on the stage.

On the platform, Brother Parker cried, "Hellfire and damnation are the price of sin," while stepping carefully to avoid the embarrassment of shifting boards.

Peering out from the shadows between the wide shoulders of smiths and carpenters, Sarah thought it would be wonderful to have a clean, white robe. Her own clothing was a decidedly unfeminine collection of castoffs, somewhat tattered and stained.

"I come in the Lord God's name," Brother Parker said, "to share the message of salvation."

Brother Parker had a close-trimmed beard, a clear ringing voice, and sharp blue eyes burning with the cold fire of his belief. Sometimes Sarah thought that he had singled her out of the group and was talking directly to her. It was an eerie feeling, and when it happened, she would slip back and hide in the dark spaces among bigger people.

She watched the governor instead. She liked his melancholy looks, as if he were dreadfully lonely. She thought he had kind eyes. Sometimes she dreamed that she was the one up there on the back of the white horse, the one who lived in the Mansion like a fairy princess. It was a silly, impossible dream, of course, and she laughed at herself for having it. Brother Parker's voice snatched her back to reality.

"The Lord God has said death comes to the one and to the many, but who believes in Him shall have eternal life."

In a world where entertainments were few, Brother Parker was entertaining enough. Most of the time he talked about things getting better. It was all supposed to happen at some vague time in the future when God would make everything right and folks would live as well, maybe, as the Old People had before the Bush Wars. Sarah didn't believe that tale much, as pleasant as it was to think about. But on the subject of death, he was scary.

In truth she would rather listen to the storyteller, who could spin dreams without lacing them with blood and thunder and threats of eternal damnation.

"Live in the Lord God, for no man may know the hour of his death. Live in Him, and the devil's fires shall not claim you."

All the Brothers and Sisters answered, "Amen," and it was like a great wave breaking on the river's shore. The flames of the torches wavered.

"Wickedness dwells among you. Crops wither. Black crows gather. Be warned. Hell burns hot. The Lord God knows what is in your hearts. Root out evil. Destroy the unbeliever. Raze the fortress of the profane. Follow me in the way of the Lord God, Brothers and Sisters.''

Sarah's attention wandered away from Brother Parker to a stranger standing close to her. His clothes were of better quality than most of the townsfolk around her, and his pockets, she thought, should yield something interesting. She was hungry, and at that moment she felt far more in need of food than of salvation.

Timing her movements to the jostling of the crowd, Sarah's hands fluttered over the stranger's clothes as softly as butterfly wings. By all rights, he should never have noticed the removal of a few coins from his jacket pocket. But just as Brother Parker was ending his sermon with his customary ''Pray for me, Brothers and Sisters'' and stepping down from his jury-rigged stage, the man shouted ''Hey!'' and made a grab for Sarah.

She ducked away and got the bulk of Tallman Morgan between her and her victim, then squirmed among the shuffling bodies as the crowd began to disperse. Annoyed grunts and curses rose behind her as the man tried to follow.

She dived into the black narrow shadows of Rat Alley where the stone walls of the buildings were scarcely an arm-span apart and the roofs almost touched overhead. The end of the alley was closed by a piece of rail fence she could squeeze through. Most adults had to go over if they were athletic, or around if they were not. Rat Alley had saved her skin more than once.

Looking backward as she ran, she bounced off the substantial belly of Butch Miller, which was preceding its owner in a spill of dim light from the side door of the Crow's Eye Tavern.

Of the five thousand or so souls inhabiting the city of Monn—it was a large community for its time—there were at least four thousand nine hundred whom Sarah would have preferred to run into.

A few years older than Sarah, Butch had always been too big, too loud, too rough—a bully. His family had some status in the city, and Butch wasn't adverse to taking advantage of it, abusing shopkeepers, insulting servants, and harassing street kids. There was enough money and influence associated with the Family Miller that he could get away with it; no one wanted to offend the Millers by complaining.

Lately Sarah had been singled out for his special favor, and his brutality had acquired a mean lewdness.

Sarah recovered herself and tried to duck around him, but there really wasn't room. His fat hand snaked out and caught her skinny wrist, holding her prisoner in the lighted space in spite of her struggles.

"Hey, Sarah, girl. You don't want to run off without even saying hello."

"Let me go, Butch. I'm in a hurry."

"You are, eh? Thieving in the square again, I bet. What have you got this time?" he asked, eyeing the closed fist still clutching the stolen coins.

"Nothing. Leave me alone." She beat at him frantically with her free hand.

He slapped her sharply, and she subsided, cheek burning. "That's more like it. You're such a wicked girl, Sarah, my dear." He pulled her toward him, and she was enveloped in the reek of smoke and beer and garlic. Crumbs of his dinner were stuck in his whiskers. "You ought to have more respect for your betters." He pried her fingers open, and the coins fell into the dust of the alley. "Ah, you wicked, wicked girl." He pulled her right against his soft, round body and wrapped his arms around her, pinning her there, hurting her. "I really ought to call the constable."

Sarah turned her face away. "Let me go, please." Her struggles renewed with renewed fear.

"What'll you do for me if I do? I could get into trouble myself, you know, aiding a thief."

"Let her go. You have no call to be terrorizing a child."

The new voice was cultured, precise, with a trace of an accent, coming from a presence that one could feel more than see in the darkness. To Sarah's everlasting surprise, Butch's arms slackened and she was able to wiggle free.

Her rescuer moved a little closer, into the backwash of light from the open door, and Sarah saw the stranger whose coins lay in the dirt at his feet. He seemed not at all impressed by Butch, and Sarah wondered briefly if he might not be a member of the Governor's Guard, or something grand like that.

Caught between the two men, there wasn't much she could do but wait and see what happened, and watch for her chance.

Butch's voice took on an ingratiating quality it rarely held. He seemed to get smaller as he talked. "You are making a mistake, good sir. This is not an honest child, but a petty street bastard, an insignificant little purse snatcher, not worth Your Honor's time."

The stranger looked down at Sarah. He was tall, though not as tall as Tallman Morgan, and square-shouldered, with a smooth, beardless, quiet face which might have been on the young side of middle age or the old side of youth. His dress was of a sort common enough in the aristocratic parts of the city, though not so common in this district. A young lord, slumming, perhaps—obviously Butch thought so—though there was that air of foreignness about him.

"She has commanded a considerable amount of your time, sir," the stranger said. "Come along, child." He turned on his heel and strode away as if he had no doubt that she would follow.

It seemed as good a move as any. She would be away from Butch at least. Bending swiftly, she snatched up the coins and trotted after the stranger.

"Hey, wait a minute," Butch said, having found some part of his courage. "Who do you think you are, anyway?"

"My name is Reese," the stranger said without turning around. "I'm living on Travellers' Way if you should feel you need to find me." He made it sound extremely unlikely that the need would arise.

At the mouth of the alley, he stopped. "You can run away now if you want to. I don't fancy another chase through the dark to catch you. But if you'd like to get fed, you'd better stick close."

Sarah's empty stomach decided for her. Wilder animals than she had been tamed with a promise of food. She chugged along silently at his side, making a little hopping step every now and then to keep up.

They walked the winding, narrow moonlit streets of Monn up the hill, away from the river, away from the close-packed houses of the lower town, and into the richer districts. Sarah rarely went into that part of the city. If it was true that the pickings were fatter, it was also true that the constables were more diligent, and Sarah had decided that the gain wasn't worth the additional risk.

They came to the Witch Road, the wide, unnaturally smooth road that divided Monn almost in half and which no human people ever used as a thoroughfare. That was because of the witch wagons that hurtled along it at terrifying speeds out of the hills and across the Witch Bridge and into the Wilderness, or else out of the Wilderness, across the Witch Bridge, and up into the hills. Nobody knew when they were coming, and all the sound they made was the awful wind of their passage. There were stories about people and animals being smashed under the wheels so fast that they never knew what hit them. Sarah hesitated to cross. She looked up and down its perfectly straight length, then scuttled over. The stranger seemed unconcerned.

A bit farther on, he led her into a side street and then into a small wooden house.

"This is it," the stranger said, opening the door for her.

It was much like any house Sarah had ever been in, a single room with a fireplace on one wall, except that the walls were made of wood instead of stone, like many newer houses were, and it had glass in the window. The only place Sarah had heard of with glass windows was the Governor's Mansion.

A lantern, turned low, stood on a rough wood table in the middle of the room, and some chairs were scattered around. A straw mattress and some bedding occupied a corner. There were shelves with nothing much on them but a couple of common earthenware plates, two bowls, a pair of wine cups, and a few odds and ends of culinary necessity. There were cupboards, but they were closed. Reese had a fine house, but he didn't seem to own much else. Sarah wandered around like a kitten inspecting a new home. The place was neat and tidy and all, but had a temporary look to it.

An object sat on the table, covered in something that looked like leather, but wasn't, and had an odd feel. It was a pretty color, though, a wine red, with some white runes inscribed on it, possibly to protect it from magic.

"What's this?" she asked, the first words she had spoken since they left Rat Alley.

Reese's eyebrow rose a bit. "It's a book," he said.

"Oh. What's it for?" It didn't look like it would be much good to eat.

"That's not an easy question. I guess the easiest answer is

that some book or another will tell you almost anything you want to know.''

''Yeah?'' Sarah said with some skepticism. ''It could tell me how I could get a nice house like this?''

''I guess.''

Sarah held the book, turned it over, and regarded it gravely. ''It's not telling me anything.''

''You have to learn how to use it.''

''Oh.'' That sounded like work. Sarah put on her most beguiling smile. ''You said you had some food?''

''Mmhm. But I think in the interests of both our appetites you should wash first.''

Sarah was taken aback, but on second thought decided that one had to expect some queer ideas from a foreigner. ''Is that the sort of thing they do where you come from?'' she asked. He nodded. Sarah took a deep breath. She wasn't keen on the idea, but she had done harder things to earn her dinner. ''Okay. Right here?''

He got a big enamel basin out of one of the cupboards and a soft cloth she could dry herself with, and a piece of something white and sweet smelling.

''What's that?''

''Soap. You use it to—''

''I know what soap is,'' Sarah said crossly, then added more gently, ''But I never saw any looked like that, or smelled so good.''

He showed her the water, in a pair of large wooden buckets near the door. Then he told her to go to it and he would be back with the food.

When he returned he had not only thick slabs of meat and onions in rich gravy in a bowl, and a loaf of coarse bread from a nearby inn, but also a change of clothes for her, shirt and trousers as if she were a boy. They were a bit large, but Sarah didn't mind.

Reese ate little. Sitting across from her at the wooden table, mostly he watched while Sarah shoveled in the food until her belly was tight and round. If her table manners lacked grace, she made up for it in enthusiasm. And when she had packed away enough meat and bread that she was sure she wouldn't be hungry for a while, her native curiosity reasserted itself, along with a few minor apprehensions.

"Are you going to fuck me now?"

It was Reese's turn to be taken aback. "Well," he said when he had recovered himself. "That's direct. I hadn't planned on it."

"Why not?"

"You're just a kid, for a start."

"I'm not."

"Nonetheless."

"I know how."

Reese closed his eyes and said nothing.

"Are you afraid of Butch?"

"No, I'm not afraid of Butch."

"Butch has a family, but I think your family is stronger."

"How did you come to that conclusion?" Reese asked, happy to be able to divert the conversation toward another subject.

"Well, you got nice clothes and a nice house, though you really haven't got much stuff. I guess maybe you got another house somewhere."

"That's true."

Sarah chewed her bottom lip in cogitation. "Not many people even with families can afford two houses. I can't even figure out why they'd want two houses. Unless maybe one was far away from the other, like in another city. So I guess maybe you're a foreign lord, and that means you got a really strong family, right?"

"You're very perceptive and very smart, Sarah."

"Does that mean I guessed right?"

"Close enough, except I am a scholar, not a lord."

"I don't even know what that is, a scholar."

"A scholar is one who tries to learn about things, to find out how things are and how they work and sometimes what they mean."

She looked at him askance. "Like what?" she asked dubiously.

"Let me give you an example. I'd like to know why you were afraid of the road back there."

She gave him a hard look. "Because."

He waited for her explanation.

"Because it's the Witch Road," she said crossly. "Every-body knows that. The witch wagons use it. You'd have to be crazy not to be afraid."

"What do you think the witch wagons are?"

"I don't want to talk about them. They're horrible Phile things, and just thinking about them gives me the creeps."

"Talk can't hurt, can it?"

Sarah thought about it. "I guess not, unless you're a witch and you're talking a spell."

"No spells, I promise. Suppose I told you the witch wagons wouldn't hurt you, that they can't possibly hurt you."

Sarah regarded him as if he had completely lost his mind. "Are all scholars crazy?" she asked.

Reese shook his head and smiled a wry smile. "Not all of them. Although it may be they tend to get that way."

They sat quietly for a few moments, each wrapped in his own thoughts. "The thing is," Sarah said suddenly, "I can't figure why you brought me here and all that."

"Should I have left you with Butch?"

"Hades, I've been having trouble with Butch for most of all the time I can remember. Besides, why would you care?"

He didn't answer the question.

"I hate Butch," Sarah said.

"Why don't you go away, to some other part of the city, if Butch is a problem?"

"Well, I thought about that sometimes when he's being more mean than usual. But I got my place, in one of the Old People's buildings, and my stuff's there. It's a good place. The rain doesn't come in much. I'd hate to leave it."

"The Old People's building. I'd like to see that, Sarah."

"Why?" she asked, instantly suspicious. There were any number of people in the city who would prey on a street kid if they had the chance, ruin her place, or take it away if they happened to like it, and steal her things, though she didn't think she had anything Reese would want.

"The Old People are one thing scholars are trying to learn about."

"They're all dead, you know."

"Yes, I know." He drew away from her then, into himself, staring down at the table as if he were looking for auguries there.

He looked heavy-hearted and sad, and it stirred strange new feelings in her to see him unhappy. She wanted very much to smooth the frown from between his brows.

"You'd better run along home, now. Will you be all right, alone?"

"Sure," she said. It was a funny question. She had been alone all her life.

Trudging back down the hill, she didn't know if she was more relieved or disappointed. Her mind's eye replayed the gleam of lamplight on hair as smooth and sleek and dark as an otter's fur.

She was going to do something to resolve the question. She didn't know what yet, but something.

Three

When the stranger walked out of Rat Alley without so much as a backward glance, Gil the Weasel giggled from safely inside the doorway of the Crow's Eye Tavern.

Butch turned on him with red-faced fury.

"Shut up," he snarled.

Gil blinked his little black eyes and shut up. He made a fair part of his living picking up the crumbs that fell like rain from the overburdened Miller table, so it was prudent of him to stifle his enjoyment of Butch's embarrassment. Gil was prudent. But privately, he cheered the stranger. he dreamed of being able to stand up to Butch one day, though he knew he never would. He couldn't help taking an instant liking to the man who did.

Butch stomped back into the tavern, boots hard on the wooden floor. There was a brief pause in the buzz of conversation. None of the other customers looked up, or said anything, but Butch could feel them grinning into their cups. The talk resumed behind him, peppered with a few snickers. Butch threw himself down in a chair at a dimly lit corner table, and the taverner arrived promptly with a mug. Gil perched lightly in the place across the table.

"Who does the bastard think he is?" Butch asked after a long sulky silence.

Gil knew better than to answer. He turned his interest to the mug that Butch was ignoring. The tirade would go on for a long dry time and probably come to nothing.

"He's not going to get away with it, I promise you. A man has his pride."

17

Gil's thin fingers flat on the table rotated the mug slightly in his direction.

"I've been insulted. The family has been insulted. Somebody's got to teach that smart-ass some manners."

The mug was squarely in front of Gil. He raised it to his lips.

Butch reached across and snatched the mug away furiously, spilling beer over his hand and onto the table. "Give me that. You find out about that son of a bitch. Who he is, what he's doing. If he thinks he's going to get away with making me look like a fool . . ."

Gil honestly believed that the Lord God had got in ahead of the stranger and taken care of that particular detail Himself.

"Well, get going," Butch yelled. The other patrons studiously avoided turning to look.

Obediently, Gil sidled around the table and slipped out of the tavern and into the night, vanishing among the shadows.

Butch brooded over his beer. Though suffering only wounds to his ego, he easily persuaded himself that the stranger had done more than injure his personal vanity. The Family Miller had a position to maintain. He couldn't think of a single reason why any insolent damned stranger should get away with insulting the family with a lot of foreign arrogance.

The darkness was thinning by the time Butch left the tavern staggering, a little subdued but under his own power, committed to preserving the family honor.

The Miller estate was situated on Mill Road, right down by the river where the water currents turned the great wheel that ground all the grain for Monnish bread, and a fair amount for other communities up and down the river. It was the mill wheel and the river that had made the Family Miller wealthy and therefore powerful in the city, but it was also the reason that the family lived in the lower town, among laborers and carters, and away from other families of its class. There were those in the city who said that the Millers had found their proper station, and some indications of that attitude eventually made its way back to the family. Some family members were just a bit sensitive about family prestige.

Butch arose late, thick-headed, just in time for lunch.

Robert Miller, presiding over his family assembled at one end of the long table in the great hall, and hearing Butch's edited version of his encounter with the stranger, suppressed his suspicions of who had offended whom where his least lovable son was concerned.

Brad Miller had no such inhibitions. "I've seen that Sarah. She ain't so much."

"Grow up, Brad," Butch growled, getting red. "That's not the point. Family honor, that's the point."

"So what'd you do, eh, Butch? Butt the starch out of him with your belly, I bet." Brad was bigger and fitter and older than Butch, so the teasing did not go down well.

"Shut up, Brad," Brian said. "The thing is, what're we going to do?"

"Butch'll probably go to his room and cry," Brad said.

Butch aimed a punch across the table. Brad leaned back, grinning, and let the blow go by. The table rattled on its thick oak legs. Loaves bounced out of their basket, and the honey pot teetered precariously. Robert roared for order. The boys subsided a little.

Gil the Weasel arrived, good timing being a necessary part of his life-style, and fine bread and honey from the Millers' table suited him just fine. He didn't have much to tell. The stranger had taken Sarah home with him and gone to the nearby inn for food; then he had sent Sarah away and gone to bed.

From a milkmaid at her early morning labor he learned that the stranger had been there about two weeks, was an early riser, ate most of his meals in the Inn of the Honest Keeper, and spent most of the rest of his time poking around in the ruins of the Old People's places.

Not a lot of information, but it was enough for Butch. Butch's plans were not elaborate, nor were they particularly inventive. The stranger would have neither family nor close friends in the city of Monn to complicate matters, so elaboration and invention were not necessary. Butch was not a man to do more work than was necessary.

The brothers squabbled among themselves like crow chicks, but when it came to family business, like chastising an impudent stranger, they stuck together. They promised each other that they would assemble in the evening around supper time at the Inn of the Honest Keeper, with the family honor on their minds.

Gil didn't wait around. The stranger, telling Butch off, had given him a moment's pleasure. Such moments were rare in Gil's life, and he hated to see the man suffer for it, whoever he might be. He thought about it after he left the hairy, overgrown, squabbling boys at the Millers' table to find a place where he could be alone for a while, sitting on his heels in the blessed peace at the water's edge, in the shadow of Mill Bridge, looking out over the river. A short distance upstream the mill wheel turned, creaking beneath the brutal sun while dusty laborers sweated under sacks of grain and flour as they moved in and out of the mill. Around them, flocks of sparrows flapped and twittered and hopped over the ground, picking up spilled wheat.

The best he thought he could do was to give the stranger fair warning. There were minor complications to be taken care of. Since he valued his own hide above all else, Gil didn't want to be caught giving away Butch's plans. Butch's slow-headed brutality could be damaging on occasion. It would be dangerous to approach the stranger directly.

But, he thought, there was no reason why he couldn't talk to Sarah, who must have some connection with the man.

He cogitated awhile longer, stood and dusted himself off, then climbed up toward the main part of the city. He stopped at the bakery and exchanged a small amount of Butch's money for a sack of stale buns, then continued uphill and into a warren of narrow streets and alleys north of Market Square.

A small house had burned, along with its owner, some years back. The broken, charred walls and chimney still stood, waiting for someone to have need of the space.

The outbuildings were being used by a neighbor to house chickens, and the smell of chicken was thick in the hot, still air. The clucking birds scattered squawking as he entered the yard. Gil pushed through tall weeds into the ruin.

Signs of habitation in this poor shelter were few—fresh ashes in the fireplace, some pieces of chipped and grimy pottery, and a tattered shirt in a heap on the dirty floor. Gil was not discouraged. He set his sack down, squatted down beside it, and waited.

After a time, he glimpsed a young boy's grubby face peering around the edge of the empty doorway.

"Hey, Martin," he said.

"Hey, Gil," Martin said, but his eyes were on the sack.

"I need some help," Gil said.

"Yeah, like what?" Martin came in and squatted down beside Gil. He was a skinny, stunted twelve-year-old with a scabby patch on one cheek. Part of the scab had peeled off, revealing a spot of smooth pink flesh beneath. Martin worried it with stained, broken fingernails as they talked.

Gil was conscious of other presences just out of sight. The kids had scattered like mice at his approach, but the promise of food was luring them back.

Martin made to take the sack. Gil moved it out of his reach. "I need to find Sarah," he said.

"She don't come here," Martin said.

"How come?"

Martin stuck out his thin chest and waggled his shoulders in imitation of a haughty dame. "She's too much of a la-de-da lady to hang around with the likes of us," he said in a prissy whine. "She got her own place, thank you very much, and thinks she's somethin', eh?"

"So where is this place?" Gil asked.

"She don't say," Martin answered with his eye on the sack. "But she hangs around the square a lot. And around the storyteller."

Gil left the sack and went back to the square.

Sarah was gathering wood for the storyteller's evening fire and telling him of the dream she had of becoming a rich lady with a big house who gave marvelous dinner parties where a hundred people came and everyone spoke sweetly to her for fear of giving offense and not being invited again.

"Does it seem weird?" she asked him. She was bent down by the stone wall laying the fire, and so somewhat out of sight. "Someone like me dreaming so grand?"

"Common enough for young girls, I guess," the storyteller said. "Hey, Gil," he called to someone out of Sarah's sight. "What's happening?" That was the storyteller's usual greeting. He was always interested in picking up bits of business to weave into new stories.

"I'm looking for Sarah," Gil said from across the wall.

"Don't tell him I'm here," Sarah whispered. If Gil was looking for her, it had to be because Butch had sent him.

"What do you want with Sarah?" the storyteller asked.

"I got to talk to her. About her friend the stranger."

Sarah's head popped up, caution forgotten. "Reese? What about him?"

"Hey, Sarah," Gil said, somewhat amused. "Let's take a walk." The storyteller usually kept the sources of his information to himself, but Gil didn't want to bet his precious skin on the man's discretion.

The matter of getting fed was a problem Reese had not adequately anticipated before coming to Monn. He soon discovered that he had no skill whatever at cooking over an open fire. The native people did, that being the only form of cooking they knew, but their disregard for the most basic elements of sanitation gave him pause. The first meal of Monnish food he had sampled had left him nearly helpless for two days while his angry intestines protested their mistreatment. Recovered, he seemed to have acquired a degree of immunity, and the innkeeper's black fingernails and racking cough were more of a psychological than a physiological problem. But there were times when he would have given half his kingdom, if he had a kingdom, for a glass of orange juice.

When he left the inn, it was already filling up with people relaxing after their day's labor. The street was quiet. Dusk was falling. A few folks in a group gossiped on the roadside. A dusty carter and his weary horses plodded home.

He intended to go home and bring his notes up to date, then head down to the square and see what the storyteller had to say. Keepers of Monnish lore, minstrel, and historian combined, the storyteller was not only entertaining, but his tales might hold valuable clues. Besides, there wasn't much else to do of an evening.

He had just cleared the north corner of the building when a harsh whisper from the shadows said, "Hey, Reese!"

He stopped and turned to see who was calling him. A fist exploded out of the darkness and smacked him in the nose.

He staggered. Pain blossomed over his face. Someone gave him a shove. He stumbled down a slope. Small branches snatched at him. His eyes watered. He shook his head and blinked, trying to clear his vision. He felt another shove. His feet found a path.

He started down it, still half-blind, thinking only to get away. Someone yanked him back by the arm.

A blow plowed into his belly and left him bent over, fighting for breath. A kick knocked his legs out from under him. He fell, hard. These guys are going to kill you, Reese, he thought. You better do something.

Lying curled on his side around the pain in his stomach, he fumbled among the unfamiliar folds of Monnish clothing. Fear clawed him until he found the stun gun in his pocket. He brought the short cylinder up and triggered it at an indistinct shadow just ahead of him. The shadow collapsed with a brushy crash.

A grunt of surprise came from behind him. He rolled onto his back and fired again, at the sound. A body dropped.

There was a wail of terror, and the sound of feet running, then the whipping sigh of damaged vegetation.

Were there more? He fought to his hands and knees, head hanging, still clutching the cylinder. He listened, stretching his ears. He heard nothing.

As soon as Gil told her what was going to happen, Sarah tore off toward the house on Travellers' Way, dashing down alleys and through yards and across vacant land, and arrived breathless only to discover that the house was empty.

She stood panting for a moment, wondering what to do next. She felt obliged to the stranger who had been kind to her. Besides, he was a beautiful man. Sarah thought she was probably madly in love with him, helplessly enchanted from the moment of meeting, like a princess in a story. She had completely forgotten that her first designs on him had been merely theft.

Besides, she owed Butch. A lot.

There was an element of danger, too, which added a delicious excitement to the spell she was under. She could imagine herself as the heroine of a storyteller's tale, a strong woman caught by forces beyond her control, the innocent victim of a passion of epic proportions which she had not asked for and could not resist. A woman who undertook great risks for her man. She could almost see the people gathered round a fire, listening with rapt attention while the storyteller's rich voice recounted the love tale of Sarah, a legend in her own time.

The inn. Probably he would be at his dinner. Getting in to warn him could be difficult. She wasn't entirely welcome there.

One of the innkeeper's daughters was sweeping out the doorway, raising a cloud of dust that all but obscured the westering sun. She laughed a nasty little laugh when Sarah approached and said she wanted to talk to the man called Reese. "For a filthy little street whore, you got big ideas, ain'cha? Get out of here. Stop bothering the customers. Leave honest folks alone, or I'll call my father."

"Come on, Angela, I just want to talk to 'im."

"Go away. I'll call my father."

"Yeah, well, my mother told your father to stuff it in his ear, so there."

The girl took a swipe at her with the broom. Sarah ducked away, stuck her thumbs in her ears, and waggled her fingers at Angela. Shouting over her shoulder through the open door, brandishing the broom, Angela gave chase. Sarah ran around the building, easily outdistancing her pursuer, and ducked into the empty doorway.

The inn was one of the few two-story buildings in Monn, diners and drinkers occupying the main floor, which was one large, smoke-darkened room of rough timber, cluttered with plain wooden tables and chairs, with a large fire pit in the center where a newly laid fire was just beginning to burn and lighten the gathering gloom. A pair of lingering diners remained and a few early drinkers had arrived, but Reese was not among them.

He must have left while she was playing fox and hen with Angela.

The innkeeper's family lived in the back of the building. From that direction Harold the innkeeper, a red-cheeked, portly man, hustled into the public room in response to his daughter's screeching. Angela by then had regained the doorway and stood guarding it with the broom held at the ready.

Sarah ducked around a table to avoid the innkeeper and was captured by one of the diners, who thought it was all great fun. The innkeeper sent his daughter after the constable and came to take over the prisoner with effusive thanks directed at the diner.

Sarah lapsed into sullen passivity for the moments it took

Harold to become confident of his hand clamped around her wrist.

"Got you this time, you little thief," the innkeeper said. Sarah kicked his shin as hard as she could. He yelped and loosed his hold, and Sarah bolted for the door.

She paused in the street only long enough to ascertain that Travellers' Way was empty. There was no sign of Reese or the Millers.

But the constable was trotting along behind Angela from the north, one hand clapped to his head to hold his feathered cap in place, the other on his hip to keep his sword from jouncing. Deciding that discretion was the better part of valor, Sarah fled along the footpath that led between the inn and the building next to it and down into the wild land of the hillside below.

The path was nearly invisible in the falling dusk, and wound among the scrub brush and tall grasses. She nearly stepped on the body sprawled face down in the dirt, and was barely able to keep herself from squeaking in alarm.

The constable was still coming. Sarah edged her way around the fallen man while keeping a watchful eye on him, and nearly stumbled over Butch, lying a few feet away. Heart pounding, she ran.

Around the next bend she stopped. No one was coming after her anymore. There was a gabble of voices back up the path where the Miller boys lay. She stopped to catch her breath for a few minutes, then moved carefully among the small trees until she could see what was going on.

Someone brought a lantern. In the circle of its light, Brad Miller was sitting on the path with his head between his hands, groaning. Down the path, Butch stirred. Brian Miller had appeared from somewhere. People were asking Brad what had happened. He shook his head gingerly and said he didn't know. The stranger had hit him with something, maybe—he didn't know what. Butch sat up looking sullen. He was as badly injured, but no one asked him what happened; they asked his older brother.

The constable looked Brad over and said dubiously that there was no mark of a blow. It was his private opinion, expressed quietly to the innkeeper when those two moved dangerously close to Sarah's brushy hiding place, that Brad Miller smelled as if he was suffering primarily from an excess of wine. "Probably fell over each other," he whispered confidentially, "and don't want to admit what clumsy buggers they are."

Sarah backed carefully away from the hubbub and came up onto Travellers' Way a judicious distance from where she had left it. She still didn't know what had become of Reese.

The door to Reese's house was open, and lantern light spilled out of it. Sarah approached with caution, not knowing what she would find.

He was inside, seated on a chair turned toward the door, with a bloody rag held to his face. He looked up apprehensively when Sarah arrived, but relaxed when he saw who it was.

"You all right?" she asked.

"I'll live," he said, his soft accents thickened and muffled. "Shut the door, will you?"

He got up then and rummaged around on the shelves until he found a small glass bottle full of what looked to Sarah like miniature white buttons. He shook a couple of them out onto the table then put them in his mouth.

"What're those things?"

"Aspirin."

"What're they for?"

"Analgesic."

Sarah wished that he would get around to using some words she understood. "Are you hurt?"

"I think the bloody nose is the worst of it. I'd sure as hell like to know who those people were and what they were after me for."

"Millers," Sarah said. She found the basin and got some water from the buckets by the door. She took the rag from him and started cleaning the mess on his face.

"Millers?" he asked crossly. "Give me that. I can do it. What millers? Do I look like a wayward sack of grain?"

Sarah parked herself in the other chair and watched him. Even ill-humored, getting puffy around the eyes, and with his nose swollen, he was worth looking at. "Butch Miller was the man in Rat Alley last night. I think you must be some kind of wizard to get away from them."

Reese's long fingers explored his face gingerly. He had truly aristocratic hands. "A pretty freaking poor kind of wizard. Mind you, a little technological magic helps."

"I don't know what you're saying again."

"Never mind. I'm probably saying too goddamned much. Forget it. There's wine on the shelf over there."

She found two plain wine cups to put it in.

He was inspecting the damage in a small metal-framed mirror when she brought it to him. The clarity of the image in the glass amazed her. It was almost as if one could fall right into it, into another world, a magic land.

"Confusion to our enemies," Reese said, raising the wine cup to her. Sarah looked alarmed, and he relented. "Don't panic, girl. That's just a dumb joke, not a curse." He swallowed half the wine in one long draught and stared into the cup at the remainder. "I'm not doing too well in Monn, am I?"

"Don't know," Sarah answered. "I don't know what you're trying to do."

He gave her a wry smile. "You're not a bad kid, Sarah." He got to his feet. "You'd better run along now. I'm going to bed."

He was turned away from her, fiddling with the bedclothes. The mirror was lying on the table. Sarah hesitated only a second before slipping it into her pocket. Then she went out, closing the door behind her.

Four

Cleo clattered down the iron stairs into the basement computer room, bypassing the lift field because walking felt faster. An air-conditioned chill wafted up to meet her, the contrast in temperature shocking. These days, the only inhabitants of the enclave who merited cool air were computers. She had chosen the loose, short-sleeved nufiber shirt and light bell-bottomed slacks in deference to a night that still held some of the heat of a melting hot day, without a thought for the computer room.

She could have watched the test on her own terminal in her office in Engineering, simply by requesting the picture from the computer. But somehow the scale of the thing demanded size.

The normally busy room was quiet. The lighting was set down to half intensity. She could hear the murmuring voices of people assembled around the big monitor and was half-afraid that she was too late. Hurrying past abandoned desks and dark terminals, she was breathless when she came upon the big semicircular conference table; she looked up at the screen that covered half the wall behind it before even saying hello to any of the dozen or so intent scientists seated around it leaning forward with their eyes glued to the display.

"What's happening?" she asked in lieu of greeting.

"T minus two point five," someone answered without turning to see whom he was talking to.

The scene that held them all spellbound was a massive structure washed by the morning sun on the other side of the world, a dun concrete doughnut set in the middle of a dune field. It dwarfed the dunes and made the power poles marching off into the distance and out of the frame look like matchsticks.

It wasn't an overly handsome doughnut. Things stuck out of it here and there, probe antennae, monitors, guys and guy stays, and mounts for cranes no longer there. Lumps marred the smooth contour of the outer surface, placed apparently at random, wherever space was needed to accommodate some bit of machinery or another.

Around the doughnut were a number of much smaller outbuildings, dollhouses by comparison—dormitories, machine shop, kitchen—all abandoned. Nothing moved but a little heat shimmer off the roofs and a thin drift of sand blowing from the tops of the dunes.

Large yellow numbers at the bottom of the screen backed rapidly down the scale toward zero. The watchers grew silent. No one dared to breathe. Hope was a palpable thing around the table.

Zero came and went. The numbers started climbing the scale again. But before anyone could react with cheers and jubilation, the screen went suddenly blinding white and then dark.

Only the numbers remained; they had stopped at 0:4.90.

The lights came up. Nobody spoke. Nobody moved.

"Shit," Arne said softly.

As if a spell had been broken, there was a general exhalation, a collective sigh. People began to wander quietly off, one at a time, not saying anything. Later, in long and vigorous discussions, lunches would be forgotten while flying pencils covered napkins with figures. Right then, disappointment made any comment seem trivial.

As crestfallen as any of them, Cleo slumped into a recently vacated chair in front of the screen.

A lot of her work had just been blasted into its constituent atoms out there in the African desert.

The failure of the fusion reactor meant that the Treasure Hunt would go on. Reese would stay in Monn, playing Boy Scout, doing his good deed.

Slowly activity in the computer room resumed. She went out, giving the people she knew a limp unhappy wave by way of greeting, and climbed the iron stairs much more sedately than she had clattered down. After a moment's indecision, she went on up a second flight, to Arne's lab.

It wasn't much of a lab as a lab was usually conceived, a small crowded space densely packed with charts and pictures and printouts and the instruments of measurement and control. The actual work went on in the computer in the basement and hundreds of miles away in the West American Enclave's underground particle accelerator. It was only controlled from Arne's lab.

Several active terminals showed screens blank except for the number 0:4.90 at the bottom. The technicians were huddled in a morose group on the far side of the room. Arne had flopped down in the chair by his cluttered desk and was staring out the window. Cleo pulled a stool up beside him. After the coolness downstairs, the air felt thick and hot.

Arne spared her a glance, took in her slight breathlessness and sweat, and asked, "Are the lift fields out, or are you on an exercise kick again?"

On the other side of the window, the lights of the city shone on the high wall that surrounded the entire Mid-American Enclave like the battlements of some medieval stone castle.

"Nothing changes in human history," Arne said. "The walls are poured concrete with a plasteel finish instead of cut stone, and they're protected by an electrified grid instead of threats of eternal damnation, but they serve the same function the walls of an early Christian monastery served—to protect the sublime thoughts of those within from the disturbances of the rude world outside." He stared at the wall and brooded.

"What are you talking about?" Cleo asked.

"Sometimes," he said, "I think we really ought to tear that ugly damned wall down and let the sun shine in."

"It's dark," Cleo said.

"You know what I mean."

"Do that, you'll let the Phobes in."

"Would that be so terrible?"

"Guess not, if you don't mind being outnumbered fifty to one by unwashed illiterate people with lice in their hair and worms in their guts involved in a replay of the Dark Ages and liking it there, who'd take over the whole enclave with arrows and spears, and we could either kill 'em or let 'em and if we let 'em we'd be right back where we were before the Separation. You physicists will be back to begging your living from people who would rather hunt rabbits than quarks and are incapable of comprehending why anyone would think differently.

"Me, I wouldn't like it. From what Reese has told me about primitive societies, I guess women don't fare so well in them."

"All right, already. It was just a thought."

"Hmph. Do some useful thinking. Give me some thoughts about the test. What happened?"

"I don't know. I'll want to see the data from the monitors first, but I think we're close." Arne swung around to face her. He was a thin, hard man with a worried expression overlying a quiet friendliness. Unruly sandy blond hair defied all efforts to control it. Triumph or disaster, Arne never changed.

"Really close," he said. "Four point nine seconds is the next thing to eternity as subnuclear events are measured. Off the top of my head, in the absence of information, I'd say we can sustain a fusion reaction, we just can't contain it."

"Fat lot of good that does."

"Yeah." He turned back to the window. "You want to know something funny? The Old People knew more about controlling fusion than we do. The theory of a fusion reaction is simple enough: smack two hydrogen nuclei together smartly and get one helium and a lot of energy. It's just the practice that's difficult. Toward the end of the twentieth century, they had some short-run, break-even reactors that didn't blow themselves up. So why don't we build on their knowledge, you say? Because it's lost, buried, hidden, destroyed, gone; energy production was a big military secret in the good old days, and you could lose your head back then for telling people how to make the world warm and comfortable for everybody. So the historians say."

"Break-even wouldn't do us much good."

"No, but stable reactors would. Think how long it's taken us to get this far."

"History, Arne. Spilt milk. The question is what do we do in the short term? What do we do tomorrow?"

"Study the data. There's no use trying to guess until we've figured out what we know for sure. And while that's going on, we'll hope there's some genius somewhere who can figure out what went wrong and how to fix it."

"The North African Enclave won't take another test. They're starting to feel picked on."

"What about the Arabians?"

"Who knows about the Arabians? They're an excitable, prickly lot."

"And that sounds just a bit prejudiced, Cleo, my girl. I guess we'd better hope the Treasure Hunters come up with the goods."

"You know what I think about that idea," Cleo said, scowling.

"Mm. 'Pig-headed adventurism,' I think you said. But, my dear, what are we going to do for energy if we can't make fusion go?"

"There's got to be a better way."

"There is, and mostly we use it." Arne frowned while he lectured. "Unfortunately, all the satellites and magnetometers and gravity meters and radiation sensors and seismic lines and all that geological jazz will tell us about fissionable material is where it used to be. The Old People pretty well exhausted all the natural deposits. So we have to look for their leavings, which are not going to be found in geologically sane places."

"I know. Still . . ."

"Energy is our number-one priority. We burn an awful lot of energy per head. You can't even get a glass of water around here without it, and if you could, it wouldn't be fit to drink. We might all properly regret the fact that our ancestors weren't more provident, but it doesn't change anything. Either we have to get fusion going, or fuel the fission reactors, or find some long-lost reserves of petroleum, or do magic. Sun and wind provide only a third of the energy we use. Less than that for the northern enclaves. Hydropower might give us another third if we dared to place very expensive, very vulnerable physical plants out there in Phobe land where no one wants to go, much less live and work."

"I know, Arne. But—"

"We're not talking about a crisis a generation from now. We're talking about next year."

"Yes, Arne, I know. You can stop preaching. I might be a damned ignorant engineer, but I'm not a total idiot."

"Sorry. I get carried away. The thing is, I'm worried. A successful test of fusion is still a long way from getting the energy on-stream. The available reserves of fuel for the fission plants are dangerously low. Even an ignorant engineer understands that, right?"

Cleo nodded. "Still, scrabbling around out there, taking terrible chances, on the basis of a rumor or a hunch or maybe just wishful thinking—it's crazy, no matter how desperate we are. We're putting good people at risk for no reason."

"Maintaining the enclaves isn't exactly no reason. If it's such a fool idea, why do you work with them?"

"Somebody's got to, or those guys would be pulling ruins down on their heads twice a week. Most of them don't know sweet pete about excavating a site."

"And here I thought it was because you were sweet on the chairman and didn't want to see his pet project get axed because of an accident."

"Who do you suppose is going to ax the chairman's project?" Cleo asked crossly, not impressed with Arne's crude humour.

"The rest of the council. Support is just so-so as it is. Chances are the kind of work you're doing is what keeps it alive. You're working against yourself."

"I don't want anyone to get hurt. I'm not about to sabotage the Hunt." Cleo pushed her hands over her face in a most unladylike gesture, as if to rub the lines of strain away. "But I don't have to like it."

"Cleo, if Reese wasn't involved, would you be so much against it?"

A spear of irritation stabbed through Cleo. She suppressed its expression with difficulty. "It's wee morning, and I'm tired, Arne," she said. "I'm going home to bed."

The shadows between those streetlights still lit were pitch black, making the streetscape a study in light and shadow which was repeated vertically up the faces of the tall buildings, an occasional lighted window among the many dark ones. Overhead was a jagged scrap of sky with gibbous moon and stars. It seemed as if there were more stars than there used to be.

The street was empty—most sensible people were asleep. Only a robot streetsweeper kept her company. It had stopped at the end of the block with a rumbling and a spewing of dust, its long hose extending, waving, searching for the hydrant, questing like a blind snake.

Cleo wondered how much energy could be saved by giving the service robots a few more smarts.

A transport pod was sitting idle just in front of her. It could whisk her home along its magnetic track in a little over two minutes. Cleo decided to walk. She wasn't all that anxious to get to her empty apartment.

She missed Reese more than she had ever thought she would.

Every time she thought about him out there, among the primitive, hostile Phobes, she got mad all over again. She was certain that sooner or later he would come to grief. And for what? Some hint, some sign of where the Old People had hidden their caches of fissionable material.

She hated Phobes. She hated their stupid refusal to be reasonable, to learn anything. She hated their animosity toward anyone or anything the slightest bit different.

Could attitudes be genetically determined? Cleo wondered. Reese would say no, that one's cultural truths came with one's mother's milk, taught, not innate. The anthropologist in him wouldn't let him admit the influence of genetics in a social structure.

Cleo wasn't so sure. If, for a few generations, one took from a population those people who were technically competent, independent thinkers, and set them up in communities of their own, surely the people who were left would be less technically competent, less independent, suspicious of knowledge they didn't understand, and breeding children of a like mind. Didn't that describe the Phobes exactly?

She shrugged. Biology was not her best subject, and what she knew of the social sciences was only what she had absorbed from Reese.

Before turning into Residence G, Cleo stopped and looked down the street toward the center of the enclave to the Crystal Spire.

By day, cunningly trapped, reflected, and refracted sunlight made the Spire into a pillar of fire rising impossibly narrow and high in the enclave's central open space. When energy had still been plentiful, the Spire had been a rainbow cascade of light at night, colors and sparkles singing among the prisms and mirrors. Nowadays one could scarcely make out its glassy form under the reduced street lighting. The physical and spiritual center of the Mid-American Enclave, beauty was its sole purpose. That the Spire should be darkened by callous necessity did more to impress upon the citizens the seriousness of the energy crisis they faced than any amount of facts and figures could.

The lighting panels in the apartment's entry came on as Cleo opened the door. The apartment was built on an open plan, with no real partitions. Functional divisions were made with furniture groupings, planters, and an occasional room divider. There were a great many plants, and a grass-green carpet on the floor. One entire wall was a kinematic mural of a seashore that varied randomly from bright sun to storm tossed. Just then it showed breakers and gulls.

The other walls were almost white near the floor, shading to sky blue at the ceiling. The whole place looked about as much like outdoors as indoors possible could. Reese said that he liked it that way, that it gave him a feeling of space. Cleo would have liked some solid divisions, some cozy corners.

It occurred to Cleo that damned nearly everything they did together, they did his way.

He really was a selfish man, doing pretty much what he felt like doing, leaving her to water the plants and feed the freaking cat and find a way to squeeze herself into the cracks of his life. She was getting a little tired of it. She didn't even like the cat.

Aurelius was lying on Reese's desk and he looked up at her with baleful yellow eyes, a look that told her that the house robot had been in to clean. After two years of periodic association and all the reassurances Cleo and Reese had been able to give him, Aurelius remained deeply suspicious of a machine that went whirring and sucking over every surface in the place. He seemed unconvinced that the robot could distinguish between dust mice and orange tom cats. His suspicions were maybe not so unreasonable. The robot did occasionally knock over a potted plant and then proceed to vacuum up the debris, leaving beautifully clean and sterile pot shards in the place the plant used to be.

Cleo sat by the desk in a lounge chair that did its best to

accommodate itself to her tense and upright posture, with minimal success.

"It sure is quiet around here, cat," she said.

Aurelius jumped down, walked over to his food dish, and
looked in. It was empty. He sat down beside it pointedly, com-
municating effectively the essential information that it was very
late and the cat had not been fed.

"You're not subtle," Cleo said.

Reminded of her own empty stomach, she went to the communications and entertainment console, got the food service menu
on the screen, and chose a couple of items without much thought.
Meals were somewhat uninteresting in Reese's absence. She gave
brief consideration to phoning Arne and seeing the night out at
the Orange Chaos where there were lights and music and laughter. Maybe if she got stinking drunk, she would feel better. Maybe
just getting out of her routine for a while would help. She rarely
went out anymore. She was becoming a recluse.

It just didn't feel right. She was too tired anyway.

While she waited for her supper and Aurelius's to arrive, she
leaned back in an easy chair, relaxing a little as it formed itself
to her shape, and let the terminal scroll through a summary of
the day's happenings in the enclaves, which she attended with
half her mind.

If energy got really tight, would the food synthesizer stop
making cat food? The enclave fed itself with a combination of
greenhouses and synthetics, both of which demanded a steady
supply of energy.

A soft ping announced the arrival of her dinner in the delivery
chute near the door.

She set Aurelius's supper out for him, which he begrudgingly
accepted, and brought her own tray back to the terminal. The
news program, sensing her return, took up where she had left it
and continued its review of events. None of it was extraordi-
narily exciting. Nothing much happened any more. Either the
enclaves were stagnating, or she was getting old and blasé. She
dozed over her food.

"Man, is that good."

Cleo came to, startled, disoriented, heart aflutter. Light was
streaming in through a window.

Reese grinned down at her, contentedly munching the sweet roll from her tray.

He was filthy and he stank, he looked as if he had run nose first into a wall, and he was still dressed Monnish fashion, a stranger wearing Reese's face. The thought raced across Cleo's mind, I've lived with him for three years and I don't know this man.

It was a fleeting feeling, and she pushed the tray out of the way so she could hug him.

He held her at arm's length.

"I've been exposed to tuberculosis, so maybe you should restrain yourself, old love, until I've been down to Medical."

"Ugh," Cleo said. "What happened to you?"

"I'm not sure. I thought I was a mugging victim, but Sarah's sure it was a guy who had a grudge from a couple of days ago when I spoiled his fun picking on a kid." He held up a warning finger. "If you say I told you so, I may never speak to you again. Besides, it's not serious."

"Yeah, okay," Cleo said dubiously. "Who's Sarah?"

"She's the kid who was getting picked on."

"How old is this kid?"

"Fourteen, maybe fifteen. I'm not sure. Neither is she."

Cleo absorbed this information without noticeable effect, but inside it didn't sit so well. "What brought you home?"

"Pure lust."

"There's nothing pure about your lust, of that I'm sure. Seriously?"

"I haven't been making much progress, so I thought I'd better come in, take a deep breath, talk to some people, and see if I could figure out what I was doing wrong. Besides which, I need some minor repairs."

"I can tell you what you're doing wrong right now."

"Yeah? What?"

"You're standing here talking to me when you could be having a shower and getting yourself fixed and certified healthy and getting back here before I attack you, tuberculosis, fleas, and all."

He started to turn to follow her instructions, then stopped. "What happened in North Africa?"

"The reactor blew up."

"Shit."

"That's what Arne said."

Aurelius had learned to distinguish the times when he would get unceremoniously chucked out of the bed from the times he could safely occupy the warm, comfortable valley between the humans. He peered over the edge of the bed and decided that it was safe at last. He had been waiting awhile.

"Aurelius, you sod, I've missed you," Reese said sleepily. Aurelius purred his appreciation of the fact.

"Are you going back?" Cleo asked.

"Yeah," he said. "Yeah, I am." His enthusiasm drew him out of his languor. "I've got leads to a couple of sites, I think. We've got the Governor's Mansion already. If we can find another reference point or two, we can start a computer search of the Old People's maps and maybe identify the old city Monn is built on. That might tell us where we should be looking, or if it's worthwhile to go on looking."

"Well, do you have to stay there? Couldn't you come home at night?"

"Mm. That's a lovely thought, but I don't think it would work."

"Why not?"

"Do you know what culture shock is, old love?"

"Sort of, in the absence of experience. The disorientation due to moving from one culture to another."

"Twice a day would be more like cultural electrocution. Adaptable as I am, I don't think I could handle it."

"I miss you, dammit. I want you here once in a while."

"I miss you, too."

"I bet you do, with all those Monnish girls chasing the handsome stranger."

"When you get a chance to see the Monnish girls, you'll stop worrying."

"Even Sarah?"

"Forget Sarah. I told you, she's a kid. And a particularly grubby one at that." He took her face between his hands and made her look at him. "What's got into you? You know me better than this."

"Do I? The way you looked when you came in, it was like I didn't know you at all."

"Well, you see what marvels a bath and a change of clothes have wrought. Underneath all that, it's the same old me."

He was smiling at her, trying to jolly her out of her mood, not taking it the least bit seriously. Her worry and resentment and anger returned.

But his hands were moving, pulling her against his lean strength, and he was kissing her into silence.

Her body responded, almost against her will. For a moment she felt remote from her treacherous flesh, wanting to disown it, with its heavy breathing and its racing heart that distracted her.

Aurelius glowered and hopped off the bed.

Five

Reese awoke feeling disoriented. Cleo had figured largely in his dreams, though not in the usual way, and he was confused to find himself in Monn, in his house, in the full light of day.

His night had been filled with the same puzzle that surfaced at odd moments in waking hours these last few days. Why was Cleo fighting him? He had dreamed of her running ahead of him, erecting barriers he had to scale, while somewhere beyond, the enclave was withering away.

He became aware of a fire crackling in the fireplace, the smell of cooking food, and the presence of another person in the house. He sat up, alarmed.

"Hey, Reese," Sarah said, smiling at him from beside the fire.

"Sarah. How did you get in here?"

Sarah fished in her pocket and displayed a crooked bit of iron she almost always carried. Its cunning curves were adequate to defeat the simple locks that closed most of the houses in Monn.

"What's that?"

"Sezmie," she said.

"Sezmie?"

"That's its name. Like in the story about 'Open, sezmie.' "

"Sesame?" Reese asked.

Sarah pursed her lips in disapproval.

"Remind me to get a carpenter to put a bar on this door before I'm murdered in my sleep," Reese said. "You got nerve, I'll give you that." He looked around the house. Most of his worldly possessions seemed in place. "Kid, I ought to paddle the living daylights out of you."

"You're mad, huh?"

"Damned right."

"Why?"

She honestly didn't know. Her ignorance defused his annoyance. "There's such a thing as privacy," he said.

Sarah thought it over, shrugged, and went back to her cooking. Reese rose and performed as much of his toilet as he felt comfortable doing in her presence. Whatever she was doing by the fire, it smelled good. She brought the results to the table and watched, fascinated, while he applied depilatory to his face and washed away the dark shadow of the previous day's growth of beard.

She noticed that the bruises were almost all gone. It was amazing. He healed fast.

"Why do you do that?" she asked.

Damned good question, Reese thought. "It's the custom in my city," was the best answer he could come up with.

"The men in your city want to look like women. I think your city is a strange kind of place."

"What have you got for us?" he asked, changing the subject. "I have to go to work sometime today."

"A rabbit," she answered proudly.

A rabbit. Well, why not? It wouldn't be the worst thing he had eaten in Monn, even if it made an unusual breakfast.

"I could go with you," Sarah said around a mouthful of roasted meat.

"I don't think that's a such a good idea."

"I can watch out for Butch, don't you see?"

"I think Butch will keep his distance."

Sarah shook her head. She busied herself for a few moments, working at the rabbit carcass until she had a haunch torn loose. She munched awhile in silence, her gaze directed out of the window, her attention directed inward.

"What do you have to do?" she asked.

"Well, first I have to find Red Allen."

"I know where," she said.

Reese sighed. She was impossible to discourage. He didn't have it in his heart to be out and out mean to her.

"All right, then," he said, thinking that he was probably making a mistake. "Let's go."

They went down Travellers' Way toward the center of the city, Reese trying to keep ahead of his unease by walking fast. Sarah trotted to keep up. The housewives out spreading their sheets and featherbeds on bushes to air no longer stopped to look. The man and the girl had been walking that route together for several mornings; the strange and mildly shocking had become the familiar. Whatever the housewives thought was going on, they kept among themselves, meager scandal to pass across the garden fences. The girl was one of the street brats after all, and the man a foreigner, so nobody really cared.

Except Reese. He would have been happy to persuade Sarah to occupy herself some other way. Just about every morning she was waiting outside his place to ambush him on the way to breakfast. She walked with him to the inn, waited for him to eat, and then stuck to him like glue for the rest of the day.

Once he offered to take her inside and get her some food, not so much because he was feeling kindly toward her as because it ruined his appetite to think of her squatting out there in the dust, waiting for him. She said she didn't think she should, because if she went inside, Harold the innkeeper would call the constable and she would get chucked in jail for ever and ever.

Once he asked her if she didn't have something better to do. She said, "No."

Now and then she would disappear on some errand of her own, but she always came back. After a bit, he gave up trying to chase her away and tried to ignore her.

It wasn't easy.

Nothing stemmed the flow of questions. She asked him about everything. This morning it was what she called The Medallion. He could all but see the capital letters on the name. "Is this a magic thing? There's nothing on it. How come it has no image? What spirit is it for? I bet you angered some powerful witch and they wiped the engraving off as a warning, right?"

Eventually, irritated and not too comfortable about the casual way she handled the tracer, nor with the way her interest in it kept her tousled head right under his chin and her warm breath on his neck, he said, "The engraving is invisible. You have to have magic to see it." That was undoubtedly another mistake.

He thought she would get the message that he didn't want to talk about it any more.

But she accepted his explanation as perfectly reasonable. "Oh," she said.

"That was meant to be a joke," he said. "You weren't supposed to take it seriously."

"Oh," she said.

"How is it a smart girl like you believes in witches and demons and magic?"

Sarah looked up at Reese to see if he was serious. He was.

"You'd have to be pretty dumb and stupid not to," she said.

"Why?"

" 'Cause."

"Pretend I'm dumb and stupid. Explain it to me."

"Well, it's things that happen all the time. Like you put something away in a special place and the next time you look it's gone and you look everywhere but it's gone and then later you find it someplace else from where you know you put it. If there isn't some wicked imps around making mischief, how can a thing like that happen?"

Reese groaned. He closed his eyes and shook his head.

Young though he was, Red Allen had a red face and red hands which would have earned him his name even if his carroty hair had not. He worked in the bakery, and so his work was nearly done for the day. When Sarah pointed him out, he was squatting in the yard beside the baker's big clay oven, tending the fire.

He looked up and saw Sarah. "That little thief's not coming in here," he said.

Sarah shrugged and vanished among the buildings. Red Allen turned back to his fire.

"Harold the innkeeper said you know of an Old People's place," Reese said.

Red Allen shook his head. "Your Honor wouldn't want to be going there. Nothing of value there anymore."

Reese counted a few coins into the dust beside him.

"The walls have started to fall," Red Allen said. "A man could get killed."

Reese counted out a few more coins.

"There's spirits of the Old People about, I think."

A few more coins.

"But if Your Honor is determined, it would be my pleasure to show the way."

They had to wait for the grumpy, flour-grayed baker to come and test the loaves in the oven by extracting one with a paddle on a long stick and thumping it soundly. Then there was the further delay while the loaves were removed from the oven and stacked on shelves inside. Reese would have offered his help, except he feared that baker and baker's helper would find his offer so extraordinary as to be frightening. So he folded his arms and leaned against the bole of the one sickly tree in the baker's yard, its meager shade welcome with the sun already hot, and waited. Much of the life in Monn seemed to consist of waiting for one thing or another.

Red Allen was finally done and came batting at his clothing to knock the flour off and grooming himself by raking his fingers through the red tangle of his hair. He led Reese through the city streets to the north, and out of the city proper into an open field where cattle grazed, and from there into a wooded area where a wagon track betrayed the activities of woodcutters. Reese was conscious of Sarah trailing along behind.

The place might have been a natural meadow, except it was unnaturally flat. Red Allen squatted and dug at the earth with the knife he had taken from his belt. In a moment he motioned to Reese to observe his shallow scraping. Beneath two inches or so of earth and grass roots, flat gray slate peeked out.

A little further on, almost lost in the undergrowth, they came upon the remains of a stone wall. Even covered with moss and struggling treelings, it was plain that the stones had been dressed by tools more sophisticated than anything to be found in Monn. Any loose stones there might have been had long since been carted away in spite of Red Allen's assurance that no one ever came to this place.

Furthermore, someone had started an excavation, straight down, cribbed like a well, just on the other side of the wall. It was cunningly hidden among small trees and bushes, and Reese might easily have missed seeing it without Red Allen's help. He laid himself out flat on the ground and peered into the mouth of the hole. Perfect, uncompromising darkness was all that he saw.

"I'll need a rope or something," he told Red Allen.

Red Allen stood well back from the opening. "There is a farmer nearby," he said, "who might loan such a thing if there were silver in it for him."

"Let's go talk to him, then."

"If it please Your Honor, it might be best if I went alone. This is a crafty man with no little greed about him, and if he were to see Your Honor's fine clothes I think the price would be much higher."

You think I'm a simpleminded fool, don't you? Reese thought. Okay, I can live with that. If I'm stupid, I'm not dangerous, and if you think money can be easily extracted, I'll get a lot more cooperation.

Reese leaned with his back against the broken wall. Red Allen went to negotiate for the equipment. There would be more waiting.

Sarah appeared, sitting on the stone wall like a ragged pixie. She was chewing on a dark, heavy bun from the baker's oven, and there were several more suspicious bumps in her pockets. "He knew you'd need a rope," she said. "He's just going to take your money for nothing."

"I know," Reese said.

"Don't you care?"

"Not much."

"That's pretty strange."

"Strangers are bound to be strange, aren't they?"

"Yeah, I guess."

The redhead returned with a coil of rope about his shoulders and a lantern in his hand. He glowered at Sarah and snatched at the half-eaten bun. Sarah evaded him and smiled a crumb-laden smile.

But nothing was going to induce the boy into the shaft. "I'll keep watch for Your Honor," he said, "lest thieves and ruffians be lurking about." Reese could have reminded him that he had said no one came there, and that there was nothing to steal in any case, but thought better of it. He tied one end of the rope to the base of a sturdy young tree and the other end to the lantern. After much mucking about with flint and steel, the lantern was lit and lowered about fifteen feet into the bottom of the shaft. Reese slid down the rope after it.

Sarah was right behind him. "Red Allen's scared of the Old People's ghosts."

"Aren't you?"

"They never did me no harm."

Like most of the sites Reese had explored, this one had been raided over the years, and anything the people thought valuable had been removed. Amid concrete walls which were beginning to crumble, he could find little evidence of what the basement had once held. In one room there were signs that metal racks had once been bolted to the wall, rust stains outlining them, but enterprising townsmen had chiseled the bolts out of the concrete and carted them away for the precious iron.

Reese had come to believe that most of the stories about the spirits of the Old People haunting these ruins were started by scavengers who wanted to keep their finds to themselves. But the stories had been told often enough and long enough to have become part of the folklore, and nowadays only the most intrepid and desperate scroungers dared to offend the ghosts.

And Sarah, who seemed exempt from all the rules.

Coupled to ignorance and native superstitions, the stories held a certain power. But in the end, the metal was too precious to give up, and the paper too valuable as a fire starter—the gods only knew how many irreplaceable documents had been used to light the smith's forge or the innkeeper's hearth—so they dared the ghosts of the Old People and took away everything they could move. They didn't think of themselves as archeologists' enemies; they were only people trying to make a living in a hard world.

The result was the same as if they had been deliberate vandals. Nothing was left to provide the urgent information about what function the building that once stood above this basement had served.

In one place, one of the concrete beams that supported the ceiling had fallen, part of it lying at an angle, the rest in huge broken chunks on the floor. The reinforcing rod that had been exposed had been cut away; Reese could see the butt ends in the broken concrete. The beam itself had been attacked by mallets, but without success. Beyond the beam, some part of the roof had fallen in, dumping earth and now dead vegetation into the hole. It did seem, as Red Allen promised, a dangerous site, and one that offered little hope of providing the data Reese sought.

"There's nothing here," Sarah said.

"I'm afraid you're right," Reese answered. Holding the lantern high, he was turning away, ready to leave, when a gleam of light caught his eye.

Beyond the broken beam and the fallen earth, something metallic returned the lantern's glow.

The scavengers had missed some bit of metal? It seemed unlikely. Reese peered under the beam, but he could see nothing. Sparing a glance to the ceiling and wishing he had Brother Parker's faith, he ducked under and made his way across the litter. He found himself confronting a large metal door.

It was painted a brownish gray, and the paint was scarred in places where tools had been applied in vain. Some of the work must have been recent, for some of the exposed steel was still shiny. A large metal wheel was mounted on the surface, alongside some fancy lockwork and a stainless steel bar which probably served as a handle. The letters "CHUBB" were engraved at the top.

Reese stared at it as comprehension slowly dawned.

"What's that thing?" Sarah asked.

"A safe. Sarah, darling, we've found a safe, which our friendly neighborhood scavengers haven't got into."

"That's a good thing, eh?"

"Uh-huh."

In safes the Old People had put money, valuable papers, and secrets. And a safe that size would probably contain something more interesting than a merchant's accounts.

Reese grinned like a kid at Christmas. For the first time since he had come to Monn, he thought his wild adventure had some small hope of success. For a moment he stood quietly with his hand flat on the cold metal. Don't get your hopes up, he told himself. Chances are it's full of the paper currency of a long-dead civilization, and the forgotten wills of folks ten generations in the grave.

Getting into it would require some help and some equipment. His mind on the logistics of the problem, he made his way back to the shaft, Sarah trailing along behind, asking questions.

The sun had risen high while they had been exploring, and

from the bottom of the shaft, Reese could see only a glare of
sunlight. He extinguished the lantern and tied it to the end of
the rope, called to Red Allen, and then went up, hand over hand.

He made a graceless exit, holding the rope with one hand,
bracing his other elbow on the mouth of the shaft, and flopping
his upper body onto the earth. Red Allen offered no assistance.
In fact, Red Allen was nowhere to be seen.

Reese turned to give Sarah a hand, but she had already
swarmed up the rope like a monkey.

"I told you Red Allen's scared," she said.

Reese dusted himself off and let her lead the way back to
town.

He knew there was trouble when he saw the door of the house
hanging open. He had closed and locked it when he left in the
morning.

Things were broken and scattered on the floor with a vicious
disregard for function or value. The cupboard doors were broken, the precious pane of glass in the window smashed. Shelves
had been cleared with a swipe of an arm, leaving untouched
items in the corners. The water buckets had been emptied onto
the bed, then thrown into the fireplace. The table had deep
gouges from a knife blade. The intruders' only interest had been
in destruction.

Reese waded into the mess and stood unbelieving, in the middle of it. He bent and rescued a fist-sized crystal cube and set it
on the table.

"Shit," he said.

"Millers," Sarah answered, but her attention was on the crystal. A shaft of light from the broken window touched it, and
inside she could see the figure of a woman. She walked around
the crystal and saw the woman from all sides. But she didn't
touch it.

She had heard about terrible, strong sorcery that could be used
to trap an enemy in a shard of amber. She wasn't all that sure
what amber was except that it was hard and clear. This could
be it. She looked at Reese with her mouth hanging open. He
might seem disheartened, standing there in the wreckage of his
home, but obviously he had been in touch with mystic powers.
She wondered if he might not find another crystal for Butch.

She didn't think she would feel too unbearably bad if he did.

* * *

In the Crow's Eye, Crazy Karen danced among the tables while patrons shouted encouragement in the form of cheers and promises of their crude sexual favors to come. They threw silver and kept the rhythm for her with their palms against the wooden tables. Crazy Karen's eyes gleamed in the firelight, and sweat rolled down her face as she kicked her legs and threw her skirts about.

In a corner by the fire, Butch Miller yelled with the best of them, egged on by the presence of the pair of well-known rowdies with him, demanding Crazy Karen's presence at his table.

But when she had danced herself to exhaustion, Karen slipped out the back of the tavern and went home with nobody. That was all right. She was crazy, and no one expected sense from her. The taverner told his boy to sweep up the coins. He would keep them for her, most of them, anyway, that the boy didn't steal, until she came for them.

But when Brad Miller came in, the taverner sent out for his eldest son. When the Miller boys got rambunctious he needed help.

Brad Miller plunked himself down across the table from his brother and would not listen to Butch's talk of Crazy Karen. He told Butch's companions to get lost. They took a good look at Brad's face and went.

"Lord God protect us from stupid younger brothers," Brad hissed in a harsh whisper that would have been a shout if he hadn't been greatly inhibited by not wanting others to overhear family business.

Butch looked at him blankly, not comprehending what his brother was going on about. Brad didn't often have kind words for his brother, but he usually had some sort of excuse for being nasty.

"Did my little brother get himself into a little old temper tantrum like a dumb kid? That was a stupid kid's trick, you brick-head. Stupid. Really stupid."

"Stop calling me stupid," Butch said.

"Ah, shut up. Do you want people to hear?"

"I don't know what you're talking about."

"The hell you don't. I'm talking about what you did to the stranger's place, that's what I'm talking about."

"So what?"

Brad turned his face to heaven as if petitioning for strength. "I don't believe this." He leaned toward his brother. "Listen, chicken brain, no matter what the constable thinks, you know and I know that bastard isn't your ordinary wayfaring stranger. What would you call a guy who went out of his way to irritate a witch?"

"A witch?" Butch turned this notion over for a while as he chewed his mustache. "You really think so, Brad?" he asked, worry for the moment overcoming filial antipathy.

"How else do you explain what happened? How else could a man be laid out like dead in the blink of an eye without a hand on him?"

"What're we going to do, Brad?"

"We? We? Did 'we' smash up a witch's house?"

"Brad," Butch cried, really worried.

Brad enjoyed his brother's distress for a moment and then relented. He was, after all, already too involved in this business himself. "Come on, then."

"What're we going to do?"

"We're going to get some help."

"Where're we going?"

"To the Temple."

Six

There were times when Brother Parker knew that he was the nexus of momentous events. He could feel God's hand molding man's fate through him, could almost, almost, grasp the Divine Plan. At those times, he would spread his arms and the Power would surge through him, filling him body and soul till he thought he would burst with it, filling him, strengthening him until he was equal to anything the unholy could throw at him, man or demon. He was in his element. He knew his way. He did the Lord God's work full of confidence and joy.

At other times he felt he was drowning in mundane trifles. His flock needed constant reassurance; the True Church needed funds to carry on the work of the Lord; he needed trustworthy followers to collect the gifts of the faithful and sometimes to persuade the faithful to be more generous; he needed accountants and guards to protect the True Church from the actions of ungodly thieves; he needed preachers and places to preach, and good converts with missionary zeal to gather up the flock so they could hear the Word; he needed to feed and house those faithful workers lest empty stomachs weaken their faith, and so he needed cooks and cleaners and custodians and hard men to bargain in the marketplace and craftsmen to maintain the Temple; and he needed to train those who would train the workers in the modesty and deportment required from men and women who represented the True Church. Also, his presence was often requested at births, deaths, feasts, and funerals, often by powerful people he could not afford to refuse; he had to mediate in internecine squabbles, bolster the faith of those who weakened, recruit new members, instruct initiates, battle endlessly with the civil authority for the hearts and minds of the people, care for his own health and welfare, and find time withal to pray to the Lord God for the strength to continue.

This night was one of the times of drowning. Brother Eric had been pointing out that contributions to the Church were woefully slim that season, and that fewer and fewer people were coming to the gatherings. The two were sitting in Brother Parker's study with mutton and wine on the table between them.

"It's the thin crops and the promise of a poor harvest that's doing it," Brother Eric said. "They're hanging onto their coins and wondering how they're going to make it through the winter. They take some persuading to get them to believe they've any to spare for us."

Brother Parker smiled to himself. Brother Eric occasionally let a rough pragmatism carry him away and would quite likely bring reluctant souls to God at sword point if not restrained. It was a characteristic Brother Parker sometimes found useful.

"There's more," Brother Eric said. "It's being whispered about that some folks are returning to pagan ways. I heard a tale of a white bull to be slaughtered in the light of the new moon on the hunchback's farm, with more than one good man ready to dip his hands in the blood and call on the ancient gods to bring back the rains."

"We will get the Brothers together with torches and put an end to that," Brother Parker said. He shook his head sadly. "They are as perverse as children. Knowing what is right, they persist in their mischief."

"There could be trouble," Brother Eric said, not unhappily. He had been looking for an excuse to bring the hunchback to heel for some time. A man with the Lord God's mark already on him should not be so arrogant.

"As the Lord God wills," Brother Parker said.

There was a hesitant knock on the door, and a Brother put his head in to announce that Brad and Butch Miller insisted on seeing Brother Parker.

Given a choice, Brother Parker would have sent the louts and their drunken appeal on their way so he could have his dinner in peace. Neither one of them could be described as a staunch supporter of the True Faith. He felt justified in a modicum of skepticism about their sincerity. However, the Family Miller could not be simply ignored. The big men shuffled into Brother Parker's study reeking of the tavern.

Brad did all the talking. Butch stood beside him, nodding confirmation like a young ox.

"God's love to you this evening, Brother."

"And you, Brad Miller. What can I do for you?"

"I trust the Lord God's work goes well."

"Well enough. It keeps me busy. What is it you want?" Brother Parker had no trouble exhibiting a little impatience, and discovered even a Miller could take a hint if it was sufficiently broad.

"Brother, we need a holy man. A real holy man. I don't know, you're probably the only one who can deal with this."

"Yes?" Brother Parker asked, pulling himself up a little straighter.

"There's a witch in the city."

"How do you know?"

"We saw him, the brick-h—my brothers and me."

"You know a witch to see one?"

"Brother, you preached often enough that there is a stink around evil that's hard to miss."

"True," Brother Parker said. "I had no idea you were listening."

"I was listening. A modest man like yourself, Brother, wouldn't realize how much influence—"

Brother Parker waved away the flattery. "Tell me what you saw."

"There's this stranger comes to the Inn of the Honest Keeper and he's got an odd kind of talk. I guess he must have put spell on poor Harold the innkeeper, 'cause he always gets the best service and the first. There's a shimmer in the air around him, like maybe a spirit eats with him, and I swear to you, Brother, he packs away enough for two good men.

"He scares people, I mean to tell you. Except maybe Angela, Harold's girl. She can't take her eyes off him. You know what I mean. I figure she's enchanted.

"You always told us to fight evil wherever we find it. What happened was the other night, when this guy left the inn, me and my brothers went after him, figuring to explain how this was a God-fearing city where our Church leaders taught us to know the Devil's servants, and how the dark powers weren't welcome around here.''

"You were not afraid?" Brother Parker asked.

"Yeah, I was, and my brothers, too. But as you always say, a man has to do his duty the best he can. We caught up with the stranger in the wild land below the inn where no honest man has business and we told him we were God-fearing men and we weren't going to stand for any hell-bound witch hanging around causing trouble.''

"That was uncommonly brave," Brother Parker said.

Brad bowed his head in modest acknowledgment. "The stranger got sore for being found out. We were going to bring him up to the Temple, thinking you'd be the man to know what to do in a situation like this. Butch went to take hold of him.

"I don't know what happened then. Maybe you could explain it to me. All of a sudden, Butch fell down at the witch's feet like he was dead. And there was this witch light glowing all around. When I went to see what had happened to the brick-h— Butch, I was knocked down, too.

"This is a strong witch, good Brother. I think it's going to take all the power of the True Church to beat him.''

"What about Brian? You have said nothing of him.''

Brad drooped as if the thought of Brian made him sad. "You understand how it is, brother. Brian is young. Just a boy, really," Brad shrugged. "He ran. Not that he got away. He hasn't had his proper wits about him since. We haven't found a way to break the spell. Maybe you could do something for the poor kid.''

Brother Parker glanced at Brother Eric. Brother Eric's eyes sparkled as he considered the possibilities. Only Brother Parker's frown kept him from spilling out his enthusiasm.

"Wait outside, young sirs," Brother Parker said. "I must give this some thought.'' The Millers obediently left the room and shut the door behind them.

The door was scarcely closed when Brother Eric blurted out, "It's perfect. It's just what we need.''

"Which is?''

"A demonstration of the Church in action. It's convenient it

should be a stranger, without family and associates to complicate the matter.''

"I suspect strangers also have families. Doesn't it strike you
odd that the Millers, of all people, should be able to provide
exactly what we need exactly when we need it?'' Brother Parker
asked. "We could not call the family enthusiastic followers of
the True Faith.''

"The Lord works in mysterious way, His wonders to perform,'' Brother Eric said.

"Truly He does,'' Brother Parker agreed, touching the cross
that hung on his chest. He did not add that the dark powers also
worked in mysterious ways. There was something eerie about
the situation, something devilish in the air.

"A man in his cups,'' he said, "even if he is a family member, does not make the most reliable witness, though I think it
would not be wise to make our doubts known to Brad Miller.

"Go to the Millers and tell them I am at my prayers, that I
will seek the Lord God's guidance. Then speak to the Brothers
and Sisters and learn if there has been any talk of a witch in the
city of late. I will be on the roof.'' Brother Parker paused. "If
we should happen to unleash the force of the True Church to
resolve a drunk's wine-soaked hallucinations, we should look,
at the very best, quite foolish. Don't you agree?''

Brother Eric left, at least a little bit subdued.

Around the tall steeple that jutted from the Temple and held
the Cross of God up to the sky, a narrow, railed platform had
been laid on the Temple's tiled roof. There Brother Parker often
retired for quiet contemplation.

The Temple rested on a small rise of ground. Enemies of
the True Church sometimes said that the mound was built of the
bones of unbelievers. That was horribly untrue. And if the
Church had to fight for truth and the souls of men at times, it
only proved the strength of the powers of darkness and richly
demonstrated the need for unwavering determination in carrying
the Word to the people.

The city of Monn lay spread out below him, the rambling
streets and jumbled rooftops displaying an innocent beauty in
the moonlight that was all too lacking by day. Brother Parker
experienced a surge of fellow feeling for the dreaming innocents

down there, wicked in their ignorance though they might be. Lost souls, every one, and it was his work to show them the Way.

An agent of the dark powers would find fodder aplenty among those wavering, uncertain hearts. They slept on, innocent of their danger.

The moon, round and nearly full, had tipped to the west, touching the cliffs above the city, the ironwork of the trestle bearing the Witch Road like filigree across its demon face. The Demon of the Moon mocked him, peeking coquettishly through the Philes' girders and beams like a lady through her lace veil.

He dragged his thoughts back to the important question of the moment, the witch. Or, more appropriately, Brad and Butch Miller.

Brother Parker did not doubt for a moment that Brad and Butch had some motive more personal than service to the True Church. In no way could he believe that the boys were anxious to hand over a witch because of a sudden attack of religious fervor or any equally sudden revulsion to witchcraft. Let some winsome maid catch their eye and they would be up the hill like a pair of goats, wheedling love charms out of Cat Anna.

It was unfortunately true that most of the young bucks of the city had a pragmatic approach to both witchcraft and religion. They believed what was convenient to the moment.

Cat Anna was another problem. If the stories were true, she had moved lords, whole families, and even the governor himself. She made no claims to magic or witchcraft, or ever said that her toothless incantations were effective, but those who went to visit the rheumy-eyed old crone huddled over her fire more often came away satisfied than not.

So if Eric needed a witch to burn, why not Anna?

Because Brother Parker wouldn't dare. Though he didn't know how it had come about, since the old woman scarcely ever moved from her stinking cave, Cat Anna had a strong influence in the community. Often she led honest folk away from the teachings of the True Church, but he dared not denounce her, for even among his own most devoted followers there were those who had been born into Cat Anna's hands and who held the wretched hag in high regard. And some in the Governor's Mansion as well.

Furthermore, in spite of Eric's enthusiasm, Brother Parker wasn't all that sure that witch burnings were effective. In the history of the True Church, stakes had from time to time stood in Market Square, and there seemed no fewer witches for that.

He must also consider the governor. There was growing uneasiness in the Governor's Mansion about the disposition of witches, which was itself indicative of deeper concerns, the encroachment of the Church upon civil matters. Or, as Brother Parker more often thought of it, the unwillingness of the secular administration to leave spiritual matters in the hands of the Church.

The new governor was young. He had yet to learn that he held his high office at the Lord God's pleasure.

Brother Parker did not want to fight that battle just yet. When all was said and done, the Church should be the final authority in all things. No man should argue with the will of the Lord God. But the time was not right for the contest. The Church did not yet have the strength to win. If it came to pass that he was to condemn a man innocent of satanic influence as a witch, the Church would lose much ground before the battle was even joined.

There was, of course, the possibility that the Millers had actually come upon a witch and had seen the wisdom and rightness of letting the True Church deal with it in the appropriate manner.

Then there was the matter of the Church as a credible force in the society. The Millers had come to him with a problem that was, on the face of it, a simple matter of the forces of good pursuing and rooting out the agents of evil. That was certainly within his mandate, and surely the Lord God would not look kindly on one of his servants who declined that duty simply because it was not convenient.

And above all that was the truth in what Brother Eric proposed. The people did need to see the True Church in action, did need to be reminded of the terrible power and justice of the Lord God, did need to be reminded not to forget the care of the spirit in the midst of their concern about the care of the body.

It was difficult to know how best to proceed.

Brother Parker knelt on the rough boards, turned his face toward the stars, and asked the Lord God for guidance. Then he went back into the Temple.

* * *

Butch followed Brad out of the Temple not a great deal less worried than he entered it. He had been forbidden by his brother to say a single word in front of the Brothers, and he was bursting with things to say.

"You lied to the Brothers," he complained. "What'd you say all that stuff for?"

"Should I have told them you got us into this mess because you fought with the witch over a snot-nosed street pig?"

"You didn't have to say that about Brian."

"Oh, shut up, you twit. You got us into this. At least keep out of my way so I can get us out."

Butch subsided, but he was not happy. He wasn't comfortable about the lies. What if the Brothers found out? What if God was angry? What should he do?

He followed Brad back to the Crow's Eye in a welter of confusion. He wondered if he dared discuss it with his father. Robert tended to be roughly impatient with his middle son.

Seven

In her secret hideaway in the Old People's place, Sarah lay under a scrap of blanket on the sheepskin on her straw bed and stared into the darkness, afraid that Reese was never coming back. In the hole under Young Albert's field, he had called her darling. "Sarah, darling," he had said. And now he was gone.

She had searched the city for him. He had walked out of the ruins of his house and closed the door behind him and disappeared.

It was funny. People had come and gone in her life before without leaving a hollow space. It was something like the way she felt when she tried to remember the shadowy figure in her childhood that she thought must be her mother.

Eventually she slept an uneasy sleep, filled with dreams. She dreamed they strode across the land together, two powerful adventurers, and no one could harm them, and it was springtime wherever they went. She dreamed that he lay beside her on the skin, here in her own place, that his strong hands drew her to him, that she was helplessly in his power, that her body, like a thing apart, was tense and quivering and waiting for him.

She woke with pounding heart, breathless, alone.

She put her hands between her legs and squeezed her knees together to close the damp and empty place.

Some people put great store by dreams. Sarah was troubled as she left her hideaway and went into the city in search of her breakfast. Some of the tension stayed with her as she climbed the rail fence into Mean Morris's yard just as the first rays of the sun touched the thatch on the barn roof and roused the rooster to his raucous song.

She had made peace with Mean Morris's dog long ago, and it came with wagging tail to greet her. The fruits on Mean Morris's tree were withered and green, but a warm brown egg under his red hen made up for sour apples.

Hunger momentarily satisfied, she found herself on Travellers' Way, climbing the hill toward Reese's house as if some enchantment were pulling her there.

Squatting in the tall dry grasses by the roadside, she watched from a respectful distance. Except for a pair of crows walking, heads bobbling, on the path leading to the door as if in search of something, there was no sign of life around the house. Peeved, she found a small rock and pitched it at the larger of the two birds. The crow jumped easily over the missile and turned its shiny black eye on her and laughed: haw-haw! Sarah hated crows anyway. They were the devil's birds, hearts as black as their feathers, and they hung around dead things. They had no business hanging around Reese's place.

She went to the square. The storyteller wasn't there, but Martin was, and she went around with him for a while although she didn't like him much. He fawned and drooled like a puppy, and he was so dreadfully young. They managed to grab a bundle of oat cakes, Sarah drawing the vendor's attention while Martin made off with the loot, then passing the goodies between them until the harried merchant gave up the chase. That activity distracted her for the length of time it took them to squat behind the pile of stone in the mason's yard and munch down their booty. But she grew restless again immediately.

She trudged slowly back up the hill to Travellers' Way, head hanging, kicking at the dust.

Nothing had changed since last time she had been there, except that the crows were gone.

She let herself in. Reese had locked the door behind them when he left the previous night. Kind of a silly thing to do, considering the state of the window. He might have at least closed the shutters.

Sezmie made it easier to go in the door than through the broken window. Inside, she picked some bits of glass carefully out of the frame and set them down against the wall, thinking there must be some use for it, even broken.

Reese's things lay scattered where they had been thrown. He had made no effort to clean up. Sarah picked the book up off the floor, dusted it off with her sleeve, and set down it gently on the table. He would come back for his stuff, wouldn't he? Surely he would.

She dragged the damp straw mattress out onto the dry grass where the sun could get at it before it got musty. She picked the buckets out of the fireplace and set them down by the door, thinking she would take them to the well and wash the ashes out of them if she could find a brush or something to clean them with. She found a shirt that still smelled of him, and hugged it to herself until she thought how dumb that was. Her cheeks reddened, and she hung the shirt up on a wooden peg in the wall and busied herself throwing chunks of broken pottery into the big basin so she could take them outside, working fast to cover her embarrassment though there was no one there to see.

There was much among the debris that Sarah couldn't identify. In her mind, that went into the general miscellaneous category of "broken stuff," though she was fascinated almost beyond endurance by the box of strange material with the little flat plate inside that shone with silvery colors like a slice of rainbow.

She turned it in the light and watched the colors swing around the plate like the spokes of a wheel. She was still playing with it when she became aware of another presence. She whirled to face the door and found a figure in the doorway, its face in shadow, the sunlight behind it making it look almost luminous.

Then he stepped into the room. It was only Reese.

Only Reese? Her heart leaped with gratitude to the fates who had given the Legend of Sarah a second chance. Now if she could only find a way to hold his interest.

"I could show you my place."

Reese turned from his efforts to make a cupboard door go back into its place and studied her. Her back to him, she was sweeping the ashes off the hearth with unnecessary vigor.

He was touched by her efforts to clean up. She had that sweet, ingenuous smile and guileless way of looking at him. If he suspended his natural skepticism, he could almost believe she was a rough-cut, artless angel child, full of nothing but good will. If it hadn't been for the missing mirror, he could almost believe it.

"You didn't want to do that a few days ago," he said.

"I didn't know you then."

"You know me now?"

"You want to see it or not? You said you did."

Well, he told himself, if you keep your stuff tied down, how much harm can she do? And that's what you're here for after all, to map the ruins of the Old People's places. Better take the chance while you've got it.

"I'd like that, Sarah," he said.

The Old People's building where Sarah lived was a couple of blocks and a short walk through wasteland away from Rat Alley, then down a steep embankment that looked as if something might have collapsed beneath it.

Broken, jagged beams of concrete stuck up through the grass and small brush, or lay half-concealed beneath it, eroded and rust-stained, a colossal skeleton moldering in the sun. It showed signs of quarrying activity by enterprising townsfolk in search of building material, but they had given up, maybe found easier pickings elsewhere. A crow lifted from the top of one of the beams as Reese and Sarah approached and flapped off heavily, hurling back at them a flurry of crow curses.

Sarah led the way along a tunnel she had worn in the greenery. It was far too snug a fit for Reese, and he had to push the growth aside, duck under limbs, and untangle clutching branches. By the time Sarah started down a flight of half-buried concrete steps that led beneath the remains of a drifted-over and overgrown wall, he was well behind her, and becoming frustrated.

She waited patiently for him to catch up.

The cement floor at the base of the stairs showed clearly the track Sarah had worn in the accumulated dust and debris. But away from the steps the place was pitch dark. Reese had to feel his way along, guided by Sarah's small rough hand in his.

After a while she let go of him and rustled around for a bit. Then a candle's small flame blossomed in the blackness.

In a small room walled off from the rest of the basement, Sarah had built herself a nest like a pack rat might build, filled with the products of her scrounging piled and stacked and hung on nails, a braided skein of onions, some items of well-worn clothing, a small rough bowl containing an interesting variety of candle stubs, some lengths of cord, a couple of burlap-wrapped bundles, part of a cheese, some brass buttons, cooking utensils, and Reese's mirror. Some of the dust and cobwebs had been removed. A loose pile of straw and a moth-eaten sheepskin served as a bed.

"This is my place," she said proudly.

But instead of admiring it as she had expected him to do, Reese asked, "Where did you get the nails?" They were not the rough products of some smith's labor, but smooth and round and uniform, albeit rusty.

Crestfallen, Sarah swallowed her disappointment. "I'll show you," she said.

She led him with the flickering light of the candle amid rooms and corridors whose extent was lost in the wavering shadows. Holding the candle high, she showed him a cavernous room with concrete pillars two feet square supporting the ceiling. Some square ducts of galvanized iron still clung to the ceiling, but most were lying battered on the floor, white and red with oxidation, but better preserved in the dry, cool, dark place than Reese had any right to expect. The insulation on the cables that swooped down came away in Reese's hands, but the metal was still recognizable as copper.

The nails lay in a heap against a pillar, whatever container had originally held them long since turned into rats' nests. There were similar heaps of other things all over the floor; intricate chromium-plated objects with most of the plating peeled off; a tangle of rough iron pipes threaded at the ends; pulley wheels; coils of wire with the insulation mouse-chewed to dust; half a dozen short aluminum ladders in remarkably good shape; stacks of rusty cans with their rainbow contents leaked out onto the floor; more nails; bolts one place, nuts another, too corroded now to fit together; some still-shiny brass screws; short lengths of hexagonal rod with flattened ends, some with their plastic handles still in place though cloudy and brittle with age; and coils and coils of plastic pipe, most black in the candlelight, but some green, with corroded metal fittings.

"Hardware," Reese said, delighted.

Sarah was becoming accustomed to his incomprehensible talk. She said only, "The candle is getting too small. We have to go back."

Enchanted by his find, Reese gave no thought to an action which to him had the ordinariness of sneezing. He reached deep into an inner pocket and removed a small package, which he bent sharply and pushed against a concrete pillar where it stayed. A cool greenish light flooded from it, brighter than the candle.

At the sound of the candle dropping and Sarah's sharp gasp, Reese realized what he had done.

He turned to her. She stared at him.

"Sarah?"

"That's magic," she said in a hoarse whisper. "Phile magic." She backed away from him. "The worst kind, that'll send you straight to hell."

"Take it easy, Sarah," Reese said. "There's nothing magic about it." He held out his hand to her, wanting to calm her.

She tucked her hands behind her.

He took a step toward her. She took a step away.

Reese stood there a moment, baffled by the impasse, and then raised his hands and turned back to the treasure trove of Old People's artifacts.

After a bit, emboldened by her safe distance, Sarah said, "Now I know how come I did it."

Reese made no further attempt to approach her. "Did what?" he asked from where he was.

"Brought you to my place. I never did that before. I never showed no one my place. You witched me."

"No, I didn't, Sarah. You don't believe that."

"You're a witch. A Phile witch." There was fear in Sarah's voice, but also an element of admiration. "Now I know how come the Millers couldn't get you. Poor dumb pork-heads, what chance against a Phile witch's power?" She laughed aloud, like it was an enormously good joke.

But she sobered quickly, glowering at the dusty floor. "But it's all right, isn't it, for an ordinary person to love a Phile?"

Reese looked up sharply from the intriguing archaic cleverness of the corroded little electric motor he had been inspecting. Great gods of the galaxy, he thought, what have I got into now?

Eight

Upstairs in the Governor's Mansion, Michael Windsor La-Roche, governor of Monn, left the marble table around which the meeting was assembled and moved about the room restlessly.

Like many of the Mansion's rooms, this one was sparsely furnished; more than half of it was empty, the walls bare, the floor uncarpeted. The fireplace at the far end was, unfortunately, no longer in use. The chimney didn't work properly anymore, and because it was made of Old People's stuff, the local masons didn't know how to fix it.

Michael shivered. He leaned his elbows on the sill of one of the tall windows that occupied most of one wall. Outside, the setting sun was cut in half by the top of the ridge, and the pinched light coming in through the glass was blood colored. The view from the windows was dominated by the sharp cliffs west of the city and by the long arches of the trestle that carried the Witch Road, a giant spider-work black against the sunset. Michael Windsor contemplated the arches bleakly, as if he considered them to be the source of his troubles.

He had a lean pale face with a meager beard which might have been called aesthetic when his thin lips weren't pursed with worry. His light hair, usually combed and oiled to fall smoothly to his shoulders, had been twisted and pulled by nervous fingers into random spikes and ropes and pushed away from a high forehead. Michael liked to think that his rising hairline had given him the wide brow of a serious thinker, but he was all too aware that shortly it was going to make him look bald. Governor or not, a man not a year past twenty was bound to worry about such things.

He turned and leaned his slight frame on the windowsill in hopes that the dying sun would warm his back. The heat of the day had vanished from the ancient stones. Michael felt even less robust than usual.

He wished he were someplace else, doing something else.

The figurative governor's mantle weighed as heavily on his thin shoulders as did the material robes and chains of his office.

Only the Lord God knew how to make it rain, and He had not shared the information with Michael Windsor LaRoche, governor of Monn. Michael knew that the crops were dying, that the people were uneasy about the coming harvest, but he didn't know what he was supposed to do about it. And those men who were supposed to be advising him only quarreled among themselves. He touched the jeweled Cross of God that hung from a gold chain about his neck and made a silent plea to the Lord God for at least the hope of a shower.

The sun vanished from a cloudless sky.

The three men at the table waited with varying degrees of impatience for Michael so that the meeting could continue. Michael wished Thomas was there. Of all the court officials, only wise old Thomas, chief adviser, confidant, and friend, showed any sympathy for Michael's dilemma.

Michael left the window ledge and returned his attention to the waiting men, sprawling himself across the thronelike chair at the head of the table. It had been padded with thick fleeces to protect his bony hips from the hard oak wood, but it was still damnably uncomfortable. The chair, like the table, had been built by the Old People. It had occurred to Michael more than once that the Old People had been either unduly fond of discomfort or had been a race endowed with resilient bottoms.

What had the Old People done about failing crops? None of the tales of the storyteller held any clue. Michael felt angry at the lack of information and knew the anger to be childish. He wished for the luxury to be a child.

The household staff arrived with lamps and unobtrusively placed them around the room.

General Brandt looked up expectantly. He had a short, square beard, gray streaked, and big knuckled hands pressed palm to palm above the table. He had the face of a hard man starting to go to paunch.

The young officer who had returned from the north with the news of warriors gathering in several cities studied his fingernails as if he, too, wished to be elsewhere. There was surely no need for him to suffer. Snatching a particle of the general's authority without a qualm, Michael said, "You can go about your business now, Lieutenant, and thank you for coming."

The officer bowed himself out of the room gratefully, and Brandt scowled.

Michael turned to his financial adviser. Creighton, round, red-faced, bald, looking always on the verge of a fit of temper, always telling him that this or that couldn't be done for lack of funds, was among the governor's least favorite of his counselors.

"I can't be reassuring, m'lord," Creighton said. "The anticipated expense of buying grain alone will leave us in serious financial condition through the winter. If the army is to increase spending, I honestly don't know where the money will come from."

Brandt snorted. "You'd buy grain, and have no one to protect it. So it'll go to feed the northern armies when they overrun the city. That doesn't sound like one of your brighter ideas, Creighton."

"Bright or not, the people have to be fed. Otherwise, come midwinter there'll be an army storming the Mansion all right, and it will be our own starving people. We won't have to wait for the northerners. If they're even coming. All you've got for proof is a lot of ifs and maybes and a few barbarians banding together, for all I know, to go bear hunting."

"Hunting? You poor benighted clerk. You'll still be counting bags of flour when the pagan hordes are raping your wife and abducting your daughters and cutting off your own silly head."

Michael considered the two men. Their furies seemed reserved for each other. They spoke of wars and starving peasants with an admirable lack of passion. Either of the possibilities was frightening to the governor. Furthermore, he knew perfectly well that each of these men could see himself in the governor's chair, and both were working toward that goal, Creighton by clutching the city's purse strings ever tighter, Brandt by constantly building his military empire. Michael couldn't trust their advice too far.

There were times when he would have been happy to give either of them the job, if only he could think of a way to abdicate and still keep his head on his shoulders. He was too young to be stuck with all this responsibility. Some older, wiser man, steeped in the lore and tradition of governance, should have it.

Of the two, Brandt was the more dangerous. If worse came to worst, Michael could chuck Creighton into jail, though his financial genius would be hard to replace. But Michael had the notion that nothing but the Governor's Guard stood between his governorship and a sudden, violent change of government by way of a military coup.

He took good care of the Guardsmen for that reason.

He would like to be able to take better care of the people, too, if only he knew the way. Desperate people would welcome change for its own sake, on the assumption that things couldn't get worse, and if Michael could do nothing, Brandt could do no less.

"This preventive action you're talking about, how long would it take?" he asked the general.

Brandt made a show of thinking it over, as if he hadn't done that long ago and had the answer ready. "If we go up the river, if the winds are fair, if we get to the barbarians and scatter them before they get too well organized, about three months."

"Three months would have the men away at harvest," Michael said.

"Forgive me, m'lord Governor," Creighton said, "but before any of this can happen, those men have to be recruited, equipped, trained, housed, fed, and paid. Either that, or strip the city of its defenses. The rivermen would have to be paid, if they agree at all."

"The rivermen will cooperate, or we'll commandeer the boats," Brandt said.

"And man them with pikemen and archers, I suppose," Creighton answered coldly.

"Enough," Michael snapped suddenly. The two graying men looked at the slip of a boy who dared interrupt them. They had a rare moment of agreement, each considering privately how unfortunate it was that this stripling happened to be governor.

"You sound like a pair of farm wives in the market haggling over the price of some stringy old hen," Michael said. "This endless bickering tells me nothing. I will seek counsel elsewhere and talk to you both later. Please send my supper to my chambers."

He stalked out of the meeting regretting that he had spoken to two important city officials as if they were mere servants, but in no way inclined to apologize.

Alone in his more comfortably appointed private chambers, the governor stripped the regalia of office from his thin body and studied the result in the cloudy mirror that had been rescued in his father's time from an Old People's building and mounted with great care on the stone wall of the dressing room.

The bones seemed more pronounced than they were, and the shadows under the eyes deeper.

Michael shrugged into a warm woolen robe similar in design to those favored by Brother Parker's flock, except that it had been dyed a pleasant reddish brown with color obtained, the weaver said, from a moss that grew in the Wilderness. He went into the main room where the floor was laid with a wool rug of rich Kolloan colors and the fireplace worked. Michael worried about the politics of Kollo and the possibility of being absorbed into the empire, but could not dispute the beauty that the dyes they traded added to a drab world. He turned his back to the fire and let the heat seep in.

He felt cold down to the core. He turned his eyes upward and wordlessly asked the Lord God if he hadn't suffered enough for whatever sins he had committed in his short life, and might not the Lord in his mercy return a modicum of health to a man who felt sorely beset.

That was a prayer he often made. It had not been answered.

Perhaps, he thought, he should find a way to spend more time in the Temple.

But Brother Parker's efforts to bring the governor to health in the name of the Lord God were expensive, in a variety of ways. The True Church milked all the public attention it could from the governor's illness. When the governor bowed his head before the altar of the True Church and prayed for health, Brother Parker made sure everyone in the city knew it.

So far, the Lord God had not answered Brother Parker any more positively than he had Michael in person, state donations to the welfare of the True Church notwithstanding. Brother Parker talked about perfect trust and patience. Michael doubted he had the time. He also doubted Brother Parker's motives. He wondered what Brother Parker truly prayed for, the governor's recovery, or his death.

Young and sickly though he was, Michael was not stupid. He did not doubt for a moment that Brother Parker could see himself as the head of a theocratic state. He had brooded for considerable periods about balancing the demands of religion, his own as well as that of the citizens, against the necessities of politics. He had prayed to the Lord God for guidance. And he had discussed the problem with Thomas, who was possibly the only person Michael knew of in his kingdom who wasn't trying to depose the governor and make himself king.

He turned as the door to his rooms opened and Thomas came in, carrying the governor's supper tray.

"You didn't need to do that," Michael said. "The kitchen boy could have brought it."

"I was coming anyway. Why disturb the boy?"

"Have you eaten?"

"Yes, I have. I dined, in a manner of speaking, with a pair of carpenters in the Crow's Eye Tavern. It was an interesting experience."

"You should not socialize with such riffraff," Michael said irritably. "It reflects on me."

"Your pardon, Michael. I mistakenly thought they were honest tradesmen and decent citizens."

How typical of the man, pleading ignorance to push Michael into seeing things in a different light. It was Thomas's fault that Michael was curious about things like where the

dye that colored his robe came from. Thomas asked questions
and tweaked Michael's naturally inquisitive mind. Michael
didn't know whether to thank him or curse him for it. It was
easier to accept the fact that his robe was brown than to imagine the terrified weaver scrabbling around in the black depths
of the forest hoping to find a scrap of the previous moss
before being set upon by wolves or snatched up by the nameless terrors hiding in the shadows, too hungry not to go, and
too frightened to be efficient.

Michael liked to think of his people as simple, happy folk,
contented with their lot in life, enjoying their rustic pleasures.
He didn't want to think about hungry street urchins stealing
because it was the only way they could live. It was far simpler
and more satisfying to dismiss them as dirty, irredeemable sav-
ages. With hints and questions and little nudges, Thomas destroyed his illusions.

The girl in Market Square had been a bright thing, though,
pretty under the dirt, smiling at him as if they were buddies
sharing a mischief as her quick hands ransacked the pockets of
the man next to her.

The governor's party had stopped there as a courtesy to
Brother Parker. Brother Parker had yet to express his appreciation.

"Did the meeting go well?" Thomas asked, drawing Michael
out of his reverie as he set the tray down on a small lacquered
table near the fire. His gesture suggested that Michael should sit
and eat before the food grew cold.

Sobered, Michael shook his head. "I am surrounded by black
crows prophesying death and waiting to feed on the carcass."
He discovered that he didn't have much appetite. His mind was
still on Creighton's prediction of starvation raging in the city by
midwinter.

"I think we are going to end up in a war," he said, "and
Brandt is delighted at the prospect. I really can't see why the
northerners would pick now to attack Monn. There's little
enough prosperity in the city this year to entice them."

"What makes you so sure they do want to attack?"

"The scouts are reporting a gathering of warriors, and battle
preparations."

"Brandt's scouts?"

Michael nodded. "I see what you mean. I wish there was a way to talk directly to the northerners. Everything I learn is colored with someone's ambitions."

"Is it so impossible?" Thomas asked. "Could nothing be arranged?"

"How?"

"I don't know, but maybe the first step would be to send an envoy to the northern cities to sound out their leaders and suggest a meeting."

Michael slumped in his chair. He felt so bone weary, as if some witch had drained the lifeblood from him. "Is it that simple, Thomas?"

"No. Unfortunately, there are reasons for supporting Brandt's war. If nothing else, it will make the people more patient about bearing the hard times to come, distract them from watching the fields dry up. Getting the bulk of the army out of the city for a while might also be wise. Brandt grows impatient with your unwillingness to die. He may decide to help nature along."

"I'm all right as long as the Governor's Guard remains loyal."

"The Guard are good men, but they are few. It is the loyalty of his own army that Brandt must overcome, lest he have his battalions fighting one another. He needs an excuse, a reason which would carry weight with his men. Hunger might be such a reason."

"So you would have me expend their lives on the battlefield instead?"

"It's no worse a fate than starvation."

"I guess not."

Michael picked at the food on his plate and wondered what the smith's apprentice was eating tonight. Anything? And he thought of the same lad with an arrow in his chest, lying on a frozen northern hill. In Michael's imagination, it was always winter in the north. At least the boy's suffering would be over then. At least one could say that.

"They expect me to do something for them, Thomas. All those people. As if I had a magic to fill withered heads of wheat with grain."

A fit of coughing racked him. When it was over, he was

panting for breath. Thomas brought a cup with a little wine in it.

"A royal wedding would please the people. The Sanjan princess—"

"I don't want to hear about that woman."

"It is your duty to marry and produce an heir, m'lord. The people grow impatient."

Michael made a gesture that suggested some considerable impatience of his own.

"There are those who might doubt your ability, you delay so long."

"The princess Donalda is a shrewish bitch with a voice like a crow and a face like a pig. She'd make a eunuch of any man, even you, Thomas. If I must play the stud horse for the entertainment of the people, bring me any girl off the street in preference. That bright-eyed one in the square will do nicely."

"This is serious business, Michael, and I suggest you treat it as such. You may play as you will, but choose your official escort with some benefit in view. Sanjo is a wealthy city and would make a valuable ally in times of—" Thomas was interrupted by a timid knock at the door.

Who, Michael wondered, dared intrude?

Thomas answered the door, and Michael saw a nervous Guardsman who hurriedly passed his message. Thomas stepped through the doorway, and Michael could hear anxious murmured conversation that tweaked his curiosity and almost got him out of his chair to investigate. Only Thomas's endless reminders to maintain the dignity of his office, meted out in generous measure in the months since the old governor had died and Michael had reluctantly inherited the Mansion, kept him seated.

Thomas returned. "Robert Miller is demanding an audience in the name of his family." The governor groaned. He had no love for the Family Miller, a coarse lot who seemed to have been admitted into the aristocracy by accident.

"I think it would be wise to hear him," Thomas said. "The good will of the family is important to you. And he does have a strange tale to tell. He says his boys were magically attacked and thrown to the ground by a wicked sorcerer and demands action to restore the dignity of the Miller Family.

"He claims there is a Phile witch in the city."

Nine

"You have to tell me," Ellen said, brown eyes bright with anticipation. "What'd he do?"

Ellen was one of few people in Monn whom Sarah could without hesitation call friend. That had been true for almost as long as Sarah could remember.

Ellen, sold as a bondmaid to the weaver when she was just a child, had little freedom of movement. Sarah brought her the news of the street to feed her insatiable appetite for gossip. In return, Ellen offered the advice of a surrogate older sister and occasional stolen tidbits from the weaver's table. She lived for the day when an ardent man would buy her freedom from the weaver. She was a thin, frail woman, well beyond twenty years, and Sarah thought privately that her chances for deliverance were not good.

"What happened?" Ellen asked. She sat on the shady step of the weaver's shop, carding wool. Through the open doorway behind her came the snap and clatter of the weaver's loom. Sarah sat beside her, picking burrs from the tangled fleece between them.

"Nothing happened. He stood there in his busted-up house, with his face like thunder. He swore a lot. If I was Butch, I think I'd buy a warding spell. Or hide out in the Temple, maybe."

"And?"

"And then he left."

"Sarah, that's not fair. We promised. We swore to tell each other everything. Positively everything."

"I am telling you everything. That's all that happened."

"What kind of a dumb witch is that? He might have at least called some gremlins or gnomes or something to clean up. He should have made some fixing magic, eh? What sorry kind of Phile have you got there?"

Sarah shook her head. "I told you he was strange."

They sat quietly for a moment, Ellen going on with her work, Sarah staring through the limp aspen leaves overhead. Ellen had reason for her doubt. In spite of her protestations, Sarah had not told her about taking Reese to her place, or about the witch light, or about the strange objects in Reese's house that Sarah had come to think might well be the wreckage of sorcerer's engines. Maybe the reason he hadn't made fixing spells or anything like that was because Butch had ruined the necessaries of magic.

Sarah's hands paused in their work. She was worried. What she had told Reese was true: she had never taken anyone to her place before. Nor had she taken anything from it that might give her secret away. The smooth nails, worth half their weight in silver in the market, and the copper, precious stuff to any metal worker in Monn, had been left untouched even when it meant she had to go hungry. She would not risk anyone trailing her back to the treasure, or catching her and making her tell where it came from.

Reese had magicked the secret out of her with hardly a word of protest. She admired his power and worried about his discretion.

"How could you for sure know a witch?" she asked.

Ellen shrugged. "They say there's always the mark of the devil on them somewhere." She paused, concentrating on the business of her hands while Sarah spent a delicious moment thinking about searching Reese for the devil's mark. Ellen continued. "They say, too, some animals can sense them. A horse, they say, will shy away from a witch every time. And a crow or a black cat will seek them out, live with them, so as to become a part of the magic. So they say. Cat Anna is the one to know."

After a while, Ellen asked, "Did you hear about Willa's baby?"

"Who's Willa?"

"John the cowman's wife."

Sarah didn't know John the cowman from John the butcher.

Half the men in Monn seemed to be John something or other.
But she had a taste for gossip herself. "I didn't hear," she said.

"It was a freak, they say," Ellen confided, her voice soft
with the fascination of the horrible. "No thing the Lord God
would have created. A monster, true, with its two poor heads
tied ear to ear." She stopped work for a moment to make the
sign that warded off evil. "It was a terrible birth, way too soon,
and poor Willa like to die. I heard Willa wouldn't even look at
it. John swears it was born dead, but there's those that say he
killed it the instant it came forth, before anyone else had a chance
to hear it bleating from its two poor mouths." She hunched her
shoulders to ease the stiffness, then took up her work again.

Sarah regarded her friend with a degree of skepticism. There
was a certain morbid bent to Ellen's chatter. She always had all
the details of the most dreadful thing going, even if she had to
make up a few of them as she went along.

"They buried it in Gray Swamp," Ellen said. "Because the
Brothers wouldn't have it in the churchyard. And the grave's
covered with camomile and witchbane. Even so, they say there's
been a will-o'-the-wisp prowling the swamp after moonset,
looking for the burial place." She put the smoothed wool carefully into a basket beside her, selected another bit from the fleece,
and laid it out over one of her spiked boards.

When Sarah said nothing, she went on. "There's talk that
there's a witch about in Monn." ·

An apprehensive shiver ran down Sarah's back. For a while
she busied herself in silence picking at the fleece, her mind's
eye replaying the sight of Reese with the greenish glow of the
witch light on his puzzled face.

Such a strong and manly face.

He wouldn't do a thing like that. He didn't even know John
the cowman or Willa to work such a horrible evil. There were
those who would say that a Phile might do a thing like that from
sheer malevolence. Sarah didn't believe it. She couldn't make
herself believe it, though in fairness to herself, she had to admit
that she didn't try very hard.

"You better watch out for your Phile if Brother Parker gets
wind of him," Ellen said. The teasing tone made Sarah look up
and catch the smile. She doesn't believe me, she thought, and

was relieved by the knowledge. She thinks I'm all addled by a fetching man.

"D'you suppose . . ." she started to say, looking down at the ground. At her feet, a small black ant was trying to move some winged thing five times its size through the stiff dry stems of grass, tugging, skidding, falling, but never giving up.

"Suppose what?"

There was a protracted silence while Sarah sought to phrase her important question without giving too much away. "D'you suppose," she said, "a person could have a witchly thing without being an actual real witch?"

She kept her eyes on the struggling ant and felt Ellen's eyes on her.

"Could," Ellen said. "Like a potion or a charm. Someone could have a thing like that."

Sarah nodded. The ant was stalled between two grass stems. "Suppose," she said, "a person wanted a potion or charm. How would they get one?"

Ellen put her work down and shot a glance behind her to make sure the weaver wasn't listening. "Are you thinking about a love potion, maybe?"

Sarah kept her head down. Her cheeks grew warm.

Ellen considered her friend for a moment, then leaned back and twisted herself around to regard the open door behind her. When she turned back to Sarah, she said in a whisper full of dramatic conspiracy, "If you promise, promise on your hope of salvation, never to tell, I'll tell you a secret."

Sarah's hope of salvation was vanishingly small. "I promise," she said, wondering.

Eyes bright with mischief, Ellen leaned close to Sarah. "I know how to get a man-catching spell."

"No, you don't."

"Do so."

"How come you never did, then?"

"Who said I never did?"

"You didn't. Really?"

"If you have to know, Raymond the wagoner doesn't hang around here to watch the looms, I don't think."

"Raymond, Ellen? Truly?"

Ellen nodded, smiling, pleased with the effect that her revelation was having.

Sarah thought about it. Would she dare? Would she really dare? Would the Legend of Sarah end when the heroine dared the dark powers for love's sake and then her beloved Phile, angry at her for encroaching on his secrets, turned her into a puff of smoke and scattered her on the wind? Would her spirit return on the spring breezes to haunt the house on Travellers' Way?

"I don't know," she said. "Maybe it's not a good idea."

"Well, if you're scared."

"I'm not scared," Sarah lied.

"It's not a really big, important spell," Ellen said after a time. "It's not like anybody really cared about a little thing like that."

Maybe Raymond cares, Sarah thought. Her early morning dream returned. It seemed so real, and so right. "How?"

"You have to have some coins for Cat Anna. You have to go up there to her place. It has to be at night. And you have to have something of his, something he keeps close, to carry the magic."

Sarah studied the ground. The ant had abandoned its treasure and gone off to get help.

Inside the crystal, a woman smiled, frozen for eternity. I am scared, Sarah thought. What is it like, trapped in there for ever and ever?

"I don't know," she said. "Besides, where'd I get money, for Cat Anna or anybody."

"Well, we could do it," Ellen said.

"How'd you?"

"What?"

"Get coins for Cat Anna?"

"There's ways," Ellen said knowingly. She turned back to her work, a sadness settling over her features.

A more pleasant thing occurred to Sarah. "If you know how, why don't you get some for the weaver, buy your own bond?"

Ellen looked up. "He'd just say I stole it. Besides, where would I go, Sarah, and what would I do?" She smiled bleakly, and Sarah thought again of the girl trapped in the crystal.

Ellen was called indoors by the strident voice of the weaver's wife. Sarah wandered idly along Monn's narrow twisting streets, kicking at the dust, watching it swirl back at her in the hot wind from the south and feeling vaguely discontented. In Market Square, she had managed to commandeer a sizable chunk of crumbly corn bread from an inattentive vendor. Munching, she trudged along and thought about man-catching spells.

Ten

Sarah decided that she didn't much like Cleo. Cleo was always chasing her away. Cleo was sharp tempered and snarly. She even snarled at Reese. Right from their first meeting, Cleo had seemed suspicious of her. And it wasn't as if Sarah had done anything to hurt Cleo.

Sarah had been sitting in Reese's house at the time, waiting for him to get back from another of his mysterious disappearances and playing with a short metal rod that she had found among his things. The rod was a little longer than her hand and about as thick as two fingers, and it flared out at one end to embrace a glassy eye. When she picked it up, a magical light beamed out of the eye. When she put it down, the light stopped. At first she was frightened, then intrigued by the way she could direct the light wherever she wanted it, into the corners of the room, up the chimney, or into the dark recesses of the cupboards.

Cleo had come back with Reese. Standing in the doorway beside him and looking as if she saw something that stank, she had said, "Who is this?" as if she had a right to know.

Reese introduced them to each other. Cleo had come in and taken the magical light machine away from Sarah. "You're going to bust something, kid."

Reese had come to Sarah's defense. "She's not doing any harm."

Cleo had looked at Reese and then at Sarah and then back at Reese. "I see," she said.

"No, you don't," Reese had answered crossly. "So don't go making mountains out of molehills, okay?"

Cleo wore a small unornamented medallion exactly like Reese's. Her clothes were of the best quality, and if Sarah thought that a short-skirted hunting costume was a bit inappropriate to the circumstances, she had to admit that it looked good on Cleo. Together, Reese and Cleo were like members of a powerful family, and Sarah was a street kid once again, on the outside looking in.

On top of everything else, Cleo was so beautiful and exotic. Her hair was tied in a knot on her neck, shining, as black as a crow's wing except where the light struck blue glints from it. Cleo's skin was an odd color, too, a smooth, even light brown. She had high, prominent cheekbones and slightly upswept eyes. Sarah had stared during that first meeting. Cleo had tried hard not to notice.

"I never saw anyone who looked like you," Sarah said when she got up enough courage to say something.

"You've got me, kid. I don't know how to answer that." She had picked the box with the slice of rainbow in it out of the basket of collected debris that sat under Reese's table, and talked to Reese over Sarah's head. "It looks like your recorder's shot," she said.

Cleo was Philish, Sarah was certain of that. Next to Cleo, Sarah felt grubby and plain and dumb.

It was sometime later that she realized with alarm that Cleo looked like the woman in the crystal. Then she felt foolish. Reese would know his enemy. If his enemy had escaped his sorcery, he would know that, too. But the resemblance was so strong, it made shivers on her spine.

In the Old People's place beneath Young Albert's field, Cleo slapped witch lights up with reckless abandon. She had no patience with oil lamps. Reese protested, explaining that the witch lights frightened people.

"Fine." Cleo spoke with the same soft accent Reese had. "But there's no one here but you and me and your little buddy and a hole in the ground. Dim, smoky damned lamps are romantic as hell, but I'd like to get one good look at least at what we're trying to do here."

She prowled around, peering in corners with light from the magical cylinder that Sarah wasn't good enough to play with. She stared at the ceiling. She beat at the wall with the sharp end of a funny-looking hammer until a piece spalled off. She took the piece close to one of the witch lights and studied it as if it might hold the key to mighty secrets.

"Why are we so afraid of these people, anyway?" she asked. She dropped the chip of concrete into her pocket.

"I don't know that we're afraid of them, exactly," Reese said.

"What would you say we are, exactly?" Cleo took note of the fallen roof. "We're going to have to shore that up before we do anything else." She gave it a second, apprehensive look before crawling over the rubble to the place where the safe was.

Reese followed after her. Sarah trailed along behind, feeling invisible.

"I'd like to think we can avoid a confrontation," Reese said. "Monnish folk are apprehensive about strangers in the first place. They're afraid of anything new. They're afraid of things they don't understand. They're afraid of raising the Old People's ghosts. Along with most forms of technology, it all comes under the heading of witchcraft."

"Humph," Cleo snorted. "Xenophobia, neophobia, phasmophobia, technophobia, and what else? No wonder they're called Phobes. I can see where I'm going to be greatly enamored of the local people and their quaint beliefs."

Reese let the sarcasm go. "I'm not sure we should be talking about them as if Sarah was deaf, dumb, and blind."

"Afraid we might hurt her little feelings?"

Reese clenched his teeth and held his temper with difficulty. "When you go out of your way to be obtuse, you do a good job of it. The thing is, if you need it spelled out, frightened people tend to get aggressive, attack what scares them. We don't want to start fighting with these people. They could cause us more than a little bit of trouble."

"With spears and swords, guy? I don't think so. Half a dozen of us armed with stun guns could stand off the whole city."

Reese shook his head, even though Cleo had her back to him and was regarding the safe with a professional eye. "Don't make the mistake of thinking they're stupid because they're primitive.

They've good warriors among them, experienced fighters—something we don't have. Also, they outnumber us about ten to one.''

"But if push comes to shove, there's no way they could win."

"I suppose not. But let's not have it come to that. People would get hurt."

Cleo turned away from her contemplation of the safe and contemplated Reese instead. She touched his cheek with a familiarity that grated on Sarah's soul. "I don't think I like the way you've changed, love. You've lost your objectivity, become too involved in Monn. Suppose there's no other way, Reese?"

"Honestly, I don't know. But can we at least try to avoid the problem in the first place?"

The moment of softness passed like a scrap of mist in the morning sun. "Okay, you tell me how. First of all, I'm going to have to bring a crew in here, robots and men, to brace the roof and do a bit of excavating to find out how big this thing is and whether it's part of the wall or if the wall was built around it. Then we're going to have to decide whether to cut or blast it open here, or move it to the enclave where we can apply more subtle techniques. In either case there's going to be a lot of light and noise and machinery to scare the shit out of your precious Phobes. And I don't see any way to avoid that. Do you?"

"Not off the top of my head." Reese took a deep breath. "Let's diagram the layout, take some pictures, and get some experts together"—Cleo gave him a sharp glare—"and do some brainstorming. Maybe someone will come up with an idea." He grew deadly serious. "But, Cleo, I don't see it's worth anybody's life, ours or theirs."

"Reese, baby, you're a romantic. You talk like these guys weren't fighting two wars a year since the dawn of time. Anyway, I'm not sure it's going to be left up to you. The enclaves are fighting for survival. We've got to have energy, or we can't go on. It if comes to choosing between us and them, we've got to choose us." Cleo put a sympathetic hand on his arm. "Now, why don't we go back to your place and take a look at the maps. Is there any chance of coffee in Monn?"

"We can make some."

"Ah, yeah. Sure. Why not? I'll take it on faith you know how."

Reese took the pot off the fire. The fire added brutally to the heat in the house, so the door had been left open in hopes of catching a slightly cooler breeze from outside. The shutters had been closed over the broken window.

"That has to be the world's most primitive coffee-making technique," Cleo said.

"It works," Reese answered.

He brought three steaming, earthenware mugs to the table, set one in front of Sarah, handed one to Cleo, and kept one himself. Leaning with one hip on the window ledge, he talked over Sarah's head, to Cleo.

"How soon do you think you can get a holographer down here?"

Cleo lifted one shoulder. "Tomorrow night, I guess, if you insist on night. I'll bring a crew, get some measurements while we're at it. I want to set up a satellite beacon, too, to locate the site exactly."

Sarah couldn't understand what they were talking about. A good part of her resentment lay in the fact that Cleo and Reese often spoke words she didn't understand. They talked about people she didn't know. They discussed events that did not fit into Sarah's world.

She looked into the cup before her. It was full of hot dark fluid that smelled good. But Cleo tasted hers and complained. "I'm not sure this witches' brew is fit to drink."

"Cleo," Reese said. "Monnish people take their witches seriously."

"Yeah, I forgot," Cleo said. She touched Sarah's shoulder reassuringly. "I didn't mean that, kid. It was supposed to be funny."

Sarah shrank away from the touch. She didn't get the joke. She didn't understand Philish humor at all. Deciding to leave the coffee strictly alone, she occupied herself with sampling the unfamiliar foods laid out on the table. The incomprehensible conversation went on above her. The long yellow things had her puzzled until she saw Cleo strip the skin from one and sink her white teeth into the soft flesh.

They cleared the food away too soon, and Cleo spread the table with a paper she unrolled over it. "Show me what you've got," she said.

They leaned their elbows on the paper and studied the colored lines on it, head to head. "We've got the Governor's Mansion here . . ." Sarah put her elbows on the paper, too, and tried to figure out what Reese was talking about. "You're in the way, Sarah," Reese said. "And the hardware would be about here just above the old shoreline."

Cleo got a thing from inside her tunic and held it to the paper. "The Governor's Mansion," she said, and drew a black cross on the paper as if to protect that spot from evil influences. Sarah's eyes widened. She couldn't imagine what kind of magic they were making. "Would you move your hand here, Sarah?" Sarah moved, fascinated to see what was going to happen, yet dreading the sorcery. Cleo made more crosses on the paper.

Reese came around to Sarah's side of the table. He pulled some coins from his pocket—there always seemed to be some in there, something like the magicians who pulled silver out of the air—and handed them to Sarah. "Sarah, would you trot down to the inn and bring us back a pitcher of wine?"

She wanted to say no, that she'd rather stay and see how the magic came out, but he smiled down at her and looked like he really wanted her to go, so she nodded and held out her hand for the money.

The coins heavy in her hand, she started away. At the door she hesitated. They already had their heads together over the paper again. Cleo said quietly, probably thinking that Sarah had already gone, "What'd you do that for?"

"I really don't think the kid should be listening to all this. I'm worried about what she's going to make of it."

"If you ever see the wine or the money, I'll be surprised."

"It's not important," Reese said.

Neck bent, Sarah plodded down the road, kicking at the dust as she went.

Not important?

There were tears in her eyes, blurring her vision. She hadn't really cried since she was very young, but she felt like doing it now. She felt like throwing herself down on the road and kicking and screaming with all her strength. She tried to swallow it down, but it was like a rock in her throat. She trudged on.

Not important?

She went around to the back of the inn, where a woman might buy wine without having to pass through the public room, and where she could deal with Harold's wife and not have Harold chasing her away. She exchanged some of Reese's money for a stoppered jug, which she carried in her arms back up the road.

When she was in sight of Reese's house again, she thought of his quiet voice saying "It's not important," and the hurt welled up again. She almost decided to go away and hide someplace. But she felt that she had to prove Cleo wrong.

The paper had been put away, and Reese and Cleo were sitting side by side at the table when Sarah got there. "Here," she said roughly, handing Reese the jug. She dropped the rest of the coins on the table, though it was against her nature to let them go.

"I can be wrong as well as the next guy," Cleo said.

"Thank you, Sarah," Reese said without looking at her. "You better run along now."

Dismissed, she did not leave Reese's house immediately, but squatted down in the dry grass outside, disconsolate, digging in the earth with a piece of stick. She hated Cleo. She hated Reese, too. She hated everyone and everything. Their voices came to her, swelling or fading as they moved about inside. She overheard Cleo asking Reese, "What are you going to do about that girl?"

"Why do I have to do anything about her?" he answered. "She's not doing any harm."

"How does a man in your profession stay so naive?" Cleo asked.

"Stick to engineering, Cleo. Psychology isn't your bag," Reese said.

"Maybe not. Just the same, though you might find this hard to believe, I was young once myself and I have some idea of the fascination a big, handsome, magical stranger can hold for a little girl," Cleo said.

Reese made a grunt of dismissal. "How about big girls?"

''Them, too,'' Cleo answered, and then Reese came and shut the door.

Sarah had never thought to question the natural order that made some folk lords of strong families, with good food and warm houses and fine horses to take them around, while other folk were forced to scratch on the fringes of society for bare survival. She never thought to question why men had all the rights and privileges and women had none. That was the way of things. But it was damnably unfair that she had been born too late. As long as Reese thought of her as a child, there was no way she could compete.

She threw the stick into the bush and trudged with hunched shoulders and eyes downcast along Travellers' Way, then turned off on Sandy Road, which went to the weaver's house. She had a gold chain in her fist that had come from around Cleo's neck without her even noticing. Cleo might be beautiful and rich and everything, but she wasn't all that sharp. It seemed fitting that Cleo should pay Cat Anna's fee.

Eleven

Before the next day broke, Cleo took a pod back to the enclave. She was out of sorts because she couldn't find her gold necklace.

In a hallway on the top floor of Residence N, she hesitated a moment before touching the door chime. Zeke would probably still be asleep. Roused, he would be gruff and irritable.

She shrugged. Zeke liked to project the image of an irascible old man, but underneath it all, he was a teddy bear, and she was fond of him. She shifted the burden in her arms, thought it was a bloody nuisance Reese couldn't have a computer terminal in Monn, and gave the chime a couple of good pokes.

"Who?" the door speaker demanded after a considerable delay.

"Me, Zeke. I've got Reese's stuff."

After another delay, the door slid open.

The apartment was dark. Cleo marched over to the window and cleared it, letting the new day come in, then looked around the cluttered space for a place to put her things down. Zeke padded barefoot around the end of a half-height wall, pushing his fingers through his just-too-long leonine mop of gray hair. His limp was more pronounced than usual, as if the muscles had stiffened overnight.

"Where can I spread these out?" Cleo asked.

"Hello, Cleo, good morning. How are you today?"

"Hi, Zeke," Cleo said, taking the criticism in moderately good humor. She never could be cross with Zeke. "Are you trying to tell me I come across a bit brusque?"

"Yes."

"I apologize."

"Grouchily accepted. You have a dawn fetish, young lady. Make that benighted machine cough up some breakfast, will you? I'll get showered and dressed. Your desperately urgent business can wait that long, can't it? Us old fogies are a bit creaky in the early morning."

"That's just an excuse for being a crab, Zeke. You're not that old."

"Don't be patronizing. I own a mirror, and I can count." Zeke peered at her through the remains of the sleep-fog. "That's quite a getup you've got there."

Cleo grinned. Her dress was a bit odd, she had to admit, a blouse of rough material, off white, covered by a long leather vest closed with a leather thong tied in front, a knee-length skirt of the same material as the blouse, and calf-high leggings also bound with thongs. She felt outlandish, and also hot.

"I just got back. You like my Monnish duds?" she asked.

Zeke shook his head. "On you they look good, but I don't see them becoming the next fashion craze. Obviously you and Reese aren't fighting so hard you can't work together."

"That's none of your business, Zeke."

"True."

"Does he tell you everything?"

Zeke shrugged. "Probably not." He turned and went back behind the wall. In a moment, Cleo could hear the shower.

She still had her arms full.

Zeke's place always struck her as being smaller and darker and more cluttered than it really was, and about twenty years out of fashion. It reminded her of a minor museum, crowded with things picked up here and there during a busy lifetime, a primitive terra-cotta figure sharing a shelf with an abstract Xstalite sculpture. Zeke often said he wasn't too keen on modern styles and saw no reason to change things just because they could be changed.

She dumped her load on a couch affair set against one wall that was relatively free of clutter, then began trying to clear enough space on the table by the window for breakfast, moving open books and printouts and disks from one place to another since there was no obvious place for them to go. She was setting

out breakfast for Zeke and coffee for herself just as Zeke reap-
peared in the room.

"You need a wife," she said.

"Umm. Want a job?"

"No thanks. I'm pretty busy. Besides, you're too snarly in
the morning."

"Just as well. Reese would kill me."

Cleo didn't answer that. Zeke busied himself with breakfast.
The sun was just clearing the wall surrounding the enclave.
Beyond the tall windows to his left, the Crystal Spire blazed into
life. Given his choice of living spaces, Zeke said, he would
choose the one he had for that view alone.

Cleo believed him. The view was spectacular.

"Not to change the subject or anything, did you want to see
the maps?" she asked.

"Umhum. Did you enjoy Monn?"

Cleo shook her head. "It's a weird place. I don't know how
Reese can stand it. Everything's so dirty. The people huddle
together and look at you like you had a horrible contagious
disease. I'm pretty sure one of them swiped my gold chain. I
have to go back this evening, and I'm not looking forward to
it."

"You adapt," Zeke said, handing her a fresh cup of coffee.
Except for his teacup, he swept the dishes off the table and
dumped them into the dispose-all slot so Cleo could spread the
maps out. "You get used to them, and they get used to you.
You find out they're people, with many of the same hopes and
fears you've got. Given time, you might even learn to like
them."

"Ugh. No thanks. Okay, here's the contour map of the river
valley with Reese's sites marked on it. This is the satellite map,
approximately the same scale. If you use a little imagination,
you could almost think these three in a row here are part of this
big complex that shows up on the satellite."

Leaning over the table, Zeke considered it. "Mm. Maybe.
It's not all that clear to me. The newer buildings make it a bit
blurry." He straightened and sipped his tea. "Is there some
good reason all this is on paper?"

"Somebody broke into that miserable hovel Reese is living
in and wrecked the recorder."

Zeke frowned. "That sounds a tad ominous. Has our boy been irritating the neighbors?"

"Who knows? It wouldn't be hard. Those people are eyeball deep in customs and traditions and rules of correct behavior," Cleo said. "And Reese can be damned irritating at times."

"You used to get along just fine."

"He didn't used to be so stubborn."

"Or you so jealous?"

"Jealous?" Cleo yelped. Her hackles rose, and she was immediately ready for a fight. "What are you talking about, Zeke?"

"Do you really want to know?"

"Yeah, I really do."

Zeke sat down with the cup in his hands and studied its interior. "Life sometimes gets boring," he said after a while. "We tend to feel envious of the people with the opportunities and the guts to have adventures." Cleo was about to argue, but Zeke didn't give her a chance. "But in your case, I think most of your resentment of Reese is a reflection of your perception of an inversion in the proper order of things. I think you, the hard-nosed, hard-science engineer, greatly resent being required to do service work for a bunch of soft sociologists and anthropologists who never have anything definite to say and who, by the hard definitions of science, barely qualify. One's sense of propriety is very deeply ingrained, and we tend to react strongly toward any disturbance."

"That's a load of bullshit, Zeke."

Zeke said nothing.

Cleo hesitated and then went on, almost against her will, "If I needed something to be jealous about, I could pick on that girl that hangs around all the time." She immediately regretted saying it. She hadn't even admitted that concern to herself.

"She's a weird kid. Reese wanted to show me the hardware site—the kid lives there, apparently—and this kid goes practically into hysterics."

"Every culture has its own concept of privacy," Zeke said. "Now you've had my wise-old-uncle lecture, are you angry?"

Cleo shook her head, surprised that she was not. "But you're wrong," she said.

"Could be." Zeke leaned over the maps again. "I'd like to

transmit this material to an archeologist I know in the British Enclave for his opinion.''

"I can't imagine there'd be any objection. I'll check with Irene," Cleo said, happy with the change of subject.

"Where's the new site?"

She pointed it out to him.

"And there's nothing there but the safe? No identifying marks?"

"Reese talked about pot shards. Or some such a thing."

"Good. Maybe we'll be able to get a date."

They spent the rest of the morning going over the pictures on the disk Reese had salvaged from the broken recorder, reading them into the computer, then displaying them on the screen. Zeke thought there was a small chance he might be able to identify some of the ruins, at least by type.

"I've seen enough broken, mossy walls to last me a lifetime," Cleo said. "Is there something special about that group?"

Zeke had isolated views of the Governor's Mansion from the others on the screen. "I keep thinking I've seen this building before," he said.

The Mansion was intact, and in use. The row of carved columns across the front and the shallow pitch of the roof were typical of the Greek Revival architecture of four and a half to five centuries ago. That in itself didn't make it too remarkable—hundreds of buildings of similar design had been built in the mid-nineteenth century in mid-America. But Monn's particular example did seem familiar.

"Have you been to Monn?" Cleo asked.

Zeke shook his head, still pondering. "In some piece of video recording, flat pictures, like these," he continued. Reese's pictures were flat because he couldn't be expected to drag holographic equipment around with him. The pictures in the record in Zeke's memory were flat because they had predated widespread use of holograms. He was recalling an old video, an Old People's tape. But where had he seen it, and in what context?

He called the main computer, and instructed it to search the old video records, ignoring fiction, for a similar building.

The computer asked for a priority, and he gave it a low one; he set his terminal on standby and got up to stretch, then rubbed his aching leg.

"That's bothering you more than usual today," Cleo said.
Zeke nodded.

"Maybe you should have Medical look at it."

Zeke made a dismissive gesture. "I don't exactly trust them up there. Excuse me a minute. I'm going to get a pill."

Cleo sighed as Zeke limped away to the bathroom. She couldn't blame him for the way he felt, but it wasn't good for him.

Twenty years ago Zeke had been doing field work in a northern community near Aver, fascinated by the place because it was being absorbed by a bigger, more aggressive tribe, the first indication he had seen that the Phobes were beginning to consolidate. He had been caught in a raid on the village, and the raiders didn't distinguish between native villagers and visiting anthropologists.

The spear hit him in the thigh. The rough medicine available in the shattered village hadn't been much help. It had taken him twelve days to make his way home while the wound festered and fever raged.

The docTRs, the medically oriented technical robots, recommended amputation. Serena, a genuine flesh-and-blood medical person, overruled them and took a chance on saving it.

Zeke and Serena had become a couple, and Zeke had quit field work, and they seemed happy together until a year and a half earlier, when a massive, unpredicted stroke had killed Serena in an instant.

Zeke had no good reason to trust Medical.

He was coming back into the room when the terminal *ping*ed its ready message.

"Good," he said. "Let's see what it's got for us."

Cleo found herself a fixed-form chair and sat erect in it while Zeke went to work at the terminal. She had a feeling that if she got too comfortable, she would fall sleep. Outside, the sun rode in a cloudless sky. She took a deep breath and forced relaxation. It was the first chance she'd had to relax since she had left Monn.

In Monn, every morning they prayed for rain.

Her brief Monnish experience had disturbed her. It was funny, seeing Reese at work. Disorienting, somehow. It wasn't exactly like finding something out of context, a fish roosting in a tree, for instance. It was as if the fish was comfortable and happy in the tree, in defiance of everything that was right and proper. Reese was just too damned much at home in that miserable place.

"Come and see this," Zeke said.

Cleo joined him at the terminal, leaning over his shoulder to see the screen.

The pictures were two-dimensional and silent, and were all the more terrible for that; the seething crowd in the foreground seemed less human for lacking sound. It was a bright summer day with a little breeze. In the middle ground three men stood on a platform with bunting draped around it. The one in the center moved a little forward, facing a bundle of old-style microphones, obviously addressing a hostile assembly. The snarling faces and waving fists of the crowd made it plain that they would rather tear him limb from limb than hear what he had to say.

"That's Clive Sheldon, isn't it?" Cleo asked as the camera moved up to focus on the speaker. She recognized the astronomer who had become the leader of the Appropriate Technology Movement from her history lessons of long ago. Obviously the pictures were from a time just before the Separation.

"Yes," Zeke said. "The man on his right is Willy Sandersen, the astronaut who was Sheldon's lieutenant."

"Will we ever get back into space, Zeke?"

"We put up two, three satellites a year."

"No, I mean people."

"You'd know better than I. I wouldn't think so. We can't gather enough resources together in modern times. I've started this a bit too far back. We'll get to what I wanted to show you in a moment. This is a historic sequence, you know, a record of the incident which sparked the Separation. At this point in history, the political systems of the world were breaking down. World trade was in chaos. The Bush Wars had been going on for about fifty years. Continental North America was beginning to feel the direct effects with self-rule movements in Puerto Rico, Quebec, Alaska, Western Canada, and with the so-called Decent Citizens' Alliance finally finding its strident anti-intellectual, anti-technology voice in Bradley Harmon. And, of course, the death throes of the trade unions and a multitude of ethno-religious struggles."

The pictures were over three centuries old, but still powerful.
Sheldon had his hands out in front of him, as if he were pleading
with the crowd.

Suddenly he jerked back and fell, an ugly red mess blossom-
ing where his head had been.

There was a moment of stunned immobility. Then the ragged,
wild-eyed crowd surged forward like a tide, broke on the platform, ripped and tore at the very boards, flowed up, snatched at
the body, overrunning those who tried to protect it, and ripped
it to bloody shreds, mouths contorted by their silent screams.
Cleo could almost hear their voices reverberating across the centuries, "Technophile—Phile—Phile."

"Okay, here we go," Zeke said. The camera swung wildly
as the cameraman was overcome by the rush of mad humanity.
Zeke stopped the motion, moving the record frame by frame,
then holding on one and expanding it until the bloating, manic
faces drifted off the screen and a background building grew in
the center. The flag on its roof, frozen in midflutter, was not the
familiar red, white, and green bars of the short-lived North
American Union that Cleo expected to see, but a stark white
one bearing a long-stemmed, asymmetric black cross.

"That cross is all over the place in Monn," Cleo said.

Zeke nodded. "I think the sequence I saw originally was the
raising of that flag, but it may not be in our library. This will
serve." The building was a bit blurry and partially hidden by
trees. Zeke called one of Reese's stills of the Governor's Mansion and superimposed it on the picture, adjusted the size somewhat, matching roof ridge to roof ridge.

"I'll be damned," Cleo said. "You mean Monn is built over
Harmonsville? The first damned New Faith community?"

"Looks like," Zeke said.

"Then we might as well abandon the Hunt in Monn. A bunch
of people dedicated to the bucolic ideal wouldn't be likely to
have anything we need."

"I'm not so sure. Bradley Harmon wasn't all that much of a
purist for all his preaching about embracing the beautiful, healing simplicity of pretechnological life. He used the television
network without any qualms of conscience until it fell apart, and
you can tell from this record, Sheldon wasn't assassinated with
a rock.

"More important, the government of the North American Union was dead set against establishing Harmonsville, which was essentially a hostile nation in their midst. Legend has it that Harmon was able to compile, through undeclared Decent Citizens' Alliance members holding high-ranking places in the government service, a list of prime military targets which he threatened to market to other, unfriendly governments if he wasn't allowed to have his place in the sun. Nuclear weapons, of course, especially concentrations of them, could be expected to be included.

"We don't know how true this story is, but that safe is definitely worth recovering, for its historical potential, if nothing else."

"There's a problem with that," Cleo said. "It'll take men and machinery to move it, and Supply and Services is busy calculating the energy requirements in kilojoules and shaking its collective head and telling me we can't afford it."

"Bureaucrats can be got around. It's too bad no one has ever been able to develop a society in which they could be eliminated."

"Also, Reese is dead set against disturbing the Phobes over it."

"We all start out as idealists, I guess. The act of living tends to teach us compromise."

"And philosophy?" Cleo asked.

Zeke shook his head. "That's the prerogative of old men."

Twelve

The moon rose big and yellow out of the river and divided itself into a river moon and a sky moon. The sky moon sailed serene and unruffled through a skiff of cloud. The river moon was shattered by wind-driven waves, pulled this way and that by the currents in the water.

It was the full moon of midsummer, the witches' moon.

Nervously Sarah left her den and crossed the empty ground, coming up the embankment on Market Road. An owl questioned her passage. She jumped, frightened. Then she had to spend time calming herself, telling herself that an owl was nothing to be afraid of. She didn't believe the story about owls carrying the souls of the unmourned dead. Hugging the book in its cotton wrap more tightly under her arm, she hurried on her way.

Monn was quiet. The common folk were abed, anticipating a hard day coming since all their days were hard, and most of the gentry had by then found their evening's entertainment. The doors were latched, the shutters closed against the ghosts and demons of the night, and the dark, narrow streets left in the care of stray dogs and prowlers.

No light showed at the weaver's house. A sense of relief seeped in as Sarah wondered if Ellen had forgotten. That would give her a perfectly good reason to put her ordeal off for another day. It wasn't as if she really *wanted* to do it. It was just that she had no choice.

But Ellen stepped out of the shadows and said, "Hey!" as Sarah approached.

"You scared me," Sarah said crossly.

"Sorry. Have you got it?"

Sarah nodded and gave her parcel to Ellen.

"What is it?" Ellen asked.

"It's a book."

"What's it for?"

"It tells you stuff."

"Like what?"

"I don't know. It never told me anything. Reese uses it a lot, though."

"Let's go, then."

"Just a minute."

"What for? We better not keep Cat Anna waiting. And don't talk so loud. If I get caught, I'll get an awful beating. I'm not supposed to be out alone, never mind in the middle of the night." Ellen handed the book back and started off down the road.

Getting caught brought a frightening possibility to mind. "Does Raymond know you made a spell for him?" Sarah asked as she followed Ellen.

Ellen regarded her friend in the moonlight. "What, you think I'm dumb enough to tell him?"

"No, but could he know? Somehow?"

"Nah, how could he?"

"I don't know. Just somehow."

"You worry too much. Don't think about stuff so much."

"Even a sorcerer or a witch wouldn't know? Even a Phile?"

"For the love of Heaven, Sarah, you've got Philes on the brain. I didn't think you'd be so scared of a tiny little spell."

"I'm not scared. Ellen?"

"What?"

"There was an owl. When I was coming."

"So? Are we going to do this or not? 'Cause I wouldn't feel too bad about going back to bed, you know."

They climbed Birch Road up the hill, following it past the Jordan Family estate all the way to the top, until it turned into a narrow track and finally into a faint path, barely discernible in the moonlight, winding along the brow of the hill among the grasses and thistles that fought for life on the rocky slope.

They came upon a wooded area where the ground was flatter for a while and where gnarled poplars struggled for a roothold and hung shadowed, knotty branches across their way. Through

the woods, Sarah could see a dim gleam of firelight coming
through the open door of Cat Anna's place. Ellen stopped. Sarah
bumped into her.

"You ready?" Ellen asked in a whisper.

Sarah nodded, forgetting that Ellen couldn't see her. "Yeah,
I guess," she said after a moment. It was deathly quiet in the
open space ahead. The moonlight lay silent and still, and even
the night breeze seemed not to penetrate. Goose bumps rose on
Sarah's arms.

Something small and dark moved at Sarah's feet. She jumped
with a small squeak of alarm. The dark form glided down the
path ahead and stopped before the open door, silhouetted in the
firelight.

It was just a cat. It looked back at the two girls as if inviting
them in, then disappeared inside.

"It's kind of spooky," Ellen whispered.

"Yeah," Sarah agreed, her voice sounding small in the night.

They crossed the open space cautiously, heads swiveling.

Cat Anna's hut was half cave, half rude building. A fire burned
near the door in a stone-ringed pit. Above it, an iron pot hung
on a tripod. The air lay warm and close and heavy with the
smells of cooking. Beyond the fire, shadows crowded in.

Huddled on a stool at the fireside sat the woman Sarah had
come to see.

Hunched under layers of shawls as if the fire no longer had
the power to heat her old bones, Cat Anna stroked the purring
animal in her lap with one hand, stirred the contents of the pot
with the other, and dreamed an old woman's dreams of better
times.

Some people swore that Cat Anna was a hundred years old.
The clawlike hand that held the spoon was wrinkled and sere
enough to make the claim believable. Some people said she was
so old that she had actually seen the Old People. Sarah didn't
think that was true. But one thing was certain—at a time when
few people made it to fifty, Cat Anna was the oldest, wisest
person in Monn. Many citizens sought out Cat Anna's help
when they were troubled, though few admitted it. She wore a
heavy silver Cross of God on a string around her neck—a gift,
they said, from the old governor—but it was said in frightened
whispers among the closest of friends that Cat Anna had powers.

Ellen hung back. Sarah warily approached the warmth of the fire and waited for the old woman to notice her.

A lean gray tom wandered in from the shadows in the back of the house, padded over to the fire, and butted his head against Anna's leg, demanding her attention. Anna reached over and scratched his ears, and he lay down beside her and watched the embers of the fire through slitted eyes.

"Sarah," Cat Anna said. "What brings you here?" The sound of her voice was the sound of the winter wind rustling dry leaves. Her eyes stayed fixed on the fire, and the flames glinted dully in them.

How did Cat Anna know her name? In spite of the warmth of the fire, Sarah shivered. She had to clear her throat before she could answer. Cat Anna had the patience of age. She waited.

"I need a man-catching spell," Sarah said.

"Truly?"

Sarah nodded.

"Tell me." She summoned the girl closer with an imperious hook of a bony finger, took the package from her, and gave her the job of stirring the pot. "Tell me of the man." Cat Anna pulled her stool closer to the fire.

Anna closed her eyes and listened to Sarah's tale. In her long life, Anna thought she had heard all the stories of un-requited love there were to hear. Most of them were perfectly ordinary occurrences distorted by the human ego which could not accept the notion that a loved one could not, would not, did not love in return. The fair maiden, apple of the eye, must surely be prevented from returning a swain's ardor by the enchantments of a jealous other. The bold, handsome man would melt before the lady's affection if it were not for a rival's spell.

The inward eye that saw things past had dimmed with age. But it seemed to Anna that witchcraft was not so much a part of her youth. There seemed to her to have been a time when stories of witches and spells would have been met with laughter. But that was such a very long time ago, and might be just part of her dreams of an easier way of life, of warmth and bright lights and music.

Sarah spoke of bright lights coming from nowhere. Anna

thought she might have known of such things once. But maybe not. So many more things seemed possible when one was young. Memories had grown elusive, and she often felt confused between recollection, reality, and the visions of the night.

But the child believed it.

Sarah watched the fire with distant eyes as she described Reese. "He is tall and square-shouldered, and his hair is smooth and shiny so you want to touch it. He smiles . . . he smiles like the sun after a storm, and his teeth are even and white like none I've seen. His hands are soft with pink nails like a baby's, but strong. He has gray eyes that watch you and don't turn away. He walks tall and long, like he owned the world." She stopped stirring and was quite for a moment. "It will have to be a strong spell. He's a witchly Phile."

"A Phile," Cat Anna said. She was skeptical; Sarah could hear it in her voice. "Stir the pot, child."

"It must be so," Sarah said.

"A veritable prince of evil wizards."

Sarah said nothing.

"What makes you think this?"

Sarah tried to think of what she might offer in evidence and remembered the crystal cube which now rode in her pocket. She fished it out, hesitated a moment, then handed it to Cat Anna. The figure within was vague in the firelight, but visible nonetheless.

Anna examined it closely, eyes squinted, head thrust forward on its skinny neck, hand like a bird's claw turning it this way and that. Then she folded it into her hands and let her hands drop into her lap in front of the sleeping cat. She sat like that, so still and quiet, for such a long time that Sarah thought she might have dozed off as old people were wont to do. Sarah leaned the spoon against the side of the pot and turned a questioning lift of the hands to Ellen standing just barely inside the door, waiting.

Ellen shrugged.

"Stir the pot, child," Anna's reedy voice said. "Do you want my supper to burn?" Sarah grabbed up the spoon and made some hasty circles.

"It's been long." Cat Anna spoke softly. "Or perhaps a dream." She straightened a little and opened her eyes to scan

Sarah's nervous face. The girl obviously believed that the old woman had taken leave of her senses. "You ask a great deal from a tired old woman, to charm a Phile. A dangerous business. You think perhaps Cat Anna grows weary of life? Is that it?"

"No," Sarah said, too loudly. "I never thought that."

"And if we weave a web so strong, what will you do with this Phile? Send him to cut hay for Mean Morris in the mornings and entertain your brats with feats of legerdemain by the fireside in the evenings? Would you have him conjure a jinn to sweep your floor and a demon to cut the wood? What do you want, Sarah?"

"I . . . don't know . . . To be with him, is all."

"Humph. Love, I suppose."

Anna seemed fiercely opposed to love, but Sarah nodded anyway.

"You younglings are all alike. Witless. You'll never believe there's more cutting of wood than making of love in life. You think getting your knees up will be the end of the heart's pain? It makes more than it cures, child."

Sarah's cheeks grew warm.

"Nothing changes," Cat Anna said, sounding old and weary. She pulled herself laboriously to her feet and peered into the pot. The cat in her lap protested being disturbed. "As you wish. You have the price?"

Sarah placed a small, heavy purse into Cat Anna's hand. Cleo's chain had brought a good price at the back door of the goldsmith's shop. Sarah had thought about reserving a few of the coins for her own use, but then decided that she didn't have the courage.

Anna weighed the purse in her hand and nodded her approval. She gave the crystal back to Sarah. "Put this back where you found it. Such things are not to be treated lightly. Are you hungry?"

It was only a hesitant second before Sarah nodded. Doubtful as she was about what might come out of Anna's pot, at her age she was always hungry.

Anna called Ellen from the doorway and sent her rummaging in a dark corner for bowls. By the time Ellen returned with them, Anna seemed to have forgotten about the food. She studied the empty spaces across the fire. "We must do this with great care," she said thoughtfully. "I shall need blood." She took a long knife out from under her shawls, and Sarah's heart leaped. But Anna only speared a round loaf of bread from the shelf over her head and brought it down.

When they had eaten, Cat Anna told Sarah to return at moon-set. The girl said her thanks, and she and her friend went away. Anna went back to her fire.

The displaced cat looked up at her with reproachful yellow eyes, an old mother going white about the ears and mindful of her comfort.

"Peace, old lady," Anna told the animal, but meant it as much for herself as for the cat. "These things must be done if we're to have a bit of meat in the pot, eh? But this is no simple love-struck girl, I think." She closed her eyes as if dozing, but her thoughts were in ferment.

To have Philes in the city again. Those had been terrible, exciting times. Anna unwrapped the book that Sarah had left and held it open in her hands, finding pleasure in the weight of it. Such things had held meaning for her once. She had forgotten. Time-blurred vision saw only a gray fog on the page.

When Sarah returned, Cat Anna led her to a magical place. It looked like a dozen other ordinary places, a small grassy space among the twisted trees a little way from Cat Anna's house. A largish rock stuck partly out of the ground. Anna stopped beside it, dug a thick candle out of a bundle wrapped in a square of cloth, then took out flint and steel. The candle was duly lighted, ceremoniously mounted in the skull of a small animal, and placed upon the rock.

It all seemed too mundane. The candle was plain tallow whose flame wavered in the currents of air like any candle. Skirts bundled into her lap as she squatted to the ground, Anna dug a circle into the grass around the rock with an implement that looked like the business end of a common garden hoe. The old woman grunted as she worked and complained of aching joints.

Sarah was not too impressed. Surely the instruments of magic should be more esoteric. She thought spells should be cast in dark, smoky corners amid runes and pentagrams and fantastic images, not out in a common meadow. Surely a witch should confront the powers in embroidered robes and high cone hat, not a tangle of uncombed gray locks and grease-stained, faded shawls. She wanted to ask the old woman if she was sure they were doing the thing properly, but she didn't dare.

Anna began chanting. She circled the stone, hobbling round and round, the tall grasses under her skirt keeping dry harmony with her rasping voice. She made Sarah sit on the rock and hold the skull with its candle in her lap while she droned on. Sarah was half-convinced that the old woman had lost what little mind remained to her, but even more afraid that fearsome and uncontrollable spirits were being lured into the circle around the rock. Every waving of grasses, every rustle of leaves, brought apprehension.

Anna gave Sarah a sprig of limp clover to hold, for health, she said; and a branch of dry washed-out wintergreen, for long life; a bit of wilted forget-me-not, for fidelity, and Sarah could only hope that the spirits or whatever were not sticklers for fresh flowers.

Then Anna wanted blood. Sarah had demurred, fearful not so much of the keen edge of the knife against her palm as of making an opening in her integral self through which dreadful things might enter.

With the sky already getting pale, Anna grew angry. "What are you playing at, child? Do you think I will leave the spell half-made? Would you have it wandering about the world uncontrolled, seeking its completion? We do not treat the powers so casually. If need be, I will make a binding spell and draw the blood from your cowardly heart."

Night was nearly ended. The danger seemed less with the coming of day. Cat Anna's fury was more imminent than that of nameless demons. Furthermore, it was generally conceded in the city that Anna was well versed in the occult lore, and must therefore know what she was doing. Sarah finally acquiesced.

The prick of the knife was barely noticeable. A drop of blood fell black upon the paper and another drop black on the assembled herbs. "You must never come back to this place," Anna said when it was done. "You will disturb the mystic energies if you do, and the spell will be shattered. Go now. You have what you think you want.''

Anna gathered up the worn herbs and stuffed them into a small leather bag which she hung around Sarah's neck. Then she packed up the impedimenta of spell-making and shambled wearily back to her dwelling, leaving Sarah to return the book to Reese so it could work its new magic.

In the house near Travellers' Way, the newborn day poked a finger of light through a crack between the shutters that closed the broken window. It touched the sleepers wrapped in each other's arms under sheepskins on the far side of the room.

Reese roused and sat up, not knowing for a moment what had wakened him. He frowned at the spot of light on the bed, then at the gap through which it came. He was sure he had pulled the shutters tight. He looked around, puzzled, feeling that something was amiss.

''That's odd,'' he said aloud.

''What?'' Cleo asked, her voice still sleep fuzzed.

''The hologram.''

''What hologram?''

''The one I had taken of you just before I left the Enclave. I had it mounted in Xstalite and brought it with me.''

''That was sweet, Reese.''

Reese shook his head. ''No, the thing is, after the place was tossed, I couldn't find it. I thought Miller et al must have carried it off. How did it get on the table?''

Cleo propped herself up on her elbows and regarded the crystalline cube sitting on the table. The sunbeam had found it, and the image looked radiant.

''Change of heart?'' she suggested.

''I don't know. Something weird is going on around here.''

''I'm flattered anyway. Turn around and I'll show you how much.''

Reese glared at the image a moment longer before turning to give his attention to the reality.

''Does this mean I'm forgiven?''

''Not exactly.''

''Cleo, for pete's sake, what do you want?''

"I want you to quit this silly business and start acting like a civilized man again. You're even starting to talk like a Phobe, you know that?"

Reese opened his mouth to protest, then closed it again. He sat up and turned his face away from Cleo and looked at the wall for a long time. "Go home, Cleo. Leave me alone."

Thirteen

Brother Parker walked with Brother Eric in the Temple's deserted gardens where in happier years Sisters would be bent over their hoes. Not a dew drop glinted in the early morning sun. The pea vines were dried to autumn crispness and the turnip leaves were already wilting. By midday they would be hanging as limp as rags. There was no need for the Sisters to labor there that rainless season. Not even weeds would grow without moisture. Head down, Brother Parker watched the dust puff out from under his sandals.

"The governor has made no move to investigate the Millers' complaint about the witch," Brother Eric said.

"I know," Brother Parker said, his mind on dying vegetables. "Robert Miller has spoken to me about the lack of action. He is greatly disturbed that his boys' complaint is not being taken seriously." He crumpled a crisp leaf in his hand and let the dust fall to the ground. "Robert thinks I have influence in the Mansion."

"Perhaps Michael is afraid," Brother Eric suggested.

Brother Parker looked up sharply. Brother Eric's face gave nothing away, yet Brother Parker felt the silent criticism from his second-in-command. Or maybe it was his conscience which told him silently, "You also are afraid, Brother, lest you be found unequal to the task."

Brother Parker let his gaze drop again to the dry earth. Every morning before the sun rose, he prostrated himself before the Cross of God in the Temple's chapel and begged the Lord God to let the rains come. Still the rains were withheld. He no longer

109

doubted that the Lord God was mightily displeased with his children in the City of Monn.

"Michael will adhere to the letter of the law," Brother Parker said. "I do not believe he will do anything until the Millers produce a witness to corroborate their story."

"Can they?"

"Not to the actual attack, it seems. Although Butch claims the witch is known to one of the street urchins. According to Brad, it was Butch's attempt to rescue the child that earned him the witch's ire in the first place."

Brother Eric shook his head. Butch Miller as benefactor to the powerless seemed unlikely. "We do not have the most reliable of informants in this matter," he said.

"True," Brother Parker agreed.

"It appears we will get at the truth of it only from the witch himself."

"Are you suggesting we act in place of, and in opposition to, the governor?"

"I see no other course, except to ignore a witch at large in the city, going where he will, doing as he pleases, to the spiritual peril of honest citizens. I think the Church must act, and should, for the salvation of souls, and for the greater glory of the Lord God."

"We do not know this for certain."

"Then we must become certain."

Brother Parker chewed at the edge of his mustache as he was inclined to do in those rare moments when he felt unsure. It was a habit he was trying to break, for it was undignified and also gave him a ragged appearance about the mouth.

"It would not do to have the True Church thought powerless to fight against evil when it is plain before us," Brother Eric said. He saw his leader's hesitation and pressed his point home. "It must be known that the Church acts on the authority of the Lord God to carry out his swift and terrible justice, and is not subject to the whims of secular rulers." Brother Parker nodded, and Brother Eric continued, "The Lord God placed his Church in your care, Brother. I believe you have the strength to carry the burden at this critical time."

Brother Parker bowed his head in acknowledgment. It was

true. The burden of decision was his to bear. And he did have the strength, once he knew the way.

"I shall go to the chapel and pray for guidance," he said, "and speak to you again later today."

Brother Eric watched Brother Parker go, watched his stride lengthen and his steps get firm as he left the garden and entered the Temple by the small, inconspicuous rear door.

Brother Eric went the other way, leaving the garden by way of a gate in the high picket fence that let him out into a narrow alley. He followed the alley to where a small dark man hunched in a doorway, waiting for him.

They did not greet one another. Brother Eric dropped two silver coins into the man's outstretched hand. "You will go to Thomas," Brother Eric said, "and tell him Brother Parker has decided to move against the witch on the Lord God's authority, and will not brook any interference by the state."

"He will ask me how I know this."

"Tell him you heard it said in the market. It will be sufficient."

The man sidled away, keeping to the shadows, and Brother Eric, satisfied with his work, returned to the Temple to await the outcome of Brother Parker's communion with God.

Fourteen

Sarah carried the book clutched against her breast with her wounded hand pressed against its cover, the small pain reassuring. The book felt subtly different to her, as if it had a warmth, a life of its own.

She no longer doubted the sorcery. She had felt a surge of power enter the strange object along with the drop of her blood that stained an inner page.

Even so, she might have declined to take the last step, except that she had found Cleo in Reese's arms on the previous night. She had stood there in the night-dark room with the crystal cube in one hand and her belt knife in the other, furious with him, and thought seriously about opening Cleo's throat. She could imagine the feel of the blade in the flesh and was horrified by her own thoughts.

With a pain in her gut, she had fled the scene, back up the hill to where Cat Anna waited.

And so she would let the spell work its magic. It was a way of getting even, among other things.

She spent a long time sitting in a patch of brush beside the road, watching Reese's house, struggling not to doze off after a tense, sleepless night. She was afraid to wait for another day for fear the sorcery would fade. She hadn't thought to ask Anna how long it would last.

Just when it seemed that he would never go for breakfast, the door opened, and Reese came out. He stopped for a moment, and threw something out onto the walk. The two crows dropped down out of the trees almost immediately and began picking it up. Sarah couldn't believe what she saw. He was feeding the crows, enticing the birds of death to his very doorstep. Was he just reckless, or so powerful that he need not worry about playing so with the dark forces?

She figured she would be smart to worry about it another time. There was one bit of satisfaction, and an indication that the magic was already working. Cleo was not with him.

As soon as Reese was out of sight down Travellers' Way, she pitched a rock at the crows, scrambled up the path, and let herself into the house.

Once inside, the main problem was finding a credible place for the book to be, supposing he had missed it when he was cleaning up. She settled for tucking it under the edge of the straw mattress of his bed. That way, even if he didn't find it, it would be close to him.

Then she went home and slept, but not too well. She saw that the Legend of Sarah had changed once again, to a tale of a desperate lover driven by circumstances to resort to sorcery to win her true love. She wasn't sure anymore how the story ended, but most of the tales the storyteller told about the making of spells ended with the spellmaker caught, even destroyed, by his own clever magic.

By midafternoon when she roused, she decided that the magic must have had time to work; she set out to find Reese and see if he was responding properly. It was dusk before she found him, trudging into town from the north, looking dusty and tired.

"Hey, Reese," she said.

"Hey, Sarah. Looking for something to eat?"

"Sure," Sarah answered, thinking that was a hopeful sign.

"I've got bread and cheese at the house, if that will do."

It sounded near ambrosial to Sarah.

But when Reese had washed up—Sarah was beginning to think he was a shade fanatical on the subject of washing—and they had shared his humble rations and a pint of beer, he sent her away. "Run along, girl," he said. "I'm beat, and I need my beauty sleep."

"I don't know what you mean," she said. And she didn't. He didn't look like a man who had been beaten.

"I mean go home now. I want to go to bed."

"But—"

"Good-bye, Sarah." He made shooing motions with his hands and closed the door firmly behind her.

She stood on the walk for a while, trying to figure out what had gone wrong.

Maybe the magic took longer. Maybe he hadn't been home all day.

Next morning she stationed herself where he would have to pass her on his way to breakfast. But he only said "Hey," and continued into the inn without even hesitating.

Instead of waiting for him as she usually did, she went off to Market Square. She hoped she might find the storyteller there, because she wanted to ask him about Cat Anna. The storyteller not only spun dreams of an evening, he was also the source of much information. But Brother Parker was holding forth, so there was no sense for a teller of tales to wait about.

"Evil, Brothers and Sisters," Brother Parker was saying. "I smell the stink of corruption, the reek of brimstone. We must be vigilant. Satan comes in many guises, wearing sweet perfumes and a pleasant smile, to lead the unwary from the paths of righteousness . . ."

Sarah went home and lay on her bed in the cool dark basement of the Old People's place and thought about what might have gone wrong. It worried her that Cat Anna might not have the power to enchant a Phile. She decided to consult Ellen on the matter.

Ellen was carrying two wooden buckets of dirty water out of the weaver's house. Sarah took one from her and the two girls staggered as far as the aspen with them and poured the water out onto the ground.

"I'm supposed to take them out there, but I don't care. This is far enough. I don't see why the spell would care who the man is," Ellen said, leaning on the bole of the tree and wiping the hair off her forehead with her arm. "The only thing I can think of is a counter spell."

"Huh?" Sarah said.

"Well, you know, like maybe he's got a warding spell that keeps other spells off him. I heard there's such a thing. Or maybe there's another, stronger spell already."

"Like what?"

Ellen considered the damp spot on the grass where the thirsty earth had already absorbed the water. "Well," she said, hunching slightly. "Some other woman?" She picked up the empty buckets and started back toward the house. "But, you know, really, you should give it time."

Time. How much time? Sarah went back home and thought about it some more. Cleo. It had to be Cleo. Sarah wished she had some Phile magic that would make Cleo disappear. Then the thought upset her. Cleo had first provoked her to consider murder, and now Philish evils. It was one thing to fool around with harmless little spells in a moonless glade. It was quite another to invoke the Philes. Maybe Brother Parker was right when he said the instant one gave the devil the slightest chance he would drag his victim bit by bit to perdition. Guilt and fear made her heart tight. The storyteller's tale was changing yet again. The Legend of Sarah was in danger of becoming one of a woman who had sold her immortal soul for her love.

That had a grandeur to it, too, of course. The ultimate sacrifice to the spirit of love. She imagined the love spirit as a fat, placid, demanding child grown thick and disdainful with all the sacrifices made to it—an altogether unpleasant being.

Next morning, crossing the square on her way to Reese's place, she ran into Butch. He roared at her to stop, but she ducked away from him and ran smack into the arms of a pair of grim Brothers.

"This is your witch?" one of the Brothers asked.

"Of course not," Butch said as he came up to them. He had an all-too-pleased look on his face, as if he had just won something. "But this little baggage has, shall we say, been keeping him company. She'll know where he is." He put his thumb under Sarah's chin, pushed it up, and smiled his toothy, garlicky smile. "Don't you, girl?"

Frightened, not knowing what Butch was up to, Sarah turned to the Brother. "I don't know any witch."

"Come with us," the Brother said.

* * *

The Temple of the True Church was the tallest building in Monn, two stories, with a steeple rising another twenty feet to hold the Cross of God high in the air. In front of the building, facing Temple Road, a single thigh-high rail fenced the Church's grounds, but around the back, tall, pointed pickets closely spaced screened the outbuildings and backyard from casual observation. Wide stone steps led to a wide, high, brass-studded front door. Sarah was hustled through that massive portal without time to really appreciate its dimensions.

Aside from listening to Brother Parker in the marketplace, Sarah had never had much to do with the True Church.

The building itself had a spooky, brooding aspect. She gave it a wide berth, and left the pockets of the Brothers and Sisters unexplored. Although she found little enough evidence of God in her day-to-day life, she thought it wise to avoid giving direct offense just on the off chance that He might be watching.

She never thought about going into the Temple, any more than she thought about going into the Governor's Mansion. She felt she was in the wrong place, her presence a transgression, against what she couldn't say. Her usually abundant self-confidence deserted her, leaving her tense and miserable.

The grim Brothers on either side did little to soothe her apprehension as they herded her along. She got an impression of cool twilight in midmorning, of bare stone walls and cold stone floors and long hallways, of muted, hidden activity.

And then she was face to face with Brother Parker, skewered by his sharp eyes as he regarded her from across a polished table in a room whose single high, narrow window emphasized the reduced quality of the light. It was as if the Temple stones absorbed all the warmth and color out of it. Sarah's pulse raced, and her hands felt as cold as the stones.

The walls were unadorned save for a man-sized, elaborately carved wooden cross fixed to the wall opposite. There was another man with Brother Parker, dressed as he was, seated as he was, on a fleece-padded chair on the far side of the table. He had a pinched, hard face and cruel eyes. His mouth was drawn down, as if he had encountered a particularly repulsive insect and was about to step on it.

Sarah shivered.

"Sarah," Brother Parker said in that resonant, awe-inspiring voice. "Do you fear the Lord God?"

She was more afraid of Brother Parker at that moment. She said nothing.

Less fiercely, Brother Parker said, "You have nothing to fear, child. Speak truly, and fully, and God will protect your spirit. The Lord God loves his children, and asks only their love and obedience in return. You have strayed in your ignorance from the paths of righteousness, given aid and comfort to the devil's agents. You must make amends, my dear, to be welcomed back into the Lord God's family."

Brother Parker speaking gently seemed no less menacing than Brother Parker thundering. Sarah had no idea how she had come to Brother Parker's terrible attention. She felt small and vulnerable.

As if reading her thoughts, he told her, "You have lain with the witch known as Reese this last while."

Startled, dumbly, Sarah shook her head. Fear for herself was supplemented by fear for Reese. She wanted more than anything to run away from there, but her feet seemed nailed to the floor.

"Do not deny your guilt, my child. It will not serve you well."

"It's not true," Sarah managed to choke out.

"We have witnesses, if it comes to that."

"They're lying."

"Do not add false accusations to the burden of sin you already bear. The Lord God is a stern Father. You have much to atone for. Bend to his will, lest you burn alongside of the evil one who misled you."

Sarah had a sudden, all-too-clear picture of herself bound to a stake in Market Square, writhing and screaming as the flames billowed up. But the lump in her throat blocked off anything she might have said. She couldn't think what to say anyway. She didn't expect Brother Parker to believe her. She was nobody, and he wouldn't believe her, no matter what she said.

"You are fortunate, Sarah," Brother Parker said. "You have

the opportunity to wipe away the stains on your soul with service to the True Church. All you need do is tell us where the witch can be found. We know he is hiding from the Lord God's just wrath. Where is he, Sarah?''

"I don't know," Sarah cried, the full and honest truth.

Brother Parker heaved a loud, somewhat theatrical sigh. He allowed himself to look very sad. "I'm sure you understand, my dear, that we cannot allow you to persist in your wickedness. A witch is a mortal danger to all the Lord God's children. The Lord God Himself has said 'You shall not suffer a witch to live.' But it would be better for you if you were to come to the right path of your own free will. Go with Brother Eric now, to a place of meditation, where you can consider how best to mend your ways.''

The man beside Brother Parker rose, came round the table, and took Sarah's arm in a grip that bruised. As he was leading her out, Brother Parker said, "Remember, Sarah, the devil has the power to assume a pleasing shape.''

Sarah was led down a long narrow hallway whose walls on both sides held a series of similar doors. The door at the end was closed by an iron bar. Brother Eric lifted the bar and urged her down a flight of stairs into a storeroom, then through the storeroom into another place crowded with instruments whose purposes Sarah didn't want to think about.

A torch in a bracket near the entry was the only light. Brother Eric stopped there a moment, used his free hand to pick up a short whip from a bench, and reached over to place it on pegs on the wall that seemed to be there for that purpose.

"At times," he said softly, "it is necessary to sacrifice the flesh to salvage the soul. Fortunately, not too often.'' He gave Sarah a push toward a small open door. The door slammed shut behind her and the latch fell. Brother Eric went away, taking the torch with him. Sarah was left in utter darkness.

She wasn't afraid of the dark. Darkness had often been her ally. But she needed space, room to move in. The place she was in was tiny. She could touch the walls on either side with her outstretched arms. She could feel the walls closing in on her. Though she couldn't see it, she was conscious of the ceiling with the weight of the Temple above it. It seemed too close and heavy. She thought she might suffocate.

She squatted down on the floor and hugged her knees close to her chest and whimpered.

Fifteen

"Hey."

Reese looked up. Two small hands gripped the edge of the table and two pale, watery eyes, scarcely above the level of the tabletop, regarded him wistfully. The weather had turned cold, and a high, sparse layer of dry cloud blocked the sun. The child shivered in its thin clothing. A drip clung to the end of its nose.

"Hey, yourself," Reese answered. "Where's your mother?"

One hand released its grip and waved vaguely toward the back of the inn. When it returned, a grubby finger popped into the mouth. The child continued to watch Reese's every move, as if any one of them might be of great significance. It was a little unsettling.

"Do you think you should be here?" Reese asked. "Shouldn't you stay with your mother?"

"I got hungry."

"Tell your mother."

"There's nothing. She said."

The child's toneless explanation caught Reese with his spoon halfway to his mouth. "Merciful Christ," he said softly, and put the spoon down.

The innkeeper came hurrying up, kneading his apron, full of apologies. "I beg Your Honor's pardon. The boy should not be here. He knows he should not be here."

"It's all right, Harold," Reese said. "He hasn't hurt any-thing."

"That's most kind of you to say, sir. Most generous of Your Honor, I'm sure."

Reese grunted something he hoped Harold would take as dismissal, which apparently he did, bustling the boy off into the back part of the inn and out of sight.

Reese picked up his spoon, intending to finish his breakfast. But the food had lost what little appeal it had held for him. He considered it for a moment, then put the spoon back down and went out.

From a dark corner of the public room, Harold watched him go with a deep furrow between his eyebrows. Then he called the child back to finish the sweetened barley. Harold was a thrifty man. There was no sense in letting perfectly good food go to waste, and he had few morning customers. While the boy licked the bowl clean, the innkeeper sat beside him, fingering the cross at his throat, enjoying his child's pleasure at this unexpected treat. The boy was Harold's youngest, his only son, and they had little enough time together.

But it was a momentary distraction from the pricking of his conscience. He had seen the coil of rope, the lantern, and the funny little hammer Reese had with him, so he knew that Reese was heading out to Young Albert's field. And he knew what was waiting for him there.

He had come to like the stranger and his soft-spoken, quiet ways; and besides, Reese was a good customer, only rarely arguing about the price of service, not like some young lords he could name who screamed as if every coin were their last.

It was no time to be a stranger in the city of Monn.

He sighed, and ruffled the boy's hair. It was early in the day to feel so weary.

"Are you sad, Papa?" the boy asked.

"Aye, it's an ugly business, lad. But you have to live in the world, do you not, that's no world you would have made if you had the making of it. So we give way when evil saints do murder the name of good, and decent folks suffer in the cause of righteousness."

The four-year-old eyes regarded him gravely, but their owner understood almost nothing of what was being said, except that sadness made Papa look old. "God loves you, Father," the boy said, mimicking his mother.

"Mmph," the innkeeper grunted, not necessarily in agreement. "You run along now," he said, patting the skinny little rump, "and tell your mother to put some meat in the pot today." Harold heaved himself out of the chair and got back to work.

No matter what else, the children had to be fed and the governor's taxes had to be paid. He stopped and looked back at the vacant table. How much harm would it have done him to warn the man?

When he had been in the site of Young Albert's field with Cleo, with some halfway-decent lighting on the scene, Reese had spotted shards of broken china in the debris around the fallen concrete beam. He had come back now to unearth a few bits to see if they were worth bothering about before the engineers arrived with their big boots and their machinery and started knocking stuff around.

It was slow work without the right tools, and Reese wished he had thought to tell Cleo to bring a properly equipped archeologist with her. But when he had uncovered three fair-sized dirty pieces and a few fragments, he decided they were nothing more exciting than the ubiquitous machine-molded crockery of late twentieth or early twenty-first-century vintage, and not even particularly good examples of that.

That was the trouble with the Old People. So much of what they made had been fashioned to standard patterns. Few artifacts were distinctive enough to carry much information. The basement he was in was a case in point. Almost all basements of major buildings for something over two centuries were made in exactly the same way, concrete poured into wooden forms. Apartment buildings, office buildings, warehouses, schools, and laboratories were all concrete and glass on steel frameworks.

The Old People had no architectural imagination whatsoever. It was frustrating.

He thought about it some more while he was gathering up his things and decided that maybe he would ask for an archeologist after all. Between them, they could uncover some of the tiles on the surface. Slate tiles were unusual. Maybe the patio would tell them something. The question was how to explain it to Young Albert and other curious Monnish folk. But so far they had accepted his interest in the Old People's buildings without any evident strain. He was a stranger. They expected him to do strange things.

He was still cogitating over it when he came to the shaft that led to the surface. The glare above told him that the sun had come out. It seemed strangely quiet up there. Not a bird chirp could be heard. The hair on the back of his neck prickled as he climbed up.

All around the opening stood solemn black-robed men.

Reese scrambled to his feet and dusted himself off. "Good morning," he said, for want of something better to say.

"Surrender yourself to the servants of God, evil one," the black-robed men said.

Sixteen

"Is this the man?" the officer of the Governor's Guard demanded.

They were in the courtyard, just at the entrance to the Temple. Brother Parker and the officer stood a little ahead of Sarah on the steps that led down into the yard. Brother Eric was just behind her. An unhappy farmer named Jonathan, commandeered from his ox-slow journey to market with honeycomb and a few eggs to be witness, stood on the ground below.

The sun was high, making the shadows small and sharp. There was no warmth in the light. It glinted off the brass buttons of the officer's uniform and from the hilt of his sword. Far away, a bird sang. A scrap of wind made a whirl of dust across the yard and then subsided. The farmer's patient ox, waiting, snuffled at the flies. The fine horse beside it shook its mane and rattled the bridle chains. Grasshoppers creaked. Sarah shivered.

Brothers and Sisters had left the Temple and gathered into a rough circle in the courtyard with a notch open toward the Temple door. In their midst was an inner circle of Brothers, and within that circle was Reese. His wrists were bound, hands palm to palm, and between his palms a wooden Cross of God had been secured with a thin cord that bit into the flesh. The cross was intended to thwart the powers of witchcraft, but the Brothers had nervous eyes and sweat-stained armpits.

A Brother came up to the group at the Temple door and presented Brother Parker with a small shallow basket containing everything they had removed from their prisoner's pockets and person. Brother Parker glanced into the basket. There was nothing particularly remarkable about it except a somewhat larger sum of money than he might have expected—a handsome donation to the True Church, which was sorely needed. A small medallion on a chain was unusual in that it had no decoration. Brother Parker picked it out of the basket and examined it more closely. It seemed to be made of two parts fitted together, like a locket. He tried to pry it apart with his thumbnails. It wouldn't open.

But he noticed a look of alarm come on his prisoner's face as he worked at it. Possibly, it could hold a magic charm, or a potion or philter, even though it was so small. He handed it to one of the Brothers. "Go to the smith and ask him to open this." The Brother went away holding the medallion gingerly in his palm.

"Could we get on with it?" the officer asked impatiently. "Look here, girl. Is this the man?"

Sarah cringed and wished that she could vanish.

Reese turned toward Sarah. There was an ugly bruised cut on the side of his head, and blood still oozed from it. The flies had found it. Reese gave his head a sharp jerk to disturb the insects. They buzzed up, but settled again almost at once.

"Sarah?" Brother Parker prompted.

Sarah shivered again under Reese's fierce glare. She could almost feel the sharp edges that shock and rage and pain had put on him. She felt ill, and bile burned in her throat like fire.

She thought—hoped—that he would surely make some mighty magic and vanish away, leaving the Brothers holding a length of empty cord. Distantly, a bird sang. Nothing else happened.

"The child can't speak," a Brother said. "He's bewitched her, sure." He grabbed Reese by the hair and yanked his head away.

"Don't," Sarah said, the syllable bubbling up through her constricted throat and bursting out onto the sun-bright air. The small explosion was all but lost in the buzzing of insects and the calling of the far-off bird.

"There is nothing to fear," Brother Parker said, more gently than was his usual manner. He came up close to Sarah, so that for the time being she could see nothing but the black of his robe and the gold of the Cross of God. He took Sarah's hands in his soft, moist ones, and her skin prickled the way it did when she encountered some of the fat toads that inhabited the darkest corners of her basement home. She tried to pull away, but Brother Parker held her fast. "You have only to speak the truth. The True Church will protect and keep you, my child. But you must cooperate. If you do not, the Church can do nothing but release the witch for want of evidence, and abandon you to find your own way against the forces of evil and the powers of darkness."

Then Brother Parker stepped aside so that she could again see the prisoner within the ring of black-robed Brothers. "Is this the man?" he asked. Everyone's eyes were on her. She had a brief but painfully clear mental picture of her probable fate if the Brothers were to let Reese go. She could all but touch his anger. It blazed out of his gray eyes like cold fire. He knew where to find her. The crystal cube might hold two girls as easily as one. There was no way out. She had to go through with it.

Miserably, Sarah nodded.

"You must speak, child. Is this the man?"

"Yes," Sarah whispered. "Yes," she cried, and snatched herself away from Brother Parker's clammy hold. She looked around her, at Brother Eric's satisfied half smile, Jonathan's blank questioning face, and the grim excitement of the Brothers and Sisters. She threw herself away from them, bumped her way unseeing among them, and ran off into the city, ignoring the officer's demand to stop.

She ran blindly, the stupid tears in her eyes blurring everything into a bright haze. But her feet found familiar routes among the crowded streets and tight alleys of the lower part of town, and when she could run no longer, when the stitch in her side had her bent nearly double and her breath burned in the back of her mouth, she found herself on the long docks that stuck out into the water where the river boats tied up while they rested from their journeys. Most of them were in. High summer was not their busiest time. They bobbed on the current, butting one another and the piers.

She walked to the end of the pier and looked out over the turbulent muddy water panting, fighting for her breath. The river was low, the water far beneath her. The gunwales of the boat called *Big Fish* were almost level with the dock.

The man on the deck working over a coil of rope looked up from his work. "Hey, Sarah," he called.

She returned his greeting with a limp wave.

"Something wrong?"

She gave her head a shake, a gesture that denied itself.

The man left his work, climbed the boat's rail, and dropped to the pier with the light-footed grace of a riverman. He came up to her, raking fingers through hair sun-bleached to the color of straw, smiling his wide, friendly smile. "You sure you're all right, girl?"

Sarah stared out over the water toward the Witch Bridge. If only one of the witch wagons would come and whisk Reese away into the Wilderness, all her problems would be solved. A witchly Phile should be able to arrange a thing like that. He could help a little, couldn't he? Why did he just stand there and let the Brothers push him around like that?

"Sarah?"

"I'm all right, Matthew. Really, I am."

"Uhuh," Matthew said, noting wet cheeks and red-rimmed eyes. "Well, at least come in and say hello to Beth. She'll be hurt if you don't."

Smearing the moisture on her face with her hands, Sarah allowed herself to be led onto the boat and down the long deck to the cabin at the rear. Beth left off the preparations of the midday meal to hug Sarah with lean brown arms.

The cabin of the *Big Fish* sheltered her from the cool breeze off the water, and Sarah felt welcome there. She had known Matthew and Beth, the couple who ran the *Big Fish* up and down the river, for so long she couldn't remember when she hadn't. Beth had no children of her own, and had at one time invited Sarah to take the place of the daughter she would never have. It was fun for a while. The river gave Matthew and Beth a good life, fish for their dinner and work carrying cargo down the river on the water's current and back up with the big square sail filling with the wind. They got to see more of the world, too, and different ways of doing things. That was one of the things about rivermen that disturbed the townsfolk—they were always bringing home queer notions. The work was hard, but it was good, honest work, and the rivermen were interesting company.

But they were also a tightly knit group, with their own tough code of right and wrong. They didn't steal from one another, even though any one of them might rob a landsman blind if the opportunity arose. Sarah could never entirely resist picking up a little something here and there. Matthew and Beth gave her all she needed, but still she had a compulsion to provide for an uncertain future, and that caused no end of trouble.

Besides, as she got older, the cramped confines of the boat rubbed on Sarah's need for independence and room to swing her arms, so she didn't stay.

In spite of the trouble she had caused for them, Matthew and Beth always had space for her on the bench nailed to the cabin wall, and a sheepskin on the floor of the neat, cupboard-lined space for her to sleep on, and a cup of the light, sweet beer that Matthew bought in Sanjo, down the river, so much nicer than the dark bitter stuff brewed in Monn.

The walls of the cabin blocked the sight of the world outside, and the slap of the waves against the hull blurred the sounds. Sitting between Matthew and Beth, sharing their fish stew, Sarah felt safe for the moment.

"You have a trip?" she asked.

"Short one," Matthew answered. "Upriver to Grassy Bend."

"Can I come?"

"Sure. Be glad of an extra hand with the wind against us. You got the constables on your tail again? You were heaving like an old horse up there on the pier. What did you do, swipe a chicken from the governor's yard?"

In the courtyard of the Temple, the Brothers who had pursued the fleeing Sarah returned empty-handed. Hampered by their long robes and larger size, they couldn't keep up with the girl who slipped like a weasel through hedgerows and bounced like a deer over fences.

The officer of the Governor's Guard frowned. He started toward his horse. Brother Parker followed him.

"If you intend to hold this man, you'll have to get her back," the officer said. "And she will have to testify before the Committee of Judges. You have no case without her."

"The Lord God will provide," Brother Parker said.

"Maybe so. Until He does, I can do nothing for you except to tell the governor what has happened here, that a man has been accused of witchcraft and that his accuser fled. And since the law does not provide for the Church to hold a man against his will, I think you'd best consider surrendering this fellow to the civil authority.''

"I can't do that. He's a witch, an agent of evil, an enemy of the Lord God. It is the right and proper business of the True Church to fight the enemies of the Lord. It is my duty to the faithful to end his dangerous influence.''

"You haven't proven witchcraft, or even given much cause for suspicion beyond the words of a frightened child. Let him go.''

"Will the state take him into custody?''

"On what grounds, Brother?''

"The practice of witchcraft.''

"Have you seen any such thing?''

Brother Parker shook his head. "But I know it to be so.''

The officer gathered up his reins and swung into the saddle. He was a man with little enough patience with mysticism of any kind, and his impatience was beginning to show. He had taken this assignment as an unpleasant necessity at Thomas's behest. The Church should not imagine either that the governor did not know what Brother Parker was up to, or that such a flagrant violation of law was going to be ignored.

There were limits to Brother Parker's influence. The officer decided it was a good time to point those limits out.

He looked down from the saddle and spoke coldly, letting Brother Parker know he was not making an idle threat. "If you refuse to give up the man to the civil authority, you, not he, may be the one enjoying the comforts of the governor's jail.''

If he thought Brother Parker was going to be properly cowed, he was disappointed. Brother Parker was secure in that aspect of his relationship with the governor. Michael was sufficiently concerned about the fate of his own immortal soul that he would not dare obstruct the True Church in its work. He met the soldier's eyes and answered with heat. "Speak to your superiors before you threaten me, and I will pray to the Lord God for you, that He soften His just wrath.''

The soldier shrugged. Wrath and threats were part of his daily life, and he had long since ceased to be impressed. "Do that,'' he said, and turned his horse into Temple Lane and up the hill toward the Governor's Mansion.

Brother Parker went back to the others still waiting in the sun.

Farmer Jonathan was fidgeting, picking at his clothes, his teeth, and his hair, uncertain of his role, and wishing he could be done with the business of God and devil, which he did not understand and which did not seem to be a proper occupation for a man of his lowly rank. He felt a bit sorry for the poor sod the Brothers were harassing, but if the man was a witch after all, he had it coming, and Jonathan's biggest concern at that moment was getting his goods to market in the hopes of finding enough bread to feed his children. Surely these matters of the holy mysteries could get along without him.

Except for those guarding their captive, Brother Parker sent his people back to their duties and turned his full attention to the witch. Brother Eric joined him at ground level, standing half a step behind as Brother Parker questioned the prisoner.

"What is your name?" Brother Parker asked.

"Reese."

"That's not a Monnish name."

"I'm from another city." Brother Parker had picked up the trace of accent. It wasn't one he recognized, though he thought he knew most of the dialects of nearby towns.

"Where are you staying?"

"In a house on Travellers' Way. The key to the door is in the stuff your people took out of my pockets, so you don't have to break anything to get in."

"What city are you from?"

There was a minuscule hesitation. "Losalla."

"Did you practice witchcraft there also?"

Reese shook his head. "I don't practice witchcraft. I never did. You're making a mistake."

"You're making a mistake if you think you can lie to me," Brother Parker said sharply. "I know the southern speech, and you do not speak it. You are not from Losalla."

"What's this all about, anyway? What do you want from me?"

"What I want is of no importance. What matters is what the Lord God wants to redeem your immortal soul."

"All right, what does God want, since you seem to think you know?"

"You have a quick and disrespectful tongue. I advise you to show some humility. You are accused of a most serious crime, and insolence will not help you much."

Reese raised his bound hands in an attempt to scrub the flies off his face against his arm. For the moment, the Cross of God secured between his hands was held up against the sun. The wood seemed almost to glow. Brother Parker knew he was on the right track.

"Tell me on your hope of salvation, are you a witch?"

"No, damn it."

"You lie."

Reese sucked in a deep breath and held it. The muscles at the angles of his jaw knotted. "Look, just tell me what I have to do to get out of this. How can I convince you you're making a mistake?"

"You will not convince the servants of the Lord God of untruths. The power of Heaven protects us from your lies and deceit. You will not make magics here."

Reese shut his eyes. "Good Lord, this is crazy."

Before Brother Parker was aware of his intent, Brother Eric stepped up and delivered a slap to the prisoner's face with all the strength that was in him. It made a sound like boards clapped together, loud in the still air. But for the Brothers holding him, it would have knocked Reese to the ground.

"You will not blaspheme," Brother Eric said with gentle menace. He was smiling.

Blood dropped from Reese's nose and mouth and made round dark spots in the dust. In the background Jonathan, alarmed by the goings-on but not knowing how to respond to them, shuffled nervously.

When he recovered from the shock, Reese glared at Brother Eric with helpless rage. Brother Eric met the glare and smiled a little more. He was breathing deeply, and a little color had come into his normally sallow cheeks.

Brother Parker put a restraining hand on Brother Eric's arm. At times he worried about Brother Eric, who seemed all too pleased with the notion of himself as the Lord God's avenging spirit.

"Take the witch to the cellar and lock him in," Brother Parker told his men. He turned to Brother Eric. "Men of God ought not shed blood unnecessarily."

"Surely it is better to scourge the body than to lose the soul," Brother Eric answered, not looking unduly contrite.

The smith had returned with the Brother who had been sent to him, mindful of his fee, no doubt. He handed Brother Parker the two parts of the medallion. In spite of his brawn, the smith was capable of delicate work. He had dented the metal a little, but had taken the thing apart without damaging the interior.

The smith tapped the outer case with the thickened, ridged nail of his forefinger. "I don't know this metal," he said.

Within the circle of one half were two very small oblong brown objects embedded in a piece of greenish translucent material. Alongside was a somewhat larger round object, possibly made of the same metal as the case.

"What is it?" Brother Parker asked.

The smith shrugged.

Brother Eric shook his head.

Seventeen

The mean little wind that blew around the Temple yard turned into a gale within the hour. It blew out of the north, bringing wracked, dry scraps of cloud to the sky, and grit off the parched land to the river. The *Big Fish* made slow progress toward Grassy Bend fighting wind and current, the great square sail canted first this way and then that as she staggered back and forth across the wide channel, beating her way upriver.

It was as if the very elements conspired to drive her back the way she had come. Matthew suggested that Sarah might try whistling down the Storm Hounds. He meant it as a joke, not really believing that any amount of melody would bring the spirits of adverse winds to heel. Sarah clung to the angle of the bow rail with her face in the gale and tried it anyway—to no avail. Half a day's hard labor was required for a run that normally would have taken a couple of hours.

The supercargo, the younger son of the Family Lockhart, was inclined not to lend a hand with the yards, tarry ropes being no part of his view of the world, but spent most of his time leaning greenly over the rail, or bothering Matthew about the damage the occasional wave breaking over the bow might be doing to his reeking bales of raw cowhides below, or grumbling to Beth that fish stew was not the sort of fare he was used to.

After suffering in silence for a while, Matthew at last told him carefully, in wholly colorful terms, that if the facilities of the *Big Fish* didn't suit him, he was welcome to get out and walk. Once young Lockhart got over the shock of being spoken to in such a manner by one he considered in every way his inferior, he did quiet down, which made everyone's life easier. Nonetheless, Sarah was happy to see the long, shallow curve of the river leading to the wharves of the Grassy Bend landing.

The hard work and the complaints of muscles largely unused since her last sojourn aboard *Big Fish* kept the images of the morning at bay. But once docked, there was nothing much to do but watch the sweating, sullen stevedores who cursed at the heavy bales of stinking hides. Young Lockhart stalked off to find himself an inn whose floor didn't pitch on the river currents, and Matthew and Beth were busy with the wharfside broker and in the tavern, looking for a cargo going south.

Grassy Bend offered little enough in the way of entertainment, a few mean buildings hugging the water's edge, some of them on high stilts, others farther up the bank squat and ugly and needing repair. Only two reed cutters were out, pulling themselves along in their wee, round, one-man boats like a pair of inverted beetles among the reeds that gave Grassy Bend its name, harvesting the long flat leaves for the baskets that were its chief export, digging up the starchy roots for the brewing of the local spirits with long-handled iron forks, tipping their potlike boats precariously.

Sarah watched them for a while, feeling a bit superior looking down from the high deck of the unladen *Big Fish*. But it didn't amuse her for long. With time on her hands, the images returned, clear and close, haunting her. She had thought to escape them, beating up the river. But they had come with her.

The wind died away to a breeze, and *Big Fish* rocked gently on the water. She heard Reese's soft, strong voice in the slap of the waves against the boat's hull, and saw the gleam of his hair where the sun gleamed on deep water. When she shut her eyes, she could see his perplexed and pained dismay as he stood in the courtyard of the Temple, the cords biting into his wrists.

The tale of Sarah the storyteller would tell now had become a terrible, ugly thing, about the woman who had betrayed her true love out of jealousy and fear. The listeners would look for her in the crowd and hate her.

When Beth returned, arms laden with supplies but without a promise of cargo, she found the girl huddled among the coiled lines on the afterdeck staring out over the water with red-rimmed, watering eyes.

"Come with me," she said, and led Sarah into the cabin. From among her packages she extracted a stoppered flask. Everything else she dropped in a corner, an almost unheard-of lack of good housekeeping aboard *Big Fish*, and poured a little clear fluid from the flask into each of a pair of cups. She handed one to Sarah. "Drink this," she said.

The liquid tasted of hot coals. It brought paralysis to Sarah's throat and tears to her eyes, and a spot of warmth to the cold knots in her stomach.

Beth watched, satisfied. "Sit, girl, and tell me what's bothering you so." She sat herself beside Sarah on the bench and sampled the spirits of Grassy Bend, waiting for Sarah's story with the quiet patience learned from spending a lifetime on the eternal river.

It was hard for Sarah to start, hard to make herself say the words. The burning liquor helped ease the way a little, still she choked on her own tongue, hearing herself disjointed and strange. Beth didn't interrupt or move except to pour another cup when Matthew came in.

When she came to describe the scene in the Temple yard, Sarah couldn't go on. She sat, hunched miserably between her friends.

"What will they do to him?" she asked after a while, wanting any bit of reassurance she could get to ease her conscience.

"Burn him, I expect," Beth answered roughly, "and you're having second thoughts a bit late, aren't you, girl?"

"I never meant for them to hurt him. I never did, Beth."

"What did you think was going to happen, eh? The Lord God knows I've no use for Brother bloody Parker, but he's no man for children to be playing games with. He's a kind of madness that's contagious, for sure, with his everlasting talk of death and demons."

"I was scared," Sarah cried. "They had me in this little place and I was scared. I thought he'd magic himself away. I never thought they'd catch him. Why did he let them?"

"Peace, Beth," Matthew said. He ruffled Sarah's hair and smoothed it out again. "Older, wiser folk than Sarah have done things of a midnight they regretted in the dawn. It's better we should talk of what's to be done to set things right."

"And what's that to be, Riverman?" Beth asked. Hard words,

gently spoken. Sarah was only beginning to understand the complexity that bound Matthew and Beth to one another, the respect and confidence beyond love that softened doubt and blunted irritation.

"I don't know," Matthew admitted. He looked at Beth for a minute. He didn't actually ask her approval, but if she was dead set against it, he would know, somehow. "But whatever it is, it won't be here. Come along and stand by the lines, Sarah. We'll go back to Monn."

"We've no cargo," Beth reminded him.

"And not too likely to find one, either, times being what they are," Matthew said. "Besides, old love, we're not starving. We can afford to make the odd empty run with a man's life at stake, don't you think?"

"You've a bad way of choosing your words, old love. Go, then. It'll be dark soon enough. I'll come take the wheel when I've got some supper for you."

The downriver run was easier, just a matter of steering the bare-masted *Big Fish* as she was carried along by the swift currents. Matthew knew the river the way a farmer knew his fields, and picked out the fast, smooth, midchannel flows almost unconsciously. Sarah kept him company at the wheel, watching the play of muscles on his arms as he twitched the spokes to keep the boat in the channel when the river would have shoved them into the bank if it was given a chance.

"River's quiet," Matthew said. "She's apologizing for giving us a rough passage, I guess."

Sarah looked up at him, but his eyes were fixed on the water. "Sometimes you talk like the river was somebody," she said.

"Sometimes, it seems it is." He glanced down at her, and seeing the intensity of her frown, hastened to add, "But that's just talk. Nobody really believes the river's a capricious spirit wandering the earth."

"I know, Matt," Sarah said. She felt a surge of affection for the strong man who would take on her problems as if they were his own. She thought if she could know her father, he would be like Matthew.

She looked out over the water. "He really is a witch, Matthew."

"Reese?"

Sarah nodded.

"You're thinking of the lights, then?"

"They were weirdly things. And the girl trapped in the crystal. And Butch, the way he was laid out like a dead man without a mark on him."

"And yet the Brothers had this witch trussed up like a Christmas goose."

"I can't figure it, Matt."

"It's queer, all right." Matthew was quiet a moment. When he spoke it was with a mood of contemplation that he rarely expressed.

"I'll tell you one thing, girl. I think there are folks all too quick to say witchcraft when something's about they don't understand. There's folks would call our Beth a witch for the way she can find a fish for dinner when every one else's net is empty. But the simple truth of it is, she knows the way of the fish and she knows the way of the water, and those that don't know cry magic.

"I've seen things in my time I can't explain. Down at Warlen on the sea, I saw a rod of wood from across the ocean that a sword couldn't cut, and there's those that would tell you it was grown in an enchanted forest and watered with human blood. In Sanjo, I saw a goat that could dance, and I guess you could say the beast was bewitched. I saw a man who ate fire, and spewed it out of his mouth like a bleeding dragon, and maybe he was a conjurer, but he was a skinny, ill-fed bugger and ragged cold in a cool autumn night, and you'd think if he was able, he'd have conjured up a joint of mutton and a warm coat better than a mouthful of flames with no comfort in it.

"Sometimes when I see a horse trainer with a wild, white-eyed animal ten times his size, and after a while he's made the creature trust and obey him, I think that must be a kind of magic. But you put the same man aboard the *Big Fish* and tell him to beat upriver against the wind, he'd have her foundered in minutes. Chances are, he thinks it takes magic to sail against the wind. But it's just the knowing of a thing, Sarah. When you know a thing, it seems natural, and when you don't know, it seems magic."

"Isn't there any real magic, then, Matthew? All that stuff Cat Anna was doing wasn't real?"

"Who could say? Maybe. Plenty of folks will tell you about magical happenings in their lives if you give them half a chance. But if magic there is, it's a lot rarer than Brother Parker and Cat Anna would have you believe."

"What about poor Willa's baby then, and the will-o'-the-wisp they say is about in Gray Swamp and all those queer goings-on?"

"In truth, Sarah, I don't know. There's a fair mountain of things I don't know."

"Could there really be a Phile, though?"

"I guess that's part of the mountain. There's enough talk about them to make a Phile out of, if the Lord God happened to have forgot. But if your witch is a Phile, with all the sorcery they're supposed to have, it doesn't seem likely that Parker would be able to hold him long without some pretty big magic of his own."

"Beth doesn't like Brother Parker."

"No, she doesn't. I can't say I'm too fond of the freakin' saint either. I wouldn't mind putting a spike into Brother Parker's schemes if the chance happened to come my way."

"You think maybe we can?"

Matthew shrugged.

"They were scared, Matthew. A bunch of them and only one of him, tied up, with the Cross of God and everything, and they were scared."

"Makes you wonder, doesn't it, what they truly believe in."

Sarah turned away again and watched the passing landscape, the colors subdued in the twilight. The banks were shallow there, and trees reached down to the water and out over it. A flock of small birds lifted as they approached and settled again as they passed. In the coal-dark shadows beneath the trees a fish jumped, making a silver ring.

"I did a terrible thing, Matthew."

"That you did, girl."

"It's the positively worst thing I ever did."

"Uhuh."

"Do you still like me? Anyway, I mean?"

"Sarah, if I only liked folks who'd never done a thing I wish they hadn't done, there'd be damned few to like, and if they felt the same way, I'd be a lonely man."

"But you never did something really awful, like maybe get someone killed, even if he is a witch." Matthew didn't answer, and Sarah turned to look at him. His face was set in hard lines, and his eyes were distant. "Did you?"

"You run along now. Go see if Beth needs a hand."

"Did you, Matthew?"

"Go, Sarah."

Beth had been coming out of the cabin to see if Matthew intended to continue the run by moonlight, and to relieve him of his steering chores while he ate if he did. Beth regretted few things about their life on the river. One of them was that when they were working, she and Matt had little time for one another. The boat demanded all their energies.

Matthew needed a brace of strong sons, and she was unable to give them to him.

They were silhouetted against the failing light, Matthew and Sarah, Sarah mimicking Matt's wide-legged stance, her arms hugged over her little breasts, looking up at him as if he were the oracle of God. A small twinge ran through Beth. The child's a child no longer, she thought, and there's trouble brewing there for sure. He works her like a boy, and she looks at him with a woman's eyes.

Jealousy does not become you, she thought. You should have more faith in your man. But she resolved to talk to Matthew.

Before Beth left the doorway, Sarah came trudging along the deck and told her that Matthew was going to anchor for the night. Sarah was so deflated and sad looking, so unlike her usual self, that Beth put an arm around the girl's shoulder and hugged her tight. Then, confused by her own shifting feelings, she led the girl into the cabin and set her down to eat.

Eighteen

"Princess Donalda's dowry—" Creighton started to say.

"I don't want to hear about it," Michael answered shrewishly.

"But, m'lord, the gold—"

"No."

Michael leaned his elbows on the table and put his head in his hands. The hard marble hurt his elbows.

He had listened to a series of small complaints: a kitchen maid had been caught thieving in the pantry to feed her family; a delegation of farmers were complaining about the lack of forage to feed their stock; General Brandt carefully delineated the need for more funds to keep the soldiers on the northern border armed and mounted, with Creighton bleating in the background that the treasury couldn't stand the drain.

The maid was dismissed, the farmers were soothed, the general was assured that his needs would be met, and finally, irritated and shrewish, Michael sent Creighton back to his counting.

The accountant managed to point out, smarting under the curt dismissal, that the city still had not secured a supply of grain for the winter. General Brandt then took up the matter of the Kolloans.

Michael was of the opinion that he had enough on his plate without worrying about a bunch of godless traders. He hadn't been ignoring them; he had information. The Kolloans had visited a few dyers and weavers, as one might expect traders to do; they had spent some time with the rivermen, which was also sensible, one might suppose; they bargained in the market, investigated the town no more thoroughly than normal visitors might, and spent most of their time in the Crow's Eye, buying beer for all and sundry. They seemed to have plenty of money and nothing much to do.

Brandt shook his head in disbelief. "Michael, go outside and look across the river. That is an encampment of Kolloans over there. Call them traders if you like, but they are the vanguard of an invasion force, believe me. Think a bit on how well you will fare under a Kolloan administration. They are irreverent folk, not unduly patient with conquered leaders. They will strip your Mansion, disperse your people, and quite possibly send you to Kollo to serve dinner to the emperor, if they don't decide to chop off your head."

He was interrupted by a commotion at the door. Angry rumbles filtered through the carved wood, and then Brother Parker's voice, loud, clear, and full of ire, said, "Soldier, if you value your immortal soul, you will let me through."

Michael couldn't hear what the Guardsman answered. He hesitated, sighed, and then indicated to Thomas to have Brother Parker admitted.

Brother Parker burst in and came to a halt before the table, then rushed with unseemly haste through his greetings and inquiries into Michael's health. Michael acknowledged him with a nod.

Brandt was not going to yield to the interruption. As far as he was concerned, the Kolloan threat was the most important issue of the day. He continued, as if the preacher were not standing there fuming. "Given time to get the army properly equipped, we might just possibly have a chance to make the cost of taking Monn more than Kollo is willing to pay. Provided, of course, we can settle things in the north first. But if we stand around here arguing about pennies, the Kolloans will take it away from both of us. Does that sink through your thick royal head?"

"General, I suggest you mind your tongue," Thomas said from his position in the back of the room. "You have no call to address the governor in such a manner."

Brandt turned to glare at the adviser. Thomas regarded him calmly from the stool by the windows, his chin resting on his fist. Brandt's hackles collapsed the way a dog's might when it knows it is outmatched. Michael wished he knew how Thomas managed to do that.

"Surely the Lord God will take care of his own," Brother Parker said confidently, anxious to have the general's business over with.

"Keep out of it, Brother," the general said. "The Kolloans eat clerics, I hear."

"You would do better to worry about the evil stalking the city now," Brother Parker continued, "rather than invoke distant, improbable invasions. Even now, demons and witches walk among us unopposed. The faithful are turning from the True Church to the practice of heathen rites and rituals. The souls of the people are in mortal danger."

"Governor," Brandt asked, "is military policy to be set by this preacher? Who exactly is running the city?"

"If the Lord God sends the Kolloans, General," Brother Parker said, "it will be his just punishment for our unwillingness to face the corruption we have fostered and cleanse ourselves of it."

Brandt swore, a soldier's curses honed to a fine cutting edge by years of practice. Brother Parker's face flamed, and he seemed to have great difficulty holding on to his temper. He muttered a swift prayer for strength. "You are not indispensable to the city, General," he told Brandt in a voice full of quiet menace.

Brandt was not intimidated. "That's where you're wrong, Brother," he said. He turned to Michael. "Maybe we could talk again, when there will not be so much interference?"

"Yes," Michael said. "That seems like a good idea."

Brandt stalked out of the room, a stiff, hard, altogether dangerous man.

"You must muzzle that barbarian, Michael," Brother Parker said. "If you let him, he will have the city endlessly at war."

Michael never let his inward smile reach his face. Thomas was right about setting his opponents to fighting one another.

He was learning the art of politics. Slowly, but he was learning.

Once Brandt had gone, Brother Parker was more or less alone with the governor. Thomas had slipped into the shadows of the room as he often did, keeping so still and quiet that a visitor would often forget he was there. Parker finally got down to what had brought him there: the witch.

"Witch?" Michael asked.

"An officer of the Guard was there when we brought him in," Brother Parker said. He was beginning to think he had made a mistake in bringing the matter to Michael's attention.

"The Miller Family's witch?"

"I believe so. The officer seemed to think that the Church is obliged to turn the witch over to the civil authority. I want your personal assurance that this ecclesiastical matter will be left in the hands of the Church."

"Where is the witch now?"

"He's being held in the Temple."

"The Church has no authority to imprison a citizen."

"He's not a citizen; he's a stranger."

"I see. And what evidence do we have that this stranger is indeed a witch? Does the witch have a name?"

Parker glared. Michael glared back, hoping he was adequately disguising his insecurity. His feeling of being in control evaporated.

"The man's name is Reese," Brother Parker said at last. Michael relaxed slightly at that small concession. The confrontation between church and state seemed a little further off. "We have a witness," Brother Parker continued.

"The witness is with you?"

"She fled. But she will be found."

"Mm."

"There are also items taken from the witch's person." Parker offered two round bits of metal, one of them attached to a length of fine chain, and a long narrow-bladed knife.

"If every man in the city carrying a knife were to be considered a witch, the whole of Monn would be in flames."

"This is no ordinary knife," Brother Parker said crossly. He searched around for something with which to demonstrate, and finally summoned a Guardsman with an imperious gesture. The soldier questioned Michael with a look, and the governor nodded.

Brother Parker pulled the knife from the soldier's belt. The Guardsman was about to stop him, but Michael held him with a gesture, his curiosity sufficiently aroused to overcome his irritation.

Brother Parker brought the edges of the two knives together and sawed away for a moment, then displayed the two, side by side. The Guardsman's knife had a deep dent in the edge, but the other was undamaged, perfect. The soldier hissed through his teeth, his astonishment too deep to hide.

Michael was impressed, but he tried to keep it off his face. He picked up the round metal objects. "What are these?"

"The witch's personal amulet, so I believe."

"Mm."

Michael called Thomas from the shadows to see the thing he could make no sense of. Thomas took it, twisted it in the light, and shook his head.

"It didn't work too well, I would say. Do we have an incompetent witch, Brother?"

"Do we have a witch at all, Thomas?" Michael asked.

"I couldn't say, m'lord. It might be best to wait to hear from the witness."

"There's been enough of witchcraft about," Brother Parker answered with some heat, "that no one should doubt. The Family Miller has been assaulted. The crows, the crops, John the cowman's baby, strange lights at night, your own illness—no one could doubt the devil's hand in it."

Michael reached over, carefully took the two knives out of Brother Parker's hands and put them gently down on the table. There was a tension in the holy man. If I let him prosecute this witch, Michael thought, if any happy event occurs within the next year, he will take the credit, and I will have lost that much more credibility among the people. If I order him to let the man go, he will refuse, and we will have to battle it out right now, and I can ill afford the fight. There is no right course.

"I want no part of burning an innocent man, stranger or not," Michael said at last.

"Nor I," Brother Parker answered. "But I cannot afford to ignore evil on that account."

"I have an obligation to the Family Miller, and to the citizens of Monn, but also to innocent travelers who should not be harassed in every moment of hysteria. It's bad for trade."

"Hysteria?" Brother Parker spluttered, but managed to control himself. He drew himself up tall. "I have an obligation to the faithful of the True Church and to the salvation of the city."

"Find the witness. Then we'll talk. In the meantime, the state will take over custody of the stranger, and Thomas will investigate the possibility of sorcery. Those Millers who are said to have suffered at his hand should be able to identify him."

Color came into Brother Parker's cheeks. He was restraining himself with effort, that much was obvious. No doubt he had made the same analysis that Michael had made and come to the same conclusion.

"This is a grave mistake in the eyes of God," Parker warned. "You seek to squabble with the True Church over the souls of men while the devil walks the streets unhindered. The devil laughs when we argue with one another and the fight against the Evil One falters."

Michael didn't know how to answer that, but Thomas said quietly, "Surely the Lord God will protect his own," echoing with no particular emphasis the statement Brother Parker had made to General Brandt just a short time ago.

"Perhaps, if we do not anger Him too greatly with our apathy in the face of evil." Brother Parker glowered first at Michael, then at Thomas, and then turned and left, as if he didn't trust himself to stay.

"That is a dangerous man," Thomas said.

"Parker is dangerous; Brandt is dangerous; if he wasn't such a frightened biddy, Creighton would be dangerous. The northern border is under attack. The Kolloans are looking us over to see if we are fat enough. It doesn't rain. Now they tell me we have witches in the city. What am I to do, Thomas?"

"The best you can, m'lord."

Michael studied the light gleaming on Reese's blade lying forgotten on the table. He wanted to know how to make steel like that. If he had the secret, Monn would be prosperous, come feast or famine. People would travel across the world to buy blades like that. They would pay any price Michael cared to set.

And what would his people think of him if they could hear his thoughts now, if they could see him lusting after arcane knowledge? That was how evil began in the world, the way the people had lost their chance at Paradise, had turned away from the Lord God, by eating of the fruit of the tree of knowledge.

That was the way of the devil, of witchcraft, of the Philes. The pursuit of secrets men were not meant to have was the road to hell. Every child learned that basic truth at his mother's knee.

Brother Parker would denounce him, surely, and give Brandt the spark he needed to accomplish his coup.

Yet how evil could the knowing be, if it meant peace and security and prosperity?

How subtle and insidious the thirst for knowledge, that it could justify itself in an instant, and drive from his mind all the teachings of the True Faith.

Was the devil on his doorstep, leading him astray?

Was the Lord God testing him?

"Thomas, are we doing the right thing?" he asked his friend.

"M'lord, that is the one question no man can ever answer in this life," Thomas answered.

Nineteen

Reese shook his head, half to clear it, half to deny the chill that was creeping up his spine. Then he sat down in a huddle in the middle of the tiny room in total darkness with his aching head on his knees and tried to get hold of himself.

Fear crowded in on him wearing the acrid smell of sweaty wool too long unwashed and the anesthetised face of religious fervor. It tried to rob him of his senses, to make a terrified animal of him. Earlier, out in the courtyard, it had seemed important that Brother Parker and his gang not know how scared he was. He held tightly to that bitter edge of pride, and it sustained him when otherwise his knees might have buckled and pitched him quaking into the dust.

Now, alone in the awful blackness, there was nothing to distract him.

How long ago had the Brothers hustled him into the Temple?

Amid black robes and set faces he had been led and driven, disoriented, through hallways and down a long flight of stone stairs into a blackness relieved only by a half-dozen candles carried by some of the Brothers. He was pushed stumbling into darkness. He fell headlong onto a rough stone floor. A heavy wooden door was closed on him, the Brothers and the candles left, and he was alone in the dark.

For a long while he lay where he had fallen, trying to master the rising tide of panic.

At first he had been able to convince himself that the argument between Parker and the soldier was significant. The soldier was a member of the Governor's Guard, so the governor would be informed of what had happened. The governor surely wouldn't go along with such treatment of innocent strangers in his city.

But that had been a long time ago. At least it seemed like a long time ago, and no rescue party was in sight.

"Okay, Reese," he said aloud to himself for what comfort could be found in the sound of his own voice. "You're here, and the whole benighted world is insane. Pull yourself together and try to figure out what the hell you're going to do about it."

A small rustling disturbed the dark around him as he spoke. Of course, he thought. There'd have to be rats or cockroaches or snakes, or maybe all of them together. The setting wouldn't be complete without them, now, would it? There were probably cobwebs around the ceiling, too, though he couldn't see them. These little details are important, he thought as black irony took the place of the terror he had managed to push a short way into the background. To make the staging complete, any moment now a demon should appear from the wings in a flash of blinding light and turn him into a frog.

His head hurt, and he could only hope that the ringing in his ear wasn't going to be permanent. He had collected a fine assortment of bruises which, now that he had the leisure to pay attention, were making their presence known. The inside of his mouth was swollen and tender where his teeth had cut it. At least his nose had stopped bleeding, but he could not tell if it was broken or not. He thought he had better mention in his reports the severe rhinohazard associated with life in Monn. The poor schnoz was taking a beating.

He wished he had a better idea of what was going on. Where did Sarah fit into it, and why had she bolted like a startled rabbit? And most of all, what in the name of the nine worlds did they all want from him? He replayed the events of the morning from the imperfect record of memory, searching for a clue.

When the Brothers had first accosted him as he climbed out of the hole in Young Albert's field, he had been inclined to take their somber presence lightly. When they demanded that he surrender himself to God, he had shrugged and smiled and said that he had an appointment in town. The hooded black ring of them seemed altogether too melodramatic and the intoned phrases too trite and too out of keeping with the bright summer sun, blue sky, and bird song, They would have been much better suited to bat-ridden midnights in decaying castles with lightning flashing around the battlements. In the full light of day they seemed mildly ridiculous.

The whole effort had an overplayed, theatrical air to it that made it hard for him to take the Brothers seriously.

But they wanted to tie him up. When he took exception to being tied up, one of those grim kooks clopped him on the side of the head with a piece of a tree, and Reese started taking them seriously.

Since then, things had become just a bit too goddamned serious.

Reese had an abiding belief that the vast majority of human beings were reasonable if they were given half a chance to be. But Brother Eric had eliminated any hope Reese had of making his captors see reason. The smack in the mouth had been bad enough, but the hot sparkle that had come into Brother Eric's eyes at the time had dashed any fool idea he had that he might be able to talk himself out of the situation.

He struggled to his feet, an action made awkward by his still bound hands. His eyes strained to adjust to the darkness, and he could make out a slightly less dark square about head high, where he thought the door would be. He reached out toward it. The arms of the wooden cross between his palms caught on the bars.

The opening was about thirty centimeters square, divided by two thick bars, cold, somewhat rough, probably iron.

Carefully, by feel, he maneuvered the cross between the bars until both arms were caught on the other side. Then he braced his feet against the door and heaved for all he was worth, hissing between clenched teeth as the cord cut into already damaged flesh.

There was a sharp crack, and he staggered backward but managed to avoid falling. His bonds were definitely looser. He wiggled the broken cross from among the cords with his teeth. Then he had enough slack to work the turns over his knuckles the same way, gnawing the knots loose. The first one went hard, but the rest were progressively easier until he was free and could shake out his numb fingers and ease his aching shoulders.

He explored by feel, running his fingers over the rough stones;

he yanked back with a shudder when something cold and muscular moved under his touch. Except for whatever the creature was that shared the space with him, the tiny cell seemed barren. He came back to the opening in the door and reached through as far as he was able, pushing his shoulder against the bars and feeling for the latch or bolt or whatever was holding the door in place. He didn't really expect to be able to reach it, and he couldn't. After a bit he gave up trying. He felt his way around the cell again. And again.

Getting himself untied was turning out to be a small victory. He couldn't find any way out of the tiny stone room, and couldn't imagine any possibility of making one.

He wondered what had become of his tracer. He had been too slow to catch on to his mortal danger to send the alarm. By the time his peril sunk into his head, they had taken the tracer away from him, along with everything else he was carrying.

He sat back down on the stone floor and waited some more.

Cleo would come looking for him eventually. Or maybe not. Maybe she would decide he deserved his captivity because he wouldn't listen to her.

The enclave wouldn't abandon him. They would miss his reports. Eventually.

The sound of movement outside got him to his feet. He could see a growing glimmer of light through the door. Boots on stone, he decided, which meant someone other than the Brothers in their soft sandals. The lanterns stopped in the hallway outside. It was amazing how bright they were.

The door opened to reveal two Guardsmen with ready swords. Behind them was their officer, the man who had been arguing in the courtyard. Further back Brother Parker waited, stiff and annoyed, with two of his minions who were looking worried. When they realized that Reese had his hands free, one of the Brothers put a fist to his mouth, and the other ducked between the soldiers to retrieve the pieces of the broken cross which lay on the floor. He held them in his open palms as if he couldn't believe what he saw, then looked at Reese with an expression that should have been reserved for coming face to face with the devil.

"Come along, witch," the officer said. He had a brusque manner and a rough-edged voice. "You don't seem so awful scary. Come on out of there, fellow. Shit, Parker, was all that necessary? Bugger looks like he's been fighting cougars.''

"You exaggerate, Lieutenant.'' Brother Parker was making no effort to disguise his anger. "You have no right to do this,'' he said. "This is a spiritual affair which properly belongs to the Church. It is not a thing to be taken lightly. I think you should know, I do intend to protest.''

The lieutenant turned to Brother Parker and clapped him too hard across the shoulders. "To whom?'' he asked with a small, sardonic smile. Brother Parker's face registered his dislike of the soldier's familiarity. "I'll tell you something, Brother,'' the lieutenant said. "The reason we're doing this is because the governor said, 'Bring the witch to me.' When the governor says 'Take the witch away,' I'll take the witch away. And the reason I do it like that is because I like my rank and my head just where they are and I'm working to keep them there. It's something you might like to think about before you start making too awful much fuss over one battered witch.'' He gestured to his men, and they herded the prisoner into the hallway with the points of their swords.

"What's your name?'' the lieutenant asked.

"Reese.''

"Okay, Reese. This isn't going to be pleasant for you, but I guess we're going to have to tie you up again. I'm sorry, but I don't see any way to avoid it.''

"I should be grateful for your concern, I suppose.''

"Aren't we tough, though? They haven't knocked all the spunk out of you yet, eh?''

Reese gazed at the small lizards clinging to the stones, blinking slow blinks in the light of the lanterns, and didn't bother to answer.

In the courtyard, the soldiers wanted him to ride a horse. Reese balked. "What's the matter?'' the lieutenant asked. "Big fellow like you afraid of horses?''

"I'm not particularly afraid of them. I just don't know anything about them.''

"More comfortable on a broomstick, are you? You're not making a lot of sense, but anyway, what's to know? All you have to do is sit there. The horse will do all the work. The alternative is to run along behind, and you wouldn't like that.''

Reese conceded that indeed he would not and suffered himself to be loaded aboard the animal. It seemed a precarious perch. The horse bent its long neck and regarded him with a doleful brown eye.

The sun was low in the west. The horses plodded along the road, hoofbeats softened by the dust that puffed up around their feet. Reese's animal was being led behind one of the troopers, and Reese concentrated on keeping his balance when the horse's back sloped as they started up the hill toward the Governor's Mansion. After a bit, the lieutenant reined back, leaned over, wadded up a chunk of the horse's mane, and put it between Reese's hands for him to hold on to. Feeling a little more secure, Reese nodded his thanks. The officer shrugged.

"What did you do to get the Brothers annoyed with you?" he asked.

"Damned if I know," Reese said.

"Damned in any case, I would say. They're going around calling you a witch."

"But why?"

The lieutenant shrugged again.

"Aren't witches supposed to be women?" Reese asked.

"More often than men, I guess. Parker seems to be of the opinion the devil isn't fussy in that regard." He looked at Reese as if gauging him. "After all, you broke the Cross."

"That wasn't hard to do. It wasn't all that strong."

"Not the point. The point is you broke it."

"Wouldn't you, if that was the only way you could think of to get yourself untied?"

The lieutenant pursed his lips contemplatively. "Either you are totally stupid, or you really don't know what's going on. The point is, man, that no true believer would have done that to save his immortal soul. Show disrespect to the Cross of God? Never. He'd die first. Don't you know that when the faithful describe the doings of a coven, they talk about the assembled witches defacing a Cross? Along with the sexy orgies and all that. If you wanted to convince the Brothers absolutely that you were an agent of the Dark Powers, you couldn't have picked a better way short of pissing on the altar of the True Church."

"Oh."

"Yeah, oh. Where have you been all your life?"

"I'm new to this city."

"That I believe. Cheer up. The governor's jail is no great place, but it'll be easier than Brother Parker's accommodations. If I were you, I'd do whatever I could to convince the governor to keep me in civil custody."

"I'd prefer convincing the governor to let me go."

"Sure you would. Good luck." The lieutenant nudged his horse and started moving up toward the head of their little parade.

"Lieutenant?"

The soldier looked back.

"The, uh . . ." Reese tried to think of a word he could use that wouldn't carry any further implications of witchery. "The medallion I had around my neck. Do you know what became of it?"

The lieutenant shook his head. "I never saw it. I suspect Brother Parker's confiscated it along with the rest of your property to serve the needs of the True Church. If that was your talisman, kiss your luck good-bye." He returned to the head of the entourage as the riders turned to pass through the massive iron gates before the Governor's Mansion.

The lieutenant was right about one thing. The governor's jail was easier to take than Brother Parker's. It was situated within a high palisade, with archers prowling a catwalk near the top, but the dozen or so prisoners wandering aimlessly inside the enclosure seemed free of undue harassment. Reese was given an opportunity to clean up a bit once he had been passed into the compound and the bonds had been removed from his wrists, and that was very welcome. At a long table out in the open, he was offered food, which was not too good and which irritated his wounded mouth, and water, which was pure ambrosia after a long, dry time without anything to drink.

Then all the prisoners were hustled into a long, narrow building in the center of the compound. The cell Reese was put into was no bigger than the one at the Temple, and the wooden door with its small, barred opening looked the same, but at least there was light enough to see by as long as the sun was up, and a pleasant absence of lizards. He even had a pile of straw to sleep on, not too moldy, which was all most Monnishmen had. A candle burning near the entrance to the building relieved the night a little.

He lay down on the straw, squirming around to find the position of minimum discomfort, with the intention of putting his thoughts in order and figuring a way out of his imprisonment. But the tensions of the day had taken their toll. He fell asleep almost at once.

The next he knew it was full daylight, and someone was calling him through the opening in the door.

"Up you get, scum," the voice said without rancor. "The governor wants to see you."

Twenty

The office in Supply and Services was decorated in pink, and the woman across the desk was dressed in a flouncy pink one-piece that irked Cleo out of all proportion to its importance. She knew the two of them weren't going to get along from the moment she saw the outfit.

The woman's name was Janneane, and she tapped the terminal screen with a long, manicured fingernail. "Just look at that," she said. "Just look at that energy profile. It's impossible. You'll have to find a cheaper way to do it."

Cleo clenched her fists as if her temper were a material thing she could hold in place with physical effort. "I will not," she said slowly and clearly, "send people into that site until the roof has been stabilized. Period."

"Well, I'm terribly sorry," Janneane said, looking not sorry at all. "I'm afraid I can't approve this."

"I thought the Treasure Hunt had an energy priority."

"Well, yes, of course, but within reason. This is not reasonable."

"Not—" Cleo bit off the rest of that thought. "You know, I think it's pretty damned stupid for us to be sending Hunters out there at considerable risk to find this stuff if we aren't going to pick it up when they do find it."

"Really, Cleo, it's not like a big iron safe was any kind of energy source. The Hunters' priority was not meant to satisfy an anthropologist's idle curiosity, now, was it?"

"Ye gods and little fishes," Cleo said. "I can't believe this."

Then the lights went out.

Janneane squeaked in alarm. Her calculations vanished off the screen, and the imperious letters, STAND BY, replaced them.

Not too gently, Cleo guided Janneane away from the console and asked the computer for a grid map to see how extensive the power failure was, but the machine wouldn't answer her. She was in the process of cussing it out when AUDIO ONLY TRANSMISSION appeared on the screen, and Arne's worried voice said, "We've got a problem. The power reactor developed an anomaly and the computer shut her down tight. And we can't get the computer to supply power from the battery backup to anything but itself. The thing has a definite prejudice. We need you in Engineering, Cleo."

It was the condition of her involvment with the Treasure Hunt that Engineering had first priority when they needed it.

"I'm on my way," Cleo said.

"I'm sorry, but I guess the theater is out for tonight," Arne said.

"That's all right, Arne. I've seen the play before," Cleo said, but she was disappointed. She needed a break. She was lonely. She needed someone to talk to. She wished Reese would get the hell home.

How come there weren't any new plays? she wondered as she left Janneane's office. She had almost committed herself to the lift field before she remembered the thing wouldn't be working. She took the stairs to ground level. Didn't anyone have time to write plays anymore?

The pods weren't running, either. She had to walk.

Hours later, the combined efforts of Engineering and Computing Science finally persuaded the computer that batteries, solar cells, and windchargers between them could support the restoration of at least some service. It had been a frustrating business. Computing was not Cleo's area of primary expertise. She went home exhausted, threw herself into the lounge chair, and tried to relax. The chair remained rigid in the form it had last taken, which wasn't at all comfortable. A luxury item, it was presently without power. Cleo groaned and squirmed and finally got up and glared at it. It had been a wearisome day.

The stupid computer had overreacted, of course. Like the

humans, it had no experience with that sort of thing. It was the first reactor failure the Enclave had experienced in its history.

The shape of things to come?

The cat came over to see if it was suppertime. Cleo patted his big orange head and scratched behind his ears, and Aurelius responded by turning his face away.

"Reese isn't coming," she told him, "so you'll have to take your comfort from me." She felt hurt. Her emotions must be really fragile these days, she thought, if she could be wounded by a cat. Aurelius ambled over to the dining area and looked into the cat dish. It was empty, so he sat down with his back to her, waiting.

A red light glowed on the communications panel telling her there was a message waiting. She tried to ignore it, but it nagged at her.

Most of the telltales on the panel were dark. There would be no incoming news service today. No video entertainment. No food service.

No food service?

"Stupid machine. Food is not a luxury," she complained to the terminal. She most emphatically did not feel like getting up and going to the cafeteria to get her supper. Maybe it would be just as easy to go without. But how would she explain it to Aurelius?

"Blast you, cat," she said. Aurelius ignored her irritation and continued to wait.

She thought about it for a long time before she could persuade herself to get moving. Living on the tenth floor was fine when the lift fields were operating, but it was a lot of stairs when they weren't.

Finally, she decided that she would fetch her dinner home, take the message while she ate, then shower and try to get some sleep. The next day there would be the reactor and the bureaucrats to deal with. Of the two, the reactor was likely to be the easier problem. Zeke had said that bureaucrats could be dealt with, but he hadn't said how.

When she got back, she gave Aurelius his share of the food, returned to the living area, and tried, out of habit, to settle herself in the lounge chair. Cursing its unyielding bulges, she pulled the fixed-form chair from behind Reese's desk to the terminal.

She reached over her tray to push a button on the terminal for the waiting message. VOICE ONLY TRANSMISSION, the terminal screen told her.

The message was brief and to the point, and made the food stick in her throat.

"Cleo, I thought you would like to know. We've lost contact with Reese."

All worries about bureaucratic obstruction vanished from Cleo's mind, along with all thoughts of energy and recovery procedures, and stubborn computers and dinner and Arne and nonexistent new plays. She sat there for a long, frozen moment staring at the END OF MESSAGE line on the screen.

Later she thought to query the computer for the time of Irene's message and discovered that while she had been busy trying to persuade the ornery system to turn the lights back on, it had been recording and notifying the Treasure Hunters' base office of the fact that Reese's transmitter had stopped sending somewhere in Monn.

That was all the machine had in its debilitated state. Any more details she wanted she would have to get from Irene in person.

Cleo leaned back in her chair, bit her thumbnail, and wondered how serious it was.

She had known all along that Reese was going to come to grief in that savage burg.

She wasn't going to get any answers by telling herself she had told him so or by chewing her thumbnail down to the bone. She punched Irene's identification number on the keyboard and hoped the local commander of the Treasure Hunters was still up and receiving.

Irene answered almost at once, her sharp, hard voice sounding ragged and worn. "I thought I'd hear from you," she said. "I didn't know it would be the middle of the night."

"I just got in a little while ago."

"Yes, I guessed you'd be busy, with the power failure and all."

"What about Reese?"

The blank screen was silent for a moment. "I don't know," was all she could truthfully say. "All we know for sure is that the transmitter stopped sending in or near the Temple of the True Church in Monn, at 1:23 this afternoon."

"How serious is this?"

"It's hard to say."

"Has the base office received the alarm signal?"

"No, we haven't. There's no reason to think he's in any kind of trouble, Cleo."

"Reese has been out, off and on, for three months. Maybe the transmitter just ran out of power. How long was it good for, anyway?"

Cleo had to imagine Irene shaking her head. "All kinds of social scientists use them in the field, sometimes for a year at a time. The power cells are pretty reliable. Besides, it's standard practice to pick up a new power cell whenever you're in, and Reese was in just a couple of days ago. I guess there must be some finite probability of a mechanical failure, but it's got to be pretty small. I don't know. I just don't know right now."

"What are you doing to find out?"

"At the moment, nothing."

Cleo's face registered her outrage. But of course, Irene couldn't see it. When Cleo started to splutter, Irene hastened to explain. "It's dark. You know as well as I do, they don't have searchlights or even streetlights in Monn. We can hardly go out and search the city with candles."

"Take some damned lights with you."

"We'd cause a panic. They'd call out the army with witchbane and swords. A lot of innocent bystanders would get hurt. Think about it. Is that what you really want?"

Cleo turned her face away from the silly, useless screen and watched the floor for a moment. Aurelius had finished his dinner and spread himself out at her feet to clean his paws, oblivious to the possibility that his favorite person in all the world might be in mortal danger.

"Are we just going to sit here, doing nothing?" she asked.

"We're getting a few of us together in an hour or so at the office for a brainstorming session. Why don't you join us? I guess you know Reese better than any of the rest of us. You might have some ideas we wouldn't think of."

Cleo would have preferred action to argument, but she wasn't going to sleep that night anyway, and there was a chance she might be able to persuade someone to do something. "All right. I'll be there."

Irene stopped in the middle of signing off. "Don't worry too much," she said. "We haven't lost a Hunter yet."

The pods were still out. Engineering hadn't even tried to put that high energy drain on the batteries. The design of the enclave made the lack of personal transportation a manageable problem.

The physical structures of the enclave were arranged in two concentric circles, the A ring and the B ring, with a large open space at the center, variously called the Plaza or the Park or the Hub, dominated by the Crystal Spire. Confined by the wall, growth had occurred upward, the original architect's plans spoiled by the stacking of story upon story, by the construction of upper-level ramps, aerial walkways, pod landings, and similar distortions for convenience. The greenhouses on the top levels were pushed higher and higher toward the sky.

For this reason no place in the enclave was very far away from any other place. While a pod could take her there in a minute, Cleo walked from her apartment in the A ring to the plain gray permacrete block of the administration building in the B ring in ten without ever descending to ground level.

Of all the buildings in the enclave, the administration building was the least architecturally inspired and the one most likely to have space commandeered to serve some urgent temporary need. Because the Treasure Hunters were considered to be a temporary project, space had been found for them on an upper floor. The lift field was out. Cleo wearily tackled more stairs.

The large enough room was made small by the crowding of data-processing equipment and map displays and scheduling boards and large numbers of replicas of paper books and documents, the originals of which had been made too fragile with age to risk moving from the library. But a space on the big central table had been cleared, and the prism of a three-faced display showed on each of its faces a street map of Monn with a red spot blinking a little west of the center. The Hunters' energy-priority rating meant that their terminal screens were working.

When Cleo came in, Zeke was holding forth to the half-dozen people around the table who listened intently.

"The thing is," he was saying, "the Old People did their level best to make the missile sites undetectable even by the most sophisticated satellite-mounted instruments, and unfortunately for us, they got quite good at it. They expected, you see, that at some time or other they would launch the things at one another, and of course the first priority targets would be the other guy's missiles.''

He looked up as Cleo came in, scraped his chair over a little to make a space for her, and said to the others, ''This is Cleo, the engineer who has been working with Reese in Monn. She knows the places he's been looking at.''

Irene came sweeping in, looking every bit as harassed and disheveled as she had sounded on the terminal, and surveyed the room. ''Where's Neil?'' she asked.

''Still with the chairman,'' Zeke said. ''The chairman is not pleased. I think we are going to get severely reprimanded. The council never was strongly in favor of the Hunt. If we've lost a man . . .'' Zeke's voice trailed off. He was fond of Reese, whom he considered to be one of his best students.

Irene shot him a look that should have withered him on the spot and then glanced at Cleo. ''We haven't lost a man,'' she said. ''The council is welcome to perform the usual sexually oriented acrobatics with itself. If Engineering shut off the power to the stills and they had to be satisfied with Phobish beer or go dry, maybe they'd pay attention. If you social-science types wanted do something worthwhile, you'd figure out a way to manage the enclave and interact with other groups without the need for the everlasting political bureaucracy.''

Zeke didn't take offense. ''Are you having a disagreement with the bureaucracy?'' he asked.

''I am having a disagreement with the bureaucracy. Those biddies are so scared that someday the Phobes will gang together and come charging in here, they're afraid to move. I keep telling them what'll happen if the Phobes ever get together is the moon will turn blue and the Phobes will be too busy looking under rocks and bushes trying to find the demon responsible to cause us any trouble.''

''That's not necessarily a good thing.''

Irene pushed a strayed lock of hair off her forehead. ''I don't share your enthusiasm for primitive people, I'm afraid.''

''Not many do,'' Zeke said.

''I'm not surprised.''

"But they are, after all, just people, albeit in unhappy circumstances."

"Sure."

"Okay, so I'm not going to convince you of the basic humanity of the Phobes. What do you want from an aging anthropologist?"

"What can you tell me about the True Church and this Temple?"

Zeke chewed his upper lip as he thought it over. "It's complicated. The True Church is a revival of elements of the New Faith sect of Christianity which rose to prominence among the Old People just before the Separation, skewed with a heavy seasoning of demonology and mysticism to suit Brother Parker's purposes. Brother Parker himself was the fourth son of a minor landowner without much future. He hit on this way of making his fortune. Though in many respects, I think he's sincere in his belief. Monnishmen generally hold a rough-and-ready religion which includes not only God but a variety of demons, good and bad spirits, sorcerers and witches . . ."

Cleo's mind wandered while Zeke lectured in his dry way. The events of the day were catching up with her. She felt overwhelmed.

"Just people," Zeke had said, unconsciously echoing Reese. Shutting her eyes a moment, Cleo imagined Reese making his way among those people, when there were maggots in the food, bugs in the bed, and folks about who would gladly cut his throat for the sake of the coins in his pocket. She shivered. She much preferred the comforts of civilization. Reese was so damned stubborn. She dragged her attention back to what the old anthropologist was saying.

". . . about the Temple, I don't know much. Brother Parker restricts access to it to those he has designated true believers, which serves well enough to give it an air of mystery and privilege. Externally, it looks like a typical Monnish stone building, approximately square, two stories with a steeple another twenty or so feet high. There's talk of underground dungeons, but then there's also talk of sybaritic orgies and perfect and holy asceticism. If there's one thing Monn is full of, it's talk."

"Assuming the worst case, that Reese is being held prisoner there, can we negotiate for him?" Irene asked.

"If they know who you are and where you come from, no chance. Would you negotiate with the agents of the devil? Otherwise it would depend, I suspect, on why he's being held. If it's a matter of simple sinfulness, like laying one of the Sisters, probably you could. But if it's a matter of preaching or practicing heresy against the True Church, I doubt it very much. Brother Parker jealously guards the power he's been able to build up, and he'd fight to maintain it."

"What about the civil authority?"

"Ambivalent. The king, whom they call the governor, is halfway hoping Brother Parker's church will be able to distract and contain and possibly give direction to a fractious population in hard times, facing war and famine. But he's also afraid of its growing influence. I think he'd try to avoid a direct confrontation. He's young and inexperienced and uncertain of his dominion, and not too comfortable with kingship. He's also seriously ill, and so somewhat distracted from affairs of state.

"Now, having said all that, what I'd better say next is that what I've told you is what Reese told me, or is in his field reports. I haven't been in Monn."

"Okay," Irene said. "I'm sorry to have kept you so long, and thank you for coming."

"May I ask what you're planning?"

"We're going to send in a team at first light to find Reese and bring him in."

"Send a man to listen in the inns and taverns. If anything major or official is happening, he'll hear. Send a man; women don't have the freedom of movement." Zeke's voice assumed a brutal tone, hiding his emotion behind a mask of hard realism. "Of course, if Reese has been mugged in an alley, you'll never know. It's such a common occurrence, it isn't a subject for gossip."

"Good God," Cleo said. The vision of Reese lying hurt and alone in some filthy doorway came all too easily to mind.

"Would you go with them, Zeke?" Irene asked. "As adviser."

Zeke thought it over, unconsciously reaching down to rub the scar on his leg. He felt old and tired. A certain rigidity came with age. He wasn't as flexible, as adaptable as he had been in his youth. He knew what culture shock was about and wasn't sure he hankered after the experience at this time in his life.

At the same time, the theoretical practice of his profession had begun to bore him. And anyone could survive a few days in Monn, tourist fashion. And he was worried about Reese, more than he had admitted to the group around him, or even to himself. The boy did tend to go off the deep end at times.

"Okay," he said. "I'll go."

"Thank you," Irene said. "I feel more confident about a person of your experience."

"I'll do what I can," Zeke said. "But you have to promise me something."

"What's that?"

"We go in as quietly as possible, and get out the same way. Monnish society is extremely unstable at the moment, and I wouldn't like to see us starting a panic or something."

Irene scratched her head, adding to her hair's dishevelment. "That's normally the way we do things," she said. "As long as none of our people are endangered. But the team is going armed, and I expect them to protect themselves."

"Fair enough," Zeke said.

Cleo closed her eyes, but her vision of Reese wounded and neglected persisted. "I'm going with you," she said.

"Bad idea," Zeke said. "You don't know what you're asking for."

"Yes, I do. At least I've been to Monn. I might not know much about it, but I know more than you guys who've never been near the place."

Irene shook her head. "It's out of the question, Cleo. Engineering will never agree at this critical time. Let Zeke and the team do the job they know how to do."

"I could go on my own," Cleo said, "but that would be a lot more dangerous, wouldn't it?"

Irene's anger flared for a fraction of a moment and then subsided because she was too weary to sustain it. "Blackmail, now. What in the name of the nine worlds have I done to deserve this?" She dug bony fists into tired eyes. "Zeke, I guess you better have the final word."

Zeke studied the engineer for a moment. "She's got a point. She knows more about the town than any of us here."

"I don't like it," Irene said to Cleo. "I want that on the record. But I don't know what I can do to stop you, short of getting an order from the council for a lawTR escort."

"Don't do that to me," Cleo said. The thought of being followed wherever she went by a robot cop did not please her.

"I'm not going to. But if you won't listen to reason, you must solemnly swear you'll listen to Zeke. And if anything happens to you, I'll never forgive you."

"You're a good friend, Irene."

Irene shook her head. "If I was a good friend, I'd lock you into a closet until you got over this nonsense."

Zeke followed Cleo out when the meeting broke up. On the walkway just outside the administration building, he said, "What you'd better do now is grab a few hours' sleep. We'll start before dawn. It should be easier to enter the city unnoticed then. I'll be around about five with some equipment. I don't know what we'll do about making you properly deferential to males."

"Don't get carried away with this, Zeke. I don't plan to turn into a Phobe."

"You see what I mean. Now listen carefully, woman. If you're not willing to be as Phobe-like as you can, say so now, and stay home. This is dangerous enough without one of us reserving the right to act stupid. We're walking into someone else's world, and they'll tear us limb from limb if they realize we don't belong there. That won't do Reese any good. Or us, either."

"Oh, Zeke, you're so masterful when you're spouting Phobish lore."

' And you, my dear lady, are not your most attractive at your most peevish." Zeke frowned at her for a moment. "You might tell me why you're so determined to do this."

"What? Because I care about Reese."

"Yeah, all right. So long as it's not a matter of doing penance for being so bitchy. No noble sacrifices, okay?"

"Zeke, sometimes I could just hate you."

"Later. Hate me later, when we get back."

Cleo went home wondering if she dared to rouse her neighbor at that hour and ask him to look in on Aurelius if she was away longer than a day.

Back in the apartment, she set the computer to wake her at five although she was certain she would not be able to sleep a wink. She even went as far as hunting up the somnetic, to induce Morpheus by electronic means, and lay down on the bed with the device in her hands and thought seriously about calling Zeke and telling him to forget the whole thing.

The next thing she knew she was clawing cobwebs out of her eyes, the computer was calling her, the door was chiming, and it was time to go.

Twenty-one

The five members of the rescue team left the pod where the Witch Road crossed Travellers' Way.

Cleo was the last to step out of its well-lighted, comfortable security into the dark, sleeping city of Monn. When the pod turned on itself and whisked back to the enclave, she felt unanchored, adrift, not knowing how she was going to cope. When she had come before, she'd had Reese's guidance, and little enough to do with the actual place.

The men squatted down and spread their map on the smooth surface of the podway, examining it by the light of a pocket flash.

Cleo crouched down beside them and pointed out the spot. "This is the house where Reese was staying," she said.

"Okay, good," Zeke answered. "If he's around, he'll show up there sooner or later. If not, well, it's a good place to look for a clue to what's happened. It'll make a good base of operations in any case. Let's go."

Zeke moved out briskly in spite of his limp and his years, continuing as they walked through the gloom the dry lecture that had begun when the team assembled in the Treasure Hunters' office in the small hours.

He was repeating many of his previous instructions, explaining Monnish currency, telling them how to behave toward family members and toward lords. Cleo heard little enough of it; the sound of his voice was reassuring, but she was preoccupied with tugging her skirt loose from thorn bushes and snagging twigs, and with keeping her footing when the rough sandals on her sockless feet twisted and slid on the ruts and humps of Travellers' Way, invisible in the failing dark.

"How come there's no buildings around the pod track?" asked Ian, a burly, young redheaded chemist.

"Reese says they're afraid of it," Zeke said. "The people call it the witch road and they think the pods will run them down or snatch them up and carry them off to hell. They know it's somehow connected with the Philes."

"What Philes?"

"You and me, buddy. The authors of all that's evil in the world. Do you remember hearing in school about Bradley Harmon, and his demands for a return to God's design for the world, how he taught that technology had made the world unfit for good, God-fearing people to live in, that science undermined faith and led honest souls from the paths of righteousness? What we have here is an extension of that notion. There's a big taboo on the enclave and everything about it. Mostly, they pretend it doesn't exist. Keep that in mind. Don't ever admit that you're a citizen. If someone asks, say you're from another city. That'll explain the accent."

"I don't have an accent."

"In Monn, you have an accent. So do I."

Sunlight touched the dusty thatched rooftops. Birds began their morning madrigals. It seemed incredible to Cleo that birds could make so much noise.

Monn was beginning to awaken. They heard a rooster, the wooden clunk of a shutter being thrown back, a distant voice calling, the whuffling grumble of a horse being brought to its work—alien sounds, for the most part unidentifiable to the team. Sunlight marched down the hill to meet them as Cleo led them onto a side street and stopped before the small wooden shack that Reese had been calling home.

They milled around, inside and out, but found nothing to indicate where Reese was.

Cleo wandered the hillside paths awhile, hoping she would spot Sarah around the house somewhere. She was pretty sure that if they found Sarah, they would find out where Reese was.

But Sarah was nowhere to be seen.

* * *

In the shadows before dawn, Arthur Browneye, loyal soldier to the governor of Monn, newly and proudly inducted into the Governor's Guard, a happy, well-laid man, was making his way back to the barracks from the hayloft where sweet young Dora had been so accommodating. He was hurrying a little in his effort to arrive before the morning call. He wasn't unduly worried. He had enough time. He did not admit to himself that he was nervous about being out alone in the dark.

Slogging along through the rough land before the Witch Road, he saw the witch wagon coming, the light of its demon eye stabbing through the night, so he stopped and waited for it to pass. The witch wagons made him uncomfortable whenever they came whipping by, but as long as he was off the Witch Road, he felt safe.

The witch wagon stopped.

Suddenly. Just a few yards from where he was. He had never heard of that before. His breath stuck in his throat. He wanted to run, but didn't dare. He was afraid to move or even breathe. He might call its attention to him. He stood there, paralyzed, wide-eyed, slack-jawed, half-convinced that the Lord God's angry eye had been on him in the hayloft, and that the just wrath of God was about to descend upon him in all its fury.

The witch wagon turned on itself, the hellish light raking across Arthur's hiding place. Arthur thought his heart would stop. The witch wagon sped off the way it had come. The pounding in Arthur's chest continued.

He sucked in a deep breath and let himself down with quaking legs to sit among the weeds and brush until he could collect his wits. Only slowly did he become aware that the witch wagon had spewed forth some beings that now squatted on the Witch Road, chittering among themselves words he couldn't make out—the language of goblins and gnomes, he was certain. A light glowed among them as if a speck of the witch wagon's eye had been left behind. He could make out eerie fragments of faces in the glow. Sweat formed on his forehead although the night was cool. It rolled stinging into his eyes and blurred his vision. By the time he blinked it away, the light was gone and the creatures were moving off, dark against the paling night, into the city.

Daylight grew stronger as Arthur sat with his head on his

knees, trying to convince himself that too much wine and too little sleep adequately explained what he had just seen.

The sun touched the tree tops on the ridge and began its slow march down the hill. The sergeant would be wondering where he was. He was afraid of the sergeant. He was afraid of the evil things he had seen. The sergeant, being more imminent, won out. Arthur skittered with his heart in his mouth across the Witch Road and started up the hill.

The courtyard of the Temple was a small area of trampled ground surrounded by a low rail fence. Tufts of dry grass stood here and there, but most of the area was worn down to the naked dirt. A young boy with half a dozen skinny goats was in earnest negotiation with a white-robed Sister when Cleo and Zeke arrived. Neither goatherd nor Sister paid them much mind.

Zeke had left a note stuck to Reese's door, telling him to wait for the team if he got there first, sent Ian to the nearby inn, a second man to the market, and the last to the Crow's Eye Tavern, with instructions to listen carefully and do nothing. He and Cleo would investigate the Temple. They would meet again at the house at noon.

Zeke marched up the short flight of steps and pounded on the wooden door. The door opened, and a Brother peered out. Zeke told a story about a search for a missing kinsman. The Brother disappeared into the Temple for a moment, then came back and invited Zeke inside. Cleo was not included in the invitation.

Left standing on the steps staring at the closed door, Cleo was furious. She glowered at the wood for a while, but that was ineffective, so, resigned, she sat down on the steps to wait, and dust be damned. Her feet hurt.

She hated that place, and when they found Reese, she was going to tell him how much. She wasn't going to let him forget too soon that she had warned him he would get into trouble and he hadn't listened. There was much satisfaction to be had in saying "I told you so."

The Sister and the goatherd were still arguing, the Sister seeming deferential even to this slip of a child. But the boy left eventually without having sold a goat.

"The Lord God's love to you this morning."

Cleo found herself startled at being addressed directly, but the Sister's smile was friendly. "Uh, yeah, thanks," she said, not knowing how else to respond to so odd a greeting.

The Sister sat beside Cleo on the step. "I think you have come a long way," she said. She pushed the hood of her robe back and shook out her hair. She was a mouse-brown creature with a flat round face, very young, not more than fifteen or sixteen.

"It's been too much walking," Cleo said.

"Are you here for the Festival?"

"Ah, no, I don't think so."

"We get to go," the Sister said happily. She was obviously looking forward to it.

"Uh, good for you," Cleo said.

"Are you thirsty?"

"Yes," Cleo said, surprised that she hadn't realized it before.

"Come." The Sister jumped up and started down the steps.

Cleo hesitated, glancing at the closed door.

The Sister waved a dismissive hand in that general direction. "They will be forever. Men talk a lot. We have time."

What the hell, Cleo thought. If worse comes to worst, I can find Reese's house again by noon. I think. She followed the Sister around the side of the Temple where tall pickets closed out the sun.

They came to a small thatched shed behind the Temple. Inside, its rafters were hung with dried leaves and seeds and skeins of onions, and its walls held shelves of earthenware pots and jars. A huge smoke-blackened fireplace occupied one end, and a heavy plank table took the middle of the space.

The air was surprisingly cooler inside. The Sister found Cleo a stool to sit on and then opened a hatch in the dirt floor, extracted a large jug with a piece of cloth tied over its mouth, found a mug, removed the cloth, poured out half a liter of milk, and offered it to Cleo.

There was a hair or something floating on the top. Cleo wished it wasn't there. But her thirst overcame her fastidiousness. She shut her eyes and swallowed a big mouthful.

The milk was cold and creamy and good. "That's delicious," Cleo said.

The Sister smiled, pleased. "Are you coming to join the Temple?" she asked, pulling up another stool.

Cleo shook her head. "Not me." She struggled for a way to put it into Monnish terms. "My friend, uh, man, he's looking for his kinsman. Fellow by the name of Reese. He'd be a stranger in your city. Maybe you've heard of him?"

The Sister shook her head. "I don't go into the city often. My faith is newly rooted, and not yet strong enough to protect me from the temptations of evil." She said this as if reciting another's words. "Yet there are few enough foreigners. Someone has surely seen him."

Cleo swallowed some more milk. It was difficult, trying to say what she wanted to say in the stilted language of this place, especially when she had to take care not to mention anything that would frighten the Sister.

"My man feels certain he came here. He'd be wanting to talk about the Old People's places." At one remove, she hoped that she would not have to explain how her man knew. "He's tall, dark hair, gray eyes, well dressed, talks like me."

The Sister clapped her hand to her mouth and stared at Cleo, round-eyed. "The witch! You speak of the witch. You call him kinsman. Am I in danger of my soul?"

"Reese?" Cleo blurted out her astonishment before she could stop herself. The Sister's head bobbed up and down, her hand bobbing with it.

Witch? Cleo wondered. What's she talking about? Is this some stupid Monnish joke? She's kidding, right?

But the girl was really frightened; Cleo could see that.

The Sister looked about to flee from her as if from an incarnation of the Devil himself. Cleo shook her head. "Hey, take it easy. There's nothing witchy about me," she said, offering what she hoped was a reassuring smile.

She hiked her skirt up a little, not knowing if that was acceptable behavior but having nothing to lose as far as the Sister was concerned, and displayed one red, blistered foot in its crude sandal. "If I had any magic in me, I'd have used it to get here, instead of getting such sore feet." I'd have witched me a different pair of shoes, or maybe traveled by broomstick, she thought.

Fear and compassion warred on the Sister's guileless features. She was an uncomplicated girl, a farmer's daughter who had been known as a kindly spirit, encouraged by a worried father to join the Church when it seemed that the farm would be unable to feed her. Concern for her immortal soul was new to her. Until a few months ago, she had hardly given it a thought.

In the end, the attitudes of a lifetime prevailed. She made sympathetic clucking noises, told Cleo to wait a minute, and went rushing out.

Left alone in the shed, Cleo didn't know whether she should wait for the Sister's return, or run for her life. For all she knew, the girl had gone off to fetch some Brothers to assist her in the capture of yet another witch. And whatever it was they did with captured witches, it probably wasn't fun.

Poor Reese. What had become of him?

Cleo felt a cold hand clutching at her gut thinking about it. She was sure the Sister knew something.

The Sister returned with strips of soft white cloth and a small pot of grease in her hand.

She squatted down beside Cleo, removed her sandals, and slathered her feet with the grease. The stuff had a rank smell, but it did feel good.

When the Sister had wrapped her feet in the cloth and replaced her sandals, Cleo told her that she was grateful, but didn't know how to repay the kindness.

"Just don't tell them in the Temple. They will think I have used our supplies unwisely."

"Okay, I won't. You've got a deal." And with that, they became conspirators, with a stake in one another's welfare.

"If only," Cleo said, trying for a wistful sigh and suitably ornate phrasing, "if only my man would find this Reese, maybe we could rest awhile. I grow weary of searching."

The Sister bent her head and studied the dirt floor of the shed. A shaft of sunlight had found its way in through a gap in the roof and touched the Sister's head. There was an insect crawling along the nape of her neck, and the Sister slapped at it idly. A louse, Cleo realized, and everything inside her cringed. The urge to get some distance between them was almost uncontrollable.

"I have seen the witch," the Sister said.

Cleo said nothing, not wanting to distract her.

"When they brought him to the Temple. I wanted to see what a witch looked like, so I sneaked out to see him." She stopped, lost in her thoughts. "I took a Cross of God with me, to protect

me, you understand, from the influence. But even so, he was
such a beautiful man, truly he was, evil thoughts came to me. I
think he is a most powerful witch. I never told anyone, not even
Brother John, who is my teacher in the True Faith. He would
be furiously angry, and punish me. But the Lord God knows
what wicked things were in my mind, and so my punishment
will come, won't it, in this world or the next?''

The girl looked so distressed that Cleo had a notion to hug
her, to comfort her. But she remembered the louse and suppressed the notion.

"I guess God is more forgiving than that," she said.

The Sister looked up, smiling a little. "Do you think so?''

Cleo nodded, thinking, What sort of faith demands punishment for a normal teenager's normal flights of fancy? But then,
what sort of faith would take Reese for a witch?

"Do you think I should tell Brother John?''

"I wouldn't. Brother John probably has lots of really important stuff to worry about. Besides, men don't understand these
things very well."

"I think that is so."

"What did they do with this witch?''

The Sister gave Cleo a sharp look. Cleo shrugged. "If he is
my man's kinsman, he'd want to know, don't you think?''

"It would be better for you if you told him the witch was
dead."

"Is he?'' Cleo asked quickly before she could decide that she
didn't want the answer.

The Sister lowered her eyes.

"Is it right to lie to your man?'' Cleo pressed on.

"I know the True Faith teaches all lies are evil. But you are
not of the Faith. It would be safer for you to go away and forget
this kinsman. To claim such a one as kin is only to bring suspicion on yourselves. He cannot help you or even himself. He
is in the Lord God's hands now. To say he is dead is almost
true."

The cold hand clutching at Cleo's gut all but paralyzed her.
She had to fight to maintain her outward composure.

"You could be right. Still, I should know, in case I have to
explain how I know this."

The Sister shook her head. "I can't say truly. They took him inside the Temple, into the cellar, I heard the Brothers say, where there is a place for keeping enemies of the True Faith until their fate is decided.''

"Has the witch's fate been decided?"

"I don't know. It is not my place to know."

"Could a person get to see this witch?"

The Sister's eyes grew round and frightened. ''Oh, no. This cannot be done. It is too dangerous. You must not even think of such—"

She was interrupted by the appearance of another Sister running full tilt, robes flying. "The stranger is leaving, but he cannot find his woman. He is very angry. Come. Make haste."

"I have kept you too long," the Sister said. "I'm sorry. Will he beat you?"

Zeke? Cleo thought. He'd better not try it. "No, he won't," she said. "He's a decent sort most of the time. But I better go. I wish you well."

When she came around to the front of the Temple, Zeke limped down the steps with his uneven gait, to meet her. "Christ," he said. "I thought I'd lost you."

"You're supposed to be angry and ready to beat me," Cleo said in a quiet voice.

"That's not a bad idea. You scared the shit out of me."

"Try it. I'll bust your arm, Zeke, so help me, custom or no custom." A couple of Brothers were standing on the steps, watching. "Let's get out of here. I've got things to tell you."

Twenty-two

Morning found Michael in the same position the previous day had left him, with the marble abusing his elbows once again. A spell of coughing on arising had left him shaken and drained before the day began. He had no enthusiasm for the tasks ahead.

The narrow-bladed knife lay on the marble table in front of him. The smith, standing before him huge and sooty and ill at ease at being summoned to the Mansion, clenched and unclenched his big right fist rhythmically.

Michael regarded the blade, wondering why such a simple thing should be such a mystery. He had questioned the prisoner about it, and the man had said he knew nothing about the making of steel. It was done, he said, by people of his city who were experts in such things. He sounded sincere. Michael could easily believe him.

But the man had also said he knew nothing of witches and witchcraft, and sounded equally sincere. Michael sent him back to the prison to think over the contradiction.

The smith shuffled uneasily, wondering if he had been forgotten while the governor brooded. Buried in his left hand was the small talisman his wife had given him. It was a beautiful thing, the likeness of the Lame Smith at his forge, artfully carved into a round of pink stone so that the grain of the stone lent character to the figure and life to the flames. Clara wore it on a thong between her breasts most of the time. She had taken it from around her neck and put it in his hand before he left to answer Michael's summons, telling him that its luck was particularly powerful, for she'd had a traveling magician add a spell to it that would protect him.

The Lame Smith was the guardian spirit of all those who worked hot metal. The smith could only hope the talisman was as potent as it was beautiful, for he could not satisfy the governor.

He felt a little guilty about those thoughts, for he was a long-term and serious member of the True Church, and the Faith had room for no charms save the grace of God, nor powers but the power of prayer.

Michael looked up, questioning.

"Your Honor, lordship, sir," the smith said in a welter of indecision about how to address the governor, for the question had never previously arisen in his life. "I can only tell you I know no way to forge such steel. I've worked iron all my life, good sir, and my father before me, and I've seen naught like it."

Michael grunted sourly, and the smith continued, nervousness making his tongue wag when he knew he should keep still. "Steel of such a temper, that does not tarnish, Your Honor, I think it can only be made by sorcery. By my faith, your lordship, it would take a Phile magician to make another such a blade."

Michael glared. "Demons, Philes, witches. That's all I hear these days. Surely what Philes can do, honest men can also do." Involuntarily, the smith backed away a pace. "An easy way to excuse incompetence, this everlasting call to magic."

"M'lord," Thomas cautioned from the background.

Michael was momentarily irritated by his adviser. The steel was important. He needed it.

After a while, he raised his head and looked bleakly out at the cliffs and the spider-work trestle. He picked up the knife still lying at his elbow and turned it in his fingers. Phile magic? Where was he going to get that?

The smith was still waiting unhappily. Michael waved a hand at him, wiping out his ill-humored outburst. "I shout at you because the Fates desert me. Forgive me." The smith's mouth dropped. His usual contact with aristocrats consisted of demands, dissatisfaction, and begrudging payment. On average he preferred to deal with six honest farmers than one plumed lord. To have the governor of the city apologize to him . . .

"I would ask one thing of you. If the knowledge of this magic metal comes to you, you will tell me that you have it." Michael shook his head to forestall the smith's worry. "The secret is yours if you can find it. Mixtures of iron and charcoal mean little enough to me. All I need is to know it can be made in Monn. Can I have that from you?"

The smith was glad to assure the governor that if such an unlikely event should come to pass, the governor would be the first to know. He's just a sickly boy, after all, and a dreamer, the smith thought, and he left the Mansion feeling more kindly toward its occupant than he had when he had entered, but a little less secure about the way the city was governed.

He did remember to squeeze the little talisman in his hand and give silent thanks to the Lame Smith for his help. Later he would go to the Temple and give his thanks to the Lord God.

Amyit the Kolloan, disguised as a peaceful trader, was holding his dancing horse before the Mansion gates and trying to persuade the Guardsmen barring his entrance to admit him to the grounds to spread his wares for the governor's household. He didn't really expect to get through, though it would be useful if he could. But he could see a fair bit of the layout of the place from where he stood and get at least some idea of the Mansion's defenses.

The smith came trudging by and was waved through as if he were expected.

That was not so strange. Presumably, the governor's household had need of a smith from time to time. But he did think it was peculiar that the smith was escorted up the front steps and into the Mansion proper. Such a thing would never happen in Kollo.

When the smith left the Mansion again a short time later, Amyit thought it might be worthwhile to have a word or two with him, so he said good-bye to the guard and set off at the trot down the hill toward the smithy. His long-legged Kolloan horse brought him there well ahead of the smith. He dismounted and pried one of his mount's shoes loose with his belt knife, apologizing to the mare as he did it.

The smith arrived dusty, hot, and unhappy, and was disinclined to accept the work at first, but a little Kolloan silver changed his mind. And Amyit was an experienced and well-trained spy. He overcame the smith's initial reserve toward strangers with inquiries about the state of his business, his family, and so forth, and soon had the story of the magic blade and Michael's ill-humored demand for the secret of untarnishable steel.

Amyit had his doubts about steel that never tarnished. That seemed like more folklore, in a class with seven-league boots and pitchers that never ran dry. Nothing one expected to exist in any real way.

That the governor should be clutching at such straws was interesting, though. Things were obviously not well in the city of Monn. It seemed to Amyit that the Kolloan emperor had taken an interest in Monn at a most opportune time. One might consider the emperor to be remarkably wise or damned lucky.

It couldn't hurt to discover what prompted the governor's desperate move. A failure of leadership made a people so much more receptive to the notion of joining the Empire.

He grew impatient for the smith to finish so he could carry the news back to the Kolloan encampment.

Michael spent the rest of the morning and a good part of the afternoon with Thomas and the representatives of the group of farming communities to the west who called themselves Lasdanes. The Lasdanes had grain to sell, but their price was exorbitant. Michael had hoped that a luxurious noon meal would persuade them that Monn's need was not great, that the purchase was a matter of providence, not shortage, and that the city could afford to wait for lower prices. The Lasdanes were not fooled. They stuck to their usury.

Michael retired from the fray defeated, overfed, and worried. He felt sick to his stomach. He was not happy to see the captain of the Guard, but could not refuse him. Nor was he happy to see Arthur Browneye, a rough, common-looking fellow in a Guardsman's uniform who didn't seem to be unduly impressed with coming face to face with his governor.

Arthur would have been more impressed if he hadn't been through his story three times already, for his sergeant, his lieutenant, and the captain of the Guard. Faced with telling it yet again to the governor, he was half expecting to be summoned before the archangels next.

"Five?" Michael said when the tale was done.

"Yes, m'lord."

"They're in the city now?"

"I believe so, m'lord."

"And you are certain they are witches?"

"They came out of the witch wagon, m'lord, in a strange light. They gathered in a ritual right on the Witch Road that seemed no proper, Godly thing, and spoke strangely. I'm not a man well taught in spiritual things, but I don't know how else it could be."

"Yes," Michael said. He put his head in his hands and wondered why the witches were picking on him. Why were they coming to his city? Didn't he have troubles enough to tax a strong man? How had he offended the Lord God so greatly, that this also had to come to him?

He addressed the captain. "You and your men begin a search for these five immediately. Let us issue a proclamation to the people to aid us in the search, with suitable rewards and penalties."

"As you wish, of course, m'lord," the captain said. "But the True Church will oppose us in this matter, as it has done before. There could be a confrontation."

"If Brother Parker interferes, send him to me," Michael said. And the Lord God only knows what I will do with him, he thought.

When they were alone, Thomas said, "I don't think involving the people was a wise move. I foresee witches multiplying like rabbits as despised mothers-in-law and difficult neighbors are included in the list."

"And if I do not act at once, Brother Parker will be denouncing me from the pulpit, and every minor misfortune that befalls the humblest citizen will be held against me. What is the right course, Thomas?"

"I believe I answered that before, Michael."

Twenty-three

Only half-joking, the townsfolk of Monn claimed that news traveled on the river with wondrous speed, with, some might say, supernatural speed. Tell a riverman in far northern Aver a secret in the morning, they said, and it would be known on the Warlen docks and be going out to sea before the day was out. They exaggerated a little.

Nonetheless, the sun had just begun its westward slant, striking jewels from the ripples in the water, when a dozen strong men and women of the river gathered on the foredeck of the *Big Fish*. That was another thing about the rivermen that bothered the townsfolk—the women of the river didn't know their place, and they set a bad example for the goodwives of Monn.

Their bantering talk might have seemed frivolous to an outsider. A small cask of Sanjo's sweet beer lay cradled in a coil of rope in the center of their circle, and often one or another approached it to refill a mug. Jokes were common, as was good-natured joshing. Shoulders were slapped and hugs exchanged. The constable patrolling the dock area came to the conclusion that the riverfolk were having a party, and stayed well clear of the *Big Fish*.

They seemed to be discussing a prankish adventure, the delight to be had from snatching a prize from Brother Parker's clutches, but the conversation had a solemn undertone. All among them had at one time or another bumped against the stark intolerance of landsmen, and they saw Brother Parker as the personification of everything they found least attractive in a strait-

laced community of burghers and farmers who knew nothing of
the world beyond the ends of their noses.

Sarah sat on the deck a little out of the circle of conspirators,
somewhat astonished by the events she had set in motion. She
watched the torchlight moving on tough, weathered features as
the riverfolk conspired against Brother Parker. It was as if she
had tapped some hidden force that had been biding its time,
waiting for an excuse to be unleashed. The language of the
discussion was light, and liberally salted with rough humor.
Now and again the meeting broke out into squalls of laughter.
But the ghosts of past injuries were near at hand—bills unpaid,
rotten rope sold for new, bad service in the taverns—and always
brought the talk back to a certain dark purposefulness.

Ryan, master of the *Wind Runner*, laid the problem out simply and clearly. "We can talk all we want," he said, "and tell
one another how tough and clever we are, but it comes down to
this: We can't get into the bloody Temple. It's built like a
freakin' fortress, and it's always full of a bleatin' mob of Parker's hell-bound sheep. Once they shut the door on us, we might
as well storm a mountain."

"I guess what we need," Matthew answered, "is someone
inside to open the door."

"I nominate you, Matt," Ryan's wife, Mavis, said. "You'd
make a good saint. How about you join the Brothers and be
ready to let us in when the time comes?"

Matthew let the ripple of amusement wear itself out. "That
wouldn't work," he said. "It would take too long even if we
could convince Parker he's recruited me, which is something he
wouldn't swallow too easily. The initiation and whatnot takes
for nearly ever. Besides, Beth would disown me."

Lucas, crewman from the *Godspeed*, the biggest Monnish
boat on the river, looked up from studying the polished boards
of *Big Fish*'s deck. He was a huge man, so huge that it was said
around the docks that only *Godspeed* was big enough to keep
his ankles out of the water; he would swamp anything smaller.
But those who fell prey to the popular prejudice that big men
were perforce stupid would be surprised by Lucas. "I take it
you got a better idea?"

"I don't know about better," Matthew said. "But we could
toss it around a bit. I'd like to hear what you people think. I'm

not much of a tactician, you know, and the art of war isn't exactly my bag of tricks, but—"

"Enough modesty. You're embarrassing us," Gordon the fisher growled from the circle. "You got a plan, let's hear it. Without all the phony protestations of humility."

Matthew looked round the circle. His friends looked expectantly back. He took a mouthful from the mug he was holding and swallowed slowly. "The way I see it, we've got two things going for us, the Festival and Sarah."

Sarah's ears perked up when she heard her name. She wiggled a little closer to the circle. Someone shifted, making a place for her, and another handed her a mug. She was startled by that mark of acceptance, but sat cross-legged on the deck with them and took the beer without comment.

"You want us to guess?" gray-haired Gordon asked. He was an impatient old man, as if he sensed his life's time running short.

"If you like," Matthew said. "But if you'd rather wait a moment, I'll try to explain." He caught Beth's glance, saw that she had anticipated him, and was doubtful. "The thing is, Sarah here can get into the Temple with no trouble. The Brothers and Sisters think she's on their side, you see. They're half expecting her."

Big Lucas shifted uneasily. He glanced over at Sarah for a split second then ducked his head and contemplated the deck once again. "I know you're fond of the girl, Matthew," he said quietly, "but the truth of it is, she's not the most reliable ally we might have. She's known about for her taking ways. She's not our kind. There's a bit of the savage in her, I think. How could we trust her not to sell us all if there was a bright bauble in it for her?"

"Hush, Lucas," Avril, Gordon's mate, answered. "You talk of a child who's grown when you weren't looking. Times change, and folks change with them. You were an unpromising lad yourself, as I remember. From what Matthew has told us, Sarah has more to lose in this than any of us."

Matthew had been careful about what he told them, and had left out all aspects of witchcraft beyond Brother Parker's accusation.

"Or more to gain, depending on how you look at it," Lucas answered.

"I don't see any other way into the Temple," Mavis said.

"Maybe it'd be easier to wait for them to come out," Ryan suggested.

"And attack the whole entire pious mob of them, and maybe the Governor's Guard to boot, with fishhooks and rope's ends? We're not warriors, Ryan, and there isn't one decent swordsman among us." Matthew grinned. "Hand to hand, one on one, I'd bet everything I have on any one of you against any landsman. But at sword point, even Big Lucas hasn't much of a chance." He shook his head. "If we're going to do this, we can't make a war of it. I think Sarah's our best chance. But if anyone wants to back out, I won't hold it against you."

An annoyed murmur ran round the circle. "Who said anything about backing out?" Lucas growled.

"Would anyone think to ask Sarah if she's willing?" Beth said. "It could be bad for her, if they decide to lock her up again. And it wouldn't do us any good, either. It's a chancy thing you're asking of her."

All heads turned toward Sarah. The girl's face flamed. The others waited politely for her to have her say. Somehow she had managed to gain a place in the circle that she thought was forever closed to her. She felt humble and privileged and suddenly close to them all, a sense of community that was completely new to her. She didn't trust herself to speak. She didn't think about the terror of the dark space under the Temple where Brother Eric smiled a lot until it was too late to back out.

She could only nod, happy in their acceptance.

Later she wished they had thought of some other way.

"All right, then," Ryan said. "Where does the Festival come into it?"

"I figure it like this. With the Festival on, most of the faithful will be out and about the town, with just a few in the Temple itself. Chances are all their schedules or whatever will be a bit disordered. The constables and the army will be mostly busy in the square, too. With Sarah to open the door, a few fellows in black robes could maybe walk right in, grab the witch, and walk out again with hardly anyone taking notice."

"A few fellows would have to have black robes," Lucas pointed out.

"Well, I figure, if those fellows were to hang around just outside the square where the Brothers were coming and going, an opportunity or two might arise."

Twenty-four

Market Square was ablaze with torches and lanterns for the Festival. Around it were arrayed a democratic collection of saddle horses and mules, ox-carts and fine carriages, drays and carts, and farm wagons attached to great blinkered draft horses looking much out of place on a city street. Around the perimeter of the light, bits of colored cloth and yarn hung from tall poles and fluttered in the breeze.

Most of Monn's population mobbed into the square and spilled out into the streets. People from a goodly distance around had come to join the noisy gathering in celebration of midsummer in the city. Even a few dour northerners, tall and prim in their embroidered buckskins, had been persuaded to join the fun and unbend a little. A pair of Kolloans with scarlet tunics, looking like perambulating flowers in a dun-colored crowd, ignored the soldiers in civilian dress who followed them everywhere.

For the evening, worries and proprieties were forgotten. Drying fields and hungry animals were put out of mind. The people sampled the governor's generosity, fed themselves to nausea, and drank themselves insensible. Whole oxen had been roasting since the previous day. Wine and beer flowed freely. A troop of entertainers had come upriver from Sanjo to join the festivities, and the acrobats among them had just completed an astonishing pyramid of their bodies piled one atop the other to an amazing height. A small white dog carrying a flag bounced over the bent backs and sat at the top with its front paws in the air, tail wagging. As onlookers cheered, a few of the wealthier ones threw coins, and the pyramid collapsed in a mad scramble for the silver before urchins and thieves disappeared with all of it.

Many family members were present, jewels and silver shining in the torchlight, rubbing elbows with carters and merchants. A contingent of the Governor's Guard was also there, horses brushed, brass and leather agleam, supposedly keeping order. But more than one soldier leaned down over the shoulder of his horse to accept a proffered cup of ale, or smoothed his beard and winked at a bright-eyed lady.

The governor was due to arrive at any moment, in full regalia, and even those who had become a bit weary of overindulgence in food and drink awaited his arrival.

A little outside the circle of light, in the shadows between a pair of modest houses, Lucas shifted uneasily. Matthew, already arrayed in a long black robe, put a steadying hand on the big man's arm and urged patience.

"It's not going to work, Matt," Lucas said. "There should be at least two of us, but the bloody Brothers stick too close together. And you can't go it alone."

"Well, I guess I could if I have to," Matthew said.

"No, Matt," Beth said fiercely.

Matthew put a cautionary finger to his lips. Two figures had detached themselves from the square and were heading up Temple Road, shadows against the glow, carrying a torch. They were hurrying, and glanced back occasionally at the party in the square as if they were reluctant to leave it.

"Can we handle two of them?" Matthew asked. Lucas shrugged. Behind them, Ryan and Mavis, watching the prisoner they already had, said almost together, "Why not?"

The men deployed themselves on either side of the road. Beth shed her jacket and revealed a blouse artfully torn to display rather a lot of skin. Too damned much, Matthew thought.

Whether charity was any part of their philosophy, and however much their religion had neutered them, the Brothers were still men, and they would stop to look, if nothing else. That was all the rivermen needed.

As the Brothers approached, a distressed and disheveled woman ran out from between the houses toward them, wailing, apparently pursued by a Brother of the True Faith, Matthew. The two hesitated and the torchbearer held his light high, trying to make out what was happening. Lucas stepped up behind him, took the torch away with one huge hand, and wrapped the other arm snugly around the Brother's neck, cutting off his cry of alarm.

The other Brother, more alert and hands free, gave them some trouble. The rivermen could only hope that his shouts would be lost in the merriment in the square. Matthew and Ryan scuffled with him until Mavis bopped him smartly on the top of the head with a club she had brought along for that exact purpose. The Brother's struggles subsided at once and he was stripped, bound with solid sailor's knots, and laid out with a rag stuffed into his mouth alongside the other two against the wall of one house. The householder would be surprised when he got home.

Lucas squirmed into the bigger of the two robes. It was a dangerously snug fit. Ryan slid into the other and warned Lucas not to take a deep breath or he would give them away.

"Put your jacket on," Matthew growled at Beth. She gave him an insolent little grin, but complied. They extinguished the torch and started en masse up Church Road toward the Temple.

"How's Sarah going to recognize us?" Mavis asked.

"She's supposed to open the door at moonrise," Matthew said.

"We're late," Lucas said. "Let's hope she doesn't get too nervous and bolt."

"She won't."

"Whatever you say, Matt," Lucas answered, not entirely keeping the skepticism out of his voice.

By the time they arrived, the moon was well above the horizon, only slightly less than full, the round-mouthed demon's face on it looking down at them and washing the Temple yard with pale light. They milled about uncertainly outside the low fence, not sure how they should proceed. Then the great Temple door opened a crack, and Sarah anxiously peered out. The pseudo Brothers, hoods up, heads bent, hands tucked into sleeves, hurried across the yard, up the steps, and into the Temple.

Left behind with Mavis, Beth wished she had someone to pray to.

"I thought maybe you weren't coming," Sarah said. She spoke quickly, nervously, with a hush, though no one else seemed to be about. "The Brothers were at me all day, you know. I was scared they were going to lock me up again. I really had to talk fast and keep away from Brother Eric. I'm supposed to see the governor's chief adviser tomorrow, so they're telling me what to say. A bunch of words, I don't even know what they are. I know the place to go, the same place in the dark they took me, but I was afraid by myself. The Brother who's supposed to be watching the door, I thought he'd get back before you came. You're late." She reached up on tiptoes to take a torch from its bracket on the wall and led them down a long, narrow hallway which had identical doors opening off it every few feet on either side. At the very end was a heavier door, closed with an iron bar. They followed, heads swiveling, trying to see in every direction at once.

At Sarah's direction, Lucas lifted the bar and set it aside, and they proceeded down a flight of stone stairs lit only by Sarah's torch.

They went through the storeroom, threading their way among barrels, boxes, and bins, into the next dark, ugly place. There were two barred doors on one wall. Both were open. Lucas took the torch and looked in one cell and then the other. Shadows swung madly around the walls.

Lucas shook his head as he turned to look at Matt.

Matthew looked at Sarah.

"I was sure this was the place. It's the only place he could be," she said.

"Well, nobody's here," Ryan said. "Let's get the hell out before some freakin' Brother shows up. We can puzzle it out somewhere else."

As his voice died away, the sound of footsteps and voices came to them down the stairs.

Outside in the moonlight, watching the Temple door for Matthew's reappearance, Beth nudged Mavis and pointed at the group of people climbing the steps. There were five of them, ordinary citizens from all appearances, except one was a woman. They fiddled at the door for a moment and then went in.

"What's going on?" Mavis whispered.

"I don't know, but I don't like it."

The door closed behind the group and all was quiet.

Beth chewed at her bottom lip for a moment. She fidgeted, then paced a few steps back and forth at the verge of the Temple yard. "Something's wrong," she said finally. "Come on."

"Where are we going?" Mavis asked, but Beth was already moving and she had the choice of following or remaining behind alone.

Beth trotted up the Temple steps, then stopped so abruptly that Mavis almost ran into her. Beth hesitated, then pulled the door open and pointed to the edge of it, standing aside so Mavis could see.

The thick iron bar that secured the door from the inside had been neatly cut through. There was a small charred spot on the wood near the bar, but otherwise no sign of how the cutting had been accomplished.

Mavis felt the hair at the back of her neck prickle. "Let's get out of here, Beth. Something weird is happening."

But Beth was already inside. "We have to warn Matt," she said. Her voice was calm, but her cheeks were ashen. At her feet was the body of a man in black robes, as still as death. Neither woman wanted to touch him to confirm their suspicions.

Standing in the barren entryway, looking down at the man, Mavis felt guilty for feeling grateful that it was not Ryan lying there. "How're we going to find them?" she asked. Dim corridors led off into the interior of the Temple. One seemed as likely as any other.

"Hush," Beth said. "Listen."

A small sound came down one hallway. It could be voices. "This way," Beth said. She started off at a trot. Mavis reluctantly followed.

"Just stand quietly, Brothers," one of the strangers said. He spoke with an odd, soft accent, standing there at the foot of the stairs, confident that he was in control. In each hand he held a device, one of which was giving off a light that made the torch Lucas was holding look as pale as water.

They were indistinct shadows behind the glare, like phantom people.

Matthew's mouth was hanging open. Sarah, hiding half-behind him, whispered something about a metal rod and Reese's magic light. Matthew didn't turn to listen. He couldn't have moved to save his soul.

Lucas, on the other hand, was frightened, and couldn't stay still. He started for the stranger.

"Please stay where you are," the stranger said.

Lucas kept going, torch held before him like a lance, and then suddenly collapsed in a heap as if he had gone to sleep in midstride. The stranger kicked the still burning torch aside.

Matthew wanted to scream his terror, but the sound wouldn't come through his stopped throat.

Two other strangers, one of them a woman, slipped behind the light holder and gave the room a thorough looking over, peering into the open cells. Away from the blinding light, they had substance, form and features. "He's not here," the woman said.

Sarah knew who she was.

"Just as well. This is a god-awful place," the light holder said. "Let's go, then."

"Cleo?" Sarah said from the shadow behind Matthew.

Cleo turned swiftly, startled, for the last thing she expected was that anyone in Monn would call her by name. "Sarah? What're you doing here, kid? Where's Reese?"

The third one, an older man who walked with a limp, studied Sarah with a deep frown line between his brows. "You know this girl?"

"This is the kid that hangs around Reese all the time. She's got to know where he is."

"I think we should get out of here," the light holder said.

The older man nodded. He addressed Matthew as if he had decided Matthew was the leader. "Your friend isn't badly hurt," he said. "He'll be a bit uncomfortable when he wakes up, but he'll be all right. We are looking for our kinsman, Reese—"

"He's not your kinsman," Sarah blurted.

"You know him? Do you know where he is?"

Matthew could only shake his head.

"The kid knows something."

"Somebody coming," another accented voice called down the stairs.

"We don't want to get caught in here."

"Can we take her along?"

The light bearer handed his equipment to the woman and caught Sarah's wrist. Sarah screeched and pulled back, yanking him forward. "I don't know, Zeke. Maybe this isn't one of your better ideas. Can you give me a hand?"

With Sarah struggling between them, they backed carefully up the stairs as if they expected Matthew and Ryan to launch an attack at any moment. The woman followed, keeping the strange device pointed toward the doorway. And then they were gone.

Sounds came down the stairway, and a voice Matthew thought he recognized, then silence.

Matthew's pounding heart, breaking, finally drove reluctant muscles into motion.

He found Beth and Mavis lying in the hall near the head of the stairs. He couldn't speak, couldn't say her name. He dropped to his knees beside her and gathered his wife's still form into his arms, rocking back and forth. Tears streamed down unnoticed in his anguish.

In the distance, Sarah's cries rose to a scream.

A long time seemed to pass, filled with a cold numbness that let Matthew's breath keep flowing and his blood keep pumping, when all the reasons for that seemed no longer to exist. Eventually, the tears dried, his capacity for them exhausted. But the ice in his gut felt as if it would outlast eternity.

He noticed a flutter of movement in his arms, then a murmured protest of pain.

"Beth?"

"I think so." Her voice was thin and trembling. Her eyes opened. She stirred weakly. There was a small noise behind them, and Matthew turned to see Lucas staggering toward them on Ryan's arm, supporting himself against the wall.

Mavis twitched and groaned.

"I feel like I've been run over by a herd of cattle," Beth said.

"Can you move?"

"Soon. What happened?"

"So help me God, I don't know. Those people . . ."

"Goddamned Philes," Ryan said. His face was as white as the moon's.

"They didn't look like demons to me, just like ordinary people."

"Matthew, what ordinary people could do this?" Beth asked.

"I don't know."

"Let's get the hell out of here," Ryan said. "We can argue about it when we're someplace safe."

They staggered down the passage, Ryan half carrying Mavis, Beth leaning on Matthew's shoulder, and Lucas following with one hand on the wall. In the entry, they passed a bewildered, moaning Brother on his knees with his head hanging; he took no notice of their passing.

Out in the moon-washed night, walking down Church Road toward the river and what they were imagining was a safe place, Matthew wondered, but didn't say, If Ryan is right, if those people were Philes, if demon Philes can march into the Temple any time they feel like it, where is safe?

What place on earth is safe?

"Where's Sarah?" Beth asked.

Matthew shook his head. He had no idea what had become of her nor any notion of how he was going to find out.

Nightmares experienced with wide open eyes were the worst kind. Asked to accompany them, Sarah might have been able to overcome her fear of Philes in groups. Caught as she was, trapped between a pair of them, she was terrified. She screamed and struggled with the men who held her prisoner, dragging her along. But they didn't let her go. Together, they staggered down the steps outside the Temple.

Normally uninterested in the presence or absence of her fellow citizens, Sarah scanned desperately for anyone who might render assistance, but the quiet, moon-silvered landscape was devoid of any sign of life. Everyone was at the Festival.

Normally she considered the Lord God a distant possibility who existed, if at all, well outside the sphere of her life. She now prayed for her deliverance, screeching her need to the heavens.

They dragged her through the night, hell-bound.

She pleaded. They did not respond.

She begged. Their set, determined faces did not change. Only the man who limped showed even the slightest sympathy, and all he did was tell her that they weren't going to hurt her. She didn't believe him too much. She renewed her screaming.

One of them tried to silence her with a hand over her mouth.

She bit into the flesh as hard as she was able. The man cursed roundly in his curious, soft voice and snatched his hand away.

Near the Witch Road, they stopped to rest.

The limping one, when he had his breath, smiled at Sarah. "Now, then, maybe we could talk. My name is Zeke, and it's very important that I find Reese. So maybe you could tell me where you saw him last."

Sarah spat at him.

He jumped away. "So much for the friendly approach," he said ruefully.

"Quit that, Sarah," Cleo snapped. "Don't be such a filthy little pagan. All we want is to know where Reese is. Nobody's going to hurt you."

"You are hurting me," Sarah complained, nodding toward the hand on her wrist. She tensed for the moment the grip would relax. She smiled wistfully at the man.

The fingers holding her loosened.

She yanked free, dived for the space between the men, and ran.

"Let her go," she heard the limping one say. "She knows the area. You'll never catch her. The pod's waiting. By the time she can get help, we'll be gone."

The crashing of her passage through the brush drowned out the response.

She slowed down. As she began to recognize the terrain, she headed toward a thicket in a small hollow she knew of, worked her way into it, and sat panting in the center like a vixen gone to earth, exhausted by fear and effort.

Dawn found her still there, shivering, starting at every rustle of leaves.

Fear seemed to be her constant companion of late. To her very great surprise, she was becoming used to it. When she thought about her unease about making the spell with Cat Anna, it seemed small and childish and far away. She could even think about the place under the Temple. There was no joy in it, surely, but she could think about it without panic making her mind stop.

Being dragged out of the Temple by the Philes was still hard to think about, but in truth, no great evil had yet befallen her, and when she had bitten the Phile, he had bled like any mortal man—and had felt pain, and cursed, like any mortal man.

Whatever they were, whatever magics and powers surrounded them, they were not invincible if common, untalented
trash off the street could bite one and make him bleed, and then
escape, unscathed.

She felt possessed of some new, profound insight, and it made
her feel stronger. Her fear did not go away, exactly, but it was
easier to live with, as if passing the night in the thicket had
worked a magic of its own. She knew what she was going to do
next.

The *Big Fish* bumped gently against the pier. Kneeling on the
deck, Matthew paused and looked out over the water. His mouth
pulled tight as if he were in pain. Then he went back to work.
Beth went back into the cabin and pretended that she hadn't been
watching and worrying.

Matthew was replacing a plank in *Big Fish*'s deck, working
as if it were the most urgent thing in the world. He had been
working so hard, the sweat rolling off him, that Beth had begun
to fear for him. She understood that it was his way of trying to
calm the turmoil in his mind; if he worked his muscles hard, his
brain would not work quite so hard. Still, now and then a thought
surfaced and hurt him, and he would have to pause until it passed.

There was an element of guilt, too. He thought he should be
doing something to find Sarah. To abandon her to the Philes
went against his deepest sense of what was right. But he didn't
know what to do or how to begin. That also was something new.
He always had a plan of action, no matter what the occasion.

So he labored to make the cedar board fit, sanding and planing
as if life itself depended on it.

Beth was coming out to him with a cup of sweet cider in the
hopes of persuading him to rest a moment when she saw the
slight figure coming down the pier. She touched Matthew's
shoulder and pointed.

"Sarah." Matthew dropped his tools and hugged Beth. He
smelled of cedar and turpentine. There were chips of wood in
his hair and beard. He turned and wrapped his arms around
Sarah. "Blessed spirits, I thought we'd lost you." He held her
away from him to look her over. "You don't look bewitched.
What happened?"

* * *

Sitting on the deck of the *Big Fish* between Matthew and Beth, sipping a cup of cider, Sarah recounted the events of the previous night. When she got to the part about biting the Phile, Matthew smiled in appreciation, but the smile vanished quickly, replaced by a frown. When she tried to tell him about how she felt different in the morning, he grew somber.

"I don't know what it means, girl. I'm not sure I know anything today. What happened last night—either I've got to start believing in witchlights and demons and Philes, or I've got to believe that folks can be knocked down flat without a hand laid on them and raised up again without a peep out of Gabriel's trumpet. But if demons are real, then I've been living in blind ignorance all my life. And if they're not, what happened in the Temple couldn't happen. But it did. Or I think it did. I don't know." He turned away from them to gaze out over the river with a melancholy expression. "I couldn't be more confused if the *Fish* sprouted wings and started to fly."

"I know this much," Beth said. "I'm glad you're home safe, Sarah. I wonder what happened to your witch, though."

"Witched himself away to a safe place, no doubt," Matthew said. Sarah looked at him. She thought he should be joking, but he wasn't.

"He doesn't know how to do that, I guess," Sarah said.

"All right, girl. I'll take your word for it. Nothing makes sense these days, so why should you?"

Sarah left feeling bad for Matthew. He had been badly shaken, she could see that, and wounded in some way she didn't entirely understand. It made him sound lost and vulnerable, he who had always been a solid, unshakable rock in her world, as if his spirit were shriveling up inside.

She had hoped that Matthew would help her. She saw that he could not.

She was on her own. She felt capable. Climbing the hill to Market Square, she marveled at the child she had been just a few days earlier.

Sarah couldn't get much from the gossip in the taverns and inns. There wasn't a tavernkeeper in Monn who wouldn't chase her away the instant he saw her. But there were places she could go where the news of the day passed quickly from mouth to mouth. She could listen in on chatter in the market; she could hold a Guardsman's horse while the smith fitted on a new front shoe. She could go to the shallows downstream from the main part of town, where the women sometimes brought their washing and their kids and their dogs to bathe.

By evening she had picked up the story of the witch in the governor's prison. One housewife, gratefully accepting unsolicited help with rounding up an escaped flock of geese, confided, "He used to walk by here every morning, you know. Going down to the inn for his breakfast, eh. Just like any man. You'd never suspect."

Twenty-five

Zeke stopped the pod well within the borders of the Wilderness, with a fair hike remaining to the city.

He muttered imprecations to the gods as he unloaded his gear. He wasn't happy with the thought of returning to Monn. Hiking was not something he did well anymore. His leg hurt at the thought of it. There just didn't seem to be any other way.

Shouldering his pack, he started off through the forest, following a game trail that led down toward the river. In the upper branches, birds had begun to chirp away the still silence of the Wilderness by night. Dawn was graying in the east, but the light did not yet penetrate to the forest floor.

He found his way by guess and feel until he was near the river. There the light was better, and the trail crossed a wider track used by hunters when half a dozen or so would gather up their courage and band together to seek game in the Wilderness. The track followed the river's edge and brought Zeke limping up to Mill Bridge by the time the sun was beginning to peek over the horizon.

Monn was strangely quiet as he made his way through the streets toward the house that Reese had been using. Few people were about, though he had the sense of watchful eyes peering from the shadows within the houses. There seemed to be a tension in the air. He paused for a few moments in Market Square and saw business being done briskly, without the usual gossip and banter. Soldiers were much in evidence everywhere.

Reese's house was empty and silent. The note he had left for Reese was still fixed to the door.

Inside, Zeke dug through his pack and reassembled the radio from its scattered parts. He did not intend to rely too much on the tracer around his neck. Tracers hadn't served Reese too well.

He tested his work by informing the Hunters' headquarters that he had arrived safely in the city, and by describing the oddities he had encountered, receiving in turn the admonition to be careful. A bit late with caution, he thought crossly.

Sighing over the thought of more walking, he picked up the pack and headed out into the town in search of information.

The Inn of the Honest Keeper was nearly deserted when Zeke arrived, although it was midmorning. Two rough young men dressed as teamsters were in the back of the public room loudly arguing the relative merits of horses they knew by name. They seemed to be the only customers.

Zeke chose a spot near the door and sat down wearily. His leg hurt. He had slept very little the previous night, and humping the weight of a trader's pack around wasn't helping. He was tail-dragging tired.

Cleo had been so upset about letting the little girl get away, he thought she was never going to get off his case.

"That little brat knows where Reese is, and you let her go. You blew our best chance, Zeke, damn it, and I'm never going to forgive you. Never."

Zeke had tried to explain. "I don't think she does. She said she didn't. Besides, we'd never have caught her."

But Cleo had only looked at him with total exasperation. "We didn't even try, dammit. You're not trying to tell me you believed her? For love of the nine worlds, Zeke, Sarah lies like a politician every time she opens her mouth. The only way we could have been sure of the truth was to bring her home and fill her full of Verisone."

"That wouldn't have done her much good. She doesn't know anything about drugs. She'd be so frightened, I don't know if she'd ever get over the shock."

"You know something? I don't think I care a whole lot. I want Reese home, before those—those barbarians get their bonfires started. And I'm going to do it, if it means giving every benighted Phobe in that miserable excuse for a city nightmares for the rest of their crummy lives." She had stomped out of his apartment.

"Quiet today," Zeke said amiably as the innkeeper came up to him.

"Aye, that it is," the innkeeper agreed. "And what would be your honor's pleasure?"

"A small beer and some breakfast," Zeke said, "and a word or two about where a trader might spread his wares in your fair city."

"If a man knew what you were trading, he might be able to make a suggestion," the innkeeper said, knowing that Zeke knew he was only trying to get the first look at whatever novelties might be available.

As the innkeeper went to fill his order, Zeke spread items from his pack over the table, some simple jewelry, buttons, tobacco, and a length of fine cotton lawn died a bright blue. When the man returned, Zeke invited him to sit. Agreeing, the innkeeper looked over Zeke's offerings without saying much. He looked over Zeke, too, with an intensity that bordered on rudeness.

"Is business usually so slow in Monn?" Zeke asked.

The innkeeper shook his head.

"I heard it said in Grassy Bend that Monn is having trouble with a witch. I've heard fear of sorcery is keeping folks indoors."

"Your honor ought not pay too much mind to vicious rumors. 'Tis a slow day, nothing more." The innkeeper held a small pearl on a chain in the palm of his meaty hand. "Such fine goods as these, I think Your Honor would have luck in the Governor's Mansion."

Zeke nodded his thanks. "Would you consider keeping that for your trouble, and for the cost of feeding me for the next day or so? I would consider it a bargain well struck."

The innkeeper's glance was more calculating than appreciative. "And I also, well struck." The pearl disappeared into the man's fist. "If Your Honor might be needing a bed for the night . . ."

"Thank you, I have found accommodations elsewhere."

"And where might that be, sir?" The innkeeper seemed to realize his breach of etiquette, for he hastened to add, "In case I might happen upon a customer to Your Honor's advantage."

"I am staying with a friend, who perhaps should not be disturbed with my customers."

"Of course. I beg Your Honor's pardon." The innkeeper bowed and left to attend to his business in the front of the room. Zeke packed up his goods and went out to try his luck in Market Square.

He thought, as he limped along Market Road, that unless things were different in Monn from the way they were everywhere else in the world, the innkeeper had been uncharacteristically unwilling to talk. And to ask him where he was staying was odd, bad manners from one who made his living pleasing a public that made much of each man keeping his proper place.

Something strange was afoot in Monn.

Harold watched the stranger's halting gait take him out of the inn and, hurrying after as far as the door, caught a glimpse of him going down Market Road. He hollered at his lazy daughters to come and look after business, then hustled himself out into the heat of the bright sunny morning, almost trotting up Foxhill Street toward the place where a troop of witchhunting soldiers had made their temporary headquarters.

As the proprietor of a business where strangers could be expected to show up, Harold had been among the first informed of the necessity of keeping a sharp eye on any foreigners who happened by, and of the rewards available for doing so, and the penalties for failure. He had an order with the governor's seal on it, and if he could read, it might say all that.

As far as Harold was concerned, the first words the trader spoke had identified him. If Reese was a witch, then this one was also, for he had the same soft accent Harold had heard Reese speaking for weeks, an accent that Harold, an expert in the queer speech of foreigners, had heard nowhere else before.

He didn't really need the confirming glimpse of the unusual, featureless metal medallion hanging on a thong around the trader's neck.

If he had no great belief in devil worshippers and covens and Old Nick in person stomping along the streets of Monn in a cloud of sulfurous smoke, he was sure the trader would be identified by someone in short order, and since someone was going to reap the benefits of doing that, Harold thought it might as well be him.

He had given brief consideration to delaying his report awhile, until he could find out where the stranger was staying. If the samples the man had spread on the table were any indication, the contents of his pack were worth a fair piece of change. Harold didn't see any reason that some dense brick of a soldier should have it. But a bird in hand was worth any number flying free. He decided to stick with what he had for certain.

At the perimeter of the camp, Harold asked to see the head man. The sentry was going to tell him to be on his way until Harold said he had information regarding the witches. Then he was shown into a small tent and told to wait. A sergeant of the Governor's Guard arrived in short order.

The trader was a total stranger. He had nothing owed him. With almost no qualms of conscience, Harold said solemnly to the sergeant, "I have found one of them. A man with a limp. He was heading up toward Market Square."

In the square, Zeke sat on the top of a low stone wall to rest his leg. It was getting close to noon. Most of the farmers were packing up to return to their farms, and the housewives were heading back to their kitchens with the morning's purchases. There was a sullen urgency about their activities, as if everyone was in a rush to get the day's business done.

A young boy with a long stick and half a dozen skinny goats came up to Zeke. The boy plunked himself down on the wall and the goats milled around trying to find something to eat in the dry vegetation sticking up around the wall.

"Hey," the boy said.

"Hey, yourself," Zeke answered.

"You're a stranger here, right?"

"Yes, I just came this morning."

"Picked a bad time."

"It seems so. What's the matter with everyone in this city?"

"Ah, they're all right most of the time, I guess. It's just right now, they're all scared of the witches."

One hungry goat started nibbling on Zeke's pant leg. The boy whacked its nose with the stick, and the animal moved off, bleating in protest.

Zeke took a few coins from his pocket and held them out. "If you know who sells beer around here, I'm buying."

The boy was meticulous about picking out two small coins. "I'll be right back." He handed Zeke his stick. "You kind of keep an eye on the goats, will you?"

The goats pushed their noses right against the stones in their search for food. The whacked one looked up, shook its head until its drooping ears rattled, and regarded Zeke with a sour saffron eye.

When the boy returned, Zeke handed back the stick and took a long appreciative pull on the mug. "What's going on with witches?"

"Well, the way I hear it, the religious guys over at the Temple caught one of 'em and there's supposed to be a bunch more running loose in the city somewhere. So the governor's got the army going through everybody's house looking for 'em, though how they're going to tell they found 'em beats me. It's not like they'd be answering the door with a black cat draped over their shoulder, eh?"

"I suppose not," Zeke said. "Still, if they managed to catch one . . ."

"So they say."

"You're not convinced?"

"They got this guy over in the governor's jail, and they say he's a witch. These are big, powerful folk who're supposed to know everything. I'm just a kid with some goats. What do I know?"

"You don't seem to be afraid of witches."

"Well, the way I figure it, if you're religious, the Lord God will take care of you, with or without witches, and if you're not, you're going to hell anyway. Me, I got no place to go but up. I figure hell is a place full of stinking damned goats, only in hell it's them with the sticks."

"You've got a good many opinions for a kid with some goats."

"Yeah, I guess. Everybody tells me to shut up. I guess I should some time."

"You know, I don't think I've ever even seen a witch. Do you suppose if a fellow went up to the governor's jail, he could get a look?"

The boy shook his head. "The way I figure it, everybody being all excited the way they are, a stranger like you so much as says 'witch,' he's liable to end up in there with him."

"You could be right."

"Everybody's scared to do anything or say anything for fear someone else takes it for witchcraft."

"Yes, I understand. I've seen it in other towns."

"Yeah?"

"It might be witches or gargoyles or enemy spies, but the hysteria works the same way," Zeke said.

"I think right there I don't know what you're talking about. Anyway, thanks for the beer. I got to get these Godforsaken goats somewhere where they can find something to eat. The mugs go back to the Crow's Eye, over there, if you would."

Zeke waved his acceptance, and the boy and his charges took off up the street and were gone from sight. Zeke picked up his pack and the mugs and wondered how he was going to get a look in the governor's jail.

He was only moments gone when a squad of soldiers trooped into the square and struck panic into the hearts of the few remaining shoppers and merchants. It was some time before anyone calmed down enough to report that he thought he had seen a man with a limp and a peddler's pack all right, but he hadn't noticed where the man had gone.

When Zeke got back to Reese's house, it was deep afternoon. He reported to the Treasure Hunters that he thought Reese was in the governor's jail and was trying to confirm the information.

He was tired. His trip around town in his guise as peddler had netted him nothing in the way of new information. People had been unusually close-mouthed. His careful approaches to the subject of witches had been turned aside. Housewives slammed their doors in his face.

He groaned a little to himself and wished that he were young and sound again, and that the citizens of Monn hadn't found it necessary to scatter themselves across six times as much territory as they needed.

He slept through the hottest hours of the day, lying down with some misgivings on Reese's straw bed. But if the straw was as buggy as he suspected, the bugs didn't bother him too much. It was late when he woke, so he had to hurry to get his job done before dark.

The term "Governor's Mansion" designated two things: the Mansion proper, and also all the buildings, lands, and holdings that were the property of the governor by virtue of his office. The latter were exceptionally extensive for the times, and Zeke walked a long time through fields and gardens and horse pastures and wood lots before reaching from the back, uphill side the huddle of buildings crowded together as if in anticipation of imminent attack.

He rested in a patch of woods with his back against the bole of a tree while he rubbed his leg and looked the buildings over. Some he could identify from their similarity to Phobish-built barns or summer kitchens in other locations. Others were anonymous, square, stone, thatched-roof structures which could have any, or no, purpose.

A little to his left was a high palisade that seemed most likely to contain the prison. He worked his way among the trees in that direction, cautious about noise.

In the trees, in the shadows of the westering sun, Zeke was well hidden and could make out the archers, still in sunlight, prowling the top, only their heads and shoulders showing above the pointed poles. But from where he stood at the edge of the woods he couldn't see into the yard. The trees had been cut back around the fence. The stakes of the palisade were a good eight feet high and planted one against the other in a solid wall.

Zeke looked around for a vantage point, but could find nothing but trees. One old poplar towered up, having escaped the woodsman's axe much longer than its fellows. Zeke regarded it doubtfully. He didn't feel much like climbing trees at his age.

But the shadows were rapidly growing longer. If he didn't get a look in there soon, he would have to spend another day in Monn.

Sighing, he manhandled a big rock to the base of the poplar and found that by balancing himself unsteadily on its top, he could reach the lower branches. Grunting unhappily, he hauled himself up into the tree.

Monnish sandals were not the best footwear he could have had for the job. His balance felt precarious. He tried to match his movements to the times the guards were looking elsewhere lest the shaking branches betray him, but it was hard to watch his handholds and keep an eye on the archers. It seemed to take forever to get high enough to see down into the yard.

Apparently, the warders were rounding up their charges for the night. There were about two dozen prisoners, but among them was one man who stood half a head taller than the others. It could be Reese. Zeke pushed a branch aside to get a better look through the leaves.

The branch he was holding with his other hand broke. Unbalanced, Zeke slid a foot or so down the trunk, scrabbling for a grip on it, saved from a fall only by the limb his leg was wrapped around.

Almost at once, an arrow smacked into the trunk about an inch above his trembling fingers.

Sparing a quick glance toward the compound, he could see the archer reaching for another shaft. Thinking he had a few seconds, he started scrambling down the tree.

Zeke had no way of knowing how fast a good bowman could get his shafts away. The second arrow caught him in the thigh of his bad leg. Shock and impact combined loosened his hold. He fell, flailing, through the branches. He crashed down into the undergrowth, missing his rock by a hairsbreadth.

He lay stunned for a moment, listening to voices shouting in the distance, only slowly realizing their significance.

He struggled to his feet. Nothing felt broken, but when he put his weight on the wounded leg, pain seared up and down through the damaged muscles. Dragging the leg, he pulled himself through the trees, trying to keep on a northwest line, trying to remember how far, on the maps of Monn, the woods extended.

After a hundred yards up the slope of the hill, his strength was exhausted. The shaft of the arrow caught on every vine and small branch, stabbing him anew with each snag. Blood had plastered his pant leg to his skin. He slid down the far side of the hill into a shallow gully and stopped to listen for sounds of pursuit. He heard nothing but his own ragged breathing.

He paused then to trigger the alarm on his tracer and to take the arrow shaft between his two hands and break it off as short as he could, teeth clenched against the jerk that was inevitable when it snapped. Then, gathering his reserves, he began his crawl up the other side of the gully.

The trees were starting to thin out when he stopped to rest again. A long stretch of open ground lay ahead of him. The sky was beginning to get dark. He wondered if he dared to wait for the light to die before attempting to traverse the meadow, but a faint sound of dogs behind put an end to that thought.

Getting to his feet, he clamped his hand tightly around his leg above the arrow and began hobbling through the dry, yellow grass. Ahead, he could see the headlight of the pod waiting on the track at the point nearest the signal from his tracer. It was so close, and yet it seemed miles away. The dogs were closing fast. He could hear them plainly. Sparing a glance backward, he could see torches among the trees.

As he climbed painfully through the scrub up the slope toward the pod track, the first horsemen broke clear of the trees and urged their mounts into a gallop. The dogs were almost at his heels. Frantically, he hitched himself across the smooth surface toward the open door of the pod. He could hear the men shouting to one another.

On the slope below, the leading bowman yanked his horse to a halt. A witch wagon was stopped on the Witch Road, and his quarry seemed to be making for it. The dogs were milling about at the edge of the road, yipping and whining with their noses down to the smooth stuff, trying to get their courage up, conscious that they were failing in their task.

The archer didn't imagine that he knew what was going on there. He had no time to think about it. He only sensed that the man was escaping.

The horse danced nervously, the light was bad, the range extreme, but his target was clearly outlined against the light from the open door of the witch wagon. And the archer's skill was legendary among his fellows.

He took careful aim and let his arrow fly.

The man was climbing into the witch wagon when the arrow hit. The impact knocked him in. The door closed, and the witch wagon took off, speeding toward the Wilderness.

The bowman's companion rode up to join him. "You got him."

The archer nodded his head. "He took a good one. He's a dead man."

"Ron," the companion said, a frown developing as he stared at the empty Witch Road. "You think the witch wagon was waiting for him? You think maybe you killed a witch?"

"Don't know," Ron said, unhappy now that he had time to think about what he had just done. "Kind of looks like it."

"What're you going to do now? They'll come for you, you know. The witches'll want their revenge, eh?"

"What 'eh'? What? You some kind of expert on witch lore? What'd'y want? Why'n hell don't you just shut up?"

Twenty-six

The wide, high collection of dials and indicators and readouts that were intended to monitor the health of the power reactor covered three walls of the hexagonal control room. They were silent, dark, and dead, like the reactor. On a fourth wall, a full-sized display showed a monochrome robot's-eye view of the reactor core. The remaining two walls were Xstalite, the toughest transparent material known. Its value there was mainly psychological.

In the observation space beyond the transparent walls, the chairman had appeared to express his concern and hopes for speedy repairs. Arne had come, too, to check on the progress of the work and to call Cleo out briefly and invite her to a performance of a dance troupe from the West American Enclave. They had a way to go, he said, before they could match the skills one could see on the Old People's records, but they weren't bad.

Cleo was supposed to be supervising the technician who was guiding the robot in an effort to recover a broken fuel element. But the technician was good at his job. He didn't need her help. She sat in the chair beside the elaborate computer console that occupied the center of the room. Her mind wandered.

She had told Zeke she was going to get Reese out of Monn, no matter what it took. She had meant it at the time. But when it came down to cases, she didn't know how she was going to do that. Sarah had been their best chance, she was certain of it, and that chance had been lost. Starting from nothing, she had no better chance of finding Sarah again than she had of finding

Reese. Less, probably. At least she knew something about Reese and his habits, where he was likely to go and what he was likely to do. Sarah lived like a clever mouse in the dim, hidden passages of other people's lives. She could pop up anywhere, or vanish indefinitely into a city she knew intimately. Cleo wouldn't find Sarah unless Sarah wanted to be found.

She was furious with Zeke for having let the girl go. But it was sterile fury. There was nothing either of them could do about it now.

"There it is," the technician said. The damaged element showed plainly on the screen, a tall narrow cylinder bent sharply out of line amid a forest of perfectly straight parallel tubes.

"Can you get it?" Cleo asked.

"No problem," the technician said.

The terminal on the console *ping*ed to get her attention. She hesitated, then answered it.

The message was from Irene. A voice from the blank screen said, "Cleo, could you come to the office, please? As soon as possible?" And that was all. Cryptic, to say the least.

The robot slowly and gently lifted the broken fuel rod out of the rack and began trundling it off the hot storage bay. The trickiest part of the job was over. The reactor should be functional again in a few hours. Cleo gave the technician her acknowledgment of his skill and went to answer Irene's summons.

A pod had been lifted off the track in front of the administration building, and two service robots were at work on it. Cleo glanced inside as she passed, but couldn't see anything obviously wrong with it except for the dark stain on the floor.

A number of people had gathered in the Treasure Hunters' office, sitting at the cluttered table or leaning against the walls. Some Cleo knew: Irene; Ian, with his bandaged hand; Gene, another member of the erstwhile rescue team; a councilor whose name Cleo vaguely associated with an attempt to oust the chairman from office. Others she had not seen before, but several of them, dressed in a variety of peculiar clothing, had the air of Hunters called in from the field for some special purpose.

"What's going on?" she demanded.

Everyone was tense and grim.

"Sit down, Cleo," Irene said. "I thought you should be in on this."

"What's going on?" Cleo asked again, certain she didn't want to hear the answer.

"Zeke's dead," Irene said.

Cleo could only stare at her.

"He was killed," the head of the Treasure Hunters continued. "In Monn."

"Oh, no." Shock made Cleo's mind slow. "But he isn't in Monn," she said stupidly. "He's here. With us. He came home with us. It doesn't make sense. You're not making sense."

Gene tried to comfort her with a hand on her arm. She jerked away. "He went back, Cleo," Ian said. "He picked up some equipment and went back. He thought he knew where he could find a lead or two."

"When?" Cleo asked, still not quite believing.

"Late last night, early this morning, something like that."

After I yelled at him, Cleo thought. After I accused him of spoiling our only chance. Damn it, Zeke, I didn't mean you should do that. Zeke, I didn't mean it. No noble sacrifices, you said. Blast you for a stubborn old fool. Why didn't you listen to yourself?

"Here," Ian said, guiding her into the chair he had just vacated.

She sank into it as if a weight were pushing her down. "It's my fault."

"It's no such thing," Irene said sharply. "The Phobes did it." She got up from her chair and paced a small circle at the end of the table. "We got the alarm, and the emergency pod went out within seconds. It came back with Zeke's body inside before a rescue team could get away. How he managed to get into the pod in the shape he was in, we'll never know, but he was dead by the time it got here. He had two arrows in him. The Phobes murdered him."

The words fell like stones in the silence of the room. No one said much of anything for a long time. Irene sat down again and ruffled the papers in front of her. Gazes were fixed on the table-top or the floor. Cleo felt a cold hand clutch her diaphragm. She struggled to get her question out.

"Reese?"

"Shortly after noon, Zeke reported in by radio. He said he thought Reese was being held in the governor's prison. He said he was going to try to confirm. That was the last message."

"What are we going to do?"

"That's what we're here to discuss."

"Get him out of there, Irene. Whatever it takes, get Reese out of there."

"Sounds good to me," Ian said. He was pounding the table softly with his uninjured hand.

"Maybe we should hear what the council has to say," Irene suggested. Given her well-known impatience with political processes, that was a considerable concession from her. It might have been a measure of the guilt she felt for having helped persuade Zeke to do something he really hadn't wanted to do. Her confidence was shaken.

Councilor Teal stood up and waited until he was sure of everyone's attention. He was dressed in a one-piece garment that was rumored to be the latest fashion derived from the costumes in an Old People's record and cut from the wonderfully shiny fabric some wag had labeled "polystar." It highlighted the bumps and lumps of an out-of-shape body to marvelous disadvantage.

"I am convinced, and I feel certain many councilors would agree, that we have been making a serious error in attempting to accomplish our goals in the Phobe communities by deception and camouflage. That policy, set by a previous council, has already cost a life and is threatening another. It's time the policy was changed. If it means disturbing the Phobes, then let us disturb them.

"A man is dead. The kid gloves are off. The pussyfooting around is finished. Let us finally, tutored by this tragic incident, approach this project in the spirit of practical efficency.

"The first order of business is, of course, to effect the rescue of our Hunter. I suggest we do this by whatever means presents itself as safe and effective." He sat down, erect, confident of his argument.

A Hunter shifted himself off the wall he was leaning on. "Excuse me, Councilor, but should we take you to mean that we ought to go into Monn with guns and heavy equipment?"

"If that's what's needed, I guess I am."

"Considering there's a lot of them and damned few of us, I can only see two possibilities. Persuasion, deception as you're pleased to call it, which has already lost us a man, and force, which is likely to be safe enough for us, but maybe pretty messy for them, and gives no guarantee we can get Reese out alive."

"They weren't overly concerned for the safety of Zeke," the councilor said. "Is Reese safe where he is?"

Gene said. "If my vote counts for anything, I favor the direct approach."

"Councilor, should we take it that your statement is official council policy?" Ian asked. "Does the chairman agree with you?"

Teal spread his hands. "I don't pretend to speak for the chairman," he said.

"Cleo?" Irene asked.

"I want Reese home."

"We may find ourselves at war," Irene said. "I am not altogether certain we could win that war."

"Against spears and arrows?" Gene asked. "Why not?"

"What choice have we got?" Cleo said.

Councilor Teal folded his hands and tried to look benign. "To simply abandon one of our own is an unsavory prospect."

"No," Cleo said, much too loud. The Hunters around the table and against the wall shifted uneasily.

"That's out of the question," Irene said. "As long as I head the Treasure Hunters, no one is going to get abandoned, whatever the consequences."

She stood up again and addressed the meeting as a whole. "You've heard what data we have. Now we have to decide what we are going to do. Let me add this so that it is crystal clear: I will categorically veto any suggestion that someone follow in Zeke's footsteps. I will have no more lone heroes and no more corpses. I will also veto any scheme which involves leaving Reese in the hands of the Phobes. Beyond that, I'm open to suggestion. I think we should come to our conclusions quickly. We cannot assume Reese has a great deal of time.''

''Also,'' Gene added, ''without the chairman's order, we can't assume Supply and Services will allow us any energy.''

''The chairman isn't the whole council,'' Teal said.

''Forget it, Teal,'' Irene answered. ''Internecine squabbles among members of the council is something we really don't have time for.''

The summons from the chairman came before the meeting disbanded, and Irene was afraid that the internecine squabbles she had no time for were going to be dropped in her lap. She resented the intrusion into her efforts to come to a decision. But as far as she knew, nobody had ever told the chairman, ''Sorry, I'm busy today.'' It just wasn't done.

The council chambers and the councilors' offices were on the top floor of the administration building, occupying about half the space. Greenhouses occupied the other half. Irene was directed to the chairman's office, a room that shared a glass wall with the greenhouse. Cleo trailed along behind, determined not to be left out of anything that was likely to affect Reese's rescue.

Something of the earthy scent of green growing things pervaded the office, and the light had a greenish tint. Beyond the glass, shadows of robot gardeners moved. The room was not large, but it was well appointed. In frames around the walls were the original architect's drawings of the Mid-American Enclave as it was first designed. Tall windows on the east looked out over the park.

The chairman rose from his seat before a large monitor screen. He was of less-than-average height, but had a hard leanness about him that belied his gray hair. He wore his years and the power of his office extremely well. He might have looked good in Teal's getup, but he wore a wide-sleeved, softly draped shirt of subdued colors and dark trousers.

"Thank you for coming," he said warmly. Cleo caught herself feeling included in spite of being an uninvited participant in the meeting. She felt flattered.

That was the wrong feeling. She knew that Irene was not happy about the summons and had come up from her sixth-floor office full of misgivings. Irene was sure she knew what the chairman was going to say.

She had explained the situation to Cleo. The council was divided. The chairman and a bare majority of members formed one faction. The opposing group were not averse to using the death of one man and the mortal danger of another as a strong argument against the Hunt and against the members of council who supported it, especially since so far the Treasure Hunt had produced no tangible results.

The chairman was fighting to hold on to his position. The loss of a vote or two in the council could put him out of office.

One way he might pull his opponents' teeth would be to stop the Hunt himself. He had the Hunters' request for an energy allotment. It would be easy enough for him to say no.

The chairman echoed Cleo's thoughts. "It would be politically expedient," he said when they were settled about a small, low table and had been served coffee from an insulated carafe by the chairman's own hand, "to order the recall of your Hunters and an end to the Treasure Hunt."

"But, Chairman," Irene started to protest. He held her with a gesture.

"Irene, I know you do not have an overly flattering opinion of politicians, so I expect you to be at least mildly surprised when I tell you I think we are going to have to set political expedience aside in favor of physical survival. In spite of recent events, I shall, with as many councilors as I can persuade to support me, press for the continuation of the Hunt."

"I'm more than surprised," Irene said. She leaned back, relaxing a little. "I was expecting you to tell me to call it off."

"Why?" Cleo asked abruptly.

"Sorry?" the chairman asked.

"If it is, as you said, politically expedient to stop the Hunt, why are you willing to risk continuing?"

The chairman's eyebrows rose a little. "A shrewd question. You are suspicious of my motives. No matter. I don't mind explaining. We are very vulnerable as matters stand. We do not even have the energy to activate the perimeter defense system for very long. When we can no longer maintain it, we will be overwhelmed like a picnic before a horde of starving ants. If the Phobes overrun the enclave, we'll be starving with them, at least the survivors will, and nobody will be the least bit better off. I believe the Hunt to be our best chance to improve the energy picture in the short term."

"Whatever the reason," Cleo said. "So long as we do something."

The chairman looked away from his guests for a moment and smiled a little. "However," he said, "there's no need to be suicidal about it.

"When Teal addressed your meeting, I doubt he intended to do me any favors. You are surprised I know that? I have, fortunately, friends in many places. I believe his support of direct action is undoubtedly intended to promote dissension among the majority of councilors who support the Hunt, but many of whom would not support physical violence. However, for once I find us in agreement. To maintain the credibility of the Hunt as well as for simple humanitarian reasons, we must get Reese out of Monn. Quickly, cleanly, and alive.

"But I think there is another, possibly more important, reason for acting quickly and decisively. Our ability to function surrounded by Phobes depends largely on the Phobes remaining afraid of us. If they discover that Philes live and die like ordinary men, much of that fear will dissipate."

"Zeke's dead. They killed him," Irene reminded him.

"And we dare not let that event go unmarked. And we dare not allow them to repeat it. We must recover Reese."

"How?" Cleo asked. "We can't even find him."

The chairman didn't answer directly. Instead, he leaned back and considered the view of the park through the windows to his left. The small smile returned.

"Before I became so involved in the administration of the

enclave, history was my study, particularly the events leading to the Separation. It struck me as peculiar that the people who eventually became known as the technophiles failed to use the knowledge and power they possessed in their own defense. Knowledge is power, make no mistake about it. But the Old People's society was able to keep technophiles isolated from one another, in competition with one another. So, although in theory they had it within their hands to exercise total control over their world—a technological society is extremely dependent on technologists—they wasted their efforts battling their society and each other for resources made artificially scarce by those who directed them.

"Another thing. During the Bush Wars, one characteristic of warfare became plain. The battles which were protracted and devastating and murderous were those between combatants of nearly equal strength. When one force was vastly superior to the other, resistance was minimal, victory, swift and unbloody.

"I believe that if we drop on Monn in strength and with all possible speed, with as much of a dazzling display of power as we are able to produce without becoming homicidal, we should be able to take over the upper levels of government and use their own internal organization to accomplish our goal.

"I realize we do not possess much in the way of instruments of war. However, we do have machinery which could be pressed into service."

"What are we waiting for?" Cleo asked.

Irene shook her head. "It sounds fine in theory. I'm not so sure it would work all that well in practice. I wouldn't hope to guess how the Monnishmen would react. Our expert in Monnish affairs is being held prisoner in Monn. It looks like we don't know as much about them as we thought we did."

"You did ask for suggestions." The chairman straightened, leaned his elbows on the table, and folded his hands. "I'll tell you what I have planned. I would welcome your criticism. I realize my knowledge of such matters is entirely theoretical." His smiled broadened and took on an edge of bitterness. "I will ask you to keep our plans to yourself, if you would, until the next scheduled meeting of council. I would not like to see an extraordinary session called that would have me out of office before this bit of business is accomplished.'' He reached over and activated the screen. ''Afterward, I suppose it is inevitable.''

Twenty-seven

Getting into the Governor's Mansion would be no problem. She was already expected there. But it meant returning to the Temple, and that took all Sarah's newfound courage.

A hush pervaded the dim, cool hallways. The usual bustle of the place was quenched almost to nonexistence. Rows of Brothers and Sisters were on their knees on the hard stone floor of the chapel, praying for their deliverance, asking the Lord God to take the witches from among them and promising to renew their vigilance against the forces of evil.

Brother Parker was prostrate before the Cross of God at the front of the chapel when Sarah slipped unnoticed into the back. "Forgive me, O Lord," he cried. "I have neglected your works for the pleasures of the flesh."

"Forgive me, O Lord," the Brother and Sisters answered like a wind rising among dead trees.

Silently, Brother Eric moved among the penitents with a short birch rod which he laid smartly across the shoulders of any who looked insufficiently pious. It was he who noticed the intrusion of the pagan girl into that most private and holy place.

He hustled among the kneeling faithful to shoo her out and into the gray, spare room where they first met.

They sat on opposite sides of the table, Brother Eric with the birch between his hands, Sarah nervously doubting her ability to go through with her plan, and the clean-cut iron bar that had once secured the Temple's front door lying on the table between them.

He questioned her closely about the events of the previous night, and Sarah answered as near to the truth as she dared. She told him about the arrival of the three men dressed as Brothers, neglecting to mention that she knew them; told him about the fruitless search for the witch, trying to leave the impression that she was an unwilling participant; told him about the coming of the Philes, about being dragged out into the night, and about her escape from them, which came across in the telling just a little more dramatic than it had been in life.

He listened carefully and asked sharp questions which kept Sarah on her mettle. When she mentioned the Philes, he picked it up immediately.

"Why do you say Philes, girl? Would not some lesser evil serve your tale?"

Sarah debated between indignation and guile and settled on flashing Brother Eric her best smile. "I don't know much about this weirdly stuff," she said modestly. "The way I figured, anyone who could work such a sorcery that could lay a man out like he was dead without even a witchly gesture or magic word, who could get into the actual Temple itself, anyone like that would have to be a Phile to have such power."

Brother Eric was not susceptible to smiles. His cold, still demeanor softened not at all. "It is an odd story, my dear. Are you completely sure you have it right? You wouldn't like to retire and think it over, as you did the other day?"

Sarah didn't have to feign terror. The thought of that cramped space in the cellar did it for her. Then Brother Parker arrived looking tired and ill at ease, and she had to go through it all over again. She didn't doubt for a second that Eric was listening carefully to see if she deviated from her first account.

"How many?" Brother Parker asked, agitated.

"Huh?" Sarah said.

"The witches who dared defile the Lord God's holy place, how many were they?"

"Three, I guess."

"Don't guess, child. Know."

"Three. Two men and a woman. No, five. There were two upstairs."

"You're sure?"

Sarah nodded.

Brother Parker rubbed his face. "They will try to assemble a coven, I'm sure of it. Now, with this evidence, the governor must listen to reason. We must destroy the one we have to give ourselves time to hunt down the others." He put his soft, clammy hand over Sarah's and patted. Sarah had to fight herself to keep from pulling away. "It is good you came back, girl. The Lord God will reward you. Do you remember what you are to tell the governor's adviser?"

Sarah nodded again.

"Come then, we will go at once."

A weight lifted from Sarah's shoulders. For a while there, she had thought that Brother Eric had forgotten all about going to the Mansion with her tale of witchcraft. She turned to follow Brother Parker's determined gait.

A hard, bony hand gripped her shoulder with bruising intensity. "Why did you come back?" Brother Eric asked.

She tried to meet his icy eyes, but had to look away. " 'Cause I'm more scared of Philes than I am of you," she lied.

Thomas, the governor's adviser, was a nice man, with a gentle way about him. Sarah liked him at once. He received them in a small ground-floor room of the Mansion that was cozy with tapestries and Kolloan dyed draperies. He poured them wine from a decanter on the sideboard into elegant, long-stemmed glasses where it glowed like liquid ruby, including Sarah in this small ceremony, sat them down in chairs of carved wood, and listened quietly as Sarah recited the things Brother Parker had told her to say.

Near the end of her recitation the governor himself came in, resplendent in his silver-worked robes of office with the jeweled chain of the city about his shoulders. She faltered then and had to be prompted.

When her recitation was through, Thomas introduced her, and the governor smiled at her. He looked so young to be governor, like a magic prince in a storyteller's tale.

"I know you," he said. "You're the girl with the bold eyes in the marketplace. I'm very pleased to meet you at last, Sarah."

"M'lord, perhaps we should attend to the business at hand," Brother Parker suggested.

The governor made a small face of reluctance to Sarah, then turned to his duty. She paid little attention to the discussion that ensued among the men. She watched the governor, intrigued by the way his long-fingered hands moved when he spoke, almost as expressive as his words.

A charming prince should be more robust, she thought, yet there was an elegance about this man. There was something utterly remarkable about sitting in the same room with Michael Windsor LaRoche, governor of Monn.

She almost forgot what had prompted her to get into this incredible situation in the first place, almost missed her chance when a fit of coughing took the governor and the men became busy with getting him wine and shawls and patting his back.

She slipped quietly out of the room. The Guardsman at the door was charged with monitoring who went into the room. He didn't much care who went out. Sarah smiled up at him and he smiled back. People smiled a lot in the Governor's Mansion. It seemed a pleasant place. For a moment, Sarah even considered returning the wine glass she had slipped under her blouse and which rode, cold and smooth, above her belt against the skin of her belly. But she thought better of it. A piece of fine glass like that didn't come her way every day.

She walked across the yard toward the stable as if she belonged there, and people went on with their work. Inside the barn, she chose her moment and swarmed up the ladder nailed to the wall into the sun-hot, dusty loft and lay down on the hay to wait out the rest of the day.

The young soldier at the prison gate sighed and wondered how he could get himself transferred to the Governor's Guard. The Governor's Guard didn't stand watch over prisons or take any of that kind of boring duty.

There wasn't even anyone to talk to. The prisoners were locked away for the night. The warders stayed inside the compound. The archers on the catwalks got to go to bed when darkness made their skills useless. But he got to stand in front of the stupid gate. What good he was doing there was beyond his ability to understand.

The early morning watch was the worst, and he was assigned

to it more often than chance would allow. The sergeant had it in for him. There was no reason for that. It was just the way things were.

He leaned against the gate post and wished the hours away. He looked hopefully toward the east. No sign of dawn had appeared. He yawned grossly and rubbed his neck. He shifted his weight to his other foot and scratched his belly. In all the cold predawn mornings he had put in standing in front of the freaking gate, not one event of note had ever occurred.

"Hey."

The greeting came out of the shadows where he could see no one. He straightened and peered into the darkness, one hand on the hilt of his sword, but not much alarmed because the voice had been soft and feminine, and there was the distinct possibility that he had imagined it, a pleasant fantasy to wile away the night.

"Who's there?" he demanded, thinking he was going to feel like a total ass if he was talking to his own imagination.

"It's just me," the girl said, moving from the shadow of the hedge that prevented the sight of the prison from offending the eyes of the important people in the Governor's Mansion.

"Who're you?"

"Nobody."

"What're you doing here?"

"Nothing. I couldn't sleep. I didn't think anyone would be here."

"All alone?"

"Umhum. It's bad of me, isn't it?"

"Damned foolish. Anything could happen."

"Well, you're here." She had come close, and he could see the moonlight on elfin features and a pleasant smile. She was no great lady, that much was obvious, but she was a good-looking girl nonetheless. Her blouse was thin cotton, and he guessed that there was nothing underneath it. The skirt was scandalously short, and the legs and feet were bare. "You'll keep the demons away, won't you? A big soldier should be all the protection a girl needs."

The soldier grunted and leaned back against the gatepost. "If I was your man and found you wandering around at night, half-dressed like that, I'd beat you black and put a damned big lock on the door.''

"The thing is, I don't have a man. Not really." She lowered her eyes demurely. "It's hard, you know. The nights are long when you're alone." She looked up again in a second, her smile grown wistful. "How long do you have to stay here?"

"Until dawn," he answered, not knowing why he did.

"That's a long time."

"Damned right."

"But if you didn't stay that long, would they beat you?"

"That would be the smallest part of it, my dear," the soldier said with a trace of bitterness.

She was right beside him now, leaning against the fence as he was, smiling up at him. He didn't have too much doubt about what she was up to, but he did wonder why. He was not a man noted for being irresistibly attractive to women.

On the other hand, his luck was due for a change. He fingered the little leather bag at his throat. He had bought it just a few days ago, from an aged hag who lived in a cat-infested cave up at the top of the hill and who swore it would improve his love life no end. He hadn't really believed it at the time; he just felt a bit sorry for a hungry old woman. He had taken a certain amount of ribbing about it in the barracks. And the truth was, he had parted with the coins not too reluctantly. He might not believe that much in charms, but it couldn't hurt.

"Of course," the girl said, "if you went away and came back, no one would ever know, would they?"

He put his hand to her chest and let it slide down over the rise of her breast. "Just what did you have in mind?" he asked.

She caught his hand and held it against her. "I'll show you," she said. Holding him, she started to move away.

He shook his head and retrieved his hand. "Come back in a couple of hours," he said.

"I can't."

He took a deep breath and blew it out as if to cool his warming blood. It didn't work. She crooked a finger at him, smiled, and started away.

He had a long time to put in. He was bored and lonely. He went after her. She was right—nobody would ever know.

This is the craziest thing I've ever done, he thought as he followed.

She led him a short distance from the prison compound to a small empty building standing open. She vanished into the nearly impenetrable darkness within. The place had a dusty, musty smell, as if it had been used to store grain.

She pulled the door almost closed until there was just a thin strip of moonlight showing.

Her small hands moved over him, assisting by feel with the straps and buckles and ties of the uniform. His sword belt crashed to the floor with a fine disregard for proper care and concern. When he tried to return the favor, she giggled and slipped away. "You first," she insisted. Her small finger dug into his navel for a moment, then her hands moved around to his hips, attempting to slide his pants down over his buttocks. He released the belt and let her do it.

He felt rather than saw her moving away, her bare feet soundless on the rough floor. The strip of moonlight at the door widened and then disappeared altogether, cutting off a brief glimpse of her silhouette. He heard the door shut firmly.

"It wouldn't hurt to have a little bit of light," he suggested.

There was no answer. Sudden alarm deflated him like a bucket of cold water. When he heard the bar clunk down outside, he knew he was in serious trouble.

For a few minutes, he couldn't make up his mind what to do. Fear and anger warred briefly, and he cursed, but not loudly. Foremost in his thoughts was that he not be caught. Yanking his trousers up, he stumbled through the pitch-darkness to the door and threw his weight against it. The bar clattered, but held. He put his eye to the thin gap between door and frame. He could see nothing.

Fumbling around, working by feel, he got dressed. It took a while.

Back at the door, he unsheathed his sword and inserted the blade between the door and the frame beneath the dark line of the bar. With both hands on the hilt he lifted it upward. The bar was reluctant to move. It took almost all his strength to lift it high enough so that the pressure of his shoulder swung the door open. He stepped out into the moonlight relieved and embarrassed and with a notion to find the girl and tear her limb from limb.

No one was about. With a little luck, the incident might possibly remain his secret. Good sense prevailed. He hurried back to his post at the prison gate.

Nothing seemed amiss. He unbarred the gate and stepped through to survey the compound. The bare yard lay empty and still beneath the watching moon. A warder making his rounds came into view at the corner of the building where the prisoners were locked away for the night. He waved.

The soldier took a deep breath, relocked the gate, and resumed his position in front of it.

In the east, a smear of red on the horizon suggested dawn.

Once Sarah had the soldier locked firmly into the shed, she streaked for the prison gate and let herself into the yard. She didn't imagine that the man would be out of circulation for long, and she most certainly did not want to meet him when he got himself out. Her Sezmie let her into the building.

Her main problem was finding which cell Reese was in. A double line of identical doors confronted her, like so many box stalls in a stable. Truly, the prison looked more like a stable than anything else and might even have served that purpose at some time.

The search was somewhat simplified because unoccupied cells had their doors hanging open, but was complicated by the warder who made irregular circuits of the building.

A candle burned on a shelf near the entrance, and an unlit lantern sat beside it. She would have liked to use the lantern, but didn't dare, for fear the light would be noticeable from outside.

The candle held high cast feeble illumination through the openings in the doors. Stretching up as high as she could to peer in, she could eliminate some candidates at once. They were small, or blonde, or were facing her sufficiently in their sleep that she could make out features. She was painfully conscious of the time slipping by.

She risked calling out now and then in a hoarse whisper as she peered through a set of bars. Once she got back a muffled curse in a voice that wasn't Reese. Once she got a crude invitation. Finally, she heard the right answer.

"Sarah?"

She fumbled with the iron bar that held the door. "Come on," she whispered frantically. He got to his feet slowly and stood there staring at her uncomprehendingly. "Come on." She grabbed at him, got a handful of his clothing, and pulled him along, stopping to close and bar the door again, mindful of the candleflame in her haste down the corridor. Some of the other prisoners had roused and were grumbling querulously.

"What's going on?" Reese asked.

"Talk later," she said. "Come on."

She put the candle back where she found it. She paused a moment to listen at the door without a thought in her head of what she would do if she heard the warder coming, then slipped out into the night. Reese seemed to get the idea at last and followed without her urging.

They still had the wide empty compound to traverse, and there was nothing for it but to trot out into the moonlight and hope for the best. Reese kept up with her, though a part of her mind registered the shambling, uneven pace.

She just got the gate barred behind them when she heard the door of the shed crash open. She pushed Reese toward the shadow of the hedge that she had originally come out of. The moon had moved across the sky; the shadow was smaller. They hugged the scratchy branches. Sarah put a cautionary finger to Reese's lips and felt the dry heat of them. She watched the soldier dash by, pause, unbar the gate, and go into the compound.

She led Reese by the hand along the hedge, sidling along, keeping watch for the soldier. The short stiff branches clawed at her bare legs. She paused partway along to retrieve the bundle that contained the rest of her clothes and the governor's wine glass. She found the low opening between the close stems where some foraging animals had worn a path. She slipped through and waited for Reese on the other side. It was a tight fit for him, and the effort seemed to take his strength.

She waited more patiently for him to recover now that the chances for immediate discovery were less.

They weren't completely out of danger yet. They were still inside the Mansion grounds and dawn was close, and Reese was not moving well.

But she knew the way now. All they had to do was get clear before the sun rose.

Twenty-eight

The robot that kept the Mid-American Enclave's inventory at Supply and Services didn't know that a request from the chairman for a dozen stun guns and four tracked earth-movers with extra tanks of fuel was an odd sort of order to come in the middle of the night from a member of council, or from anyone else, for that matter. Nothing in its instruction set suggested that it should question such a thing. All the instructions it was ever given specifically regarding the chairman was that a request from the chairman did not require administrative approval and should go to the head of the priority queue.

It made a note to itself that the order pretty well exhausted the enclave's supply of earth-movers and of weapons, and issued the requested items in the chairman's name. In the morning, someone was bound to notice the curious, high-energy change in inventory, but by that time the items would be in Monn, or the whole scheme would have fallen apart.

Though his purposes were served at the time, the chairman was a little disturbed that weapons were so readily obtained. The enclave, he thought, really ought to keep more careful control over its guns than it did over its wrenches, and he made a mental note of his own to remedy the situation later, when he had the time, if he was allowed the time. He was standing on the wide, permacrete apron behind the supply building, bidding his invasion force good speed, admonishing them to keep themselves safe above all, and wishing that he was going with them on the most adventuresome thing any enclave had done in a century.

He stopped to speak for a moment to Cleo. In the brief time he had known her, he had been impressed with the woman's furious determination to proceed with the uncertain enterprise. He had perceived strength, intelligence, and a fierce loyalty, and that strange undefinable ability to get people going in the direction she wanted them to go, coupled to the instinct to know if it was going to take desperate pleading or aggressive leadership to do it. He thought he might, in the leisure that was about to be induced by the loss of his position, learn more about her. Power was a heady wine; once tasted, it was difficult to forego. That he was to be personally thrown off the council did not mean that his influence there had to end. He might groom a successor. It was a bit late for the first round, but there would be another.

Furthermore, in his newly induced leisure time there would be opportunity for aspects of his life that had been somewhat neglected of late. Cleo was a beautiful woman, youthful without being girlish, and the thought crossed the chairman's mind that it might be expedient to leave Reese in Monn and out of the competition.

Expedient, but poor strategy, and not exactly ethical. He sighed.

"When you return," he said to Cleo, "I would like to talk to you about your future. I have a feeling you are being wasted in Engineering."

Cleo heard him, but the words didn't really register. It didn't seem possible that they meant what they seemed to mean, and there was no time to puzzle through them, for Ian was urging her up into the cockpit of the dozer.

Then they were off, roaring and clanking through the night, following the podway, leaving the chairman behind in their dust to stave off the opposition as long as possible.

The dozers were slow-moving compared to the pods. The journey that normally took less than an hour by pod took the lumbering earth-movers more than four. Breaking dawn found them still in the forest lands east of Monn locally known as the Wilderness.

The pod bridge looked a bit frail when confronted by the heavy dozers. But the big machines were eased across one at a time and the bridge held with only minor groaning. When they were reassembled on the west bank of the river, the invaders got down to the ground to stretch cramped muscles. The dozers were not designed as passenger vehicles, and three people per unit meant that two of them were miserably uncomfortable. They changed places periodically, but everyone was feeling bloodless and stiff.

They breakfasted on field rations in self-warming packs and scrupulously picked up after themselves, for plastics were nothing if not solid fuel, and aluminum was worth its weight in electricity. Cleo gathered her little group together and held a council of war.

"We've undoubtedly been spotted by now," she said. "Only the Great Bird of the Galaxy knows what the Phobes have made of us. I think our best bet will be to move as quickly as possible on the Governor's Mansion. The less time they have to think it over and assemble their defenses, the better.

"We're going to be ruthless, people. I want it understood. Until we reach the Mansion, we're not going to stop for anything. We're going over or through whatever opposition we meet. Anyone who can't live with that should call a pod and go home."

She waited a moment, and when no one made a move to leave, she said, "Okay, keep your weapons ready. Remember, spears and arrows look primitive, but they can kill you. Let's go."

Twenty-nine

Butch Miller prowled the extensive rooms and stone-walled passages of the Miller house like an all-too-corporeal ghost, restless, grouchy, and filled with a sense of impending disaster.

He snapped at the servant who came to tell him that breakfast was prepared. He was off his feed, too, a unique circumstance that everyone in the family had commented upon at least once by then. Butch was a bit sick of hearing about it, and sick of his family's feigned concern, and sick of the world in general, and felt not much restored by the sight of his brothers bearing down on him obviously full of important news. He would have fled their unwelcome company if he had been able to summon the necessary vigor and if he had been able to think of any place to go. As it was, he settled down in the big leather chair in the main hall, poured himself a cup of fresh milk from the silver ewer he had the servant bring. He was avoiding going to the table and facing the family. It was just his luck that the troublesome family came to him. He sat at the window and saw the morning sun sparkling on the river and the great mill wheel turning, and tried to ignore Brad and Brian when they came in.

Brad would not be ignored, of course. He hitched his hip onto the windowsill smack in front of Butch, with his back to the river. "Boy, little brother, you're in real trouble now."

"Yeah?" Butch grunted, not too interested.

"Yeah," Brad declared, not grinning his usual enjoyment of his brother's predicaments. He looked serious.

"How come?"

"The witch escaped," Brian said. Brad glowered at him for spoiling the story.

Butch's jaw dropped, his attention caught. "What're you talking about?"

"It's all over town this morning," Brad said.

"A bunch of them came yesterday morning, you know, in the dark," Brian said.

"A bunch of what?"

"Witches, you twit," Brad answered. "What do you think? Looking for their buddy, eh? Not like they would abandon one of their own like that. I expect they were looking for you, too, seeing as how you gave one of them such a bad time."

"Me?"

"Anyway, the witch is gone, vanished right out of the governor's prison. There's those that say they hexed the whole entire prison and everyone in it. There's those that say he made himself into a crow and flew out over the wall as neat as you please and nobody could stop him. I expect he's going to be just a tiny bit peeved about being locked up and all. I don't know, Butch. Your ass is really out there. What're you going to do?"

"Me? What am I going to do? What about you? You're in this as much as me."

Brad shook his head. "Oh, no, you don't. This is your problem, little brother. I didn't try to take any girl away from any witch. I'm not that dumb."

"That's not what happened. Anyway, you're the one who told the Brothers all that stuff."

"Just trying to help out. Not that I expect any gratitude. Anyway, it's all yours now, brother." He slid off the window ledge, picked the milk cup out of Butch's numb fingers, swallowed the contents, and replaced the empty cup in Butch's unmoving hand. "I think I'll go downriver for a couple of weeks, see what's happening somewhere else, away from this dumb burg."

"Wait a minute, Brad," Butch called, but Brad was gone. Butch frowned at the empty doorway. It was entirely possible, he thought, that Brad was just playing games, trying to get him all upset so he could have a good laugh at his brother's expense. Brad would do a thing like that. He often did.

"Is this for real, Brian?" Butch asked.

Brian shrugged. "That's what they're saying around town. Some time last night, they say. But you know, chances are the guy just plain lit out running for his life and is trying to get as much distance between us and him as he can. Don't you think?"

"You think so?"

Brian lifted his hands palms up to display his ignorance. "Well, shit, Butch, what do I know about witches, eh?"

At the river's edge, Butch hunted among the bridge supports for Gil the Weasel. But Gil was nowhere to be found. Butch thought about going up town to look for him, but in truth, when Gil wasn't hanging around mooching his dinner, Butch had no idea where he went.

Probably, it didn't matter. Gil was a low-class shithead parasite anyway, and wouldn't tell Butch how to deal with witches if he knew, which he didn't. He wouldn't be worth spit in this situation.

It would have been a comfort, though, to have someone to talk it over with.

He went into the mill, but the workmen told him his father had gone out to see the smith about repairing a broken bearing. They didn't expect him back before noon. They didn't have time for extended discussions. They were busy. They returned to their work.

Butch felt like he was being deserted, isolated, so that the witch's wrath when it fell, would fall on him alone. It wasn't fair. He never meant anyone any harm, really. All he had ever wanted was a bit of fun. That wasn't such a wicked thing, was it?

He thought about joining Brad downriver, but realized at last that nothing would prevent the witch from following. He could hide, but where, and for how long, and doing what?

He needed help, but didn't know where he would find it. He was afraid to go back to the Temple, afraid Brad's lies had been found out, afraid of God's fury as well as the devil's, and Brother Eric's more than either.

He did know of one expert in the magical mysteries, and if she wasn't inordinately fond of Butch Miller, her services could be bought. He would have to go up the hill to see Cat Anna.

Thirty

Sarah knew she was going to have to get help.

Back in the prison, from the moment of opening the cell door, when he peered at her out of the gloom, frowning as if he had never seen anything quite like her before, she had known there was something dreadfully wrong with Reese. He didn't catch on to what was happening. He kept wandering off in the wrong direction when she was trying to get him back to her den. He either didn't hear, or didn't understand her, and looked at her blankly when she spoke, as though the words had no meaning.

Now he was groaning and thrashing on Sarah's bed, calling people she had never heard of. His hands were hot, and his cheeks flushed, and his eyes glittery with the fever. She brought him food, but he wouldn't eat it. She brought him water. He drank, but threw it all up a few minutes later.

The wound on his head had gone bad; it was red and swollen and ran thick ugly pus that matted the hair down into an encrusted mass.

She was reluctant. She couldn't take him anywhere the way he was. She would have to bring the help to him, to her place. She would once again have to give away the secret of her refuge. She didn't want to do that. She caught herself resenting him, wishing that he had never come into her life, since all he had ever done for her was fix it so she had to tell somebody her precious secret. She waited out the early morning hours hoping that by some miracle or exercise of his witchcraft he would get better. It didn't happen. Some curse beyond his powers must be on him. She had to go.

To find a healer was one thing. To find a healer with power against curses was entirely another. Sarah knew only one person who might be of help. She climbed the hills to Cat Anna's cave.

The passage was less terrible in the light of day. But the wizened old woman crouched at the front of her cave by her fire was every bit as dreadful as Sarah remembered.

Busily drying some dark, limp leaves on a rack woven from green willow switches suspended over the fire, Anna was not overly enthusiastic. "You think I want to go all the way down the hill and all the way up again? That's a long way for someone my age. And what do I get from it, besides exhaustion?"

"What do you want?"

Anna turned the limp leaves one by one with the awkward quick movements of arthritic fingers trying to avoid a scorching. "When last you came," Anna said, "I pulled these old bones up to the top of the ridge at midnight to watch the sky for signs of augury. Do you know anything about auguries, girl? I suppose not. The old mysteries are being forgotten, and the more people forget, the more frightened they are."

"Could we go now? Reese needs you now."

Anna went on turning leaves as if she hadn't heard. "I sensed a difference more than could be accounted for by infatuation with that unfortunate man you've done the disservice of labeling a witch. The sky was quiet until dawn was near. Then there came an owl, and after the owl, a pair of eagles. Death and royalty are in your life." She stirred the coals with a long, fire-blacked stick and was quiet for so long that Sarah was about to remind her once again of the urgent problem of Reese when Anna pulled out of her reverie and spoke again.

"How do you suppose old Anna can work wonders beyond the ability of a Phile, child?" she asked, working herself closer to her fire as if age had formed a second skin around her, preventing the warmth of sun or fire from reaching her.

Before Sarah could answer, Anna fixed her with a faded eye. "A strange vehicle for old Destiny to choose to carry the Fates." She pulled herself to her feet, leaning on her blackened stick. "Come. Let us see to your wounded Phile. We will discuss the matter of fees another time."

* * *

Butch leaned against the bole of a tree and rested. It was a long uphill walk from the mill to Cat Anna's, and Butch was not up to a superabundance of athletic endeavor. He bent his knees and let his back slide down the trunk until he was seated on the ground. If he hadn't been so frightened, he would have given it up as a bad job and treated himself to a mug of ale at the inn instead of getting tired and sweaty climbing the benighted hill. He was thirsty and he didn't feel like walking anymore—and he was only halfway there.

He leaned his head back and closed his eyes. The morning breeze, already hot, dried the sweat from his face. In the branches above him, one by one the birds resumed their twittering—then stopped, abruptly.

The sudden quiet was startling. Butch's eyes opened. He couldn't see anything. But in a moment he could hear something: voices, and slow steps approaching around a bend in the road.

The tall dry grasses by the side of the road would mask him from observation unless one was really looking for him. That suited Butch. He didn't want to be found sitting by the roadside in the dirt like some common farmer. He held himself rigid so that the walkers would pass him by.

As they came round the curve, Butch recognized both of them, Sarah and Cat Anna, with Sarah obviously trying to hurry the old woman's deliberate pace. Butch almost called out to them, but held himself back at the last moment.

Something was going on there.

A largely unused brain labored to assess the situation. Sarah was closely associated with the witch. That was what had gotten Butch into trouble in the first place. Cat Anna, for all her protestations of ignorance, bore an aura of witchery and magic. It could not be accidental that those two should be together at that particular time. Something was happening. Something involving the witch. Butch was sure of it.

In any event, there was no point going on up the hill if Cat Anna wasn't there.

When they were well past, Butch pulled himself to his feet and followed, keeping his distance so they would remain unaware of him. They kept up their steady pace through the heart of the town. When Sarah led Anna around the back of the Crow's Eye, Butch took the short cut through Rat Alley and arrived at

the fence at the end of it in time to see the two women crossing
the scrub land, moving toward the river. They disappeared into
a patch of brush and didn't come out again.

"I need light," the old woman said. "More light." Sarah lit
candle after candle and wished for one of Reese's witch lights.
Anna's clawlike fingers probed the wound with surprising gen-
tleness. Even so, Reese, half-conscious, groaned.

Anna rummaged around in the copious leather sack that Sarah
had carried down the hill for her and withdrew from it a narrow
blade of Old People's steel. It gleamed in the candlelight. "We
must let the poison out," she said. "And you must do the work.
These old hands shake too much, and these old eyes are dim."

Sarah eyed the blade with a queasiness in her stomach. The
candle flame trembled in her hand. She thought about the knife's
edge biting into damaged flesh, about pain and blood.

She shuddered. "I can't," she said.

"Then he will surely die."

I can't do this, Sarah thought. If he dies, he dies. No one can
make me do this. And Reese's eyes opened, staring past her into
the black face of Azrael, into the endless night.

Sarah took the knife in her hand. The handle was slippery
with her own cold sweat. It was hard to concentrate on Anna's
instructions. Then the old woman put her hands on Reese's
shoulders, leaned her frail weight against him, and nodded to
Sarah.

Sarah tried not to think, only to do.

Reese screamed and cursed, but the blade was keen, opening
the wound to let it drain. It was done almost before he could
react. Anna was tossed into a heap of angular joints and bundled
clothing. Sarah's stomach heaved, and she was afraid she would
have to drop the knife and run except that her legs felt too weak
to carry her. Reese's eyes turned up, and he fell back, limp.

"Good," Anna said, gathering herself together and straightening her shawls. "It's better he should be insensible awhile."
She worked over the wound, pushing at the edges of the swelling
until the blood ran red. When she was satisfied that the wound
was as clean as she could get it, she set to mixing a poultice
from a bundle of plantain leaves she took from her bag. Then
she sent Sarah down to the river's edge for willow bark, which

they steeped in water heated in Sarah's big black iron pot over the small fire they had built on a flat bit of Old People's stone above Sarah's place.

When Reese showed signs of regaining his senses, Anna forced a little of the bitter infusion between his lips with one of Sarah's cracked cups. "Do this as often as you can," she said. "It will help with the fever and the pain."

"Will he be all right?" Sarah asked.

"I don't know. The corruption has gone deep. It's up to whatever gods or demons oversee these things now. I've done all I know to do." She looked down at Reese's pale, sweating face with its stubble of beard. "It's a damned sorry excuse for a witch you have here." She gathered up her things and prepared to leave.

"Anna?"

"You have courage, child. I'll remember my fee when the time comes."

"Anna, is the death in my life Reese?"

Anna looked back at Reese, who seemed to be sleeping easier now. "Owls only ask for names, girl. They never give any."

Butch scrambled and slid down the embankment toward the place where the women had disappeared, but when he got down to that level there were dozens of brush patches, and they all looked about the same. He sat down on a boulder to rest. He wondered if he wasn't being just a little bit dumb, scrabbling around in the bush looking for he-didn't-know-what. He didn't even know what he was going to do if he found whatever it was. He would be more sensible, he thought, to go back to the Crow's Eye, get something to drink and something to eat, and try once more to persuade Brad to help him out of his trouble.

He heard a muffled scream, like some poor soul in torment, and it made his hackles rise.

But it seemed appropriate to the terrible enterprise he was engaged in, so he loosened the knife in the sheath at his belt and forced himself to proceed cautiously a short way in the direction of the sound. He paused again to look around, and could see nothing but the ruins of an Old People's building sticking up through the undergrowth.

Then Sarah appeared, hurrying, preoccupied, heading for the

river. She moved like a rabbit through the brush and vanished from his sight in no time.

He moved toward the spot from which she had appeared.

He didn't see her come back. He smelled rather than saw the fire. He picked his way carefully closer, his nerves as taut as bowstrings. He stopped again. Still he could see nothing out of the ordinary.

Cat Anna shuffled by, scarcely a stone's toss away. He half expected her to hear his startled gasp and strike him down with a gesture, but she continued on her way, arms hugging a leather bag, head bent to watch her footing.

Butch didn't know what to do. Should he continue to search for Sarah, or should he go after Cat Anna? Life was infinitely complicated. He risked sufficient movement to scratch his head in puzzlement.

Reese was sleeping quietly, so Sarah took the opportunity to go up onto the ruins and bring the iron pot with its infusion of willow bark down into her den. It was dreadfully heavy, especially half-full of water and bark, so she wiggled and bumped it to the edge of the wall above the entrance with the intention of lowering it down on a rope. Then she could scramble down herself and pick it up.

"Sarah."

She jumped at the sound of her name. She looked down. Butch Miller looked up.

Her heart sank. He was standing right in the entrance to her place. He had found her sanctuary. She no longer had a safe place to go. She could feel her whole world crumbling around her.

Not only that, but Reese was inside, unknowing and helpless.

"Get down here, Sarah," Butch said.

"No." she said. "Please go away," she said, knowing there was no chance he would do that.

"If I have to come up there, you bitch, you're going to be bloody sorry."

He stood there with his hands on his hips and his face turned up, her enemy, her nemesis. Her consciousness closed down to that one reality. Everything else faded out of being. For the moment the whole of the universe consisted of her and Butch frozen in that tableau.

She was scarcely aware that she had dropped to the ground, that her feet lashed out with all her strength against the iron pot.

The bump and clatter of the pot on the stones below brought the rest of existence swimming back into her ken. Trembling, she dragged herself to the edge of the wall and looked down.

Butch lay sprawled half down the steps. The iron pot had vanished into the hole below. There was blood.

Thirty-one

"What am I going to do, Matt?"

Matthew put his palm on Sarah's cheek. "Hush, now, girl. You're not the first, nor the last. We'll think of something."

The *Big Fish* rocked gently on the river currents. In the cabin, Beth held Sarah's hand in her own to give the girl reassurance. Head bowed, Matthew listened to Sarah's story. His face grew grave, and he bit his lip as Sarah told how she had finally taken hold of her courage and climbed down to where Butch lay blocking the entrance to her home.

She had exhausted her strength rolling him over, the limp weight of him bringing bile to her throat. With some effort of will, she had put her ear to his chest. Nothing moved in there. Butch was quite dead.

Shock and horror had held her immobile for long, wrenching minutes that seemed to slide sideways through the bright morning. She had expected some monumental upheaval of the natural order to mark the terrible deed. She half expected a demon to appear before her and smile and suck her soul away.

Nothing happened.

A calling crow at last roused her from her paralysis. The world was as it had always been. The sun poured down. Birds chirped. Leaves hung limply from dying trees. In the distance she heard the voices of people going about their business.

Getting her trembling legs under her, she had fled the scene, and arrived more by instinct than by conscious thought at the *Big Fish*, in search of help and comfort.

"I got to get him out of there, Matt," she said.

Matthew nodded. "Or else," he said, "you've got to move."

"No," Sarah said. Matthew's face questioned her. "I don't want to leave my place."

"I don't know that 'want' comes into this. You don't want to be hanged for murder, either. Butch Miller was bound for a bad end from the day he was born, but I don't think the Miller family is going to see it that way."

Sarah's spirit rebelled. She resisted the thought with all her heart. But Matthew appealed to her head.

"You can't be certain," he said, "that Butch didn't tell someone where he was going, or that someone won't track him, looking for him."

She could see the sense of it. Somehow she had known, from the time she had first taken Reese to her place, what was going to happen, that she would lose the one precious thing she had. The storyteller had many tales of lives ruined by passion. The Legend of Sarah was becoming one of them.

It wasn't even passion any more. Not really, not much. More a sense of responsibility, a sense of duty to one she had injured. More a feeling that saving Reese was the only thing that could justify the things she had done.

"The sooner we do it, the better," Matthew said. "The longer we wait, the more likely the body will be found."

What would she do about Reese? "I can't leave. There's somebody."

"Who?"

Sarah hesitated.

"If I'm going to help, girl, you have to be honest with me this once. I'm willing to take you aboard the *Fish* till you get straightened out, but I'm damned well going to know who it is I'm taking."

Sarah studied Matthew with the frowning intensity of a stray dog studying the butcher, divided by hope and fear. She didn't know how Matthew would react. "It's the witch," she said softly.

"The witch?"

"He's sick. He can't even walk."

"The witch we didn't rescue from the Temple?"

Sarah nodded.

"Saints preserve us," Matthew said. "Soldiers are everywhere, digging in dark corners for signs of sorcery. Most kids pick up stray cats and orphaned puppies.''

"I'm not a child, Matthew.''

Matthew considered this for a moment. "That's true,'' he said. "You're not.'' He caught Beth's eye, and in their silent language, he and his wife came to an agreement. Beth, conscious of the risk they would be taking, had seen Matthew's spirits revive in those past few minutes, seen something of his old self return to animate his features. It was as if Providence and Sarah had conspired to give him the opportunity to redeem himself for what he—and he alone—saw as his failure in the Temple. Should all the demons of hell appear before her and threaten to drag her straight to perdition if she agreed, Beth could not have told him no.

"Show me the way,'' Matthew said.

Monn was suddenly brimming over with experts on the perils of the black arts prognosticating woe, making the signs against evil when they spoke to one another, drawing pentagrams on their doorsteps, casting anxious glances up the Witch Road and conducting their business in haste.

Witchbane graced the doorways of the city. The Temple was crowded. People were afraid. They had no defense against the mysteries of witchcraft save the mysteries of God.

They feared the witches, and they feared the soldiers seeking witches. The governor's prison was fast filling up. With malicious humor, a soldier told a suspect that they would soon have to execute a few prisoners to make room.

Sarah was afraid, too, not of fiends and soldiers, but of the people.

If anyone in town discovered the *Big Fish* harboring a Phile, honest, upright, God-fearing townsmen would kill them all; or, worse, haul them off to the Temple to await burning in Market Square. She felt vulnerable, for herself and for Reese, and for Matthew and Beth. Without finding anything particularly evil about Reese, she had come to terms with the idea that he was a Phile. But she didn't trust anyone else to come to that understanding.

It was no sorcerer she had hidden, so pale and wasted that her heart ached with guilt for having been away too long.

She led Matthew through the wild land to the steps leading down to where Butch's body lay.

Matthew nodded shortly, then told her to get her things together, that he would be back with Lucas to see what could be done.

Sarah entered her sanctuary for what might be the last time, full of pain and melancholy. The room was dark. The candle had gone out. It was taxing her supply to keep one burning all the time, but Reese seemed more comfortable with a light. She felt her way to her dwindling hoard to get another, realizing as she did that it didn't matter anymore, not the candles, not anything. Tears brimmed up. She stopped to let the moment pass, gritted her teeth, and continued on, resolutely in search of a candle.

She stumbled over something in the way. Nothing should have been there, but it felt unyielding against her foot, and sounded, clattering against the floor, like the big iron pot.

But she had left the pot where it had fallen, at the foot of the stairs.

She got a candle lit, lifted the pot out of the way, and realized that the room was empty. Reese was not there.

She searched the rest of the rooms of the basement as quickly as she could without losing the candle flame in her haste. He was not in any of them.

Where could he have gone? How could he go anywhere?

No, her heart cried. She couldn't have gone through all that only to lose him.

For a moment she wondered if the sorcerous Philes had found him and magicked him away. But she didn't really believe it. The taste of Phile blood in her mouth was fresh in her memory.

She climbed up onto the mound of debris above her home and scanned the terrain for some sign of him. She couldn't see anything. She tried to imagine him leaving. Where would he go? Not toward the river, surely. And wouldn't he pick the easier going along Birch Road? He wouldn't try to cross the wild land, would he? She scrambled down and raced across to Birch Road.

An ox cart with an empty barrel in it was coming toward her, the driver nodding, half-asleep behind the plodding ox.

Sarah hailed him and asked him if he had seen a sick man walking.

The driver blinked and stared. "I know you. You're Sarah."

Sarah nodded, a swift head bob indicating haste. He seemed vaguely familiar to her, but she didn't stop to wonder where they had met.

The man pointed back up the road. "You better get after him, girl. He looks in a bad way."

She ran up the road, pausing at the intersection to look, and realized that there was no way she could tell what direction he had taken. She tried to think. Where would he go? With only half his wits about him, where would he go? If one of the Brothers saw him, or the witch-hunting soldiers . . .

Maybe his house. It was a place to look.

She tore down Travellers' Way. She was getting winded. She clutched her side where a stitch made breathing hurt.

Behind her, the man in the cart called the ox to a halt, climbed up onto the top of his barrel, and stood with his hand shading his eyes, watching her race away. When she vanished around a bend in the road, he climbed down again, shouted the ox into motion, and sat on the floor of the cart chewing his lip as the beast resumed its slow pace.

The shutters were closed over the broken window in the house off Travellers' Way. The light filtered between the boards in dusty rays and made the shadowy interior seem cooler than the bright sun outside. Sarah stood in the middle of it with the sweat of her headlong run dripping down her face and stinging her eyes. Reese wasn't there. She wanted to scream her frustration and fear, but she didn't have the breath remaining for such a luxury. She held onto a corner of the table and tried to make her churning brain think of what she was going to do next.

"Where is he?" she demanded of the empty room. All his Philish things were there waiting for him, but he hadn't come back for them. The girl in the cube was waiting on the table, faded in the dim light, as if she needed sunshine to live. She could not answer. The shadowed silence swallowed up the question and offered no suggestions.

* * *

Brother Wayne held his thick head.

He was crossing the Mill Bridge on his way back to the Temple. It was hard for him to accept the fact that the entire night and a good part of the morning had passed.

He had received with a modicum of unease the previous evening's invitation to visit the Kolloan camp. He knew the Kolloans to be a godless people who worshipped, when they bothered to worship at all, little clay statues of a woman all bust and belly that stood naked and unadorned on their spare altars. Those statues were offensive to any decent man and, he was sure, an abhorrence in the eyes of the Lord God, a foul parody of the proper reverence men should afford their Maker. If he went, some might interpret it as tacit acceptance of pagan idolatry. He might become contaminated in some way he could not even understand.

But the Kolloan who had stopped him on the street with goodhearted questions of simple earnestness about the True Faith seemed such an ingenuous fellow who truly wanted to understand, it was hard for Brother Wayne to think ill of him. It would be no small triumph for the Lord God, and for Brother Wayne, to convert a Kolloan idolater.

The Kolloan said his name was Amyit and that there were others in the camp who would be interested in hearing Brother Wayne's message. A small risk for a significant gain, and ultimately Brother Wayne felt secure enough in his own faith to allow himself to be persuaded.

He had been escorted to a blood-red tent, which, he was happy to see, contained no altar, only some low stools and a small table. Three other gaily dressed Kolloans joined them, making Brother Wayne feel a bit dowdy in his coarse black wool. He was offered skewered lamb with an astonishing variety of dried fruits to nibble on, and a sample from a large copper jug of wine which had been cooled in the river. Because there were no women among the Kolloans, Amyit served his guest himself, and Brother Wayne was not so ignorant of Kolloan ways that he was unconscious of the honor being done him.

That left him with a dilemma. The True Faith frowned upon indulging in wine, though it was not strictly forbidden. But Brother Wayne did not wish to offend his hosts by refusing. He wanted the most sympathetic hearing he could get.

He decided to accept a glass as a sign of good faith, and to merely hold it during the conversation so he wouldn't be offered another. But when Amyit asked him how it compared with Monnish wine, he had to taste it, and found it smooth, not sweet, and tartly refreshing.

The Kolloans were easy to talk to, and attentive listeners. Their hard, clipped speech made them sound reserved, but they asked good questions. At one time, Amyit excused himself and went to the river to fetch another jug.

And suddenly it was dawn, and Brother Wayne was wending his way home amid bird song grown harsh and loud to his overly sensitive ears.

"Brother?"

The hesitant query had come from the water's edge. There was an ox cart there, with a barrel in it, and a man with a bucket in his hand. "You got a minute, Brother?"

"Of course, of course, my good man," Brother Wayne mumbled, making amiable sounds by conscious effort, deeming it reasonable penance for the state he had allowed himself to get into.

"Name's Jonathan, Brother. Who was took off the street a while back to be a witness when you was accusing that witch."

"What can I do for you, Jonathan?"

The man was nervous and shy. He kept his head bent and he fiddled with the bail of his bucket. He had the directness of one who had struggled to pump his courage up and must complete his business before it failed him.

"I heard it said around how the Church is looking for a bunch a witches that're in the city. A terrible thing, Brother. Terrible."

"Surely," Brother Wayne said. He peered at the man through the wine-fog, trying to divine his purpose.

"I heard it said if a man knew where a witch was, he's supposed to go tell the Brothers, who would, well, sort of, uh, make it worth his while."

"Yes. Though a pious man might do this for the greater glory of the Lord God's name alone."

"I'll tell you, Brother, I'm as much for God as anyone. But I got a wife and kids, eh?"

Brother Wayne leaned against the flank of the ox, drew a handkerchief from the sleeve of his robe, and mopped his face. The risen sun glinted on the river and made his eyes water, and the pressure behind his brow was building into a headache. His forced amiability was sliding away into irritation.

"You know something about this?" he asked.

"Could be."

"Then tell me, man."

"Well, you know how it is, Brother. I'd feel better about it if I had something in hand. A sign of good faith, eh? You know what I mean?"

"You think the True Church would cheat you out of your due?"

"Not me, Brother. Never. But my woman, she don't trust nobody, you see."

"What's your woman to do with this?"

The man shrugged, helpless to explain.

"Well, Jonathan, I do not carry about with me gold and silver on the off chance of finding one whose concern with his purse outweighs his enthusiasm for the battle against the devil."

"Tell you what, Brother. I'm done here. I could take you to the Temple in the cart. Save you the walk. Save a lot of time, eh?"

In his conference room the governor of Monn hugged himself against the morning chill untouched by sun in this westward-facing room, and argued with his adviser with a kind of numb stubbornness.

"No, Thomas," he repeated, sullen, inflexible, and unhappy.

Thomas busied himself arranging the folds of Michael's robe and setting the chain of office properly on the thin shoulders in an effort to produce some appearance of majesty. The governor tended to be careless of such details. Michael was leaning with his elbows on the marble table, his head in his hands, not making the job any easier.

"People are beginning to think it strange you are so opposed to marriage, Michael. Many are likely to come to entirely wrong conclusions."

"I'm not opposed to marriage. I'm opposed to the Beast of Sanjo."

"I don't think you should refer to the princess in such terms. Sanjo could be a valuable ally. We need allies."

"We've been through all this before. If I must be mated for reasons of state like some prize stud, then send me a serving girl, or that elusive street urchin Brother Parker had here, better than the Beast—Princess."

"Michael, please."

"Leave it, Thomas. We have more important things to worry us these perilous days. Admit the captain of the Guard. Let us see what is disturbing him."

The captain came in looking agitated, and Michael had the horrible thought that the Kolloans had made some overtly hostile move to which he would have to respond with his seriously depleted forces.

But the captain's concern was both less and more worrisome. Armies could be dealt with in some rational way.

Some hours after rumors had already wormed their way into every nook and cranny of the city, the governor was informed of a most curious event.

"M'Lord Governor," the captain said, "the witch has escaped from the prison."

Called to attend the governor, the chief warder was apologetic, frightened, and worried. He was unaccustomed to addressing the leaders of his city and uncertain as to how responsible he was going to be held.

"In truth, Your Honor," he told Brother Parker, "I can't see how it could be, save for sorcery. With all the doors locked and all, and the soldier at the gate swearing no one passed him, how else could it be?"

"That is the question we would like you to answer, of course," Michael said. He hugged himself, feeling that a greater chill had come into the room with Brother Parker. He had hoped to keep knowledge of this business from Parker at least until he had explored the possibility of recovering the witch. He had hoped he wouldn't need to inform the True Church at all. But Brother Parker's spies in the Mansion were ever vigilant. Brother Parker had arrived almost on the captain's heels, full of righteous indignation.

"I warned you, m'lord," Brother Parker said, "that the disposition of witches was the province of the True Church. It's best to have Divine assistance when dealing with the dark powers. Had you not interfered . . .''

"The Philes would have him," Michael said. His own spies weren't completely asleep.

Thomas came with a fur wrap to place over the governor's shoulders. It spoiled the effects of his earlier work, but the shivering was more than he could bear. He spoke to the chief warder. "I mean no criticism, Robert, but if your missing prisoner had a friend who could gain entry into the compound, might we not see the same locked doors?"

"It could be, m'lord Thomas, except that I don't know how the witch and his friend left the compound unseen by the patrols. We found no ladders or ropes that might have been used to scale the walls."

"Have you asked the other prisoners what occurred last night?"

"You do not expect crooks and ruffians to be anxious to help out just and honest men, do you?" Brother Parker inquired coldly.

"In truth, Your Honor," the warder agreed, happy to be able to agree with someone for a change, "they'd like as not lie themselves blind for the pure mischief of it."

"You're undoubtedly right," Thomas said. "Still, it might be interesting to hear what they had to say."

Michael glared at the warder. "You told me, or Thomas, that the witch was sick unto death," he said, sounding petulant because he was a bit frightened. "Now you say he's disappeared. There's too much of disappearing around here. First the girl right out from under our noses. Now the witch from the prison. Can't we keep track of anyone? What manner of men do I have about me that people come and go without so much as a by your leave?"

"They are undoubtedly related, those disappearances," Brother Parker said with more certainty than the circumstances warranted. "The girl, after all, denounced the witch. He will want his vengeance."

"Oh, yes, undoubtedly. So the witch made himself invisible, flew out of the prison, into the very Mansion, snatched up the girl, and flew out again without disturbing a hair, without open-

ing a door or window, just to leave us baffled, and he deathly
ill, without so much as a broomstick to aid him."

Brother Parker chose to ignore the governor's sarcasm.
"There are enough stories of demons who can make themselves
invisible."

"And stories of flying horses and men who spin gold from
straw. Perhaps the storyteller could solve this mystery."

That was about all of that Brother Parker could stand. His
face became quite red and his voice quite loud. "Knowing what
you know, you make jokes at my expense. I warn you, there
will come a time when everything possible will be too little. I
warn you in the Lord God's name, take up your duty, Michael,
else others must take it up for you."

Somewhat taken aback, Michael didn't know what to say.
Thomas's quiet voice came from the shadows of the room. "Are
you now preaching treason, Brother?" he asked mildly.

A soldier burst in before Brother Parker could reply.
"M'lord," he said, wide-eyed, speaking to the governor as if
no one else was there, "Something strange is happening on the
Witch Road. I think your lordship should take shelter at once,
sir. The demon Philes are coming into the city."

The warder, nonplussed by the high-level squabble going on
around him, had backed away from it into a corner, hoping that
he might become a little bit invisible himself. He stared slack-
jawed at Brother Parker, wondering how the preacher's prediction had come to pass so soon.

The Guardsman at the door muttered a quick incantation or
prayer.

The governor looked unimpressed with the news. "What
makes you think so?" Michael asked calmly. Demons and Philes
and witches were so much a part of his life lately that he found
he was becoming used to them.

"Sir, you can see them from the windows across the hall."

Everyone piled out of the conference room and into the hall
where the windows looked out over the city toward the Wilderness. The cloud of dust raised by the demons' passage blocked
half the sky, and the dark forms beneath it were visible through
the dust.

"Lord God preserve us," Brother Parker said. "They've
come to claim their own."

"Please, Governor. Come now," the soldier urged.

"Go, Michael," Thomas said quietly. "Release the soldiers to do their work. They cannot fight demons with one eye and watch for your safety with the other."

Michael bowed his head and pulled the fur wrap close about him, then followed the soldier down the hall.

Brother Parker went with them, though no one had been particularly urging him to a safe place. Stubborn though Michael might be, it was Brother Parker's duty, after all, to go along and guard the governor's immortal soul.

The men of Brother Eric's hastily assembled troop had prepared themselves for battle with a profusion of crosses and medallions blessed by the saints on thongs about their necks where also rode a goodly number of talismans with other, less pious, devices. A cross-hilted sword was prominently displayed, as were wooden staves and a pike or two, and not a few sprigs of witchbane were concealed on their persons, for all Brother Eric condemned the practice as pagan. If one was rushing off to attack the forces of evil directly, it only made sense to carry all the protection one could get. Brother Eric addressed them as soldiers of the Lord God, but they felt decidedly unsoldierly.

Their preparations made them almost too late. Brother Eric prodded them on, his sense of urgency making his manner sharp. With Brother Parker away at the Mansion, Brother Eric felt he had an opportunity to show his worth, to make an impact with the capture of a witch that neither the Church nor Parker could ignore. He hustled his reluctant conscripts along and turned a deaf ear to their grumbling.

The house on Travellers' Way was deserted. Brother Eric was grateful for the inspiration that had prompted him to put Jonathan astride a long-legged mule and send him on ahead to keep watch. The man had not approached the house too closely in spite of the promise of a gold coin, but was able to tell them that the girl had left a short time before, heading toward the Witch Road, which seemed a logical place to go to find a witch.

The Lord God's motley soldiers crowded close to Brother Eric as they crossed the wild ground along the Witch Road, milling about more like a mob than a troop of the righteous.

Hesitant, stumbling over and bumping into one another, they

came upon the witch lying face down in the hollow of ground just before the land rose toward the Road itself, where a witch had been killed only the day before. Above him, like a hell hound protecting its demon master, the girl Sarah stood.

"Bewitched," Brother Eric informed his followers, reading the situation with a practiced eye. "Enchanted, doing the devil's biding despite herself." Holding the Cross of God before him, speaking benedictions, he approached while his troops prudently waited. Sarah flung a rock at him, and it bounced smartly off his kneecap. He yowled in a most unseemly manner, then stopped and gave the situation grave consideration.

Calling upon the Lord God to extend his protection, Brother Eric urged his men to join him at the top of the ridge surrounding the little depression. They were not too anxious to go in spite of his invocation. With a round dozen facing one witch and one street urchin, Eric thought his people might have more faith in the forces of good overcoming the forces of evil.

"Surrender yourself to God, evil one," he shouted over the intervening distance. "Sarah, put your faith in the Lord God and surely no harm can come to you."

Sarah bent to pick up another rock.

Brother Eric was aware that the young Brother next to him had unlimbered his sling. Around him, the warriors of the Lord moved uneasily.

Brother Eric needed the witch alive. The man was worth far more that way, for Brother Eric was not insensible to the value of the magic steel. He would be worth more alive as object lessons to the people, too. Bonfires in Market Square might inspire enough fear to bring obedience, but not belief. He needed a living witch to show the Brothers and the people that Brother Eric served the true power of the Lord God in all His mercy.

If he could be seen to be doing the Lord's work, seen to be cleansing the city of evil, seen to be saving souls from the devil's eternal fire, the people would understand and give him the honor and recognition he was due.

A man of honor could bring so many more lost souls before the altar of the Lord God.

He turned to stay the eager Brother's hand and saw the look of horror on the young man's face. The man was paralyzed with fear. He turned again, looking past the fallen witch and the girl, and saw the great cloud moving toward them along the Witch Road faster than a man could run. Dark forms moved within the cloud with a snarling roar and a clanking of chains as if all the damned souls of hell had been loosed among them.

There was a loud cough from the foremost demon, like a bit of aborted thunder, and some dreadful imp flew up with a wavering howl, leaving a trail of sparks and smoke. It climbed the sky until it was almost overhead, then exploded into a colossal glittering many-fingered hand shimmering and expanding to encompass the entire group before fading away into smoke.

The doughty Brothers scattered, running flat out, as if they thought that with speed they could escape the wrath of God. Brother Eric fell to his knees in a paroxysm of holy terror.

Ian grinned at Cleo. "Pyrotechnics," he shouted over the dozer's motor. "Fireworks. The Old People used to use them for celebrations. I found a description in the library. I didn't know if it would work. I never made one before."

"Looks like it was pretty effective. What would have happened if it didn't work?" Cleo shouted back.

"Just a fizzle, I guess."

"You guess?" It was hard to do justice to alarm when she was already talking at the top of her voice.

Ian was slowing the dozer. The roar dropped a little with the speed. "Anyway, it didn't work that well. Two of them didn't run. Is this where we start being ruthless? Tell me quick. Do we go around or through?"

Cleo studied the scene ahead. One man was on his knees with his arms flung up as if in supplication. The other had turned to face them as if to stand them off with his bare fists. *Her* bare fists. Recognition came with a crash.

"It's Sarah," Cleo shouted. "Stop this thing. Stop. It's Sarah."

Ian wisely said nothing about tough words on the river's edge. He brought the machine to a halt. By then he had recognized the girl, too. He still had a bandage on his hand.

The coming of the demons neatly divided the population of Monn into several parts. There were those who snatched up their children and hid in their cellars trembling with fear, and there were those who raced out into the street or climbed onto rooftops to get a better view of a most incredible sight. There were those who fled into the Temple and threw themselves on the Lord God's mercy, and those who trusted more the old ways, the signs and symbols and chants that warded off the devil's henchmen.

Cat Anna, making her slow way up Birch Road toward her cliffside home, was one of those who stood wherever they happened to be, with their mouths hanging open, staring toward the Witch Road, immobilized by the infernal apparation.

The sun shone brightly. The air was warm and still. In the preternatural quiet, she could hear the distant roaring. Above the awful sound an enormous dust cloud rose and grew as if the demons of the thunderstorms had dropped to earth to do their mischief. Beneath the cloud were the demons themselves, huge, dark, and terrible.

They turned abruptly and started down Travellers' Way, four of them, menacing in their purposefulness.

A dog barked hysterically. A horse screamed in panic. Anna frowned, puzzled by memories, or dreams, or memories of dreams—what was it? She cursed the ravages of age that clouded the mind. Such things had seemed more possible once, as if in her youth they had been less dreadful. But it could be she remembered only youth. So many more things seemed possible when she was young.

She stood for a long time in the silent sunshine after the demons had passed, listening to an inner voice. The day of reckoning had come sooner than she expected. She turned and started toward the Governor's Mansion, knowing that it was time to collect what Sarah owed.

On the roof of the Governor's Mansion, Thomas watched the demons come. The track of their passage was plain where they left Travellers' Way and started overland toward the Mansion— a wide path of flattened earth and grass and trees, a wake of destruction.

Ahead of them was the high stone wall that marked the perimeter of the governor's property. They stopped before it and huddled together, muttering and grumbling with their deep, ground-rattling voices. Then one of them advanced to lean against the wall, roaring. Before Thomas's incredulous eyes the wall bulged inward and then collapsed, leaving a great gap and a scattering of stones.

They came on again, toward the Mansion. Thomas scrambled back down into the building as fast as his old bones would allow to lend what aid he could to its defense. But deep inside he felt certain that what the defenders needed most was a troop of wizards. Soldiers, he was sure, would not be effective there.

The captain of the Governor's Guard had deployed his men across the front entrance of the Mansion, where the rank of pillars would offer them some cover while they stood between the oncoming demons and the governor.

He was proud of them. Not a single one broke, though the demons had come right up to the steps, all but choking them in dust. They were good men, the best. He would match them against twice their weight in Kolloans any day. Against supernatural forces, he was not so sure. He felt certain that he was staring perdition square in the face. But he could not be less strong than the men who looked to him for leadership. He held his place though his knees felt like water and every instinct screamed for him to run. With a shaking hand he made the signs to ward off evil and said his silent prayers.

The demons just stood there, murmuring to themselves in deep-throated syllables that seemed to make the air vibrate. Sun glinted off their smooth hides, shimmering with the tremor of their rumbling. A suspicion grew in the captain's mind. What kind of demons were made of iron? In truth, they looked a lot like machinery. Weird, outlandish, gigantic machinery to be sure, but with identifiable wheels and levers and such.

His speculations ended when one of the things opened up and some strange-looking people came out, as if the demon were regurgitating its last meal of poor damned souls.

He unsheathed his sword and called to his men to be ready. But all about him, his men were falling like wheat before the scythe. And then he was falling, too.

Thirty-two

In the center of the Mansion's basement floor, a small room had been fortified and reinforced to serve as a refuge for the governor in times of danger. It was a small space, poorly ventilated, containing a meager cot, a candle, and the most rudimentary of sanitary facilities. When the governor was inside, the door was barred from without as well as within, and two brawny Guardsmen defended it.

When he first ascended to his office and was introduced to the sanctuary, Michael thought that if his enemies should ever catch him in it, it would make a fine prison. Once inside, he was wholly dependent on someone outside to let him out. Such old thoughts gave him a degree of claustrophobia.

Brother Parker's presence made his confinement no easier to bear. The man paced and mumbled, saying his prayers, Michael assumed. He stirred up the dust, which made Michael cough, used up the air, and made the place smell strongly of sweaty wool. Michael lay on the cot with his face to the wall and tried to doze the time away. He didn't do a remarkably good job of it, and he was still alert when the knock came on the door.

"Open up, Governor," someone called, voice muffled by the heavy wood.

Michael's heart rate doubled in an instant. His people did not address him in such a fashion. He sat up on the edge of the bed and stared at the door, half expecting a demon to pass through it.

Brother Parker was backed up against the opposite wall, holding his cross up before him like a shield.

When further demands for entry went unanswered, the voice on the other side of the door warned them to stand clear. A thin finger of light probed the room between the door and the jamb, glowing ruby-colored among the dust motes. The smell of charring wood filled the air, and the light descended slowly to meet the bar. Where they met, the iron parted with small sputtering complaints. Michael stared, openmouthed. Brother Parker's prayers became louder and more fervent.

The door swung open, still smoking at the edge. The bodies of the two Guardsmen lay on the floor. Three strangely dressed people stood in the doorway.

"Which one of you is the governor?" they demanded. Two of them each held a short, shiny metal rod. The third was fiddling with a complicated device. When he was done, the finger of ruby light had vanished.

Michael gathered up his furs and his courage and got to his feet. "I am Michael Windsor LaRoche, governor of Monn."

"Okay, you come with us, Governor."

"Begone, foul fiends," Brother Parker cried, "or surely you will feel the furies of Heaven. You have no business with just and honest men. The Lord God is terrible in his wrath."

The third stranger regarded Brother Parker from under raised brows.

"Who're you?"

"Brother Parker, by the grace of the Lord God leader of the True Church."

"You better come along, too, Brother. You might turn out to be useful to us."

The Philes barricaded themselves into the conference room on the upper floor of the Mansion, commandeering an assortment of chairs from other rooms for themselves and their prisoners, and blankets and quilts for the wounded witch. Brother Parker suggested that they had chosen that room because they feared a place that overlooked the Temple. General Brandt smiled sourly and shook his head. "It's a defensible position in the short term. These people, witches, whatever, aren't stupid."

The prisoners were huddled in one corner of the room. With them were Thomas and the captain of the Governor's Guard—all the leaders of the city, captive in one place. It was a good move, which General Brandt could appreciate from a professional point of view. It also suggested two facts about the invaders: there were likely not more of them than he could see there, and they did not plan a long-term occupation.

Thomas was questioning the captain of the Guard closely about his experience when the demons first came, when the captain thought he had surely been killed and yet awoke some time later to discover that he was neither in heaven nor in hell, but lying on the Mansion steps, bruised and stiff and uncomfortable, but definitely alive, and all too much still in the world.

At the opposite end of the room, near the defunct fireplace, the Philes had formed a loose circle around their sick friend and plotted their strategy in soft-accented murmurs. They were unremarkable from that distance, pretty much like any tall healthy folk, albeit dressed strangely, men and women alike, in loose shirts and trousers of light smooth fabrics in subtle colors that a Kolloan might envy.

Overall, their dress was not so odd as the garments sorcerers were reported to wear, and there was not a rune nor cabalistic sign among them.

The most peculiar thing about them was the women. The storyteller had tales about warrior women, but none of the Monnish folk in the conference room had ever expected to meet any. Their immodest clothing might have been scandalous under other circumstances. As it was, it merely went to prove the basic shamelessness of the devil's minions.

More worrisome, according to Brother Parker, was their number. Counting the sick one, they were thirteen—the number of ill fortune, of evil. The number of a coven.

They attended the sick man with strange rites, and with instruments of glass and steel and unknown substances. They dosed him with what might have been the white eggs of minuscule birds. The Phobes watched nervously, uncertain, not knowing what to expect.

Between the two groups, Sarah sat at the table with her arms resting on the smooth marble surface, looking first at one group and then at the other, bewildered and unsure about where her loyalties lay. She was too numb to try to sort it out. Too much had happened already today, and the day had a way to run. She felt overwhelmed and soul-weary, and when she shut her eyes, she could still see Butch sprawled on the steps like a great, gape-mouthed fish.

When the governor saw her watching him, he sent her a quick, sad little smile, meant, she supposed, to be encouraging. She smiled weakly back because he was a nice man in his way, even when his face was all screwed up with worry. He was overcome with coughing suddenly and turned away until the spasm passed.

There was a small sound, like the sound made by spitting onto a hot fire, and General Brandt jerked his hand away from the door, surprised and also sheepish. One of the Philes looked over from their circle with a raised eyebrow and shook his head.

The Philes had warned their prisoners that they would get hurt if they tried the brass-bound door. Brother Parker had immediately marched up to it, announcing that the servants of the Lord God were not about to be balked by any Philish trickery, and made to open the door. That sound had occurred, and Brother Parker had cried out and jerked back with a shocked look on his face. Whatever had happened, it seemed not damaging, but it was obviously extremely unpleasant. Brandt had hoped that while the Philes were busy with one another, he could sneak the latch open. But the spell on the door was still firmly in place in spite of their inattention.

For whatever reason they had been gathered there, they would have to await Philish pleasure.

Gene turned back to his fellow rescuers. "If they keep that up, the battery'll be gone in no time."

"It should be okay," Cleo said. "Even cattle learn to respect an electric fence. But we can recharge the battery from a dozer engine if we have to." She turned to Ian. "How is he?"

Ian had been kneeling beside the sick man. "I don't know," he said, straightening. "I'm not a medical expert. I wish we had a docTR with us. "I've got him to take a broad-spectrum anti-biotic. I hope it does some good."

Cleo squatted down and touched Reese's hot, dry forehead. He opened his eyes and gave her a weak scrap of a smile. The effort seemed to exhaust him. He slipped back into unconsciousness. "Damn you, Reese," she said softly to his senseless form. "Do you see how much trouble you caused because you're so freaking stubborn?"

Cleo could feel Sarah glaring at her, but the girl didn't move from her place by the table.

"It wouldn't hurt to wait a few hours," Cleo said to the rest of her group.

Sheila called Cleo to the window with a crook of her finger. "I'm not so sure about that," she said, pointing out. Cleo caught glimpses of armed men in the hedgerows and behind trees and bushes. "Now we've got us in here," Sheila said, "I hope we've got some plans for getting us out."

Ian stood up and dusted his hands against one another. "I think we should get Reese back to the enclave as soon as possible. Can we get out?"

Cleo took a deep breath. "What we're supposed to be doing is talking our way out. We've got business to do, so let's get on with it." She called to the group of Phobes huddled together in the far corner waiting for the earth to open up and drop them into hell. "Gentlemen, we have to talk. Would you sit down, please? Who's in charge here?"

"I am governor of Monn," Michael said. He strove for the imperious emphasis the announcement was due, but his voice quavered a little. Sarah looked up at him, impressed with the way he stood up to the Philes in spite of being scared half out of his wits.

"You're just a boy," Cleo said.

Michael didn't dignify that with an answer.

"My name is Cleo," the Phile said. "There are a few things we need from you, Governor. We can fight each other for them, or we can sit down here and negotiate a business deal. Which is it going to be?"

"Business?" Brother Parker squeaked. "Honest, God-fearing men do not do business with the agents of the devil."

"Who are you?"

"Brother Parker, by the grace of the Lord God leader of the True Faith and guardian of the souls of these good people."

"Well, you just sit still, Brother. If we need some religious help, I'll let you know."

Parker spluttered into silence. Michael, no less unhappy about his circumstances, experienced a fleeting moment of warmth toward the brash, shameless lady witch. Thomas leaned close.

"I begin to see where these Philes might be useful to you, if we can handle them properly," he said quietly.

General Brandt whispered in Michael's other ear. "If we can keep them busy with talk until the northern armies can arrive, I think we'll show them a fight they'll not forget, witches or no. It'll take more than Philish magic to stand off our good fighting men."

Confused and overwhelmed by events, Michael moved away from them both. Since the woman called Cleo had commandeered the governor's fleece-padded chair at the end of the table, with the Philes clustered around her, the governor sat down across from Sarah. And because she regarded him calmly, and because it had been on his mind for some time, and because it was a moment of relief from the confrontation with the Philes, he asked her, "How did you manage to disappear right out from under my nose the other day, past a Mansion full of guards and soldiers and whatnot?"

She gave him a smile sparkling with elfin mischief, enjoying his puzzlement. "I didn't disappear. I just walked out when you men were arguing with each other. Your guards and things don't pay much attention to who goes out. They watch who goes in."

Her smile was contagious. She obviously felt good about confounding the most powerful people in her city, and not too much threatened by whatever Philish disaster was awaiting them now. Michael felt better just looking at her. "I guess we ought to do something about that."

Sarah shrugged. She was indifferent to the defense of the Mansion.

"You're very bold," the governor said.

"That's what people say. The more fainthearted they are, the more they say it."

Michael wisely changed the subject. "Did you really ride inside the demon?" he asked.

She nodded.

"What was it like in there?"

"Noisy. I spent the whole time holding my ears."

Michael smiled at the thought of this innocent girl worrying more about her eardrums than her immortal soul.

"Michael!" Thomas's voice, not loud, but reproving and somewhat strident, reined him back to the business at hand.

Michael dragged his attention to the hard woman sitting in his chair at the head of the table. He felt quite helpless to deal with the Philes. He didn't know what Thomas expected of him.

"Now," Cleo said. "I would like to make the situation perfectly clear. You people are essentially hostages here until we can be assured that our demands will be met and that we have safe passage out of the city."

Thomas had settled himself next to Michael. Negotiation, argument, was what he was good at. "You spoke of doing business together. Yet you begin with threats and demands. This does not appeal to me as an auspicious beginning."

Cleo regarded him with surprise. Well, she thought, Zeke, may he rest in peace, warned me not to underestimate the Phobes. "How would you like to start?" she asked.

"It might be best if you told us what it is you want."

"We want the man who killed our kinsman."

"Who would your kinsman be? And who the man, that you think he might be ours to give? He is a citizen of Monn? If so, you cannot expect us to hand him over like chattel goods." Thomas would concede nothing if not forced to it.

Cleo liked an argument, too. She felt a twinge of guilt because she was anticipating the contest. "Don't play games," she said, deciding that a hard line would play Phobish fears to her best advantage. "You know, and we know you know. However you go about reconciling it internally, we want him. We also want the safe."

"Safe?" Michael asked. "Safe what?" The word was not a noun to him.

"A big metal box in one of the Old People's places in Young Albert's field," Sarah said.

"Oh."

"We also want your leave and protection to explore other archeological sites in the city, and permission to take away with us such items from them as we find are valuable to us."

"What are these ark-kee-oh things?"

"The Old People's places," Sarah said.

"Oh."

"I doubt we could agree to let you carry off whatever you fancy without compensation to the city," Thomas said.

Michael caught himself feeling relieved. He didn't like the

thought of sacrificing Ron the archer. He didn't like the thought of Philes mucking about the city indefinitely. But at least they weren't asking for the destruction of the True Church and twenty souls a day or something horrible like that. Thomas's hand on his arm prevented him from expressing his relief, though. And Michael was willing enough to follow Thomas's lead.

"And supposing we were to agree to all this, what would we get in return?" Thomas asked Cleo.

"What do you want?" Cleo asked, conscious that the initiative had been taken away from her and wanting to get it back.

There was a moment of silence around the table while the leaders of the city tried to think what they would have the magic Philes do for them. It was something like being offered three wishes by a fairy godmother, and the storyteller's tales were full of examples of people who chose unwisely. It gave a man pause.

After a time, Michael asked, "Can you make it rain?"

"No."

"Can you get the Kolloans off our necks?" General Brandt suggested.

"What are Kolloans?" Cleo asked.

"They are some mean people who trade in dyes and make wars and take over other people's cities," Sarah said.

"I see. Possibly. I'm not sure we want to get involved in a war."

Thomas had been scratching his beard and staring out into space. If one must deal with magical people, he was thinking, one should take advantage of the magic. "Can you restore the governor to health?" he asked.

"That I'm pretty sure we can do," Cleo said. "Provided we can get the governor's cooperation. He might find the procedure a bit frightening."

Michael straightened suddenly and glared around the table, defying anyone to argue with him or condemn his thirst for knowledge. "I want the secret of the magic steel," he said.

Cleo looked at Sarah. Sarah shrugged, unable to supply an explanation.

The governor pulled the long, narrow knife from the belt under his fur. "Watch him," Cleo said sharply. Almost immediately, a short shiny cylinder appeared in Cleo's hand. The captain of the Guard cried out in alarm.

Michael laid the knife on the table. The Philish weapon was also laid on the table.

"That's Reese's blade," Cleo said. A definite chill descended between them.

"I want to know how to make steel like that," Michael said, undeterred.

Cleo looked at Ian. Ian shrugged. "I don't see how they could handle chromium in this place, never mind tungsten. They just don't have the technological knowhow, the infrastruct—"

"Madness. Abomination. Unspeakable evil."

Brother Parker was shouting. He came to his feet, his face a mask of horror. He waved his fist under the governor's nose. Startled, the governor drew back.

"You risk eternal damnation for us all, treating with these godless fiends from hell. You barter your immortal souls like goats in the marketplace. Think you to defy the Lord God who charged you to fight with all your strength against the powers of darkness?"

Maybe it was that he had seen the Phile woman get away with showing a disrespectful attitude toward Brother Parker without any ensuing bolts of lightning coming out of the sky to blast her into hell, or maybe he just had too many other things to worry about at the moment, or maybe he saw Brother Parker clearly for the first time as a frightened, power-hungry man who was seeing his power slipping away, but whatever it was, at that moment Michael felt annoyed with the Brother and a little bit sorry for him, but, for the first time ever, not the least bit afraid.

"Sit down, Brother," he said firmly. "And be still. Leave affairs of state to statesman." He caught Thomas's almost imperceptible approving glance.

"I will not sit down," Brother Parker shouted. "I will not stand by while you call hellfire and damnation down upon us."

Michael turned to the captain of the Guard. "Captain, will you take Brother Parker in hand and see to it that he stays quiet?"

"My pleasure, m'lord."

Stunned, Brother Parker sat down. Michael could almost pity him. He had received too many strong jolts for one man in one day. But there was no time to be gentle.

The Philes picked up their internal dialogue apparently where they left off.

"Could they work ingots?" Cleo asked.

"In open forges? I don't know," Ian said. "What we need to do is get a metallurgist to talk to their—what?—smith?"

They went on some more about softening temperatures and coal and charcoal. Michael didn't understand them, and he was distracted by a movement across the table.

Sarah had left her place and walked round the end of the table to the sick Phile. She looked down at him for a moment and then started away. Michael moved to intercept her.

"You weren't thinking about disappearing on me again, were you?" he asked.

Sarah's silence strengthened his suspicions.

"I would like you to stay," he said.

"Stay?"

"Yes."

"Here?"

"Yes."

"In the Mansion?"

"Yes."

"You're making some kind of a joke, aren't you?"

"No, no joke. Listen to us around the table. We can scarcely talk to one another. You are the only person here who understands both sides. I think we are going to have a great need for you as our intermediary, our envoy to the Philes."

She regarded him suspiciously, still expecting to become the butt of some incomprehensible high-society trickery.

"Governor," Cleo called from the table. "All we can promise you about the steel is to try to work something out."

Michael returned to the conference wondering if he had convinced Sarah, if she could possibly escape the Philes' charm on the door, and if his motives were as pure and disinterested as he had represented them to be. His ruminations were interrupted by a most incredible turn of events.

The door of the conference room opened.

In the opening stood a very old, very small, hunched, wizened hag under a burden of dirty, faded shawls. She had the end of one of those shawls wrapped round and round the hand that held the door latch.

"Damn, how did she figure that out?" one of the Philes asked of no one in particular.

Beside the governor, Sarah breathed with a degree of awe, "Cat Anna."

"Sarah," the aged crone wheezed. "I've come for my payment."

Thirty-three

The long day bent toward evening. A mutter of thunder in the west added a distant, eerie voice to the tableau before the Mansion's doors.

The city garrison of the Monnish army, looking grim and nervous, was drawn up on one side of the lawn. The governor's household staff, a hairsbreadth from hysteria, was mobbed on the other side. Any citizen who had sufficient curiosity to overcome his terror had been admitted to bear witness to the proceedings. They weren't many. They made a thin, restless, murmuring crowd.

On the portico between the pillars, the leaders of Monn stood in formal order, with the governor in front bearing up bravely under the regalia of his office. Beside them, looking a little lost, were the Philes. Sarah and Cat Anna looked on, feigning approval, whatever their private thoughts might be. There, also, was the sick Phile, in a litter borne by four brave members of the governor's household.

Michael and Cleo clasped hands in the Philish fashion, palm to palm, then in the Phobish gesture of friendship, each with a hand on the other's shoulder, which both of them accomplished with a degree of unease.

That was a demonstration for the benefit of citizens and soldiers. The governor did not feel as yet so comfortable with the Philes nor so trusting of them as the tableau suggested. During their negotiations, rather one-sided under the circumstances, though much less so once Cat Anna had broken the magic on the door, Michael had insisted on his healing first, as a test case with limited consequences if it should go bad. Some might consider that an act of courage. Michael considered it an act of sheer terror. He was desperately afraid of the Philes and their spells and engines. He no longer doubted the value that could be had from them, but that didn't make him less apprehensive, and he wanted them working where he could see them.

Bent, stinking old Cat Anna. The look on the Philes' faces when she had walked right through their holding spell was worth whatever demands the witch woman would make on him. The governor had begun to think kindly of her. Every ruler should have a sorcerer at his side, as in the legends.

It was probably worth whatever it cost to let the Philes know that Monn was not without magic of its own.

The gestures of friendship ended. The wooden smiles stayed in place. The Philes tried hard not to let their nervousness show as they walked down the steps of the Mansion between the Guardsmen ranked on either side.

The Guardsmen were scarcely less nervous, and though they held their positions like stone men, their muscles were rigid with tension, and a fair proportion of them were silently petitioning the spirits of war to bring forth the word from their captain which would allow them to reach for their weapons and revenge themselves for their earlier humiliation.

The litter bearers stopped at the bottom of the stairs, refusing to approach the iron demons any closer. Philes took up the burden and arranged their man as comfortably as they could in the belly of a demon.

A gust of chill wind ruffled the watchers as the Philes piled into their weird conveyances. The rumble of the demons wakening to life drowned out the answering rumble from the sky.

The first movement taxed the courage of soldiers and civilians alike. And then demons and Philes were gone in a plume of dust, driving straight for the Witch Road.

The soldiers were dismissed, the governor returned to the Mansion, and the citizens went back to their hearths, all feeling that the world had changed in subtle ways, all finding it odd that cattle still had to be fed, dinners prepared, and babies nursed and bathed and put to bed as if nothing had happened.

* * *

Throughout their stay in Monn, the Kolloans had been amused by the persistent reports of witches and sorcerers going about doing mischief there, certain that such reports were nothing more than the active imaginations of a highly superstitious people. They had felt a certain nose-lifting superiority toward the Monnish administration which sent its soldiers coursing through the city in a frantic search for clandestine magicians.

But the passage of the demons was no idle rumor. Good, honest, hard-headed Kolloans had seen them, heard the roar of them, and choked in their dust. They were no figment of Monnish imaginations. They were real, and incomprehensible.

The commander of the encampment was even less inclined toward the supernatural than were most of his people. He did not believe the things were demons. But if they were not, then what were they?

It seemed provident to find out. It was his job, after all, to ensure that the army of the emperor of Kollo met with no surprises.

After conferring in the red tent with his second-in-command and a few trusted advisers, he decided that the best way to solve the mystery would be to capture one of the alleged demons and have a good look at it. To that end he assembled his warriors in battle dress. He realized, of course, that such a move would blow his fiction of peaceful trade to the four winds, but it was almost time to do that anyway, and it seemed worthwhile to find out why those things had stationed themselves at the Governor's Mansion, and what they were doing there. He deemed it not impossible that they were a new type of weapon the Kolloan army should become aware of.

Amyit did not agree with his leader.

Though he had no serious belief in phantoms, ghosts, spirits, or any of that mystical baggage, Amyit felt it unwise to tempt the gods by going out deliberately hunting for demons. There were certainly things he would rather do.

Furthermore, black clouds had formed over the ridge above the city, and a flash of lightning stabbed through them. A storm was brewing. They were probably going to get wet doing the commander's business.

Amyit's mare danced away from him as he prepared to mount, and he swore at her, his mind more on the imprudent nature of the upcoming foray than on the fact that such behavior was unlike her. It wasn't really fair of him. He was uneasy, and she was taking her mood from him.

Discipline was a fact of Kolloan life. However he felt, Amyit took his place in the double ranks of mounted men preparing to cross Mill Bridge. Though they didn't expect any opposition from Monnish forces, they carried iron-tipped lances at the ready. Archers looked to their bows. Who could tell what weapons might be needed to subdue a demon?

A scout came pelting across the bridge at the gallop. He dropped from his lathered horse at the head of the column.

"They're on the move," he told the commander. "Down the Witch Road, the way they came."

The commander stroked his beard and thought it over, then decided on a change of tactics. "Good," he said. "Let them cross the Witch Bridge. We'll catch them against the river."

The dozers paused at the bridge and lumbered over one at a time, then regrouped on the other side. Earlier, they had stopped at the podway to summon a pod for Reese and Gene. It meant a more comfortable ride for the sick man, and quicker medical attention.

But the brief halts worried Cleo. She felt reasonably secure as long as the dozers were in motion, but who knew what sort of Phobish mischief might jump out of the bushes at them when they were standing still?

The enclave's little invasion force gathered on the bank, milling around uneasily before starting the long grinding trip home. There had been a lot of tension and not much action, and they had a load of nervous energy to discharge.

Suddenly Ian said in a voice made loud with amazement, "Holy shit!"

Cleo swung around to see what had disturbed him.

Between the water's edge and the fringe of the forest was the wide sandy shore shading into grass. Along that strip came the Kolloans at the trot, six abreast, bright battle flags aflutter, lances preceding them like the quills of a Brobdingnagian porcupine.

"Who called out the cavalry?" Cleo asked crossly. "Get aboard, everybody," she shouted.

"Can we outrun them?" Ian asked as he climbed into Cleo's dozer beside her.

"I don't know," Cleo said. "I've got a hunch it would be bad tactics to try. I don't suppose you've got more fireworks hidden away?"

Ian shook his head. "Sorry."

The demons roared into life, turned on their outrageous belt-like wheels, and moved toward the oncoming Kolloan force. Amyit's mare bounced and shuddered and threw her head up, all but jerking the reins from his hands, eyes white-ringed, nostrils flared. She was terrified. Amyit wasn't far from that condition himself. He fought her for control.

Along the bank of the river the demons came, crunching down brush and small trees, rumbling and crashing and clattering. The mare jerked her head loose from Amyit's numb hand, gave a couple of tremendous stiff-legged jumps that left Amyit in the dirt, and ran screaming for the shelter of the forest. Amyit was much inclined to join her, and did after several of his fellows passed him, heading in the same direction. Behind him, the demons thundered by, heading toward the camp.

They crunched over the tents and flattened them. They came to a stop, turned on themselves, and smashed through the camp again; they came growling back through the scattered Kolloan force without hesitating and continued on to the Witch Road, then turned east and disappeared into the Wilderness. It was some time before any of the shaken Kolloans could bring themselves to return to the wrecked tents to see what could be salvaged from the ruin.

Ian looked back at the flattened camp. It was a mess. He had to shout to be heard over the engine of the dozer. "I greatly approve of the way we use knowledge and reason to achieve our ends; it's so much more graceful than brute force and wanton destruction," he said bitterly.

''Power has its uses,'' Cleo shouted back. She had a gleam in her eyes as she guided the dozer along the riverbank toward the pod track.

''You're enjoying this, aren't you?''

Cleo nodded.

''Do we even know who those people were?''

''Kolloans.''

''What makes you so sure?''

''The colored tents and flags. It has to be them. We may have prevented a war here, guy, by smashing down a few tents. Is that such a bad thing?''

''That's a politician's question. I'm supposed to think that because preventing a war is a good thing, what we just did is a good thing.''

''Well, it should put us in solid with the governor, anyway.''

''You really should go into politics, Cleo.''

''Someone else told me that. I'm beginning to think you're right.''

Ian subsided into silence. It was crazy trying to carry on a philosophical discussion at the top of his voice.

Thunder cracked, almost overhead.

A farmer plowing down his ruined crop stopped his horse and looked up. There was a general hesitation in the business of life. Grazing cows lifted their heads. Birds sat silent on their branches. Even the stones seemed to lie more still than usual. The light was strange and shadowless.

Black and boiling, the sky was split by a shaft of lightning that forked up into the heavens. Thunder smashed down and left earthbound creatures breathless.

A small pattering began on tree leaves and dusty roofs, scattered, hesitant at first, then growing steadier. The taste of the air changed, taking on a remembered flavor.

All up and down the river valley, wherever they happened to be, people paused in their labors or stood on their doorsteps to observe a phenomenon they had not seen for over a year. They brought their babies out to experience the wonder. They turned their faces to the sky and held their hands up with the palms cupped to receive the long-awaited gift from heaven. The fat cold drops washed dust-encrusted sweat from their brows and penetrated deep to ease the desiccation of their souls. The pinched specter of a hungry winter faded a little.

In the city of Monn, it rained.

Thirty-four

Sarah's place in the Old People's building was ablaze with lights and hardly recognizable. The brush and grass had been cut and replaced with strings and flags as the archeologist laid out his grid. In the basement, cataloguing had already begun.

Sarah's nest had been grubbed out and thrown away. Sarah didn't need it anymore, and contemporary materials cluttered up the dig. Reese could understand the necessity of all the work, but there was a sadness to it. They were irrevocably changing the Phobes' world, and there was nothing the Phobes could do about it.

It wasn't hard to imagine Zeke's ghost hanging over the site, shaking its disapproving head. Eyes closed against imaginings, Reese paused a moment to let the pain pass. He missed Zeke more than he had thought possible.

He left off his tour of the site then, and walked the dark streets of Monn toward Market Square.

The archeologist tossed aside Sarah's pitiful collection of worldly goods because it was in his way. The enclave treated the Phobes' culture in a similarly cavalier manner. The Phobes were learning to accept lights and machinery without understanding what such things were all about. They were becoming dependent on Philish resources without realizing it. There would be no going back.

Off the coast of France, members of the West European Enclave were battling Phobes over an underwater radioactive site. Phobish fishermen there were convinced that the Philes' activities were angering the sea god and destroying their harvest. It was turning into an armed conflict.

Was that better or worse than what the Mid-American Enclave was doing in Monn?

Reese wondered what life would be like if the technophiles who were his ancestors had had the guts to take charge of their world when it was falling apart, racked with disease and starvation and crumbling institutions in the wake of the Bush Wars. Could they have saved some part, at least, of their civilization if they hadn't turned their backs on the willfully ignorant mass of humanity and walled themselves up in their ivory towers to preserve their precious intellectual achievements from a society going to pieces around them? Would he have done anything differently if he had been there?

Clouds covered the moon. The shadows were black, relieved only by the flickering glow of the flames. The storyteller sat cross-legged on his bench, leaned his back against the rough stones of the wall around Market Square, and regarded the crowd gathering in the light of his fire. A good-sized group was assembling, and he watched them carefully, trying to pick up bits of their conversation and to assess their temper, weighing it to determine which tale would suit them that evening.

Around him the night was warm, the air heavy, freighted with moisture from the recent rains. The earth gave forth a fragrance of renewal, of fresh growth, of recovery. He felt good, filled with a sense of the rightness of things. He looked for a reflection of that feeling among the shopkeepers, carters, farmers, and farmers' wives buzzing like a swarm of colossal bees as they exchanged the gossip of the day and waited for him.

At the front of the slowly forming semicircle, Reese was already in place, having accurately judged how close to the speaker courtesy would allow the listeners to come. He sat on the ground like any Monnishman, with his red-eyed little god-in-a-box beside him. He came to hear the tales most days, and the citizens were slowly getting used to him, though there was still a tendency among them to leave some space around him even when a large audience had gathered and space at the front was in high demand.

It was almost a month ago that the Phile had come to the

storyteller and asked his permission to attend the gatherings. The storyteller had questioned him about his god-in-a-box. The Phile tried to explain about what he called recordings, and did something to the box whereupon the god closed its red eye, opened a green eye, and astounded the storyteller by producing his own voice out of the box, using his own words. All the storyteller's hair had stood on end, and his gut had tightened. It was extremely unsettling.

When he got over his reaction, the storyteller said that anyone, even a Phile, was welcome to listen to him, but he would be eternally grateful if Reese could keep the god quiet in his presence.

Philes were everywhere. They had excavated a pit halfway to hell in Young Albert's field while Young Albert sat as rigid as stone on the edge of a chair in his kitchen with his eyes shut and his fists clenched waiting for an angered Beelzebub to burst forth from the hole on a pillar of flame and incinerate everything for a mile around.

The Philes said that they had the governor's blessing. There were folks who said that the devil rode at the governor's right hand. If so, it was doing the man a world of good. The storyteller had never seen Michael looking so well.

The arrival of a pair of Guardsmen escorting two women on white mules caused a stir at the back of the crowd, and a murmur of recognition passed like a wave through the people.

The women dismounted and made their way through the crowd, which parted willingly enough to allow their passage, except for a few disgruntled grumblers. Not everyone was in wholehearted agreement with the governor's choice of advisers, nor happy with his willingness to disregard tradition.

One of the women was very old. She shuffled slowly along, leaning heavily on the arm of the other, who was very young and very lovely.

The storyteller recognized Cat Anna at once, in spite of the artfully dressed hair and fine clothes. No one else in Monn was so ancient. But he didn't know the young one until she was near the fire and flashed him that familiar smile.

The Guardsmen laid a rug on the ground near the Phile, and the women settled on it.

"Hey, Reese," the young one said.

"Hey, Sarah," the Phile answered. "You're looking good. High society agrees with you."

"I guess." She arranged her embroidered skirts with studied gestures. Modesty did not come naturally to her. "I thought you might come to the Mansion once in a while, you know."

"I don't think that's a very good idea. I've heard the gossip in the city about a royal wedding. The old folks are thoroughly scandalized. You probably shouldn't be here."

"I don't see why I can't listen to the storyteller the same as anyone else," Sarah said defensively. Her voice rose, and heads turned her way.

"I thought finally people wouldn't always be telling me what to do," she said more quietly.

"It doesn't work that way, girl."

She didn't answer; she just looked at him with the special eyes women reserve for the men they care about. He appeared to be in good health, and the scar over his ear was almost hidden in the new growth of hair that had come in white. The white patch made him look even more exotic.

"Are you happy, Sarah?" Reese asked.

"I guess. Michael is a nice man."

"Nice?"

"It's nice to have a bed to sleep in, and people to bring you food whenever you want some, and people to look after you. It's nice to belong someplace. I only wish . . ." Her voice trailed off wistfully, and she turned to face the storyteller, presenting him with an expression in the flickering fire light that reminded him of the bittersweet triumphs of youth.

"Butch wasn't such a bad person," she said.

"He was a thoroughly nasty piece of work, Sarah. Some people will tell you anyone who's safely dead lived a saintly life. You don't have to believe it."

A group of lords and family members had joined the audience, taking the choice spots as if by divine right and causing a certain amount of shuffling annoyance among the people.

"Where's Cleo?" Sarah asked.

"Home. Busy. She's got a notion to get herself elected to our ruling family. We don't see each other much these days."

Sarah turned to him with eyes full of rising mischief. He shook his head. "You're doing fine," he said. "Don't spoil it."

* * *

Gradually, the shuffling and muttering among the people faded into an expectant silence. The storyteller sat up straighter and looked into the darkness beyond them. He knew which story he would tell that night.

His rich voice flowed out over the crowd.

"This is the Legend of Sarah."

About the Author

LESLIE GADALLAH was born in a small town in northern Alberta on October 8, 1939, graduated from the University of Alberta in 1960 with a B.Sc. in chemistry, and spent the next fifteen years or so plying her trade and raising a family before abandoning the practice of science for the opportunity to write about it.

Ms. Gadallah has written popular science extensively for newspapers and radio, and served as a technical editor for the Alberta Research Council for a number of years. This work represents her second foray into the field of science fiction.

Ms. Gadallah lives with her family on a small farm just outside of Edmonton, Alberta, which they share with four cats, five chickens, a goat, and an uncertain number of rabbits. There they pursue the firm but distant goal of becoming independent of the supermarket.